SPRINGTIME IN BURRACOMBE

The village of Burracombe is looking forward to the coronation of Queen Elizabeth II but the year of 1953 is to prove one of heartbreak as well as celebration. As Stella Simmons begins to plan her wedding, sister Maddy is coming to terms with the loss of her fiancé. At the big house, Hilary Napier asks herself if love will find her and across the village Val and Luke Ferris are wondering if they will ever become parents. Meanwhile, the life of the village goes on, with all its ups and downs, feuds and dramas.

For my dear son Philip
1959–2008

Springtime In Burracombe

by

Lilian Harry

Magna Large Print Books
Long Preston, North Yorkshire,
BD23 4ND, England.

British Library Cataloguing in Publication Data.

Harry, Lilian
    Springtime in Burracombe.

    A catalogue record of this book is
    available from the British Library

    ISBN   978-0-7505-3164-1

First published in Great Britain in 2009 by Orion Books
an imprint of The Orion Publishing Group Ltd.

Published in Large Print 2010 by arrangement with
Orion Publishing Group

Magna Large Print is an imprint of Library Magna Books Ltd.

Printed and bound in Great Britain by
T.J. (International) Ltd., Cornwall, PL28 8RW

Chapter One

Burracombe, Devon, March 1953

On the afternoon of the accident, the village of Burracombe was just waking to Spring after a long, cold winter.

Jacob Prout whistled to himself as he cleared ditches of the debris of the most recent downpour. He always felt that this was the true beginning of the year and an afternoon like this, with the promise of longer, lighter days, and new growth starting up wherever you looked, was one that filled him with hope. It's going to be a good year, he thought, what with the new Queen's Coronation and all. A good year in Burracombe.

'Jacob – *Jacob!'* He turned quickly and saw old Minnie Tozer hurrying as fast as her ancient legs would carry her, out of Constance Bellamy's gate. They'd had a word or two not ten minutes earlier, when Minnie had passed him on her way to see Miss Bellamy with a basket of broad beans for sowing on the Easter full moon. She'd been as chirpy as a cricket then, but now her face was as grey as her wispy hair and her eyes frightened. Jacob dropped his spade and ran towards her.

'Whatever's the matter, Minnie? You look as if you've seed a ghost.'

'It's Miss Constance – her's had an accident.' Minnie stopped, gasping, and put a hand to her

7

side. 'I've not run like this since I don't know when! Quick, Jacob, us needs help.'

'What happened?' They were both hurrying now, back towards the gate set in the high wall around Miss Bellamy's house. 'Have she had a fall?'

Minnie nodded. 'Pruning that old plum tree, if you'll believe it. I told her as soon as I walked through the gate, you never ought to be up that ladder at your age, I said, and her just looked at me cheeky-like, and said "I'm not as old as you, Minnie Tozer, and you'm not my nursemaid now!" and then not two minutes after that, she were lying in a heap at the bottom of the tree and I come straight out to get help. There she is, look – hasn't moved.'

They went closer and bent over the crumpled figure. Gently, Minnie laid her hand against the weatherbeaten face, as seamed and brown as a walnut, and to their relief Miss Bellamy's eyes opened and she looked up at them in bewilderment.

'What's going on? What am I doing here?' Her gruff, well-bred voice was little more than a whisper, and she frowned. 'What's the matter with me?'

'You fell out of that old plum tree,' Jacob told her. 'Which you never ought to have been up in the first place. And why you had to be pruning it now I don't know – should have been done a fortnight ago, before the sap started to rise. You should have asked me to see to it for you.'

'I always do it myself,' the old lady said with a touch of her usual stubbornness. 'That was my old grandfather's tree and he always did it first week in March, and so do I. I've told you over and over–'

'And this isn't no time to be telling him again,' Minnie broke in. 'Here you be, laying on the cold ground with the good Lord knows what injuries you've done to yourself, and arguing about pruning fruit trees. And you'm no better, Jacob Prout. Now, Miss Constance, where have you hurt yourself? Us can't move you until us knows that.'

'You don't need to move me at all,' Miss Bellamy said, beginning to struggle to get up. 'There's nothing wrong with me that a cup of tea won't put right, and I hope you'll both– Oh!' She fell back again, grimacing with pain, and Minnie Tozer looked at her with exasperation.

'You always were an obstinate little toad. Never would stay in her pram, once her could toddle,' she told Jacob. 'Had to be out, stumping along the road as if her was setting out on a day's march.' She addressed her charge again. 'Now, what have you done to yourself? Hurt your leg? And you must have had a nasty bump on your head too, that ought to be looked at.'

'It's my ankle. It's just a bit of a sprain, that's all. If Jacob will get me up and help me into the house... There's nothing else, Minnie, and I do not need to be "looked at".'

'That's what you think,' Minnie said grimly as Jacob helped the little woman to stand up, leaning heavily against him. 'Bumps on the head aren't things to be took lightly. You might be concussed. Soon as we've got you settled indoors, I'm going round to fetch Dr Latimer.'

'Don't be ridiculous,' Miss Bellamy said, but her voice was feeble and her legs wobbled. Jacob put his arm round her and held her up as they made their way slowly up the path towards the house, with Minnie following anxiously behind. She slipped ahead to open the back door and the little procession filed through the porch with its clutter of Wellington boots and waxed jackets, and into the big, untidy kitchen. Jacob lowered Miss Bellamy gently on to a battered old sofa, unceremoniously pushing aside a resentful dachshund, and he and Minnie stood for a moment or two, looking down at her.

'I'll put the kettle on,' Minnie decided, going over to the range. 'Sweet tea, that's what you need for shock. And as soon as she's had that I'm going for the doctor, no matter what her says.'

'You needn't talk as if I'd lost my senses,' Miss Bellamy said sharply. 'I can still speak for myself, and I don't want Charles Latimer dragged round here on a fool's errand. I'm just a bit shaken up, that's all, and a cup of tea will put that right. And then if you'll be good enough to make a poultice for this ankle and put a bandage on it, I can look after myself for the rest of the day. A good night's sleep and I'll be right as rain.'

'So you might be,' Minnie said. 'But I'm calling the doctor just the same. What do you think people would say if Jacob and me left you here to fend for yourself and you were took poorly with that old concussion? Us'd never heard the end of it.'

'I haven't *got* concussion!' Miss Bellamy retorted, and as the two old ladies glared at each

10

other, Jacob hastily intervened.

'My stars, look at you – like a pair of fighting cocks! Now, you make that tea, Minnie, and have one yourself, because if you ask me you've had a bit of a shock too, and *I'll* go for the doctor, and no more arguments. And I won't say no to a cup myself, once I get back.' He went out, shutting the door behind him, and the two looked at each other and smiled reluctantly.

'I suppose he's right,' Miss Bellamy admitted. 'And so are you, Minnie. It's better to be safe than sorry and I wouldn't want the village at your throat. You always were a good nursemaid to me and my brothers.'

'Maybe so, but I didn't expect to be still doing it at eighty-seven. And I didn't expect to find you climbing trees, neither. It's time you realised your own age and stopped being so foolish. Jacob would have looked after that tree for you.'

'I know, but I wanted to do it for Grandad. I meant it to be the last time.'

'Very nearly the last time you did anything at all,' Minnie told her grimly, pouring boiling water into the big brown teapot. 'Now, where's my basket? I suppose I must have dropped it in the garden. I've got some broad beans for you to put in, and Alice sent down a few scones as well. I'll just slip out and fetch them in.'

She bustled out and Constance lay back on the sofa. Truth to tell, she did feel rather shaken, and her ankle was throbbing painfully. It was a good thing Minnie had arrived when she did, for nobody else was expected that day and she was aware that she could have lain there for hours,

11

possibly even all night. A fine state I'd have been in by morning, she thought, and here I've been biting poor Minnie's head off as if it was all her fault!

Constance had known Minnie Tozer all her life. She hadn't been Minnie Tozer, of course, when she had been Constance's nursemaid, she'd been Minnie Dodd, and she hadn't been an old woman, either; she'd been a slip of a fourteen-year-old in her first position with the Bellamy family, accustomed, as the eldest of seven, to dealing with small children and standing no nonsense from Constance and her brothers. She had left them four years later to work as a maid at the Tozer's farmhouse, and three years after that she and Ted's father had married. But there had always been a firm friendship between the two women and Minnie still, at times, treated Constance as the little girl she had been over seventy years ago.

If I had to fall out of that tree, Constance thought, while not admitting that she should never have been up it in the first place, there's no one I'd rather have found me than Minnie.

'Wherever can she have got to?' Alice Tozer asked, looking out of the kitchen window. 'It must be well over an hour since she went down to Miss Bellamy's with that basket of beans. I suppose they'm sitting in the kitchen chewing the fat over a cup of tea you could stand a spoon up in. Those two never stop talking when they gets together, but her ought to be home soon or it'll be getting dark.'

'Would you like me to walk down and meet her?' Joanna asked, settling the second of her baby twins in their cot in the corner. 'These two should sleep now for a couple of hours. I wouldn't mind a bit of fresh air.'

'Well, you could do. I don't want her to think we're fussing over her, but there's a cold wind getting up and she hasn't long got over that chill she had a week or two back. It's all very well to be hale and hearty, but we've got to remember her age, even if she won't, and I don't want her chest getting bad again.'

'I'll go to the shop for something,' Joanna said. 'Then I can meet her by accident. I'll pop an extra scarf in my basket. Robin can come along too.' She called her small son from his game with a handful of wooden bricks, and they set off down the track and crossed the village green. As usual, there was plenty going on. Alf Coker was busy shoeing a horse at the entrance to his forge, and the butcher's van was standing outside Bert Foster's shop where Billy Friend was heaving out a side of beef. He stopped when he saw Joanna and grinned his wide grin at Robin.

'That looks heavy, Billy.'

'It is, but I'm strong.' He lugged his burden into the back of the butcher's shop where Bert would chop it into joints, and then came out for another. 'I've got good muscles,' he said proudly, stretching his arms to show them off.

Joanna smiled and went into the village shop, where Edie Pettifer was serving Betty Culliford with her sweet ration. 'That's two ounces of sherbet dabs,' she said, pouring the sweets into a cone of blue paper and folding in the top. 'That's threepence, please, Betty.' She took the three-penny bit the child handed over and passed back

13

the cone of sweets. 'I'm thankful the sweet rationing's stopped,' she told Joanna as Betty skipped out, already unfolding the top of the cone. 'There's only a few things left on ration now. I seem to have been counting out little squares of paper all my life. I'd never have believed when it started that we'd still be doing it nearly eight years after the war ended. You'd never think we'd won, would you? Oh!' She stopped suddenly. 'I should have asked you straight away – how's old Mrs Tozer?'

Joanna stared at her. 'She's all right. Why do you ask?'

'Well, I thought she might be a bit shook up, you know. It was her found the old lady, after all, or so I heard from Freda Dawe when she came in not ten minutes ago. I dare say it'll be all round the village by now, the way news travels in Burracombe. Why, I remember–'

'What accident?' Joanna broke in. 'What will be all round the village? What's happened, Edie?'

'You mean you don't know? Miss Bellamy fell out of her plum tree, apparently, and it was your gran that found her. Got Jacob Prout to help her get the old lady indoors and he went for the doctor. I'd have thought someone would have sent up to the farm straight away. You didn't hear nothing about it?'

'No, not a word. But Mother was out in the barns all afternoon, seeing to the hens, and I've been upstairs with the babies – if anyone had come to the door or telephoned, I wouldn't have heard them. Is Miss Bellamy badly hurt? Have they taken her to hospital?'

14

'Not that I've heard. You'd better go straight round, Joanna, and see what's what. It's bound to have been a shock for your poor gran.'

'Yes, I will.' Joanna took Robin's hand and led him out, ignoring his protests. 'I'm sorry, love, we haven't got time to stop for sweets and it's not our day anyway. We bought some yesterday, didn't we? Come on now, let's see what's happened to your great-granny.' She hurried him along the lane towards the school, where they met Charles Latimer coming out of Miss Bellamy's gate.

'Ah, Joanna,' he said, sounding relieved. 'Just the person. You've heard what happened?'

'Only that there's been some sort of accident and Granny Tozer was there. Is she all right? Is Miss Bellamy badly hurt?'

'Not too badly, but both ladies are a bit shaken. I was just coming to find someone to go in with them for a while. Can you spare the time? What about your babies?'

'They should be all right for an hour or so, and Tom's mother's with them. But what happened, doctor? Edie Pettifer said they were climbing trees but surely that can't be true.'

The doctor smiled. 'It's not far off, actually. It seems Miss Bellamy was pruning her grandfather's plum tree and she fell just as old Mrs Tozer came through the gate. Jacob Prout was working nearby, as luck would have it, and he got them both indoors and came for me. Luckily I was just back from my afternoon rounds. They're in there having a cup of tea together, but I don't want Miss Bellamy left alone and your grandmother ought to be at home, where she can rest

15

properly. At the moment she's fussing about like a mother hen and talking about staying the night.'

'Oh, she mustn't do that,' Joanna said quickly. 'It's because she used to be Miss Bellamy's nursemaid – she feels she must look after her. But did Miss Bellamy hurt herself badly?'

'A nasty sprain to her ankle, and a bump on the head, which is why I don't want her left alone. That sort of thing can have a delayed effect and if she starts to be sick or feel drowsy she may need to be taken to hospital for observation. To tell the truth, I'd like her to go anyway, but she flatly refuses. I wondered if your sister-in-law would be willing to stay with her.'

'Val? I'm sure she would. She's very fond of Miss Bellamy – we all are. I think she's home now – shall I go and ask her?' Joanna hesitated.

'No, I'll do that. You go and find your grand-mother and try to get her to sit down. She's made tea but when I came out she looked all set to start a bit of spring-cleaning!'

'My goodness,' said Joanna, who had been in Miss Bellamy's kitchen and knew what that meant. 'She'll be there until next spring if she does that.' She hurried through the gate and along the garden path, with Robin still clinging to her hand, while the doctor made his way to the cottage where Val Ferris lived with her husband Luke. Val was a nurse at Tavistock Hospital, and the best possible person to keep an eye on the old lady.

Joanna knocked on the back door and made her way into the kitchen without waiting for an an-swer. As predicted, she found Constance Bellamy on the old sofa she kept there, with her legs

16

stretched out and her dachshund beside her. Minnie was busy at the range with an old rag.

'Grandmother!' Joanna scolded. 'Whatever are you doing? The doctor said you'd got to sit down and have a rest. You've had a nasty shock.'

'I'm not the one who fell out of a tree!' Minnie retorted, and looked round. 'Oh, it's you, Joanna. What are you doing here?'

'Looking for you. Mother was getting worried about why you'd been gone so long. Now, sit down, do, and drink your tea.' Joanna turned to the other woman. 'And how are you, Miss Bellamy? You had a bad fall, didn't you?'

'Not that bad, no,' the old lady said, but her voice had lost some of its accustomed robustness. 'Had plenty of falls worse than that in my young days but these old bones don't bounce like they used to.'

'Old bones indeed!' Minnie snorted. 'You'm still a good few years younger than me, Miss Constance, but you'll never be any wiser. Scrambling about up trees pruning branches – you were lucky you didn't saw your own leg off!'

'Don't,' Joanna said, shuddering. 'And please, Granny, sit down. If there's anything that needs doing, I'll do it. I'm sure Miss Bellamy doesn't want you fussing about her kitchen.'

'No, I don't,' Constance said. 'But she won't be told. Always a bossy-boots, Minnie Dodd was. Mind you, I'm glad she was here when this happened. I could have lain there all night, and Rupert never get any supper.' She fondled the dachshund's ears and he growled softly and licked her hand.

'Rupert would manage,' Minnie said grimly, catching Joanna's eye. 'There's enough bits and pieces lying about on this table to keep him fed for a week. How long's this ham been on this plate? And those biscuits are as soft as new bread.'

'I like them like that,' Miss Bellamy said defiantly, and untruthfully. 'And the ham was left over from lunch. Not that it's any of your business.'

'I really think you ought to rest,' Joanna said. 'Both of you. And try not to talk too much. The doctor said you'd had a bump on the head, Miss Bellamy. If you get overexcited you may have to go to the hospital for observation.'

'Overexcited! I'm not likely to get overexcited reclining here like a princess,' Constance retorted. 'It's that old busybody over there you want to be talking to. Stop fussing about that range, Minnie, and sit down and drink your tea, as your granddaughter tells you. And then she'd better take you home and leave me in peace.' She moved her leg and winced. 'I'll probably stop here for the night. Be more sense than trying to get up those stairs.'

'Yes, it might,' Joanna said, handing Minnie her tea. 'Val will be here soon and we'll see if we can make you up a more comfortable bed.' She turned as the back door opened and her sister-in-law came in. 'Oh, there you are, Val. We were just saying, it might be better for Miss Bellamy to sleep down here tonight.'

Val came over and knelt by the sofa. She put her hand on the old lady's forehead and looked into her eyes. Then she turned her attention to

18

the sprained ankle, which the doctor had ban-
daged, and felt it gently. 'Does it hurt much?'

'A bit,' Constance admitted. 'No more than
you might expect. I'll be right as rain in the
morning.'

'Yes, you probably will,' Val agreed. 'But I'm
staying tonight, just in case. No arguments, now,'
she added in her best nurse's voice. 'It's doctor's
orders – that or go to hospital. Which do you
want it to be?'

'Oh, very well,' Constance said grudgingly. 'But
you can send these two home. Minnie Tozer
needs to be in her own bed by the look of her,
and this young woman's got those twins to see to.
Not that I'm not very grateful to you both,' she
added, and they knew she meant it, 'but if young
Val is going to be here there's no need for anyone
else. And to be perfectly truthful, I'd like to have
a bit of peace and quiet now. It's been a busy
afternoon.'

'Come on, Gran,' Joanna said. 'And you,
Robin. Let's go home.'

They went towards the door but just as they
reached it Miss Bellamy called them back and
they turned.

'I thought you said you brought me some broad
beans to put in,' she said to Minnie. 'Don't you
go taking them home with you. I'll be out in the
garden again before you can blink, and I want to
be sure of getting them planted.'

Minnie picked up her basket and took out a
paper bag which she laid on the table. 'Don't
cook them by mistake,' she said. 'And here's the
scones Alice sent down for your tea. But just you

be careful if you go out in the garden for the next few days, see? No more pruning – understand?'

'Yes, Minnie,' Constance said with unaccustomed meekness. 'No more pruning.'

She waited until they had left, then looked at Val and winked.

'I'd just about finished anyway,' she said.

Chapter Two

'Oh, my dear soul alive!' Dottie Friend exclaimed, running down her front path. 'Come you here this minute, my flower, and tell your old Dottie all about it. And don't you worry about a thing. You'm home now and nothing more's going to happen to you.'

Maddy Forsyth climbed out of the red sports car and stood shakily at the gate as the plump little countrywoman folded her in her arms, taking care even in the warmth of her welcome not to jar the arm that was encased in plaster. She rested her head on the comfortable shoulder and the tears began to seep from her eyes.

'I'm sorry – I didn't mean to do this. I just can't help it, somehow.' She wriggled her good arm free and felt for a hanky. 'I'm making your dress all wet.'

'That don't matter a scrap, and of course you want to cry. 'Tis only natural, after what you've been through. Come along indoors now and have a cup of tea – and never mind about your bits and

20

bobs,' she added as Maddy waved a helpless hand towards the car. 'Felix and Stella will bring them in and take 'em straight up to your bedroom. You just come along with me.' She led the weeping girl firmly round the side of the cottage to the back door. There, even though it was only March, the sun was warming a garden bright with daffodils and primroses, and a camellia was smothered with deep pink flowers. A bench stood by the door and a large black cat lay stretched on the flag-stones, his stomach exposed to the warmth.

Maddy bent to stroke him. 'Albert. Oh, it's good to see you.'

'He'll be pleased to have you back too,' Dottie observed. 'The whole of Burracombe is, Maddy, but we're only sorry it had to be in such sad circumstances. And you know you're welcome to stop here as long as you want, don't you. You ought to have come here straight away instead of being on your own at West Lyme.'

'I know, and thank you, Dottie.' They passed from the sunlight to the dimness of the cottage. 'But I wanted to go back to work. And I don't like turning you out of your own home like this.'

'Bless you, my pretty, 'tis only a step across the road to Aggie Madge's spare room at night, and I can be here all day, same as ever. Don't you think no more of it. Now, sit you down there while I make the tea. There's some fresh scones just out of the oven. I dare say young Felix won't say no to one of they, neither. Where's he to?'

'Here, Dottie,' the young curate said, ducking his head to follow them through the door. 'I'll just take Maddy's case up, shall I? Stella's bringing the

21

rest.' He bumped the suitcase up the narrow stairs to Dottie's room, where Maddy was to sleep, and Maddy's sister Stella came in, festooned with bags and boxes. Maddy sank into an old wooden armchair, padded with cushions, and Dottie bustled about, moving the kettle on the range and spooning tea into the fat brown teapot, while footsteps above indicated that the luggage was being dispersed about the tiny bedroom.

By the time the two came down, the tea was poured into the best bone china cups and Dottie was arranging golden-brown scones on a flowered plate. She set it on the middle of the table, flanked by another plate of thinly-cut bread and butter and a Victoria sponge, and they drew up their chairs.

'There's home-made strawberry jam from last year, and some fresh lemon curd I made yesterday, and I don't want too much left because you know how quickly it goes off,' she instructed them. 'Now, Maddy m'dear, I know you won't feel like eating much, but just have a bite or two to please me, there's a good girl. You needs to keep your strength up, you know. You'm looking as pale as a pan of whey.'

'I'm all right, Dottie, really. Just tired.' Maddy took a slice of bread and butter. 'Everything seems to have happened so quickly – and yet I can hardly believe that it's such a short time since ... since...' Her voice wavered and she put down the slice of bread and rested her forehead on her fingertips. 'I'm sorry... Would anyone mind if I just went upstairs for a while?'

'Of course not.' Stella was on her feet at once,

but Maddy waved her away. 'I'll bring your tea up, shall I?' Her face tight with anxiety, she spread jam and lemon curd on to a few slices of bread, and put them on to Maddy's plate together with a buttered scone and a slice of sponge. Dottie passed her a tray and she loaded it up and followed her sister up the stairs. Felix and Dottie looked at each other in concern.

'Poor little maid,' Dottie said after a minute or two. ''Tis a hard thing to lose your sweetheart, but to see him knocked down before her very eyes, and on the day they got engaged as well – it don't bear thinking about. It'll take her a while to get over that.'

'I don't know if she ever will,' Felix said soberly. 'Oh, she'll go on living, and we hope and pray she'll even enjoy life again – but a wound like that never completely heals. She'll always grieve for Sam in some corner of her heart.'

Stella and Felix had gone to see Maddy at West Lyme that morning, arriving just before lunch in Felix's little sports car, Mirabelle. Maddy was waiting for them, acutely aware of how much she had missed her sister, and as soon as Stella got out of the car she flung herself forward.

'Oh, Maddy,' Stella exclaimed, holding her away to look at the tears streaming down her cheeks. 'Maddy, don't cry. We're here now. I'm sorry we're a bit late. You weren't worried about us, were you?'

'No – it's not that.' Maddy sniffed and wiped her eyes on her sleeve. 'It's just – I hadn't realised how badly I've been wanting to see you.'

'You ought to have come back to Burracombe with us,' Stella said gently, pulling her close. 'I knew you shouldn't be on your own.'

'I haven't – the Archdeacon and Mrs Copley have been so kind to me. They've told me to go downstairs and be with them any time I like. And I did want to be by myself some of the time. But … oh, it's just that you need someone of your own, you know.'

'Yes, I do,' Stella said, thinking of how she'd longed for so many years for the little sister she thought she'd lost. 'Maddy, why don't you come back with us today? Stay as long as you like. Or just take a few days, if the Archdeacon can't manage without you. I really don't think you should be here without us.'

'I can't. There isn't room.'

'There can be,' Stella said firmly. 'Dottie said she'll go and sleep over at Aggie Madge's, so that you can have her room. I didn't ask her – she told me she'd been thinking about it and she wants you to come back. We all do.'

'I think it would be a good idea,' Felix said from behind Stella, where he had been waiting quietly for the sisters to complete their reunion. 'She'll only sleep there; she'll be in her own cottage all the rest of the time, so you'll have company while Stella's at school. After all, Dottie's as near family to you as anyone could be.'

'Yes, she is,' Maddy agreed, thinking of the times Dottie had bathed her grazed knees, brought her Friar's Balsam to inhale in bed when she had a cold, and nursed her through chicken-pox and measles. 'She really brought me up, after our mother died and Fenella adopted me. Well ... if you're sure it will be all right.'

'Absolutely sure,' Stella said. 'What about the Archdeacon? Can he spare you?'

'I expect so. In fact, I think he's half expecting it – they've both been dropping hints all week about Burracombe.' She gave them both a rather wobbly smile. 'But we don't need to rush, do we? Lunch is nearly ready, and I promised Archie a walk on the beach this afternoon. I shall miss Archie,' she added regretfully, 'but I don't suppose Dottie would want me to take him as well.'

'Dottie might not mind, but Albert would!' Stella laughed, picturing the dismay of Dottie's elderly cat if a large black labrador should burst into his domain. 'Anyway, he'd never squeeze into Mirabelle. In fact, I'm not quite sure how you will, with luggage as well. I suppose you'll want to take the usual ton.'

Maddy shook her head. 'Just a couple of changes of clothes. We won't be going anywhere smart, will we? It will be nice just to be there.' She linked her good arm through her sister's and drew her up the steps. 'Come on. We seem to have got everything arranged and you haven't even managed to get through the front door! And you must be frozen.'

They turned to go inside, Stella giving Felix a smile of relief. All the way here, they'd been discussing how to persuade Maddy to come back to Burracombe with them, and it had been achieved almost without their knowing it.

I'll be able to look after her now for a while, Stella thought thankfully, and followed her sister

25

through the door.

Now, Stella was sitting on her Dottie's narrow bed, her arm around Maddy's shoulders.

'You don't need to be sorry for crying,' she said softly. 'Dottie's right – you should cry as much as you want to, and there's nowhere better for you to do it than here, with us. It'll be better for you in the end.'

'It's not just me,' Maddy said, through her sobs. 'It's those poor people at Bridge End – Dan and Ruth Hodges and that dear little girl Linnet. They thought the world of Sammy. Mr Hodges had already lost his older son, you know, in the war, and Mrs Hodges has lost her "little evacuee" – she still called him that sometimes – and now Linnet's lost her big brother. And if we hadn't stayed so long in the New Forest that afternoon, if we'd gone straight to Lizzie and Alec's like we'd said we would, maybe it would never–'

'It's no good thinking like that,' Stella said, knowing that Maddy was tormenting herself with blame. 'Nobody knows what would have happened if things had been different. Nobody ever *can* know. It was nobody's fault. Nobody's.' She hesitated, then said, 'And he must have been very happy, you know. Just getting engaged to you, looking forward to the party, and his new job and everything. He must have been on top of the world.'

'So why couldn't he stay there?' Maddy cried. 'Why couldn't we have been engaged for the next two years and then got married and grown old together? That's all we wanted, you know. We

26

wanted to be together all our lives. And now – now he's gone, and I'm all alone. I shall never have anyone like Sammy again, never!' The tears broke out again and she turned and clung to Stella, who rocked her like a baby in her arms, murmuring wordless consolation as best she could, but feeling dismally inadequate even as she did so.

'I don't know why it happened,' she said at last. 'I don't know why any of it happens. Why did our mother get killed in the air-raid, and our baby brother? Why did Daddy get lost at sea? Why did they separate us when we were children and send us to different children's homes? None of it makes sense, and there doesn't seem to be any point in looking for any. We just have to keep going, Maddy, and doing the best we can, and hoping that some things, at least, will turn out right.'

'Some of them do,' Maddy said. 'Look at you and Felix.'

'Yes,' Stella said, feeling uncomfortable at having her own happiness brought into this conversation. 'But we don't know that life will always go smoothly for us, do we? We don't know what might happen in the future.'

'I hope nothing happens,' Maddy said passionately. 'I don't want *anything* else to go wrong in our lives. We've had enough, Stella. It's our turn for things to go right now, and if it can't be me and Sammy, it's got to be you and Felix. If it isn't, I just shan't want to go on with it any more. I'll lose all the hope I ever had.'

Stella gathered her sister close against her. She laid her cheek against the soft, wet face and closed her eyes.

'You mustn't say that, Maddy,' she whispered. 'It's been terrible, but we mustn't lose hope. We must never, never lose hope.'

Downstairs, Dottie and Felix nibbled at their food until at last Felix put his scone down with a sigh.

'It just doesn't seem right,' he said apologetically. 'Tucking into one of your teas as if nothing had happened, when poor Maddy's in such a state. I'm sorry, Dottie, I honestly don't think I can eat a thing.'

'I feel much the same,' she admitted. 'It's as if we'm all at sixes and sevens. Maybe it's just a drink of tea us needs to set us on the right track again.'

Felix smiled. 'Tea – the cure for all ills. Well, perhaps not all,' he amended sadly. 'I don't think it will do much to cure Maddy's ills just now.'

'No, but it'll make her feel a bit better just the same. And her'll come round in time, you know, Felix. 'Tis a tragedy, what's happened, but it's true what Vicar said in church the other day – time is a great healer. And the poor little maid's in the best place for healing now, down here in Burracombe with her friends. It's where she belongs to be.'

The bedroom door closed and Stella came back downstairs. She looked drawn and tired, and Felix jumped up and urged her into a chair. 'Sit down, sweetheart, and have a cup of tea. Dottie says it'll make us all feel better, and she's right.'

'Of course I am,' Dottie said. 'If you can't eat, you can always drink, and tea's the best thing. Not that you'd know it from the way some of those folk up at the Bell knock back the beer,' she added, 'and talking of which, I ought to be

28

getting ready if I'm to be behind the bar at opening time. Now, you two just rest easy here and listen out for that poor maid upstairs, and eat whatever you can manage. I'll be back soon after ten – Bernie said I could slip away at closing time and leave the clearing up to him and Rose. I'll look in and see how things are before I goes in to Aggie's.'

She bustled about, getting herself ready for the evening's work at the inn and, after she'd gone, they sat quietly for a few minutes. Then Felix reached absently for a slice of bread and butter.

'How d'you really think she is?' he asked quietly. 'She hardly said a word all the way from West Lyme.'

'I don't know,' Stella said miserably. 'She seems absolutely stunned, doesn't she? Except when she cries – I think Dottie's right, you know, it's good for her to let it out. But apart from that, it's as if she was carved out of stone.'

'We must just let her go at her own pace,' he said. 'Don't force her to do anything. Just let her heal slowly – go for walks on her own if that's what she wants, or go with her if she needs company. Listen when she talks, but don't ask too many questions. And hope that the rest of the village leaves her alone, too.'

'Oh, I'm sure they will,' Stella said wryly. 'You know what people are like when someone's had a bereavement. They don't know what to say, so they cross the road when they see you coming to avoid saying anything. That's the worst thing of all.'

'I know. A squeeze of the arm – well, not the broken one of course! – or a friendly "I'm sorry" is often all that's needed. But I'm sure Burra-combe people understand that. And they nearly all know Maddy and love her.' He glanced at her plate. 'Eat some tea, darling. I'm sure you'll feel better for it. It's no use letting yourself starve; you'll be no help at all to your sister then.'

Stella smiled and picked up her scone. They ate in silence for a while and then, to their surprise, they heard footsteps on the stairs and Maddy appeared at the door, carrying her tray.

'I thought I'd bring this down,' she said, her voice shaking a little but threaded with determination. 'I'd rather be with you than up there on my own.' She sat down at the table and lifted her chin as she looked at them. 'Why don't you tell me what's going on in the village these days? How are those little Tozer twins? And what's the village going to do to mark the Queen's Coronation?'

Chapter Three

Constance Bellamy's ankle kept her immobile for several days but, as usual, the villagers of Burra-combe rallied round to help and a constant stream of visitors passed through the high gate and into the kitchen where she and Rupert held court. In fact, as she told Minnie Tozer who came in every day to take charge, there were almost too many visitors.

'I hardly get a moment to myself,' she grumbled. 'They're all very kind and I do appreciate it, but I

30

don't even get time for a half-hour nap in the afternoon. And I've got to admit, it does seem to have shaken me up a bit. I feel quite tired at times.'

'Our Val said you would,' Minnie said, passing her a cup of tea. 'That first night's sleep did you the world of good, but you need more rest than that. I'll sit outside for a bit and stop people coming in.' She gathered up her knitting and a couple of shawls and went out into the garden to sit on the old bench Constance had placed in an arbour, sheltered from the wind but catching the sun.

Val had spent the first night at the house, but Constance had slept well and woken without a headache, and Dr Latimer had declared her out of danger of concussion and said her ankle would be better in a week. 'You're a very lucky woman,' he'd told her. 'You could have injured yourself very badly. I want you to promise me that there'll be no more climbing trees. Or even stepladders. I don't even want you standing on chairs or stools.' He tried to think if there was anything else Constance might stand on that he should forbid. 'Or boxes,' he added. 'Or ... well, anything at all. Keep your feet firmly on the ground.'

'I suppose you'll allow me to go upstairs?' she'd asked grumpily. 'Or do I have to spend the rest of my life down here on this old settee?'

'Of course you can go upstairs,' he said, knowing that she was being sarcastic but choosing to take her seriously, 'but be careful how you come down. I mean it, Miss Bellamy. I've seen too many people having to spend the rest of their lives in bed or a wheelchair because they took foolish risks. You don't want that to happen to

31

you, do you?'

'No, she doesn't,' Minnie interposed, still in nursemaid mode. 'And I'll see she doesn't, Doctor. I'll make sure she don't do nothing foolish.'

He smiled. 'But you won't be here all the time,' he pointed out. 'At some time you're going to have to go home and leave this obstinate lady to look after herself. And I know you're a woman of your word,' he went on, turning back to Constance, 'so if I have your promise not to do any of those things – or anything else you know you shouldn't do – I can be sure that you'll keep it. Can't I?'

Miss Bellamy sighed and folded her lips tightly. 'I suppose so,' she said at last, in a grudging tone. 'All right, Charles, I promise. But I'm still going to look after my garden,' she added fiercely. 'If I can't do that, I might as well give up altogether.'

'And none of us wants you to do that,' he agreed more gently. 'You enjoy your garden, Miss Bellamy. It's a credit to you. And now I must go. I've got really sick people to look after, you know.' He went to the door, pausing beside Minnie. 'And you look after yourself as well, Mrs Tozer. Let some of those visitors do a few chores about the place. I don't want you falling ill as well.' He went out and the two women looked at each other.

'And you can stop crinkling up your mouth like a Cornish pasty,' Minnie said sharply. 'Doctor's quite right. You'm too old to go clambering about on ladders and up trees, and if you wants anything like that done, you can get Jacob in, or one of the village boys. Young Micky Coker's a handy youngster, he'd do an hour or two for you if you paid him a tanner. Get your wood in for the fire, that sort of thing.'

Constance had agreed, and Minnie had got Micky and his friend Henry Bennetts along the next day to bring some logs down from the top of the garden and pile them near the kitchen door, and do a few other jobs around the outside. They knew both old ladies and chatted cheerfully to Minnie now as she sat outside, knitting in the pale March sunshine. After a while, she got out a tin of Alice Tozer's home-made biscuits and they sat at her feet, munching.

'I bet you remember a lot of things about Burracombe,' Micky said, his mouth full. 'My dad says you're one of the oldest people here.'

'So I am. I was born when Queen Victoria was on the throne. Us had got the railway in Tavistock a few years before I was born and my old father used to take Mother to Plymouth on it some-times, for a treat. A lot of the Tavistock that you know today was built around then too – proper slum it was before that, so I been told, with hovels for the miners and their families to live in. Then the old Duke of Bedford – him whose statue stands in Bedford Square to this day – he built all the Bedford Cottages and the Town Hall and Pannier Market and Bedford Square. I grew up with all that.'

'You mean you're nearly as old as the Town Hall and Bedford Square?' Henry Bennetts asked in awe. 'Are you as old as the church, too?'

Minnie laughed. 'My stars, no! That were part of the old abbey – nearly seven hundred year old, that be. I might be getting on a bit, but I'm not a miracle!'

'My dad says you are,' Micky said. 'He was saying to my mum only the other day, after you found Miss Bellamy laying on the ground half-dead, and got help, and looked after her, that Minnie Tozer's a flipping miracle, he said.'

'Oh, did he indeed?' Minnie said, trying to sound cross but looking rather pleased. 'I shall have to have a word with your dad, talking about people behind their backs. And now,' she added, looking up at the sun, which had started to go behind a tall conifer, 'I'm going back indoors. 'Tis getting chilly out here. And you two boys had better get back to work. There's a ton of logs up at the top end of the garden want bringing down, and I'd like the box filled up in the kitchen before I goes back to the farm.'

The two boys scrambled to their feet and ran off, and Minnie got up more slowly, colder and stiffer than she'd realised. Miss Constance would have had her rest now, she thought, and be ready for a cup of tea, and then Joanna or Val would probably arrive to walk back to the farm with her. Later on, Alice or one of the others would call in to make sure the old lady was comfortable through the night and Minnie would be back in the morning.

Nearly as old as Bedford Square! she thought with a sense of wonder. Why, I haven't thought of that for years. But still – she smiled – not *quite* as old as St Eustachius church...

She paused, her hand on the rough bark of Constance's plum tree, and thought of all that she had lived through and all the changes she had seen. And yet Burracombe itself seemed always the same. What changes there had been had hap-

34

pened slowly, almost unnoticeably. It was the people mostly who had changed as the years passed by. Old people dying, new lives being born. Children growing up, taking over from their parents, passing away in their turn.

One day it'll be me, she thought. But not just yet. I'm not ready to leave all this for quite a while...

'I called in to see Miss Bellamy this afternoon,' Hilary Napier told her father at dinner at the Barton that evening. 'Minnie Tozer's guarding her like a dragon. Wouldn't let me in until she'd checked that Miss Bellamy had finished her afternoon nap and the best cups were out for tea. And she seems to have got half the village lending a hand around the house and garden – boys all over the place, bringing in logs for the fire, Jacob Prout finishing the winter digging, Alice Tozer and Dottie popping in with meals on plates. Poor Miss Bellamy hardly has a moment to call her own.'

Gilbert Napier grunted and wiped his lips with his napkin. 'People are pretty good in the village – always ready to lend a hand. Not sure they'd be so ready if it was one of the Cullifords, mind.'

'Oh, I don't think they'd let anyone go neg-lected,' Hilary said, but she knew that he was partly right. Feckless Arthur Culliford and his slatternly wife Maggie wouldn't be exactly neg-lected, but there wouldn't be a constant stream of well-wishers and helpers at their door as there was at Constance Bellamy's. 'People rallied round when Shirley's arm was broken,' she added, and saw her father's face darken. He never liked being reminded of the time when Travis and the game-keeper had gone after poachers one dark night and someone's gun had gone off, injuring a small girl. 'Anyway, I thought you'd like to know about Miss Bellamy,' she added quickly.

'Of course I do. I hope you gave her my regards. I'll call in myself tomorrow. I suppose Mrs Tozer will let me in?'

'If you give the password,' Hilary said solemnly, and they both laughed.

'She's getting on a bit herself,' he said thoughtfully. 'I remember going round to the farm as a boy, for cream and eggs, and she'd been married to Ted's father for a few years then. Ted was in his pram. My, that seems a long time ago. We've had two world wars in that time.'

Hilary nodded. Gilbert, a retired colonel, had served in both wars, and she had been an Army driver in the second. And it was in that war that her brother Baden, the heir to Burracombe, had been killed, changing the lives of all of them.

'She's very spry, all the same,' she said, referring to Minnie Tozer in the hope of steering her father away from the subject of war. 'You'd never think she was ... what? Eighty-six, eighty-seven?'

'Something like that,' he nodded. 'And as tough as an old oak. But she won't go on for ever. None of us does that.' He poured himself more coffee and Hilary waited, afraid that he was going to start talking yet again about her 'duty' (as he saw it) to find herself a husband and produce new heirs for the estate. Instead, to her surprise, he continued with the subject of Minnie Tozer. 'You know, she must have seen more changes than any of us. And more monarchs, too. She was already a wife and mother when Victoria died and she's seen every coronation since. I don't suppose she'll see another after this. Think of that, Hilary – born when a queen reigned over Britain, and will probably die when another's on the throne.'

'Yes, it's quite a thought,' she agreed. 'Which reminds me, Father, there's a meeting in the village on Friday evening about the Coronation celebrations. Do you want to go?'

He shook his head. 'No. You go along, see what's being planned. I dare say you'll have a hand in it yourself anyway. I'll help with the finances, of course. They won't be able to do a Coronation celebration on a shoestring.'

Hilary nodded. Gilbert always supported the village events and usually attended, but he never took part in the planning. That was for the village, he said, and he would only be a dampener on the proceedings. Nobody would feel free to be themselves.

Hilary thought he was right, but she was surprised that he realised it. For herself, she liked to be part of what was going on, and had every intention of attending the meeting, as did Travis Kellaway, the estate manager, and she was fairly sure she didn't damp things.

The world was changing, though, and it was for people like herself to change with it. And she was looking forward both to the coronation itself and to the village's celebration. If you could say nothing else about the villagers of Burracombe, she thought – and you could in fact say plenty – they always knew how to have a good time.

Chapter Four

Joyce Warren smiled charmingly at the group of people gathered in Burracombe village hall. Only someone who knew her well would have seen in that smile the determination to take charge from the outset. As it happened, most of those present knew her all too well.

'Thinks she'll take over the whole caboodle,' Alf Coker muttered to George Sweet. 'If us don't stand up for ourselves from the start, us won't get a look-in. 'Tis always the same with outsiders.'

If Joyce Warren had heard this remark, she would have given the blacksmith a sharp reminder that she had lived in Burracombe for the past fifteen years. However, she heard only the gruff murmur of his voice and sent him a reproving glance before continuing with her little speech.

'I've called this meeting tonight to discuss Burracombe's plans for celebrating the Coronation,' she began. 'I think you'll all agree that the pageant the year before last was a great success, as was the summer fair last year with the children's performance of *A Midsummer Night's Dream,* but I'm sure that for something as wonderful as the Coronation of our young Queen we can do something even better. Now, I've sketched out a few rough ideas of my own, but I'm sure that lots of you will have suggestions as well, so perhaps we can start with those.' She gazed benignly at the

38

rows of faces, knowing perfectly well that nobody would say a word. 'Dr Latimer, perhaps you'd like to give us a start.'

Charles Latimer gave a start, but it wasn't the sort Joyce had been thinking of. He'd been miles away, as it happened, dreaming wistfully of the holiday he and his wife were planning in Scotland later in the year. He looked blankly at Joyce. 'Er ... well, I'm afraid I haven't really had time to think about it much, but...'

'We've all had since February last year to think about it,' Joyce pointed out. 'We knew as soon as the King died that there would be a Coronation.'

'Yes, I know,' the doctor floundered, 'but it's been a busy winter for me and...' He glanced around for someone to help him out. 'Felix, you're usually full of ideas.'

Felix grinned. 'But I'm not going to be in Burracombe by then,' he said. 'I'll be across the river as vicar of Little Burracombe. I expect we'll be arranging our own celebrations.'

The villagers stared at him. They all knew, of course, that he was to be inducted as vicar on Easter Sunday and that they would lose him as part of their own village, but none of them had really considered the meaning of this. Felix had only been with them for three years but he wasn't an 'outsider' as Joyce Warren was. As Basil Harvey's curate, he had a special place, and he'd more than filled it – visiting the school once a week, organising a drama club and producing the first village pantomime since before the war, and even getting himself engaged to the young schoolmistress, Stella Simmons.

Ted Tozer cleared his throat. 'Seems to me it might be a good idea for the two Burracombes to join forces over this. As Mrs Warren says, 'tis a big event and us ought to celebrate it proper. And with curate going over the river, it might be a good chance to do summat really big.'

There was a flurry of bemused whispers. Join forces with Little Burracombe? Such a thing had never been heard of. The two Burracombes had been rivals since ... well, ever since there'd *been* two Burracombes. Or so Alf Coker declared, setting himself firmly at the head of the dissenters.

'I don't see how it could be done,' he maintained. 'There'd have to be a village party, for a start, and where would us have that? In Little Burracombe, or over here? Burracombe folk wouldn't want to go traipsing over there, and I dare say they wouldn't be too eager to come here, neither. I don't even know as they've got anywhere suitable for the children's sports and games, and then there's the teas and the dancing in the evening. Neither of the village halls is big enough to hold everyone. And there's getting back afterwards, not to mention the refreshments. Can't just keep it to tea and orange squash, not for a Coronation. I tell you straight, Mr Copley, I wouldn't fancy coming back over the Clam with a skinful, and I don't reckon nobody else will, neither. And they Little Burracombe folk are an uncivilised lot, as you'll discover when you gets to be vicar – they can put it away even more than us here. Send 'em home in the state they'll be in, and you'll be holding funerals for the drownded for the next three weeks.'

Felix, who had often crossed the Clam – a narrow wooden bridge which had once been no more than a large tree-trunk, laid from bank to bank – laughed. 'It looks as if I'm going to have some interesting times in my new job. But at least you've answered quite a few questions.' He cast the blacksmith an amused glance. 'Alf seems to have set out the programme for the whole day – children's games and sports in the afternoon, teas and a dance in the evening. It sounds like a good start. And I've got a suggestion to make about that, if no one minds. If the two villages are indeed to combine, then why not use those two fields down by the river, one each side? They're nice and level for games, and we might be able to put a big marquee in one for teas and so on. We could even make use of the river itself – have a greasy pole across it, for instance. A greasy pole is always fun.'

'Oh, I don't really think–' Joyce began, but Ted Tozer was speaking again.

'Us'll need to lay on some special bell-ringing,' he said firmly. 'Me and some of the others have been talking about this and we reckon there should be ringing at the same time as they'll be ringing in London, at Westminster Abbey. That'll be as the Queen is on her way there, and again when her comes out. Then everyone will know just how things be going on.'

'Isn't it going to be on the wireless?' George Sweet asked. 'Folk'll be indoors listening, won't they?'

'Yes, but if they leave their windows open they'll hear the bells all right,' Ted asserted, and the others nodded. It was only right and proper,

41

after all, that the bells should be rung on such a day.

'Well, we're thinking of buying a television set,' Joyce said, a little self-consciously. 'They've agreed to let the cameras into the Abbey itself, you know. We'll probably have a better view than many of those who are actually there.'

There was a short silence. Most of the villagers had seen television, usually in Towls' shop window in Tavistock, or in Plymouth, but as yet nobody in the village had acquired one. Val Ferris nudged her husband and whispered, 'I expect she'll be asking a few favoured friends in to watch. She'll be quite unbearable afterwards – we'll never hear about anything else.'

'Didn't you say Hilary's father's going to get one as well?' Luke murmured, glancing towards the front row at the Squire's daughter.

'Mm. The Colonel wanted to go to London to be with his old regiment, but Dr Latimer won't let him. He's not giving in very graciously, but he finally agreed to the television, and Hilary says we can go along and see it if we like.'

'Could we have *everyone's* attention, please?' Joyce Warren enquired in a tone of exaggerated patience, and the two culprits grinned and turned their eyes to the front again. She gave a little nod, satisfied that she was once more in control, but Alf Coker had more to say.

'How long be this Coronation going to last? From what I've read, it'll be going on most of the day. I can't see as we'm going to have much time for jollification – the village is going to be like a ghost town, with everyone sitting indoors listening

42

to the wireless or staring at a television set.'

'It finishes some time in the afternoon,' Joyce said firmly. 'Plenty of time for afternoon games, tea and a dance in the evening. But as I was going to say, we really need–'

'And there's us ringers too,' George Sweet broke in. 'We're not going to hear much of it, if we're over in the church. How be us going to know when it's time to ring, anyway? You know what it's like with weddings – they never starts on time, what with the bride not being ready or the best man losing the ring, and by the time they've chucked in an extra hymn or two they never finishes on time neither. This Coronation could go on till teatime for all anyone can tell.'

'It will start and finish exactly on time,' Joyce stated, irritation beginning to edge her voice. 'They organise these things rather better in London than we seem to manage here in Burracombe.' Having now offended almost everyone present, she went on, 'And if I may have a moment to outline my own ideas, I really think we need something more than children's games and a dance in the village hall. As I said at the beginning, we've done very well in the past with our pageant and summer fair, and I'm sure we can pull something extra special out of the hat – or the crown! – for an occasion as wonderful as this.' She paused, giving a little laugh at her quip, then went on a little less certainly, 'Felix, you're usually full of ideas.'

'Yes, but as I've already pointed out, I'm not going to be here. I'm really sorry, Mrs Warren, but unless Little Burracombe agrees to combine,

I don't feel I should suggest what Burracombe should do after I've left.'

'Perhaps you shouldn't have come to the meeting then,' she said rather sharply. 'But I'm sure we can trust you not to take any of our ideas to your new friends and parishioners.'

Felix flushed and Stella's blue eyes darkened. 'There's no need to treat him like a spy,' she exclaimed. 'Felix has to carry on doing his work while he's here, but he's quite right to keep out of any discussions about what's going to happen after he's left.'

'Look,' the young curate said, putting his hand over hers, 'you all know how much I've enjoyed being in Burracombe but I'd have had to move on eventually and the thought of being so close is more than I could ever have hoped for. But it does present certain difficulties. From my own point of view, it would be ideal if the two villages could join together to celebrate the Coronation, but Alf's right, it might not be easy. Meanwhile, perhaps it would be better if I left the meeting, so that there's no problem about whether I should join in the discussion or not.'

There was an instant outcry, over which Alf Coker's booming tones could be heard.

'As long as you'm in this village, Mr Copley, you'm welcome at any meeting that gets held. And us'd like to have your opinion, even if you can't make any suggestions, which I should think we'd all understand.' He glowered at Joyce Warren, whose back stiffened with indignation. They had had more than one difference of opinion during the pantomime which Felix had written and produced in the village hall just before Christmas. Mrs Warren, accustomed to making herself the leader of any village event she could reasonably take over, had been distinctly put out to find Felix effortlessly taking charge, and – worse still – that Alf Coker's portrayal of the Dame had been so good that his word too was treated as law.

All the same, she had called this meeting and was determined to remain in the chair. As she glanced around, she noticed that Basil Harvey seemed to have something to say, and she raised a hand for silence and nodded to him.

'I just thought you might like to know that arrangements are being made for the service to be broadcast in the church,' the Vicar said, his round, rosy face wreathed in smiles. 'So all those who feel they'd like to join in, as it were, will be able to come in and listen. It's a long service, so I wouldn't expect many to remain the whole time,' he added, 'but it will be useful for the bell-ringers to know exactly when to start ringing.'

'That sounds lovely,' Stella said. 'We can all enjoy it together instead of being shut away in our houses.'

Joyce Warren looked nonplussed. 'Well, that certainly sounds very nice for those who won't be able to see it on television,' she agreed, letting it be known that she wouldn't be one of the de-prived. 'But it doesn't solve the problem of how to spend the rest of the day.'

'I already said,' Alf Coker retorted. 'Games and sports for the little tackers in the afternoon, and a bit of a hop in the evening. I daresay Bernie Nethercott'll send down a barrel or two from the pub to keep things festive, like. And the river field would be the ideal place for it, so long as nobody tries going home over that there greasy pole!'

'And there's plenty of help to do the teas, and a few sandwiches and sausage rolls and cakes and so on for both,' Alice Tozer said after the laughter produced by this quip – rather more successful than Mrs Warren's joke earlier – had died down. 'I'm sure me and Dottie Friend and a few of us can take that in hand.'

'I must say, it sounds a good idea,' Felix said. 'But I think Mrs Warren is right too. An event like a Coronation does demand something special.'

Nobody could deny this, and the faces that had been so wooden a few minutes ago were now furrowed in contemplation.

'Well,' Joyce said, when she'd allowed long enough for ideas to develop but not long enough for anyone to express them, 'as it happens, I do have one little suggestion to make. It occurred to me that, as this is the Coronation of a new monarch, we might do a representation of all the monarchs through our history. Most of them have a story to tell, and we could arrange tableaux of their stories – Elizabeth the First, for instance, knighting Sir Francis Drake, or Richard the Lionheart riding to war.'

'Or Henry the Eighth, chopping off Anne Boleyn's head,' Vic Nethercott said, grinning.

Joyce frowned. 'I'm sure there are plenty of other stories about Henry the Eighth we could illustrate,' she began and everyone laughed as Vic chuckled and said 'I bet there are!'

'Well, anyway,' she went on with a quelling

look, 'even if we can't find a story about a particular monarch, we can portray him – or her – in
a typical scene, with their subjects dressed
appropriately. What does everyone think?'

'You know,' Alf Coker said after a pause, 'it ain't
such a bad idea at that. There's quite a lot of 'em,
after all.' He held up an enormous hand and
began to count on fingers so huge that the local
butcher's sausages were known as 'Cokers'. 'You
can go back a long way, when you think about it.
Harold, getting his eye put out at Hastings–'

'Nobody's sticking an arrow in my eye,' Vic
said, grinning again.

'–and Alfred burning the cakes, and that queen
who had those knives sticking out of her chariot
wheels – we could use Ted Tozer's horse and cart
for that – and...' He ran out of ideas. 'Well, that's
a few to be going on with, anyway.'

'There aren't many parts for the children,' Miss
Kemp, the head teacher, said dubiously. 'Or
women, come to that.'

'Oh, I think there are,' Joyce said. 'We have at
least three queens – Boadicea, Elizabeth and Victoria – not to mention Henry the Eighth's six
wives, and Queen Anne, and the two Marys–'

'One of them was Queen of Scots,' George
Sweet butted in. 'My missus was reading a book
about her only the other day and she told me all
about it. You can't have her in it.'

'Well, there are still plenty,' Joyce retorted. 'All
the Kings would have consorts, wouldn't they?
Six, in Henry the Eighth's case. And as for the
children, there are plenty of princes and princesses, not to mention some subjects – courtiers

47

and peasants – for the tableaux which don't have much actual story.'

There was another short silence and then Hilary Napier said, 'I think it has definite possibilities. It'll be colourful and fun to do, and it's appropriate for the day. And it will remind everyone of our history, too.'

'There is that, certainly,' Miss Kemp agreed, and glanced at Stella. 'We could do some extra lessons on kings and queens.'

Stella, thinking of wallcharts and paintings and the stories the children could write, nodded with enthusiasm and Mrs Warren looked pleased and satisfied.

'Well, shall we put it to the vote? Unless anyone has any other suggestions to make?' Nobody spoke, and she said, 'Hands up all those who agree to put on a pageant of British Monarchs Through the Ages.'

A small forest of hands went up, and she said, 'Well, that seems to be unanimous. Now, we haven't much time to prepare – the Coronation Day is on June the second so we'd better draw up some plans. Who's prepared to take part?'

'Us'll need a committee,' Alf Coker said, determined not to let Joyce run things entirely her own way. 'I don't mind being on it.'

Felix reminded them once again that he wouldn't be a part of the village by then. 'Although I'll pass on your suggestion that the two villages join forces. I know they're holding their own meeting on Friday and I've been invited to be there.'

'I don't suppose they'll be interested,' Alf Coker

said. 'Always been a bit independent, Little Burracombe have.'

'Don't you tell 'em about our plans, mind,' George said. 'Not unless they'm willing to join up with us.'

'I won't breathe a word,' Felix promised. 'Even if they come up with the same idea.'

'Oh.' George looked nonplussed. 'Well, maybe if they do that, you'd better tell 'em. Look a bit daft, both villages doing the same thing. And you can come back and tell us what they be planning,' he added.

'I can hardly do that,' Felix said, and Alf agreed.

'If us don't want Mr Copley telling them our plans, he can't come back here and tell us theirs, can he, now? Fair's fair, George. And the more you think about it, the more sense it makes for the two villages to join up. 'Tis a happy occasion, after all, and one that don't happen too many times in a lifetime.'

'Well, we seem to have had a very productive meeting,' Joyce Warren declared. She shuffled her notes together and beamed at the assembly. 'I suggest that the committee meets at my house as soon as possible to start making plans. There'll be plenty to do – floats and scenery for the tableaux, costumes, props, not to mention the refreshments and the organisation of the rest of the day. And we haven't a great deal of time – the Coronation is only three months away, and there's Easter in between.'

There was a scraping of chairs and general buzz of conversation as people began to get up and make their way out of the hall. A few stayed

49

behind to stack the chairs in the small room off the main hall, and Hilary approached Stella, who was talking to Val.

'How's Maddy now?' she asked quietly. 'Is she getting over what happened? It was a dreadful thing for her.'

'Yes, it was,' Stella said. 'Val's just asked me the same thing. She seems to be managing pretty well, all things considered. We brought her back with us the other day, but she still wants to go back to West Lyme as soon as she can use her arm more. She says she'll feel better if she gets back to work. But she misses Sammy terribly. It's going to take her some time to get over it.'

Hilary nodded. She had lost her own fiancé during the war, but at least she hadn't seen him killed before her eyes, as Maddy had.

'On the very day they'd got engaged, too,' she said. 'That makes it even more heartbreaking. Poor girl. I feel so sorry for her. Do pass on my commiserations, won't you, and she's welcome at the Barton if she feels like coming over.'

Stella nodded. Her own eyes were filled with tears and she was glad to go out into the darkness with the other two. They walked through the village together, with Luke a little way behind, discussing floats and scenery with Travis Kell-away. Felix caught them up after a moment or two and linked Stella's arm through his.

'Dottie says I'm to come in for a cup of cocoa and a slice of toast,' he said.

'Well, there's a surprise,' Stella said. 'Don't you always? And I don't suppose you gave her any hints, did you?'

'Certainly not,' he said with dignity. 'She suggested it herself. Anyway, what do you all think of Mrs Warren's plans?'

'She seems to have made all the decisions beforehand and swept us all along with them, as usual,' Hilary said wryly. 'Just as she always does! But without people like her, nothing ever would get done, so we mustn't grumble. I think it sounds a good idea anyway, and I expect you and Miss Kemp are glad of the chance to teach the children a little history, Stella.'

'Are you insinuating that we don't do that anyway?' Stella enquired. 'But you're right, it's always good for them to have an extra incentive to learn. I do foresee some trouble though. Micky Coker is bound to want to officiate at Anne Boleyn's execution and his father probably has an axe in the forge that he can borrow.'

'You'll be pleased when he and Henry Bennetts go to big school in Tavistock after the summer,' Hilary remarked, but Stella laughed and shook her head.

'They add quite a lot of interest to the average school day! Mind you, the Crocker twins are rapidly taking over from them. They don't seem to have the same charm as Micky, unfortunately. I think I'll see if I can get them cast as the Princes in the Tower, and then I can lock them up!'

They parted at the corner. Stella and Felix turned to go down the lane to Dottie Friend's cottage, and Hilary and Travis walked on through the village towards the Barton, where Hilary lived, and the farmhouse where Travis was still lodging. Val and Luke watched them go and then set off for their own home, Jed's Cottage – still named after the grumpy old man who had lived there until last year.

'Do you think anything's going to come of Hilary and Travis?' Val asked after a moment or two. 'Hilary hated the idea of having an estate manager, when she was doing the job perfectly well herself, but she seems to have come round to it. They seem quite friendly these days.'

'The pantomime helped,' Luke said. 'And Travis helping her to save her horse's life. He seems a decent sort, anyway. It would be silly for her to go on being hostile to him.'

'Mm. I was wondering if they weren't getting a bit more than friendly, though. They spend a lot of time together – not just working. You often see them out riding together, and they obviously came to the meeting together tonight.'

'Well, they both live in the same direction.' Luke turned his head and looked at her. 'You don't think...?'

'Well, why not? It's time Hilary found someone. It's years since Henry was killed, and there's never been anyone since, though I did wonder for a while about Felix... But Travis would be much more suitable. He understands the estate, and that's important for Hilary.'

'But he's an employee,' Luke said. 'And there's his whole background... I can't see the Colonel taking to that idea.'

'We're not talking about the Colonel,' Val pointed out. 'We're talking about Hilary. She's a grown woman in her thirties. And she might have given up a lot of her life to look after her father

52

and run the estate, but she's not going to let him dictate to her about who she marries. And if she decides it's Travis she wants, I don't give much for Colonel Napier's chances of stopping her.'

Luke smiled and slipped his arm around her waist. 'I think you're right about that, my love, though I'm not so sure you're right that it is Travis she wants. But time will tell.' He chuckled. 'That's what I like about village life. All you have to do is stand back and watch, and the whole pageant will unfold before you. Just like Mrs Warren's History of British Monarchy. Did you notice how she slipped that past everyone, by the way? *British* Monarchs – not just English. She'll be able to include Mary Queen of Scots after all!'

Chapter Five

Travis and Hilary walked along the road in silence for a few minutes. Then he said, 'Well, that was all fairly predictable, wasn't it?'

Hilary felt herself prickle immediately. Although she and Travis had reached a better understanding in the past few months, she was still sensitive to anything that might be construed as a criticism of her beloved village. Her voice sounded stiff and tight as she replied.

'I don't know what you mean. I thought Mrs Warren's idea was quite a good one.'

'Oh, I'm not saying *that* was predictable, although I suppose it's fairly obvious really,' he said, making her prickle even more. 'I meant the way the meeting went – just like every other village meeting I've ever been to. Takes a while to get going, while everyone tries not to get drawn in, then someone starts an objection which leads to a bit of an argument, someone else throws in the idea they'd thought of in the first place, there's a bit more argument and the next thing you know you've been given a job to do. That's unless you're wise enough not to say a word, and make sure not to catch the chairman's eye.'

Hilary chuckled a little reluctantly. 'That *is* more or less how they go,' she admitted. 'And Joyce Warren always seems to end up in charge. It's strange how we let an outsider run our affairs.'

'Ouch,' he said ruefully. 'How long has she been here? Fifteen years, and still an outsider? I'd better be very careful what I say, then, after only a few months.'

Hilary laughed outright. 'That'll be the day, when *you* start to be careful what you say! Anyway, you know what villages are like. You have to be not only born here but have ancestors in the churchyard to be considered a local. I expect it's the same in Dorset.'

'It is. But our family did have ancestors in the churchyard there, so I could say what I liked. It's quite difficult to bite my tongue at times in Burracombe, but believe it or not, I do manage it occasionally. And it's easy to understand why the village lets an "outsider" run things – it's so that they can have a good grumble about it without causing offence amongst themselves! Now, which queen do you think you'll play in this march-past

54

of British royalty?'

'Me? Oh, I'm not going to be in it. I'll do something behind the scenes.'

'That I very much doubt. You have quite a regal air about you at times. And with that flash of temper you display when things aren't going your way, I think you'd make a very good Boadicea. You could use the old governess trap I've seen in the stables; it's much more the style than Ted Tozer's hay cart.'

Hilary was still gasping with indignation at his reference to her temper. 'You make me sound like a spoilt child!'

'Not at all. You just have a strong personality – exactly right for the dear old battleaxe. Not that she was old,' he added quickly. 'At least, I don't expect she was when she was leading her battalions of females to war. That's another thing you need, a female battalion. Plenty of parts for women, and it will look most impressive. In fact, I think you should lead the procession, since you'll probably be the earliest queen there.'

'You seem to have got it all arranged,' Hilary said, struggling between laughter and annoyance. 'You're not in Joyce Warren's pay, by any chance, are you?'

'If I were, I wouldn't tell you. In any case, I'd be more likely to take the side of the men in this pageant. We're definitely going to be taking second place.'

'I don't see why. It's a parade of monarchs, not queens, and most of them were men. And talking of kings, which do you fancy playing? Henry the Eighth?'

'With all those wives tagging along behind him? No thanks! Anyway, I haven't got the build – Alf Coker is much more suited to the part. Who do you fancy for William the Conqueror? And then there was Rufus, who got killed in the New Forest – we'll need someone with red hair for him.'

'I can tell you who Stella suggested for the two little princes who got murdered in the Tower,' Hilary said with a grin. 'The Crocker twins!'

They strolled on. Hilary's brief irritation had faded and she looked up at the stars and thought how pleasant this was, to be walking at night with a man she felt pretty well at ease with. Not all the time, of course – there were still moments, when she was with Travis, when she was either annoyed or uncertain of herself. But now, she thought, they could call themselves friends. Apart from Felix Copley, whom she had befriended when he first came to the village, it was a long time since Hilary had had a male friend.

'I'll say goodnight, then.' Travis broke into her thoughts and she realised they had reached the big gates leading to the drive of the Barton. 'Unless you want me to see you to your door.'

'Of course I don't!' Hilary said quickly. 'I've been walking along this drive in the dark since I was a Brownie. Goodnight, Travis.' She hesitated, but he simply grinned, tipped his hat to her, and strode off into the darkness, whistling softly. Hilary watched him for a moment, and then turned to walk up the familiar track, aware of a certain bleakness and thinking that it might actually have been quite nice to be seen to her door. Then she scolded herself for behaving like a young girl coming home from a village hop with a boy she fancied, and quickened her step. It was time she was home. Her father would be waiting for her to tell him about the meeting, and then he'd want a nightcap. As time went on, he seemed to need these moments of companionship more and more, and Hilary was the only one who could provide them.

I'm turning into a kind of substitute wife, she thought, climbing the steps to the big front door. That seems to be the pattern of my life these days – a substitute for my brother Baden, a substitute companion for my father, a substitute estate manager. And how does Travis see me? As a substitute for an employer, probably! But where am *I* in all this? Where's the real Hilary?

Ted Tozer stopped in the farmhouse porch to take off his boots before going into the big kitchen. Alice, who had somehow managed to keep her shoes clean on the walk through the village, went in to find Joanna listening to the wireless and darning a pile of socks.

'You've missed *Take It From Here*,' she said as they came in. 'It was really funny. Ron and Eth were a scream. How did the meeting go?'

'Much the same as always,' Alice said, going to the larder for a jug of milk and pouring some into a large saucepan. 'Mrs Warren took charge, of course, and made sure it'll all go the way she wants it. I could have told you that would happen before we went.'

'I've got an idea you did,' Ted said, winking at his daughter-in-law. 'A couple of times, if I

57

remember rightly. But you got to be fair, she do have some quite good ideas, and she don't mind putting in a bit of work.'

'She don't mind telling other people to put in a bit of work, you mean,' Alice retorted, getting cups and saucers out of the cupboard. 'I take it you'd like a cup of cocoa, Joanna?'

'Yes, please.' Joanna bit off the darning wool and wound it into a ball. 'There, that's this week's lot done, and if Tom wears holes in his heels before the next wash, he'll just have to put up with them. Some of these darns have got darns of their own.'

'He'll have to ask his gran to knit him some new ones,' Alice said. 'Where is she? Gone to bed already?'

'Yes, she said her cold was a bit worse so she made a poultice and took a hot-water bottle with her. She's not been gone all that long, though. She might fancy a cup of cocoa.'

'I'll take one up.' Alice fetched a tin of flapjacks out of the larder. 'D'you want one of these, Ted, or would you rather have a bit of cheese on toast?'

'I wouldn't say no to both,' Ted said with a grin. 'Our Tom'll be glad of a bite too, if he's been out in the lambing pens all evening. I'll take a turn out there when I've had mine, and he can come in for a hour or so.'

'So what's been decided about the Coronation?' Joanna asked.

'We're all going to have to be kings and queens – well, those of us daft enough to want to dress up on a sweltering June day. Which won't be me, because I'll be busy doing the teas.'

'It won't be me, neither,' Ted said. 'I'll be busy

58

ringing. We've decided to keep the bells going all day, on and off, as well as when the service starts and stops, and I can't do that in fancy dress.'

'I don't suppose it'll be me either,' Joanna said. 'The twins are still going to need a lot of attention. Robin could go as a little prince, though. He'd look sweet in a lace collar.'

'You might have a battle on your hands to get him to wear it,' Alice commented, mixing cocoa, sugar and a little cold milk in five large cups. 'Did they all get off to sleep all right?'

'Out like lights,' Joanna said. 'Not that it'll last long. The girls will be sure to wake up soon for their ten o'clock feed. It's like clockwork, the way they do things together, little as they are. I'm never sure if one sets the other off or if it's just automatic, like they're really one little person. It's quite frightening sometimes.'

Alice, pouring hot milk into the cups, looked at her curiously. 'How d'you mean, love?'

'Well – you know, if one's a bit poorly I somehow expect the other one to be the same. And I heard someone say once that if a twin dies, the other one soon follows. I don't know what I'd do if that happened.'

'Now look,' Alice said, setting down the milk pan and going over to her daughter-in-law. She put her arms round Joanna's shoulders. 'You're not to think that way. We got them through their first few weeks, didn't we? And there were plenty of people who thought we'd never do it, they were so tiny. And look at them now, as hale and hearty as any baby could be–'

'They're still small for their age, though. And

59

not sitting up yet.'

'Well, that's nothing to worry about. They'm only just five months old, and look how early they were. If they'd been born to time, they'd only be three months and you wouldn't even think of expecting them to sit up. And small don't matter. They'm putting on weight regular, and all from your own good milk, that's the main thing. You couldn't give them a better start than that.' She went back to the cocoa. 'You're tired, Joanna, that's what 'tis. It was a shock, having two when you thought there was only one, and it's been hard work for you ever since. You'll feel better when they're a bit older and the nice weather comes along.'

'I don't know about hard work,' Joanna said, brushing the back of her wrist across her eyes. 'I think I get it easy, with you and Gran to help, and Tom does all he can too.'

'It's still you that bears the brunt of it.' Alice finished stirring the cocoa and handed her a cup. 'There, you drink that and I'll take Gran's up to her. I'll do the cheese on toast when I come down.'

Joanna smiled and took a sip of cocoa, then put the cup down on the hearth beside her. 'I'll do the toast,' she said to Ted. 'I may be a bit tired but I'm not an invalid and Mum does too much as it is. And I'll toast a sandwich and take it out to Tom. You put your feet up for a bit, Dad, before you go out there to take over.'

Ted did as he was told, stretching out in his armchair beside the range and putting his feet on the battered old stool that Robin sat on when he was downstairs. He watched his daughter-in-law working, thinking what a good girl she was and how handy she'd become around the place since coming as a Land Girl during the war. They'd been lucky to get her, and lucky to keep her when Tom had come home and fallen in love with her. She fitted in well with the family, happy to live in the farmhouse with the rest of them, and they had a good marriage.

If only he could say the same for his own two daughters. Not that he could complain about Val, she was happy enough with young Luke, and he seemed settled enough now he'd stopped trying to make a living from those paintings of his and got a proper job, teaching art in Tavistock. But as for Jackie ... he frowned a little, thinking of his younger daughter, working in a big hotel in Plymouth and living away from home when she didn't need to. He ought not to have too much to worry about, since she was living with Jennifer Tucker who had said she'd look after her, but it wasn't the same as family, when all was said and done.

The air was filled with the savoury smell of toasting cheese when Alice came down the stairs again, her lips drawn in and her brow creased.

'What's the matter?' Ted and Joanna said together. 'Is it one of the children?' Joanna asked, already halfway to the door, and Ted added, 'Mum's not worse is she?'

'Well, I think she is a bit,' Alice said, and put out her hand to Joanna. 'No, it's not them, love, I looked in and they're all sound asleep. But I do feel a bit worried about Mum. It's gone right

61

down on her chest, and she's wheezing and looks as if every breath's hurting her. I'm not sure but what we ought to call Dr Latimer in.'

'What, at this time of night?' But Ted was already getting up and going to the door for his coat. Alice wasn't one to panic, and if she thought the doctor was needed, he wasn't going to argue. 'Well, he ought to be home now, unless someone else has called him out. He was at the meeting.'

'Yes, and I dare say he's just settling down to a bite of supper before he goes to bed.' Alice chewed her lip. 'I don't know, Ted. I don't know what we ought to do. You go up and have a look at her, will you? I don't want it to be just on my say-so.'

Ted went up the stairs. Alice stood by the kitchen table, resting one hand on its scrubbed surface and Joanna looked at her anxiously.

'Have a drop of cocoa, Mum. It'll steady you a bit.'

Alice nodded but made no attempt to pick up her cup. She rubbed one hand across her face and glanced up at the low ceiling where Ted's heavy footsteps could be heard moving across the bedroom. After a few minutes, he came down again.

'I'm going round for the doctor now,' he said. 'Go up and sit with her, Alice, will you? I don't reckon her wants to be on her own, just now.'

He dragged his coat around his shoulders and went out to the porch to put on his boots. The two women looked at each other and then Alice turned away and went up the narrow staircase.

Joanna sat undecided in her chair, the toast and cheese forgotten. It was only a few moments before she heard footsteps at the door and started to her feet. Surely Ted and the doctor couldn't be back already?

'What's going on?' Tom's cheerful voice enquired as he took off his boots in the porch. 'I thought someone was going to bring me out some cocoa. What does a bloke have to do to get a drink around here – die or something?'

Chapter Six

Minnie was suffering from a severe bout of bronchitis. Dr Latimer came straight round and put her on tablets, which made her very sleepy and confused but seemed to ease her breathing. He told Alice that they would have to keep an eye on her cough, because it could turn to pneumonia.

'I'll come again in the morning,' he said. 'Though I'll probably have to fight my way through the crowd, once people hear that Mrs Tozer's ill.'

'She's a popular woman, all right,' Alice said. 'But us'll look after her, Doctor, don't you worry. She's a tough old party, she won't let this keep her in bed for long.'

'So long as she stays there until that cough's gone,' he warned, going down the steep stairway. 'I don't want her getting up and about too soon after this. The weather's treacherous at this time of year.' He paused on his way through the kitchen and spoke to Joanna. 'And how are those twins of yours, and young Robin?'

'They're all fighting fit,' Joanna said, not wanting to tell the doctor of her superstitious fears. 'Robin's getting excited about Easter, and the babies are growing well. Though they're still quite small, of course,' she added, unable to prevent a small note of anxiety from creeping into her voice.

'They've got quite a bit of catching up to do still,' he said comfortingly. 'But if you're at all worried, I'll have a look at them.'

'Oh no, I'm not really worried. Just a bit over-anxious,' she smiled, but he gave her a closer look.

'I'll check 'em over anyway, when I come to see old Mrs Tozer tomorrow. We have to keep an eye on these precious little people.'

Alice came down the stairs as Joanna was getting ready to go to bed.

'She seems a bit easier now. Going off to sleep, where I hope she'll stay if that cough don't wake her up again. Where are the men – back out in the sheds?'

'No, Tom's gone up for a few hours' sleep. He said he'd set the alarm for four. I'll be waking up to feed the babies then anyway, so I'll look in on Gran as well. You ought to get some sleep too, Mum.'

'I'll sit with her for a while first,' Alice said. 'I can start thinking about refreshments for Coronation day.'

'But that's months off! You don't need to do that yet.'

'I do, if we're going to do something special. Me and some of the others are thinking of making a big cake, like a wedding cake. Three tiers, we thought, though we might need more if the whole

64

village is going to have a piece. I reckon we'll need a good half-dozen.'

'It'll topple over,' Joanna said. 'And how big will the bottom one have to be? Has anyone got a tin—'

'I mean half a dozen *cakes*,' Alice said. 'Three tiers each. That's a lot of baking and you know a fruit cake needs to be made well in advance, especially if it's got to take the weight. And then there's all the icing and decorating to do as well. It's going to take a lot of thinking about.'

'You'd better start now, then,' Joanna agreed. 'Who's going to do all this icing and decorating? You're talking about eighteen cakes! What's it all going to cost? And where are you going to get all the fruit from, and the sugar?'

'Maybe it do sound a bit ambitious,' Alice admitted. 'Perhaps us should just stick to the one decorated cake for show, and have some others already cut up in the back for serving out. George Sweet can give a hand with the baking too, and I dare say plenty of folk will be ready to give up a bit of fruit and sugar for them. There'll be Coronation mugs to think about as well, though I expect that'll be done through the school. I'd better talk to Miss Kemp. Anyway, you get yourself off to bed and I'll go and sit with Gran.'

The two women went up the stairs, leaving the kitchen lamp burning low for Tom when he came down at four o'clock.

'I hope she'll be better in the morning,' Joanna said softly as they parted on the landing. 'I don't like to think of anything happening to dear old Gran.'

'None of us do,' Alice replied. 'But her's well into her eighties, and it's got to come sometime. We'll stave it off as long as possible, though. There's a lot of life left in her yet. And you don't want to go worrying yourself too much about those twins, neither, maid. They come of long-lived stock and they'll still be here when they'm in their eighties, too.'

'Goodness, I can't imagine it!' Joanna said with a smile. 'My little twins, in their eighties! I hope you're right, Mother.'

'I am,' Alice said firmly. 'I know I am.'

When Joanna peeped in a few hours later, Minnie was sleeping, propped up against a mound of pillows, and the chair next to her bed was empty. Alice must have gone to bed, satisfied that the old lady would be all right for a while. Joanna stood for a moment looking down at the face, as wrinkled as an old apple, the pale lips drawn in over toothless gums. Thin grey hair lay flattened against Minnie's scalp and her breath wheezed slightly in her chest. She looked very old indeed, and Joanna tried and failed to imagine her children at that age. I can't even imagine myself at that age, she thought, turning away to go and begin feeding them.

Tom was up and dressed, bending over the cot where the twins slept together, one at each end.

'What it is to be a baby,' he said, straightening up. 'All tucked up cosy and warm with a nice mother to come and attend to your every need. No wonder they say it's the best time of your life – I just wish I could remember it! I'll bring you a cup of tea. How's Gran?'

'Better, I think. But she looks so old, Tom, without her teeth in and her hair all anyhow. And she's so tiny. You don't realise it, somehow, when she's bustling about downstairs, but there's nothing of her. I hope she pulls through this.'

'Of course she will. She's a Tozer!' Tom pulled on his thick socks and padded to the door. 'I'll be back in a minute. Want anything else? Some toast?'

'I wouldn't mind a slice, if you're making it.' She knew that he would fry some bacon to go between two slices of toast for himself, and take some out to his father. By the time Ted came in, Alice would be downstairs to cook him a proper breakfast before he got a few hours' sleep and then went out to attend to some of the other jobs around the farm. At this time of year it was like living in a lamb factory and there were usually two or three orphans in a cardboard box in front of the kitchen range, but at least his cousin Norman would be coming up to do the milking. They couldn't have managed without all the help they had from Norman and the other farm workers.

Joanna settled down in bed, one baby on each breast. To begin with, she'd fed them in turns but Nurse Sanders had shown her how to hold them, one under each arm, so that they could suckle together, and there was no doubt that it saved a lot of time. She liked to think it was better for them too, to be feeding together, and she looked down at the tiny faces, eyes closed in blissful concentration, and felt a warm rush of love for them. I thought I was only expecting one, she reflected,

67

but if I was asked now which one I'd have chosen, I couldn't answer. They're both so precious.

She remembered the time just after their birth, when Heather, the elder twin, had suddenly seemed to fail. It had been touch and go for some time, but they were now both strong and healthy, and putting on weight fast, despite being small for their age. I'll be glad when they're a year old, Joanna thought. I shall start to feel safe then.

Tom came in with her tea and toast. She could smell the bacon frying downstairs and almost wished he'd brought her a rasher too. She smiled at him and he bent and kissed her, and then both babies.

'Look after yourselves till I get back. Tell you one good thing about farming, you can nearly always pop back to see the wife and little uns. I wouldn't like to have to catch a bus into Plymouth every day and work in an office. Nor even to Tavistock, like Luke does, though I suppose a school's not so different from a farm in one way.'

'How's that?' Joanna asked, and he grinned.

'You're working with wild animals in both places! Well, no, that's not really true – farm animals aren't wild.' He winked at her and went out, closing the door quietly behind him. Joanna chuckled and lay back against her pillows.

The twins were falling asleep, replete with warm, sweet milk. She removed them gently from her breasts and made sure they were still clean and dry before laying them back in their cot. She covered them with their soft blanket and stood looking down at them for a moment, her heart aching with love.

My little precious ones, she thought. My precious little girls.

The village grapevine was extra busy next morning, and news of Minnie Tozer's illness was already spreading when the shop opened. Mabel Purdy, the school cleaner, had heard it from Norman Tozer's wife.

'Got bad bronchitis, so Betty told me – her Norman was called up there to do the milking early on, and it seems they called the doctor round late last night after the meeting. They're frightened it's going to turn to pneumonia.'

Edie pursed her lips. 'That don't sound too good. Poor old Minnie Tozer's getting on for ninety, isn't she? Has their Val been up to the farm at all, do you know?'

'I'm not sure she'd have known about it. She was off early this morning to catch the bus to Tavvy with her hubby. I saw them walking out to the main road together.'

'Well, maybe it's not that serious then. They'd have sent down for Val first thing, if it had been, her being a nurse and all. Did you go to that meeting last night? I'd got some new stock in so I couldn't manage it.'

Mabel gave her a quick résumé. 'I suppose you'll be shutting for the day, Edie,' she observed. 'Us'll have to get everything in early that week. I'll have half a pound of tea, and a pound of sugar, please.'

''Tis only for one day, Mabel, we'm not setting up for a siege,' Edie told her, weighing the sugar into a blue paper bag. 'I'll probably just open for

69

an hour or so in the morning to get the papers out of the way. It wouldn't be no good staying open all day, not if everyone's going to be indoors listening to the wireless and then having a bunfight and games after.'

'I hear that Mrs Warren's getting a television in,' Mabel said. 'Don't suppose her'll be inviting the likes of us round to see it, though.'

'Of course not. She've got her own friends. Anyway, I've seen television sets in Towl's window in Tavistock, not much bigger than a seaside postcard, they be. You get a better picture of the Queen on a postage stamp. And Bert Foster says they're going to make a film of it, in colour, too, that we'll be able to see at the Carlton. I'll be happy to wait for that.'

'You can go with Bert and have a cuddle in the back row,' Mabel said with a grin, and Edie's face flushed. She had never got used to being teased over her friendship with the butcher next door. Mabel laughed and went on, 'I wouldn't mind going up to London and seeing it on the day. A proper sight that'll be, with Pall Mall all decorated and everything. They say people'll be sleeping on the pavements the night before to make sure of a good place.' She took the bag of sugar and the packet of tea. 'And a quarter of Callard and Bowser's toffees.' She handed over her ration book for the groceries. ''Tis nice to be able to buy as many sweets as we want. I'm surprised you didn't run out when they came off ration last month.'

'We got a good stock in, and the government let the manufacturers have extra sugar to allow for it.' Edie snipped off the sugar token and handed the book back. She began to weigh out the toffees and rolled up a cone of blue paper to tip them into, folding its top over as she talked. 'You're not really thinking of going up to London and sleeping on the pavement are you, Mabel? I can't say I'd fancy it much myself, even in June.'

'What, me? I can't even get my Fred to take me to Plymouth for the day. But I wouldn't be surprised if Down's don't run a few coaches from Tavvy, you know. There's sure to be some people would like to see it.'

'If Mrs Warren wasn't getting a television set, she'd probably be going herself,' Edie remarked. 'You know how her likes to go one better than everyone else. Not that I can see her sleeping on a pavement, not even for the Queen!'

They were both laughing at the idea of Joyce Warren sleeping on a pavement when Jacob Prout came in. He looked at the two women and said, 'Well, someone's got summat to be happy about. What's the big joke?'

'Oh, nothing much,' Mabel Purdy said. 'We were just talking about the Coronation. Will you be going up to London for it, Jacob?'

'Me?' he said, as if she'd just suggested he go to the Moon. 'Go to London? Don't talk so far back, Mabel. You know I never goes further than Plymouth these days, and that's only to please my Jennifer now and then.'

'I don't know why she don't move out to Burracombe,' Mabel said. 'She's got that cottage next door, what young Val Ferris and her hubby live in. She could move into that and go in to Plymouth on the bus every day.'

71

'I'm hoping she will, eventually,' Jacob said. 'But she won't turn Val and Luke out, not until somewhere else comes up for them to live. And young Jackie Tozer's staying with her now, so 'tain't so easy for her to give up the house there.'

'I heard as Jackie wants to live in at the Duke of Cornwall hotel,' Edie remarked. 'That'd be a good thing for her, I reckon. She could get on there and make something of herself. I always did think she was too good to be a housemaid up at the Barton.'

'Here, what did you think about the meeting last night, Jacob? D'you reckon this pageant idea of Mrs Warren's will come to anything?'

'Don't see why not. Us'll all be badgered into it one way or another anyway, you know what she's like when she gets an idea. Not that I'll be taking part in it,' he added firmly, in case anyone was about to dragoon him into fancy dress there and then. 'It's the village itself I'm concerned about it. I wants it to look its best for the day, and there's a few gardens could do with a bit of care and attention. I dare say you all knows which ones I mean.'

'Arthur Culliford's, for a start,' Edie said with a sniff. 'I don't know why he can't throw out some of that rubbish he lets pile up, and pull out a few weeds. Then he and Maggie could grow some veg to feed the little uns. She's always in here pleading poverty but what I say is, when you grow your own veg you've always got something for the pot, and that's what your garden's for. What were you wanting, Jacob?'

'Packet of ten Woodbine, please,' he said,

fishing a few coins from his pocket just as Dottie Friend came in with her shopping basket over her arm. 'Morning to you, Dottie. Us was just chewing over the meeting last night. I reckon us ought to have a think about what sort of decorations we can put up, don't you? There's that bunting we gets out for the summer fair every year, but to my mind that's looking a bit tired.'

'A few Union Jacks, that's what we want,' Dottie said. 'But I don't know where the money's going to come from. We could do something in the gardens, though – I was thinking, if we could get everyone to plant red, white and blue flowers it would look patriotic, wouldn't it? I could make a start on those barrels we got outside the pub.'

The others gazed at her with respect. 'All the gardens red, white and blue,' Jacob said thoughtfully. 'Now, that'd make a good show. But there's not much time if we'm going to do that. Maybe us ought to put up some notices, put the word round, like.'

'I could put one in the window,' Edie offered. 'And I'm sure Jessie Friend will, and Bert Foster and George Sweet. 'Tis a pity you didn't think to suggest it last night, Dottie.'

'Well, last night was just to get us started. There's supposed to be another meeting soon. But there's a Flower Club meeting next week too – that's the place to start it off.'

Two or three more women came into the shop then, and Jacob Prout departed to work on clearing the churchyard. There was a patch of nettles in one corner that he never seemed to be able to get rid of entirely and he was determined to make an early start on them. They were just showing above the ground now, a bright, fresh green. He began to hack them down, remembering that his wife Sarah would have used them to make soup. He wouldn't do that – he'd never liked it anyway, and only eaten it to please her – but it did him good to do something energetic.

While he was working, the Vicar came out of the church carrying some bits of rubbish to put in the bin. He saw Jacob as he came round the corner and walked over, his black cassock brushing the wet grass.

'Hello, Jacob. You're doing a good job there. Those nettles would be a foot high by the weekend.'

'They do grow master fast.' Jacob took a swipe at the last few and straightened up. 'I hear old Mrs Tozer ain't too clever today.'

'Yes, so the paper-boy told me. I'm just popping round to see her now, once I've finished a few jobs in the church. Not that the Tozers have called me,' he added quickly, seeing Jacob's dismay. 'I don't think she's that bad. It's just a friendly visit.'

'Well, 'tis to be hoped so. Only I heard it might be turning to pneumonia. Doctor was going in again first thing, so Norman's wife told me. I wouldn't be surprised if her don't get took to hospital.'

'I doubt that,' Basil Harvey said, thinking that if Minnie were that seriously ill she was more likely to be left at home, to slip away peacefully with her family around her. 'Minnie's too tough to let a touch of bronchitis beat her. But perhaps

I'd better go before I do the jobs I'd meant to do. They're not urgent, anyway.'

'Well, if her's still in her senses enough to understand what you says,' Jacob said, evidently determined to think the worst, 'you tell her from me she've got to get better for this Coronation malarkey. She's the oldest person in the village, not counting old Silas Rudge, and he don't hardly know which way's up. A bit of village history, old Minnie Tozer is, and ought to have a special place in whatever we do.'

'I'll tell her that,' Basil promised. 'And now, I'd better go. The Rural Dean is coming this afternoon and I want to have the church tidy and looking its best for him. If you can spare time to clear around the south side of the church, I'd be very grateful.'

'I'll do that, Vicar,' Jacob said, and Basil hurried down the path to the lych gate and along the village street towards the track which led to Tozers' farm. Despite his encouraging words to Jacob, he felt anxious. He didn't know exactly how old Minnie was, but was pretty sure she was nearer to ninety than eighty, and spry though she might be, age was age and nobody could defy it for ever.

It would leave a big gap in the village when Minnie went, and an even bigger one in the Tozer family. And the last thing they needed just now was more anxiety, when they'd had already a hard winter getting those little twins through their first few months. But spring is round the corner, he thought, noticing clumps of primroses like patches of fallen sunshine along the grassy banks, and once it starts to warm up a bit we'll all feel better.

Alice Tozer was in the kitchen when he knocked on the back door of the farmhouse, and she let him in at once. She looked tired but her flowery pinafore was fresh and clean, and there was a smell of new bread baking. On the table he saw a pile of chopped swede and onions, and a second pile of beef, cut into cubes, with a bowl of flour waiting to be turned into pastry. The Tozers were going to be given a good dinner, no matter what else was wrong.

'Come you in, Vicar, and forgive the mess,' she said, rubbing lard into the flour. 'I hope you don't mind me getting on with this, only I want to get a few pasties in the oven before Joanna comes down. She's taking a turn with Ted's mother – I don't know if you've heard her's poorly.'

'I think half the village has heard. Jacob told me just now so I came straight round to see if there's anything I can do. How is she?'

Alice stopped halfway through stirring water into the pastry mix and looked at him. 'I'll be honest with you, Vicar, I've never seen her as low as this, not in all the time I've known her. She seemed to get better in the middle of the night, then about five o'clock she started to cough and wheeze so bad I thought she'd turn herself inside out. She didn't hardly have strength to breathe when she stopped at last.'

'Oh dear,' Basil said, his round face creased like a baby's. 'I am sorry. Would she like me to pop up and say hello, do you think?'

'I'm sure she would. She could do with seeing a cheery face. Her door's the second along the landing. And you could tell Joanna I'll be up in a few minutes, as soon as I've got this lot in the oven. Once they're in, I won't have to worry about dinner until the men come in at midday. Don't matter what else is happening, they still got to be fed, and they'm so busy now, what with the lambs coming thick and fast like a snowstorm.' She began to roll out the pastry, using a plate to cut it into circles.

'It's a busy time for you,' Basil agreed, making for the stairs. He climbed them quickly and found the door, standing ajar. Giving it a light tap to let those inside know he was coming, he pushed it open and peeped into the room.

Minnie was lying in the big iron bedstead he guessed she'd had ever since she was first married, but if he hadn't seen her wan face on the pillow he'd have been hard put to it to decide if there really was anyone under the piled blankets and eiderdown. Beside her, Joanna was sitting on an old kitchen chair. She was leaning forward slightly and holding a small, wrinkled hand, stroking it gently and murmuring in a soft voice. She glanced up as Basil came in, and started to rise to her feet.

'No, don't get up,' he said quietly. 'I just came in to see how she was. Is she awake?'

'I'm not really sure. I think she's asleep most of the time, which is a blessing, but she seems to know I'm here. If I try to let go of her hand, she clasps my fingers as if she doesn't want to be left alone.' Joanna looked up at him, her eyes filled with tears. 'It's so sad, to see her like this.'

'I know, my dear. We all love Mrs Tozer and we don't want her to suffer.' He gazed down at the old

77

face. He'd never known her anything but old, he reflected – she must have been in her late sixties when he'd first arrived in the village, her face already seamed with fine lines – but she'd always been a steadfast member of his congregation, sitting in her pew halfway down the church, and he had scarcely ever seen the farmhouse kitchen without her. Always busy doing something too – shelling peas, stringing beans, mixing cakes, darning socks, knitting for the children, working out the harmonies for a new tune on the handbells that hung from the beams. In summer, she would have been outside on the garden bench, but still her hands would have been active. And now those same hands lay idle, one clasped in Joanna's, the other pale and thin on the sheet, the fingers restless as if they felt they ought to be at work.

'Would you like me to sit with her for a while?' he asked softly. 'Your mother-in-law said she'd be up in a minute, but if you want to go downstairs and rest, I'll be glad to take over.'

'I think Gran would like it,' Joanna said. 'And I'll need to see to the twins soon. It seems so cruel!' she burst out, lowering her voice again as soon as the words were spoken. 'She's been such a tower of strength ever since they were born, telling me how she kept her tiny one alive and helping me with them. I did so want her to see them grow up.'

'And so she will,' Basil said comfortingly. 'I'm sure the good Lord would like to have her for His own, but she's nowhere near her time yet. There's more work for her to do here, and He's got all eternity. She'll come through this, Joanna, I'm sure of it, and our faith and strength will help her.'

'Do you really think so?' Joanna stood up and gave Basil the old hand to hold as he took her place. 'She was so good to me when I came here as a Land Girl, you know. I wasn't much use around the farm then, but she always stood up for me and said I had the makings of a real countrywoman. I don't know if I would have stuck it without her.'

'Go downstairs and have a cup of tea,' he said. 'And you can have one ready for me when I come down, too. I'll stay with Mrs Tozer for as long as you like.'

Joanna left the room and he heard the murmur of voices in the kitchen below as she joined Alice. He sat close to the bed, holding Minnie's hand, as fragile as a tiny bird, in both of his, and looked down at the old face.

'I really think you will have to get better, you know, Minnie,' he said quietly. 'They still need you, you see. And there's a lovely spring just beginning, and all the excitement of the Coronation. You're not going to let that happen without you, are you? Of course not!' He paused as he felt a tiny pressure on his hand, and saw a flicker of expression cross the crumpled cheek. 'Let's just say the prayer that Our Lord himself taught us, shall we? You don't need to say it yourself if it's too much for you – just think the words along with me. *Our Father...*' He went through the prayer, his eyes closed as they always were when he prayed, and it wasn't until he came to the last word that he opened them again.

Minnie's lips were moving very, very slightly.

There was a faint tinge of colour in her cheeks. And as he bent closer, he heard a thread of a whisper.

'Amen...'

Chapter Seven

Stella's suggestion that the Crocker twins should be given the parts of the Princes in the Tower came into her mind again that morning, as she took the register and found that only one was present.

'Are you George or Edward?' she asked, annoyed at having to reveal, yet again, her inability to tell them apart.

'Can't you tell by me jersey, Miss?' the boy enquired innocently.

Stella gazed doubtfully at him. After many ideas had been mooted and discussed it had been agreed with Mrs Crocker that the boys should wear differently coloured jerseys – red for Edward and green for George. This wasn't an ideal solution, as the boys were perfectly capable of swapping jerseys, and often did, but short of taking up Felix's suggestions of tattoos or ear piercings, which had been briskly dismissed, there seemed to be no better way.

'You're Edward, then,' she said, and couldn't help adding, 'Aren't you?'

A wicked grin spread across the child's face and she sighed and wondered if she had been too hasty in rejecting the idea of a tattoo. There were days – five a week, approximately – when it seemed to make a lot of sense.

'All right,' she said. 'You're Edward.' She was almost past caring which he was. They were both bright boys, who would probably do well once the novelty of deceiving everyone wore off – if it ever did – and neither seemed to suffer much from being mistaken for the other. Since they obviously took great delight in making sure it happened, it didn't seem likely that they would. They'll change, once they get interested in girls, she thought, but that was a good many years ahead and meanwhile she and Miss Kemp had to struggle along as best they could.

At playtime, she stood outside with a mug of tea in her hand, watching the children race from one end of the playground to the other, screaming so shrilly that she could well understand the phrase 'letting off steam'. Miss Kemp came out and stood with her.

'We ought to have a chat at some time about Mrs Warren's latest idea. She's sure to want the children to be involved and it would be nice if we had some plans already made, to present to her.'

'It seemed to go down quite well with the meeting,' Stella said. 'And some of those costumes we used for the pageant ought to be all right.'

'Yes, but I'd like it to be more than just a march-past. I think the children should put on some kind of performance – something appropriate to the occasion, of course. If we can think of something fairly soon, we can plan it over the Easter holidays and just have time to rehearse it before June.'

'Yes, we could,' Stella agreed. 'Have you

81

thought of anything already?'

'Well, I've had one or two ideas,' the head-mistress admitted with a smile. 'But let's give ourselves a few days before we start to talk about them, shall we? We might both think of some-thing better. Why is George Crocker wearing a red jumper, by the way? Isn't that supposed to be Edward's colour?'

'It is Edward,' Stella said. 'At least, that's what he told me when I was calling the register.'

'Oh no,' Miss Kemp said confidently, 'that's George. There's no doubt at all about that.'

'How on earth do you know? Have you found some way of telling them apart?' Stella heard the eagerness in her voice. 'It would be such a blessing if we could.'

'I'm afraid not. But Mrs Crocker sent a note along this morning to say that Edward wouldn't be in until playtime. Look – here he comes now.' They watched as the second twin raced in through the school gate and merged with the crowd, becoming immediately indistinguishable from his brother since they were both now wearing red jerseys. Stella groaned.

'For a moment there, I thought all our prob-lems were solved. Now I won't have a chance for the rest of the day. Why is he late, anyway?'

'He had toothache in the night and his mother was taking him to the dentist in Tavistock this morning. I'm sorry – I meant to tell you, but then Shirley Culliford fell over and I had to administer first aid, and by the time I'd done that it com-pletely slipped my mind. So George pretended he was Edward, did he? Well, he'll have to be punished. You'd better make him sit in the corner for the rest of the day.'

'That's if I can find out which one he is,' Stella said gloomily. 'Honestly, I shall be glad when those two go up into your class. And even more glad when they go to the big school!'

'I dare say we shall live through it,' Miss Kemp observed, watching the two boys who were now in the centre of a group of children. 'They're popular enough, anyway. And, do you know, I've just thought of the perfect parts for them to play in the Coronation play!'

'Don't tell me,' Stella said. 'I've already thought of it myself.'

After school, Felix came into Dottie Friend's cottage and the four of them had tea together. Maddy was looking better after a good night's sleep and a walk beside the river, but her face was still pale and she wasn't eating much. She was very quiet too, and hardly joined in the conversation at all.

Dottie had made three different kinds of scone – cheese, sultana and ginger – and a Victoria sponge filled with her own strawberry jam. Today, they were set out on her everyday china, a set she'd bought in Gamages when she lived in London before the war, working for the actress Fenella Forsyth.

'Don't you start on the cakes yet,' Dottie told Felix severely as he eyed the loaded table. 'Bread and butter first, if you don't mind, and there's fish paste or Marmite to go on it.'

'It's just like being at home with our nursemaid,' Felix said. 'Aren't you ever going to stop treating us like children, Dottie?'

'I might, when you stop behaving like them,' Dottie said. 'Especially you, Felix. Nobody would think, to look at you now with jam on your chin, that you were going to be a Vicar in a few weeks' time.'

'No, they wouldn't,' Stella agreed. 'Honestly, Felix, you need a bib. I'm not sure the parishioners of Little Burracombe know what they're letting themselves in for.'

'Well, they ought to. I've been going over there long enough, even before Mr Berry was ill. Not that they've seen me having tea, much. They still have that pleasure to come.'

'Pleasure!' Dottie snorted. 'I'd better get word to them to start saving up. I'd as soon feed an army as you, and that's the truth.'

'I hope you're not implying that I'm greedy,' Felix said with dignity, and Dottie threw up her hands.

'As if I would! Now, who wants the last ginger... Oh, I see you do. And suppose your fiancée had wanted it?'

'I asked her. At least, I looked at it and then at her and she smiled, so I knew.' Felix finished buttering the scone and took a bite. 'I really like these ginger ones, Dottie. You haven't made them before, have you?'

'No, Maddy and me have been trying out some new ideas for the Coronation tea, haven't we, Maddy? Thought I ought to do summat special.'

'Well, these are certainly special.' Felix started on the second half. 'And Maddy's turning into just as good a cook as you. You know, I'm really going to miss dropping in here for tea when I'm living over the river.'

'We'll miss you, too,' Dottie said. 'Burracombe's not going to seem the same without your silly face, and teatimes are going to be very quiet.'

'You'll have to come over to me instead,' Felix said cheerfully. 'Stella will anyway, won't you, darling?'

'Yes – I suppose I will,' Stella said, faintly startled. 'I hadn't actually thought much about teatimes, to be honest. There's been so much else... But you won't always be around then, surely? You'll have to have tea with your parishioners, and at Mothers' Union meetings and things like that.'

Felix paused, the last piece of scone halfway to his mouth.

'So I will.' He put it down slowly on the plate and stared at her. 'You know, I'm beginning to realise just what this means. Once I'm at Little Burracombe, we're hardly going to see each other.'

'It's not that bad,' she said uncertainly. 'We're only across the river from each other.'

'And it might as well be a hundred miles.' He put his hand over hers. 'We're going to have to think about this.'

Dottie looked from one to the other and got up. 'I'll put the kettle on for some more tea,' she said, and went out to the tiny scullery, shutting the door behind her. Stella and Felix gazed at each other.

'We shall still be able to see each other quite a lot,' she said, her voice wobbling a little. 'Shan't we?'

'Of course we will! Don't look so upset, sweetheart. We just need to think about it, that's all, and make some plans, so that it doesn't come as a shock when I'm there. And ... there's something else I've been meaning to say, but that'll have to keep for later.'

Stella turned to her sister. 'How are you really feeling, Maddy? You do look a bit better, you know. Has Dottie been making a fuss of you?'

Maddy nodded. 'She's been a real mother hen. I wasn't sure she'd let me out by myself, but I had a nice walk along the river. There are primroses out.' She crumbled the remains of a scone on her plate. 'It's lovely to be back in Burracombe, but I think I'd like to go back to West Lyme at the weekend. I need something to occupy my mind.'

Stella gazed at her in dismay. 'Already? I thought you'd stay at least two or three weeks. Don't you think you should?'

'Not really. Other people have to pick themselves up and get on with things, so why should I be any different? I've got a job, and however good the Archdeacon is to me, it's not fair to leave him for too long.'

'I'm sure Uncle wouldn't mind,' Felix observed. 'He and Auntie Barbara think the world of you, you know. They wouldn't want you to go back until you felt ready.'

'Well, I do feel ready. At least, I will by the weekend. Look, nobody else can take two or three weeks off – Mr Hodges has had to go back to work, and Mrs Hodges has got to make things better for Linnet, and it's just as bad for them as it is for me.' Her voice shook a little but she went on determinedly. 'I've been looked after and pampered all my life – well, ever since Fenella adopted me, anyway – and it's time I learned to stand on my own two feet. Not that the Archdeacon and Mrs Copley are any more likely to let me do that than the rest of you are,' she finished ruefully.

'Well, if you really feel that's what you want to do,' Stella said with some reluctance. 'I know they'll look after you.' And as Maddy started to speak again, she held up her hands and said, 'Yes, I know you're saying you don't want to be looked after, but I'm afraid you're just going to have to put up with it! We all care about you too much to leave you to manage on your own after what's happened. And you *are* on your own – the Hodges have got each other.' She saw the pain in Maddy's eyes and stopped abruptly, biting her lip. 'I'm sorry, I didn't mean to say it like that. But don't try to be too independent, darling – not yet.'

'Stella's right,' Felix said. 'Take it gently. I think you should go back to West Lyme, if that's what you want, but don't try to get back to normal too quickly. And if you want to come back here for weekends, or at any other time, just let us know and we'll come and fetch you.'

The door opened again and he turned as Dottie came back in. 'Maddy's talking about going back at the weekend, so you'll need to make the most of her for these few days.'

'Already?' Dottie set the teapot on the table. 'I haven't been working you too hard, maid, have I?'

Maddy laughed a little shakily. 'You haven't

been working me at all. That's just the trouble – I need more to do. I want to feel useful.'

'You're useful enough here, just being company. But if that's what you want, that's what you must do, so long as you can manage with that arm. You know there's always a bed for you here if you want to come back.'

Maddy gave her a grateful smile. 'It's not that I don't love being here, Dottie. I just want to be in my own place – I've got a nice little flat in the Archdeacon's house, you know, and I think I need to be on my own for a bit. And I don't suppose I'll be asked to do any more than I feel able to do.' She paused, looking at the tablecloth. 'Ruth and Dan Hodges said I could go to them as well, at Bridge End. I think I might want to do that, at some point, so that I can be with people who knew Sammy.' She got up suddenly. 'I'm sorry – I think I'll just go upstairs for a minute. I need...' She went out quickly.

'Oh dear,' Stella said. 'I hope we haven't upset her.'

Felix shook his head. 'I think it was talking about the Hodges that brought it all back to her again. It's bound to happen. And it's a good idea for her to go to them sometime.' He put his hand on Stella's. 'People have to do what they feel is right for them at times like this, you know. However much we may want to help them, sometimes it's best just to stand by and wait.'

'I suppose you're right,' Dottie said with another sigh. 'It was a cruel thing to happen, though. And him such a nice young fellow, by all accounts.'

'He was,' Stella said. 'And it does seem cruel.

But he saved his little sister's life. We have to remember that.'

They were quiet for a few minutes, and then Dottie remembered the teapot and picked it up.

'I reckon us can all do with a fresh cup,' she said. 'And I dare say you might want another piece of my sponge to go with it, Felix. What about you, Stella?'

Stella shook her head and they began to talk about Felix's induction in his new parish. For some time before the previous vicar's death, he had gone over to take services, but it had been by no means taken for granted that he would be offered the living as new vicar. As he'd told Stella, the parishioners might want someone entirely new to the area, and the bishop himself might not like the idea. In the event, however, everyone had agreed that Felix was the man they wanted, and he was to be installed on Easter Sunday.

'Us'll all come over for the service,' Dottie declared. 'I suppose Marge Lillicrap will be in charge of the refreshments. I might walk over and see if her wants any of us to bring anything.'

Felix grinned. The rivalry between the two villages, one each side of the river, had gone on for as long as there had been villages, and he was pretty sure that Mrs Lillicrap, whom he had met several times, would refuse any help from Burracombe. Still, Dottie's offer would be appreciated, and the knowledge that there would be people from the bigger village attending the service – and the tea afterwards – would put the new parishioners on their mettle.

'It'll be a tea such as has never been seen

before,' he said to Stella afterwards as they went for a walk down to the ford. 'And that's saying something, round here!'

'I hope you're not going to encourage them,' she said sternly. 'A little bit of friendly rivalry is all very well, but we don't want them at each others' throats.'

'Don't worry, I intend to bring the two parishes together as much and as often as possible. While still making sure they keep their own individuality, of course. And these Coronation festivities are a marvellous opportunity to make a start.' He leaned on the stone parapet of the little hump-backed bridge and gazed down into the tumbling water. 'That's not what's worrying me.'

'What is, then?' she asked, leaning beside him and turning to look into his face. 'I know there's something you're not happy about, darling. Are you getting cold feet about the work? You really needn't. I know we tease you a lot, but that's all it is – just teasing. You'll be a good vicar.'

'No, it's not that. I don't expect to be the best vicar in the world, mind – well, not to start with, anyway,' he added with a sideways grin. 'But you must know what it is, Stella. It's being away from you so much. It wasn't until we were having our tea just now that it really hit me. I mean, I've known in my head that once I was living over the river I wouldn't see so much of you, but I hadn't quite *realised* it, somehow. Not being able to come to tea at Dottie's, not seeing you come out of her gate in the morning just as I'm coming out of Aggie Madge's. Just not being *here*. And it's going to seem very strange, living in that big

90

vicarage all by myself instead of in two rooms at Aggie's cottage,' he added.

'You'll have a housekeeper, though. Mrs Pridham said she'd come in every day, like she did for the Berrys, didn't she?'

'Yes, though apart from cooking my supper and flicking a duster round the place I can't see that there'll be much for her to do,' Felix said, bypassing the need for more regular or thorough cleaning, bed making, washing, ironing, shopping and all the other odds and ends that seemed to happen by themselves – if you were a young curate with blue eyes and a winning smile. 'But she's not going to be company, exactly, is she? She's not going to be there in the mornings when I get up or in the evenings when I want someone to talk to. Or love,' he added, with another sideways glance.

Stella's lips twitched. 'I certainly hope not,' she said demurely. 'So what are you going to do about it, Felix? Ask me and Dottie to tea every day?'

'No, I'm not! Well – yes, of course you can come to tea every day if you want to. I hope you will.'

'But not Dottie,' Stella suggested slyly.

'Well, she can come sometimes, of course. I'll always be pleased to see Dottie. She's been a good friend. But it's you I really want.'

'And Dottie's cakes and scones.'

'Oh, stop it, you little demon!' he exclaimed, turning to shake her gently by the shoulders. 'You're just teasing me. You know perfectly well what I mean.' His face sobered and he looked down into her eyes. 'I want you there with me – living with me. All the time. I'm going to be so dreadfully lonely without you.'

The laughter faded from Stella's face and she nodded. 'I know. And I'm going to miss you. But we've only been engaged a few months.'

'That doesn't mean we can't get married. It's all the more reason not to wait – everyone knows about it.'

'We meant to wait at least two years.'

'Two years is a lifetime! Two years, all by myself in that huge great vicarage, miles away from you–'

'It's only one mile, at most, if you go across the Clam.'

'It might as well be a hundred miles,' he said. 'Stella, please think about it. You know we're meant to be together. Why wait? Mrs Berry has left quite enough furniture there, we don't need much more of our own, and there would be wedding presents. I honestly can't see any reason not to get married as soon as we possibly can.'

'Oh yes,' Stella said, 'and have all the gossips watching me for the next six months to see just why we suddenly brought the wedding forward. A fine start for a new vicar that would be.'

'Well, perhaps not as quickly as that, then,' he admitted. 'But–'

'And besides,' she went on, 'I'd have to give notice at the school. A term's notice. So it couldn't be before the summer anyway, and we've got all these Coronation celebrations right up to June. We're both going to be too busy to think about weddings.'

'After the summer then,' he said. 'Look, suppose we made it Christmas. We'll have been engaged a year by then. That should be respectable enough for anyone. And we'll have all autumn to get ready.'

'Christmas term's dreadfully busy,' Stella said, but he could tell by her voice that she was wavering. 'And it will be just as bad for you. All those parties and extra services...'

'One more party will be neither here nor there, then,' he encouraged her. 'Suppose we make it just *after* Christmas. You can finish your school term and I'll do all my carol services and parish parties and so on, and then we can have a week or two to ourselves to settle in – we might even manage a honeymoon away somewhere. What do you think?' He looked into her eyes again, and then added more quietly, 'It's not just that, Stella – me being lonely and all that, I mean. And I know I shouldn't feel like this, because it's almost like a feeling of superstition and priests aren't meant to have such things. It's ... it's what's happened to Maddy that's on my mind. Losing her fiancé like that. I ... well, I'll feel a lot happier when you're safely married to me, that's all. Not that anyone's ever entirely safe,' he added.

Stella looked up him. Her eyes were as serious as his as she said, 'I know. I feel it too. Sammy's life was taken away so suddenly, it makes you feel you want to hang on tightly to everything you've got. But that's another reason why we can't get married too soon, Felix.' The tears came into her eyes. 'I just can't do it to her. We've got to let her get over it, as much as she can, before we even say a word about it.' Her voice shook a little as she said, almost in a whisper, 'It's like flaunting our own happiness, when she's lost all she had.'

Chapter Eight

For a while, after the Vicar's visit, Minnie had seemed to rally. Her breathing had eased, the terrible rattle in her chest had softened, and a tiny web of colour had appeared on her wrinkled cheeks. 'The roses are coming back,' Alice said, looking down at her. 'She'm on the mend.' And she'd lifted Minnie's bony shoulders from the pillow and helped her to sip some cool, fresh water. 'Drink this, Mother, and then I'll give you some of that medicine the doctor left for you.'

Minnie's nose furrowed and Alice laughed a little. 'And you needn't make that face, neither. As bad as the kiddies, you be. Anyway, 'tis cough syrup, got honey in it. You couldn't do better than that.'

Minnie swallowed the medicine obediently and went back to sleep. But later that evening, Alice found her twisting in her bed, her thin arms wrapped around her head as if she were in pain, and she called Joanna up to have a look. Together, they gazed down at the pale face and listened to the laboured breathing, and then met each other's eyes.

'She've got that wheeze again,' Alice said in a low voice. 'I don't like it, Jo. I thought she were getting over it.'

'Shall I go for the doctor?' Joanna asked, and Alice bit her lip in indecision.

'I don't like to keep bothering him, specially at the weekend... Send Tom to fetch our Val, will you? She'll know what to do for the best.' Without taking her eyes off Minnie's face, Alice felt for the bedside chair and sat down on it, holding one of the old lady's hands in hers. I never realised how thin she was getting, she thought. She's all skin and bone. She's got no strength to fight this no more, that's what it is. She's just too worn out.

Less than fifteen minutes later Val ran in, a jacket thrown round her shoulders and her face anxious. She bent over the bed and looked intently into her grandmother's face. The roses had faded from the cheeks now, leaving them white and papery, with the eyes sunk deep into sockets as dark as bruises. The narrow chest rose and fell so slightly that the movement was barely visible, but the wheezing sound went relentlessly on, painful to hear yet bringing a strange reassurance that at least the old lungs were still managing to work. Every now and then, there was a deeper sound – a moan, a sudden rattle, that made both Alice and Val catch their own breath, afraid that this was Minnie's last moment; yet every time, after a terrifying pause, the struggle to breathe was won again, and Minnie made another sound, a faint whimper, as if it were all too much for her, and both Val and her mother felt tears aching in their throats.

'I reckon us ought to fetch the doctor,' said Ted from the doorway, and Val looked up to see both him and her brother Tom, standing fearfully just outside the room. She nodded.

'I think you're right. Tom...?'

'I'll go,' he said quickly, and disappeared. They heard his footsteps on the stairs and then the slam of the kitchen door. The house fell silent again. The children were all in bed and asleep. With luck, they would not stir again until the twins needed their feed at two a.m.

Dr Latimer arrived with Tom, both breathless from hurrying through the village and up the farm track. He looked gravely at Minnie, listened to her chest and took her pulse while Alice, Ted and Val watched anxiously. Eventually, he straightened up.

'Let's go downstairs.'

'I'll stay with her,' Joanna said quickly, coming to the door, and the others followed the doctor down to the kitchen where he stood regarding them sombrely.

'It's bad news, isn't it, Doctor,' Alice said quietly.

'Well, it certainly isn't good, but it may not be as bad as you fear. Mrs Tozer is very poorly, and I am very much afraid she may develop pneumonia. But she's a fighter as we all know, and I've seen people older and frailer than she is recover from bouts like this. Now, the question is, would you like her to go to hospital or would you rather nurse her at home?'

'Oh, at home,' Alice said instantly. 'I'd rather she was here with us, and anyway I know she'd hate to go into hospital. Begging your pardon, Val,' she added apologetically, 'but good as you nurses may be, you're not family to your patients, and your gran wants her family around her. Take her to hospital and her'd go out like a light.'

'I know, Mum. It's all right – I'd feel just the same. And you know I'll help as much as I can.

96

You ought to think about it though, just the same,' she added. 'They've got all the right equipment in the hospital, like oxygen, and doctors are on hand if she needs anything special.'

Alice chewed her lip. 'I don't know what to do for the best,' she began, but Ted put his big hand on hers.

'You don't have to make the decision, m'dear. She's my mother when all's said and done, and I reckon her'd want to stop home where she knows everyone, and us can all pop in to see her from time to time. And it don't matter how good the nurses are up at the hospital, there's not a single one of 'em better than you or our Val, specially when it comes to looking after Mother. So what I say is, she stops here and we'll all do whatever Doctor says is necessary to do.'

Alice nodded, relief in her eyes, and Dr Latimer looked satisfied.

'I'm sure that's the right decision, Ted. Now, there are some special medicines I'd like her to take – I'll give you a prescription and perhaps someone will be able to pop into Tavistock for it tomorrow. One of the chemists will be open – it'll tell you which one in the *Gazette* or the *Times*. I've got something in my bag to give her now, to make her a bit more comfortable during the night. And remember, if there's any change or you're at all worried, all you have to do is let me know. You've got a telephone, haven't you? Use it – that's what it's for. No need to waste time sending Tom, or anyone else.'

Ted looked abashed. 'I don't always think about it,' he admitted. 'Us only had it for the farm, and us don't use it much for ringing village folk up, not when they're all practically in shouting distance.'

'Well, remember it next time you need me,' the doctor said. 'I'll come as quickly as I can. But try not to worry too much – as I said, old Mrs Tozer's a fighter and she won't give in easily.'

He went out, and the family looked at each other.

'What d'you think?' Alice asked.

Ted shook his head. 'I'm not sure he's as hopeful as he makes out. Mother might be a fighter, like he says, but she'm pushing ninety and it's a battle we all lose in the end. I reckon there's a chance, like he says, but it's not all that good. But don't you take on,' he added, putting his arm round his wife's shoulders as she began to cry. 'Us'll do our best for the old lady, and give her all the company us can, and nobody in all the world can do more than that.'

Prayers were said in church next morning for Minnie Tozer and when Alice came out after the service she was surrounded by people asking for news. She answered them all as best she could but Stella, who had left Maddy behind thinking that she would be the one who was centre of attention, could see that the farmer's wife was itching to get back to her patient.

'Our Val and Joanna are looking after her now,' Alice said, trying to answer a dozen questions at once. 'They knew I'd want to join in the prayers... She got through the night all right, with the medicine the doctor gave her, but I'll feel better when we've got the prescription from the chemist.

Our Tom's gone to Tavvy now, in the lorry.'

'My stars!' George Sweet exclaimed. 'How many pills has she got to take, then?'

'He's not bringing back a whole lorry load,' Alice retorted, rolling her eyes. 'Not as far as I know, anyway. He took the lorry because it would be quicker, that's all.' She turned away and Bert Foster grinned.

'She got you there, George. Not that it be any laughing matter,' he added quickly, and deepened his voice a little to speak to Alice. 'You give her all our best regards anyway, and I dare say you wants to get off home now. Come on, you lot,' he said, addressing the small crowd, 'you've heard all there is to hear for the time being, and I know the Tozers'll be grateful for all our concern. Minnie's a grand old lady and us don't feel ready to lose her yet.'

'No, that us don't,' several voices agreed, and they cleared a path for Alice to make her way out of the churchyard. Basil Harvey was standing at the lych gate and he took her hand as she paused beside him.

'Thank you for the prayers, Vicar,' she said. 'Mother'll be master pleased to hear about that. I wouldn't be surprised if I don't walk in the door to find they've started working already.'

'Neither would I,' he said. 'The power of prayer is surely a miracle. But don't linger here, Alice. You get off home and don't forget to have a rest yourself, now and again. We don't want you wearing yourself out.'

'I'll not do that. The girls are looking after me, although they've got plenty of their own jobs to

99

do, especially Joanna. They've been a godsend, though, both of them. And Tom, too, of course – and even Luke's helping where he can on the farm, to give Ted a bit of time with his mother.'

'You've got a good family,' Basil said. 'And how about young Jackie? Has she been out to visit her grandmother?'

Alice looked awkward. 'To tell you the truth, Vicar, we haven't let her know yet. There didn't seem much point, until we knew what the situation was. But I'm sure she'll come home the minute she finds out.'

Basil looked at her thoughtfully, wondering if there was something wrong here. As far as he knew, Jackie Tozer came home most weekends, when Jennifer Tucker came to stay with Jacob. But Jennifer hadn't been in church this morning, so perhaps they'd both decided to stay in Plymouth this time, and perhaps Alice was a bit put out about it. He hoped it was no more than that.

He turned away to hear Joyce Warren explaining about the television set she and her husband were purchasing, and smiled his thanks for her offer to come in and watch the Coronation on it. 'Or, indeed, anything else you might be interested in,' she added. 'I believe they're going to start some very good dramatic productions. We might be able to learn something from them for our own little offerings.'

'Why, we're not proposing to make our own television programmes, are we?' he asked, rather startled, and she smiled indulgently.

'Of course we're not. I meant for our little drama group. There'll have to be some changes

100

there anyway, with the curate leaving us soon.' A chance for her to step in again, Basil thought, but his mind wasn't really on the conversation. He was still thinking about the Tozers and young Jackie. Ted and Alice really don't need any more trouble at the moment, he mused. Not with those little twins only just out of the woods, and now Minnie lying at death's door.

'...a few friends round, and we can have drinks afterwards. Make a little party of it,' Joyce was saying, and he dragged his mind back and ordered it to stand to attention. 'We'll have to make an appearance at the village festivities, of course, but we needn't stay long. After all, we'll have worked hard to organise it all and there's the Grand Parade in the afternoon – we'll have done our stint, don't you agree? I don't imagine the sort of junketing that will be going on in the evening is any more your cup of tea than it is mine, Mr Harvey.'

Basil felt a sudden uncharacteristic surge of anger. Before he could stop himself, he said: 'I'm sorry to disappoint you, Mrs Warren, but the sort of junketing that will be going on in the evening is very much my cup of tea. You see, one of the reasons why I enjoy being a village priest is because I like the villagers so much. And I especially like to join them in their celebrations, especially when, as you say, we'll have worked so hard to organise it all. In fact, it will be the high point of the day for me, after listening to the service broadcast in the church. As I hope it will be for *all* the villagers.' He paused for a moment, savouring the astonishment on her face, and then went on. 'And now, I'm afraid I'll have to ask you to excuse me. There are a number of other people I want to talk to, and I really must slip in to see how old Mrs Tozer is before I go home for lunch.'

He turned away before she could speak, and crossed the churchyard swiftly, his cassock flowing about him as if he were a great black bird about to take flight. Even as he strode between the gravestones, his heart thudding, he knew that he would come to regret his hasty words. His flashes of temper were rare, and he usually managed to keep them in check, knowing that he would be the one to suffer the pangs of guilt afterwards. But just at the moment he was glad he'd said what he did. And what if I do feel guilty later, he asked himself robustly. It'll be worth it, just to remember that look on her face. I've never in all my life seen anyone look quite so much like a landed codfish!

Chapter Nine

Stephen Napier had seen Stella briefly the week before and learned that she and Felix had brought Maddy home with them. He knew that she wouldn't want a visit so soon, and merely asked Stella to tell her sister that he was thinking of her, but he'd made sure to be home again this weekend, and he was in the church in good time, occupying the family pew at the front.

By the time he realised that Maddy wasn't coming to church, the service was just about to begin and he could hardly get up and walk out. Knowing the service by heart from years of attendance, he sat, knelt and stood automatically, and only took in half of what Basil Harvey said in his sermon. He did notice that prayers were said for Minnie Tozer, and joined in a sincere 'Amen', for he'd known the old lady, and all the Tozers, from his babyhood and was genuinely sorry to hear that she was ill. Apart from that, however, he fidgeted impatiently in his seat and, as soon as the Vicar had walked down the side aisle to say farewell to his parishioners at the door, he hurried to catch Stella before she could disappear.

'She didn't really feel up to it,' Stella told him as they stood in the lane just outside the churchyard. The bright new green of the high grassy banks was crowned with tiny wild daffodils and above the murmur of voices a few birds twittered as they squabbled over nesting places. To Stella, trying to imagine how Maddy must feel, coming so sadly to this place where she had been happy, it was a bittersweet moment and she brushed her hand across her eyes. 'She knew that everyone would want to speak to her and ... well, she just couldn't face it.' I'm not even sure I can, she thought, wishing she'd been able to escape before Stephen had caught her.

'I'm sorry,' he said. 'I don't want to intrude. But I did want to know how she is – and let her know I'm here, if she wants me. I mean, if there's anything I can do...'

'Thanks. I'll tell her.' She gave him a brief smile and half turned away but he put out a hand and she paused again.

'How long is she staying? I'd really like to see her – just as a friend, you know. We got along so well, before...'

'I know.' Stella looked at him consideringly. 'But I'm afraid she's going back later today. We were hoping she'd stay a few weeks, but she's decided she needs to be at work. To keep her mind off things.' She stopped and gave a small shrug. 'To be honest, I don't think she really knows what she wants to do. When she's here, she wants to be at West Lyme and when she's there she wants to be here. Or maybe somewhere completely different. She's just looking...' Her voice broke and she looked down quickly.

'She's searching for *him*,' Stephen said quietly. 'That's what it is. Nowhere's right for her, because he's not there, so she goes somewhere else and he's not there either. Only perhaps she doesn't quite realise that's what she's doing.'

Stella looked up again, startled, and he grinned ruefully.

'I'm not quite the heartless dilettante you might think,' he said. 'I knew a girl once... Well, more than knew her, if I'm honest. We were very close... And then ... she died... It wasn't sudden, like Sam Hodges ... she'd been ill for some time. But I felt the same way. I couldn't settle anywhere until I finally came to terms with the fact that she just wasn't going to be around any more.' He paused, looking at his hands. 'I think that's what's happening to Maddy now, and there's nothing anyone can do about it. She has to come through it in her own time.'

'And how long will that be?' Stella asked, but

he shook his head.

'Everyone's time is different. We all think it's the end of our world, and so it is, in a way. The end of the world we hoped for, anyway. But eventually, we come to realise it's the beginning of the world, too – a different one, but a beginning just the same.' He grinned suddenly. 'Listen to me! I don't think I've ever talked like that in my life. Father and Hilary would never believe it!' And then, serious again, 'Tell Maddy I'm here, won't you? Tell her I'll do whatever I can, even if it means staying away until she's ready to see me again, as a friend. And if she wants a lift here from West Lyme any time, I'll be glad to provide it. I could take her back this evening, if you like – but maybe that's a bit soon.'

'Yes, I think maybe it is,' Stella said. Then she looked at him and smiled fully for the first time. Holding out her hand a little shyly, she said, 'Thank you, Stephen. I'll tell Maddy what you've said. Would you mind if I told her all of it – about the girl as well? Unless she already knows, of course.'

'No, she doesn't know. Not many people do. Not even Hilary.' He paused, considering, and then said, 'But you can tell Maddy. Just so that she realises that I do understand – a little bit. And tell her she must take her time – about Sam, and about everything else. Including me.'

'I will.' Stella smiled at him again and then walked away, thinking over all that he had said. Until now, she'd always thought Stephen something of a lightweight – a rich young man with everything handed to him on a plate, flitting

105

blithely through life, discarding the responsibilities of the estate which his father believed he should take on, and going his own way with not much thought for others. But their conversation had left her with an impression of something deeper, of blows which he had suffered alone, and her respect for him had increased.

I wonder who the girl was, she thought as she approached Dottie's garden gate. Someone he met while he was first in the RAF, I suppose. And he must have been very young at the time, so I expect she was too. And then she died, and he bore his tragedy all alone.

Maddy was in the back garden, sitting on the old bench and stroking the mound of rusty black fur that Albert turned himself into when in the sun. It was sheltered there, and Stella sat down beside her, tilting her head and closing her eyes so that the sun shone pinkly through her lids.

'Was it a nice service?' Maddy asked.

'Much the same as usual. We sang "All Things Bright and Beautiful" and "All People Who On Earth Do Dwell". And we said prayers for Minnie Tozer. She's very poorly.'

'I'm sorry about that. She's a lovely old lady. I used to go up to the farm when I lived here, and she'd let me help her skim the cream.'

They were quiet for a moment or two, then Stella said, 'Stephen was there too.'

'Was he? He doesn't often go to church – he says he gets enough of it on the station.'

'He came last week as well. I think he was hoping to see you – he asked after you. He offered to take you back to West Lyme tonight, if you'd like

106

a lift.'

Maddy was silent, looking down at her fingers. Sammy's ring was still on her left hand, as if she couldn't bring herself to take it off and see her finger bare; as if that might be a final acknowledgement of his death, a betrayal of his memory.

'He just wants to be your friend,' Stella said gently. 'He told me specially to say that.'

'I know,' Maddy said in a dreary tone. 'I know that's what he *says*.'

'I think it's true. He wants to help you, and he really wouldn't try to make it go any further than that.'

'Even if he feels differently inside? People can't help what they feel, you know, and if Stephen...' She fell silent again, still staring at her fingers, stroking the tiny diamond that was all Sammy had been able to afford. 'I just don't think I can deal with him,' she went on in a low voice. 'Not now.'

'But you and he were friends.' Stella remembered the day she and Felix had taken Maddy back to West Lyme and found Stephen waiting for her at the Archdeacon's house, and remembered too the way her sister had run into Stephen's arms. More than friends, she might have added.

Maddy shook her head. 'There are too many reminders,' she said hopelessly.

Stella waited for a few moments, then she said, 'Don't just dismiss him, Maddy. He really does care, and he understands how you feel. He–'

'How can he understand?' Maddy burst out. 'He's never lost anyone, the way I've lost Sammy. He can't have any idea.'

'He can,' Stella said quietly. 'He told me this

morning – there was someone for him, once. A girl he obviously cared for very much. And she died. So I think he *can* understand. And – he didn't mention this, but remember he lost his mother too, when he was quite young. He's not had life all his own way.'

For a little while, Maddy said nothing. Stella sat without speaking, watching the fingers move within each other, pitying Maddy the plaster on her arm that must be a constant reminder. In a week or so it would be off, and that would perhaps be another step on the long road to healing. Accepting Stephen's friendship might be another.

'It's not his fault,' Maddy said at last with a deep sigh. 'And I'm glad you've told me about the other girl. But I'm just not ready yet for anything, not even just being friends. I really don't think it would be that easy. It's too soon.'

'He knows that too,' Stella said. 'He says you have to take your own time, and everyone's time is different. You know, I saw quite a different Stephen this morning – a wiser one than I expected. He'll be a good friend to you when you're ready, but he'll wait until you are.'

Dottie poked her head out of the back door, her face flushed from the heat of the oven.

'So there you be, you two, basking in God's good sunshine, and why ever not? But come you in now – dinner's on the table and Felix is just coming down the road, so you'd better be ready to start. You know how hungry he always is after service.'

The two girls got up. Stella turned towards the door, but Maddy laid a hand on her arm and she turned back again.

'I won't forget what you've said, Stella. I won't forget Stephen either. But he was right – I have to take my own time.'

Alice had hurried back to the farm as soon as the service was over, hoping that her mother-in-law hadn't worsened while she'd been in church. You just never knew with these things, and a person as old as Minnie could just slip away in the blink of an eyelid. In many ways, that would be a blessing – nobody wanted the old lady to suffer – but not yet, she prayed. Not just yet. We're not ready for it...

The small exchange with the vicar had brought other worries to her mind. She knew he'd wondered a bit about Jackie and, now she came to think of it, Alice knew that it did seem strange that they hadn't let her know about Minnie's illness. But it had only just happened, she argued with herself. Up to now, it hadn't seemed too serious – and anyway, there was no telephone in Jennifer Tucker's house and they'd expected Jackie home for the weekend. But if something did happen to her grandmother, and they hadn't let her know, the girl would be justifiably upset. I'll ask Ted to send a telegram, she thought, the minute I get in and see how Mother is.

She opened the back door and let herself into the kitchen. Joanna was at the sink, scrubbing carrots, with the babies in their cradles beside her and Robin lying on the rag rug playing with the toy farm Tom had made for him. For a moment, the big kitchen looked as it had always done – a warm, welcoming space where the family could all gather and exchange news, gossip or read the papers. But Minnie's chair was empty and the sight pushed her worries about Jackie to the back of Alice's mind.

'How's Gran?'

'About the same, I think,' Joanna said, putting down the carrots and going to the range to shift the kettle on to the hotplate. 'Tom came back with the pills about half an hour ago, and Val's up there with her now.'

When Alice quietly pushed open the bedroom door, she found her daughter leaning over the bed, supporting the frail body so that Minnie could swallow her pills with a sip of water from a cup. As Alice watched, Val gently laid the old woman back on her pillow, smoothed back the straggling grey hair and pulled the sheets up to her chin.

'I think she'll sleep now,' she whispered, stepping back beside her mother. 'She's had a warm drink and the pills will help her to rest.'

Alice moved closer to the bed and looked down. Minnie seemed almost like a ghost already, her face waxen against the white cotton, and her eyes were sunk deep in their sockets. There was scarcely any movement at all from her breathing but, as Val had said, she did seem more restful.

'I'll stop with her now,' she murmured, but Val shook her head.

'Go downstairs and have a cup of tea first. I'll make sure she's settled. Luke's coming round here for his dinner, so I can stay as long as you want. And – I've been thinking, Mum.' She hesitated as Alice turned back from the door. 'I don't think there's any need to panic, but – well,

110

d'you think we ought to let our Jackie know? Just in case she'd like to pop home? I'm sure it'd do Gran good to see her.'

Their eyes met. 'I've been thinking the same thing,' Alice said quietly. 'I think we ought to send a telegram. I'll get your dad or Tom to do it. The girl ought to be here. It's times like these...' Again, her voice trailed away. She stood hesitant for a moment, then closed the door softly behind her and tiptoed down the stairs.

In the kitchen, she found a cup of tea waiting for her and the carrots finished. The potatoes were already in the oven, roasting alongside the meat, and Joanna had started on a large pile of Brussels sprouts. Alice picked up a knife and began to help.

Luke had arrived and was kneeling on the floor with his sketch pad, showing Robin how to draw farm animals. With a few strokes of his pencil, a yard full of ducks and chickens took rapid shape, and as they watched he added a cow looking over the gate. He gave Robin the pencil and guided his hand for a moment, until a cat appeared, sitting on a shed roof, and then a yelping dog.

'There,' he said. 'You can do the rest yourself. It doesn't matter if they look a bit funny to begin with.' He glanced up at his mother-in-law. 'How is she?'

'About the same, I'd say. We're lucky to have Val to help look after her. Luke, Val and me think us ought to let Jackie know. I want to send her a telegram but you know what I'm like on the telephone, I get all of a dither. Would you do it?'

'Of course I will. Just write down what you

want to say and I'll do it straight away.' He tore off a scrap of paper and handed it to her with another pencil. She chewed her lip and handed them back.

'I don't know what to write. You do it, will you? Just something about her gran being poorly and asking her to come home to see her. I don't want to frighten her, mind,' she added quickly. 'She thinks a lot of her gran, and I don't want her upset when there's no need. Just...' She turned away to pick up her teacup and drank quickly. 'Well, you'll know how to put it. I'll go back upstairs now, give Val a bit of a spell.'

She went quickly out of the kitchen, and Luke and Joanna looked at each other.

'She's really worried,' Joanna said after a moment. 'If you ask me, it isn't Jackie she doesn't want to scare – it's herself. Putting it down on paper would make it seem more real.'

'I know.' He wrote a few words and showed her the paper. 'Will that do, d'you think?'

Joanna read the short message. *'Gran poorly, think you should come and cheer her up.* Ten words. Yes, I think that's all right. She'll know it's a bit more than an ordinary cold or anything – we wouldn't send a telegram for that. Tell you what, if we don't hear from her by tomorrow morning, we could ring the hotel. I know they don't like the staff having personal calls, but I'm sure they wouldn't mind passing a message, if Gran's worse.'

'Let's hope she won't be,' he said, and went to the telephone. 'I wonder what young Jackie's up to, down there in the big city. She usually comes home at the weekends, doesn't she?'

'Usually,' Joanna said, with a dry note in her voice. 'But anyone could see that wasn't going to last. I reckon Jackie's a city girl, for all she grew up out here on the farm. I don't think she'll ever come back to Burracombe to live.'

Chapter Ten

Jackie arrived in time for tea, getting off the bus at the main road and walking the mile to the village. As she walked along the lane between the high, Devon banks, the spring sun shone on an unfolding coverlet of new primroses, and here and there she could see peeping between them a purple hint of violets. Soon, they would be a glory of amethyst and gold; and then the bluebells would appear, their nodding heads lifted above the grass on slender stems of pale green, and after them the pearly white of milk-maids, the froth of Queen Anne's lace and the deep pink of campion and foxgloves.

Jackie paused to pick a few white violets from their hiding-place. She had seen these things all through her life and sometimes paused to enjoy them, sometimes taken them for granted, but today they seemed to thrust themselves upon her sight, as if she were seeing them for the last time.

It isn't me, though, she thought. It's because Gran might have seen them for the last time. For she was under no illusion about the significance of the telegram. Nobody sent telegrams just because someone was 'poorly'. Not in her family, anyway. The small brown envelope that the telegraph boy brought on his red bike could, in some families, have meant no more than an invitation to tea. But not when it came from Jackie's parents, and she had stared at it with misgiving, half afraid to open it.

'You'd better see what it says,' Jennifer said after a minute or two, and she nodded and slit the envelope with her thumb.

'I'm just scared it's one of the twins.' She read it quickly. 'No, it's not them. It's Gran. Poorly, Mum says.' She turned frightened eyes on the older woman. 'They want me to go home.'

'You better had, then.' Jennifer understood the significance as well as Jackie did. 'You can catch a bus this afternoon and be home in an hour.'

'Maybe I ought to go straight away.'

'Dinner's almost ready,' Jennifer pointed out. 'Your mother would want you to have that first. There's no sense in starving yourself.'

'I'm not likely to do that, going back to the farm,' Jackie said with a small grin. 'You know what Sunday's like there. But I suppose I might as well, seeing that it's ready.' The smell of roast lamb and mint sauce was drifting along the passage and when she reached the back room Jennifer was already setting dishes of roast potatoes, carrots and cabbage on the table. They sat down together and as soon as dinner was over, Jackie made to carry the dishes out to the tiny kitchen.

'I'll do that,' Jennifer said. 'You get yourself ready and get off. You'll catch the two o'clock bus

114

if you go soon. And it might be a good idea to take your toothbrush and nightie, just in case you decide to stop the night. You're on late morning, aren't you?'

'Yes, I suppose I could do that.' Jackie looked at her with fear suddenly in her eyes. 'You – you don't suppose it's really serious, do you?'

'Don't worry too much,' Jennifer said, laying her hand on the girl's arm. 'But your gran is well into her eighties, isn't she? She's as strong as an ox, but nobody lives for ever.'

'No.' Tears filled Jackie's eyes, and she turned away quickly. A moment later, Jennifer heard her footsteps on the stairs, and she sighed and began to run the tap to start the washing-up.

She had almost finished when Jackie came down again, her face pale and her eyes a little red-rimmed, carrying a bag. She came over to Jennifer and gave her a quick hug.

'I'm going now. How will I let you know if I'm stopping at home?'

'I'll just take it that you are, and expect you when I see you. You can ring me at work tomorrow to let me know how things are going.' Jennifer was a senior fashion buyer at Dingle's, the city's main department store. 'And if you do need to stay any longer, I'm sure the hotel will understand.'

'Yes.' Jackie's eyes filled again and she turned towards the door. 'All right, then. I'll probably see you this evening, but if not...'

'Just do whatever you need to do,' Jennifer said. 'And give my love to the family. And your gran, of course.'

But as Jackie approached the village, the fear

115

that had been with her all through the bus journey grew and she began to wonder if her grandmother would still be there to hear that Jennifer had sent her love.

The last quarter of a mile seemed endless but at last she was passing the gates to the Barton and turning up the track to the farm. The primroses were even bigger here, turning smiling faces towards her as she hurried along, but their smiles seemed false now, like the smirk of an enemy who knows more than you do about your fate. Jackie shuddered and turned her head away as she opened the gate and shooed away the chickens which came rushing at her, hoping for food.

Her sister Val was in the kitchen, washing up with Luke at her side drying the dishes. They both turned when Jackie burst in.

'Jackie! Good lord, I thought it was a herd of elephants.' Val came quickly across to hug her, holding hands frothed with suds clear of Jackie's coat. 'You were quick. You got the telegram?'

'Yes. I got the first bus I could, only Jennifer made me have my dinner first.' Jackie shrugged off her coat and draped it over a chair. 'How is she?'

Val made a face. 'Not too clever. The doctor's worried it could turn to pneumonia, and she might not be able to stand up to it. Mind you, you know what they call that – the old man's friend. There's many that have gone quick and without too much trouble when pneumonia's set in.'

Jackie drew in a sharp breath, and Luke moved forward to take her arm. 'It won't necessarily come to that,' he said gently, with a warning glance at Val. 'She's weak from not having had

116

much food for a few days, but we all know how strong she is really. And she's got a will of iron – if she's not ready to go just yet, she won't.'

'Can I go up and see her?' Jackie asked, and Val nodded.

'Mum's with her now. Joanna's feeding the babies and Dad and Tom are milking. Robin's out there with them.'

Quietly, Jackie mounted the stairs and peeped through her grandmother's door. Her mother was sitting with her back to the door, leaning towards the bed in which Jackie could see the pathetically small mound made by Minnie's body. As Jackie came further into the room, Alice turned and saw her.

'Jackie!' She stood up quickly and stepped away from the bed to kiss her daughter. 'I didn't think you'd be here so soon.'

'I came as soon as I got the telegram.' Jackie looked down at the bed and asked again, 'How is she?'

Alice's answer was much the same as Val's had been. 'But she's holding her own. Tom went and got her some medicine this morning and I reckon it's done her a bit of good. Doctor says it's just a matter of waiting to see if she turns the corner now.'

Jackie leaned over her grandmother and Alice saw that the girl's face was softened as she had not seen it for months, and filled with love and pity. She's a good girl really, she thought, her earlier doubts pushed aside. She'll always be our Jackie, even if she does move away and live her own life.

'Gran,' Jackie whispered. 'Gran, can you hear me? It's Jackie, come specially to see you.'

Minnie's eyes remained closed, but her head moved a little on the pillow. Jackie sat down on the chair Alice had vacated and took the bony old hand in hers, gently stroking the fingers. She leaned closer and went on talking in a low voice.

'I've come on the bus from Plymouth. You remember I live in Plymouth now, with Jennifer Tucker? I'm working at the Duke of Cornwall Hotel and I really like it. But it's nice to come back and see you and the rest of the family. D'you know, the primroses are out now, all along the lanes, and they look so pretty, like little patches of sunshine. The sun's quite warm this afternoon. You ought to be out there now, in the garden, letting the sun shine on your face like it's shining on the primroses. It would do you good. And guess what, I saw some white violets as I was coming along, near that old oak stump that was left when the tree fell during that thunderstorm on my birthday when I was thirteen – remember that? I've never seen them there before. I've brought you a few.' She held the little bunch against the withered cheek. 'You know, if you got better quickly, you could go along and see them too. There are quite a lot there. Only you'll have to be really quick, because they'll only be there for a week or two. Why don't you try, Gran? Get better in time to come along the lane with me and see the white violets...'

The murmuring voice went on as Alice slipped out of the room and down the stairs. Val and Luke had finished the washing-up and were making a pot of tea. They looked round as Alice came into the kitchen.

'My dear soul,' she said, sitting in Minnie's old rocker by the range. 'I've never heard our Jackie talk like that in all my days. Prattling on like poetry, she is, all about primroses and sunshine and white violets and I don't know what else. If that don't make Mother sit up and take notice, I don't reckon anything will.'

'Jackie's a good girl,' Luke said, passing her a cup of tea. 'She must have come the minute she got the telegram.'

'It's all right, Mum, you don't have to feed her,' Val said as Alice began to get up again, casting anxious eyes towards the larder. 'She had her dinner first. Did she say how long she'd stop?'

'Didn't really have time to talk about it. She sat straight down and started talking to Mother like there weren't nobody else in the room. And I reckon the old dear knew she was there too, you know. Moved her head on the pillow for all the world as if she was listening. It fair warmed my heart to see them.'

'Gran always did think a lot of Jackie,' Val commented. 'Well, I think it was a good thing we sent that telegram. It must help her, to know that so many of us want her to get better.'

'It'll give her strength,' Luke agreed. 'And that's all she needs, really, once she's beaten this. In a couple of weeks she'll be trotting about as good as ever, you mark my words.'

A knock on the door caused them all to turn their heads. Val opened it and exclaimed in surprise.

'Why, Miss Bellamy! How nice to see you. Come in.'

'I just called to see how Minnie is,' Constance Bellamy said in her gruff voice, still limping a little as she stumped into the kitchen. 'Don't want to intrude.'

'Of course you're not intruding. We're pleased to see you. Would you like a cup of tea? I've just made a pot.' Val went to the dresser and took down another cup and saucer.

'Won't say no, in that case. I've just had lunch with the Harveys. I joined in the prayers this morning too, of course.' She accepted the cup and nodded her thanks. 'Couldn't let the day go by without calling in. Known Minnie all my life, since she used to take me and my sister out for walks along the lanes when she was our nurse-maid. And it's not much more than a fortnight since she found me on the ground under that plum tree. I could have been there all night if it hadn't been for her.'

'Jackie's up there now, talking to her about how lovely it all looks out there today,' Alice said. 'Telling her about the primroses and some white violets. She brought a few with her.'

Constance Bellamy nodded again. 'I saw they were out, by that old oak stump. Haven't seen them for a year or two – it was good to see them back. Jacob Prout always says we ought to cele-brate New Year in spring, when everything's growing up fresh and starting again, not in January when it all seems dead, and I'm inclined to agree with him. Well, Minnie will enjoy the flowers and the scent will remind her of when we were young. A bright little thing, Minnie was in those days, and had half the village boys after her when she was our nursemaid. I remember when she left us to work at the farm, and took up with your Ted's father. To tell you the truth, none of us thought it would last.'

Val laughed. 'Well, I'm glad it did or we wouldn't be here now. Miss Bellamy, why don't you go up when Jackie comes down and talk to her for a while? I'm sure it does people good to hear a familiar voice talking about old times.'

'I will, if you think she'd like it, but I'd have thought it was her family she'd want round her at a time like this.'

'It's friends as well,' Val said firmly. 'Especially friends like you. I'll go and tell Jackie you're here. She's probably ready for a cup of tea herself – she went straight up the minute she got here.' She passed the sugar bowl. 'Did you bring Rupert with you?'

'Left him at home. He's getting old and crotchety these days and those short legs of his won't stand the distance, even from the Grey House to here. I'd rather take him for walks he'll really enjoy, like down to the ford or up on the moor, though he can't go far then. I sit on a rock and let him fossick about for a while and then we totter home.'

'I can't see *you* tottering,' Val grinned. 'You march around the village as if you were steam-powered. And that ankle of yours doesn't seem to be stopping you much.'

'Oh, that soon got better,' the old woman responded. 'Life's too short for sitting about. Too much gardening to do, to waste what time we're given. Unless it's to do something like sniff at those roses Jessie Friend grows over her fence, or the honeysuckle in your father's hedges, or look at the sunset. Mustn't ever forget to enjoy the bounty. Always the same, and always different, that's the beauty of it all.'

'Ted's mother says much the same sort of thing,' Alice said. 'Always busy, but always got time for a minute's appreciation. Us ought to put that on her headst–' She stopped abruptly and turned away.

There was a moment of silence, then Val said quietly, 'I'll pop up and see if it's all right for you to see her, Miss Bellamy.'

Left alone together, the two women looked at each other. Alice said, 'It's good of you to come. I know Mother will be pleased.'

'I won't be offended if she's too tired to see me,' Constance said. 'You can just tell her I popped in.'

The staircase door opened and Joanna came in, a twin under each arm. 'Hullo, Miss Bellamy. Have you come to see Gran?'

'Just looked in to see how she is. And how are these two? I haven't seen 'em for a couple of weeks.' She stared at the white bundles. 'These are never the same babies you had then, surely? They're double the size!'

Joanna laughed. 'They're growing fast. Still a bit small for their age, of course, but they're catching up. Dr Latimer says they're as healthy a pair as any he's seen.'

'And so they are. They'll be growing out of that pram before we know it.' Constance had provided an old twin pram, a giant contraption with huge wheels and a hood at either end, which had been left unused in one of her outbuildings for years. Tom had refurbished the bodywork, and Alice and Minnie had re-upholstered the interior so that it was almost like new. Joanna had become a familiar sight wheeling her twins around the village in their smart carriage.

Val reappeared, with Jackie behind her. 'She's dozing off, but if you don't mind sitting beside her for a little while I'm sure she'd be pleased. Jackie's been talking to her about the spring flowers.'

Miss Bellamy stood up. 'I'll ramble on a bit about old times. We've got a lot of memories to share, Minnie Tozer and me.' She stumped across the kitchen and up the stairs and Val poured some more hot water into the brown teapot and passed Joanna a cup of tea. Jackie went to the sink to wash a cup and poured one for herself.

'She *is* going to get better, isn't she?' she asked, her voice quivering a little.

'Well, if she don't,' Alice said, 'it won't be for want of trying, on her part or any of the rest of us. I'm glad you came back, Jackie.'

'I had to. I couldn't let...' She let the sentence trail off and went to sit on Robin's stool, holding her cup between both hands. 'I'll stay the night, if that's all right.'

'Of course it's all right! This is your home, and your bed's always ready for you.' Alice stopped, feeling that her voice had been sharper than it need be, and added, ''Tis kind of Miss Bellamy to call in, isn't it? Her's a good old soul.'

'There'll be plenty of people wanting to know

123

how Gran is,' Val said. 'But those two have always been friends. Miss Bellamy's probably known her longer than almost anyone else in the village. Does anyone know how old she is?'

'She must be well into her seventies. If Mother were her nursemaid, she'll be about twelve years or so younger, and Mother's getting on for ninety, so–' The back door opened again and the men came in, taking off their boots in the porch. Robin stumped in, in much the same way as Constance Bellamy had stumped, and looking important.

'I milked Cora,' he announced. 'I squeezed her titties and got out lots of milk. She didn't mind a bit.'

'Well, isn't that good,' Joanna said admiringly. 'You're a proper little farmer, aren't you? Come over here and wash your hands, and that face could do with a scrub, too. There's muck all over your cheek.'

'There's nothing wrong with a bit of honest muck,' Robin asserted, and they all laughed.

'You got that from Mr Prout,' his mother told him. 'But he doesn't let it stay on his face, and he doesn't take it indoors with him either. His cottage is as neat as a new pin.'

'Why is a new pin neat?'

'Goodness me, I don't know. It just is. Come here, now.' Joanna damped a flannel under the tap and wiped it round his face. 'Hands. That's better. Now you can have a drink.'

'Can I have one too?' Tom asked, presenting his hands to be washed, and she flapped them away, laughing. Alice fetched a plate of sandwiches and

124

another of buttered scones from the larder and put them on the table, and Val made a fresh pot of tea. As they were gathering round, Miss Bellamy came down the stairs.

'We've had a good chat and she's sleeping peacefully now. No, I'll not have anything else, thank you, Mrs Tozer. I'd better be going. I've got any amount to do in the greenhouse.'

'D'you mean she actually woke up?' Alice asked. 'She knew you, and talked to you?'

'She did, I'm pleased to say, and we had a good yarn about the old days. I'd say she's turned the corner, not that I'm any expert of course. You'll know more when you see her for yourself.'

'I'll go now,' Alice said, and made for the stairs with Ted behind her. 'We'll just look in quietly and see.'

Val saw Miss Bellamy to the door. 'Thank you so much for coming. I'm sure it's done her good. And you too, Jackie,' she added, after she had seen the old lady off. 'Knowing you were there must have made all the difference.'

'I'll just pop the babies in their cot and come down again for my tea,' Joanna said, following Alice and Ted upstairs. 'Oh, I do hope Miss Bellamy is right, and she's on the mend. We just aren't ready to lose her yet.'

'I don't think we ever will be,' Tom said, his usually merry face serious for once. 'She's been there all our lives. I don't see how we can ever be ready to let her go.'

Chapter Eleven

'What time did Felix say he'd be coming round to collect you?' Dottie asked, popping her head into the living room where Stella and Maddy were sitting, surrounded by Maddy's luggage. 'I'd have thought he'd be here by now.'

'Six o'clock, he said,' Maddy answered looking at the clock on Dottie's mantelpiece. 'It's gone half-past. I can't think what's keeping him.'

'He did say he had to go over to that farm by Wheal Sarah to see the old man there,' Stella said. 'They sent for him this morning, straight after the service. But he was sure he'd be back by now.'

'Perhaps the old chap's really ill and he can't leave,' Maddy said. 'But he'd have tried to let us know, wouldn't he? Are they on the phone?'

'What, up at Wheal Sarah?' Dottie exclaimed. 'They haven't even got the electric up there. I'm not sure they've even got as far as having oil lamps.'

Stella smiled, then said, 'There must be someone there who could bring a message, though. I hope nothing's happened to him.'

They sat anxiously for a few minutes, looking out at the darkness in the hope of seeing Mirabelle's lights approaching. But the village street was dark.

'You don't think he's had to go and take the service at Little Burracombe after all, do you?'

Maddy asked. 'He might have called over on his way back to make sure that Mr Chadwick was there and found he couldn't be, and had to stay. That could have happened.'

'But then he'd have rung up from the vicarage and let Mr Harvey know, and he'd have got a message to us.' Stella got up restlessly and craned her neck to see further out of the window. 'Oh, someone's coming now. It's him! Oh, thank goodness.' She ran to the door and opened it. 'Felix! Whatever's happened? We were getting really worried. And where's Mirabelle?'

'Broke down,' he said, coming through the gate and leaning wearily in the doorway. 'I had to leave her up at Winlake and walk all the way back. I'll have to get someone to go out and look at her tomorrow.'

'Oh, Felix!' Stella led him into the room and pushed him into a chair. 'That's a good eight miles. You must be exhausted. And in the dark, too.'

'Well, it wasn't dark when I left,' he said wryly. 'But it got dark pretty soon after, and it's a rough track most of the way. And of course I didn't have a torch. Thanks, Dottie, you're an angel,' as she handed him a cup of tea. 'But never mind all that. What about Maddy? How are we going to get her back to West Lyme?'

'She needn't go,' Stella said decisively. 'She can stay here an extra day or two. It won't hurt to have a bit more holiday, and I'm sure the Archdeacon will understand. Won't he?' she added, turning to her sister.

'Well, yes, of course he will,' Maddy said doubtfully. 'But I did promise to be back, and I know there's a job he specially wanted me to start on tomorrow. The Bishop's coming to see him later in the week and there are all sorts of things that need to be attended to.'

'Well, if you can't get back, you can't,' Stella said a little impatiently. 'It's obvious that Felix can't take you.'

'No,' Maddy said, 'but there's someone else who could.' Her eyes met Stella's.

'Stephen? Would you really want to ask him?'

'Well, he did offer.'

'Yes, but...' Stella looked at her again. 'You didn't want to see him just yet.'

'I know. And I know I could stay on here, but now I've got myself all prepared to go – well, I just want to be back at work, doing something useful. And Stephen's not going to be silly over it. It's practically on his way back to White Cheriton, after all. And you said he just wants to be friends.'

'Yes, and I'm sure that's true. But it's how you feel that matters. If you're sure–'

'I'm sure,' Maddy said quietly, and Stella turned to take her coat from the back of the door.

'I'll go up to the Barton and see if he's still there. He may have gone already, mind. You'll have to stay then.'

'No need for that,' Dottie said. She already had her own coat on. 'I'll ring the Barton from the inn. It won't take me two minutes to run across, and I'll come straight back and tell you. Give that poor man something to eat, Stella, he must be starving.'

Stella did as she was told, making Felix cheese on toast and another cup of tea, and by the time

128

he was sitting down to eat it, Dottie was back. 'He says he'll be pleased to take you,' she told Maddy. 'They're just sitting down to their high tea that they have of a Sunday, but he'll come straight after that – soon after eight, if that's convenient. And he'll ring the Archdeacon to tell him you'll be there about ten or so.'

'Oh, that's kind,' Maddy said in relief. 'Thank you, Dottie. And it'll save Stella and Felix that long journey there and back, too. Really, I don't know why I didn't accept Stephen's offer in the first place.'

'You had your reasons,' Dottie said. 'Anyway, seems to me it'd be a good idea if we all had a bite more to eat, since you're going to be late. That cheese on toast smells good. Why don't we all have some?'

'I'll make it,' Stella said, glad to have something to do. 'And by the time we've finished that, he'll probably be here.' She smiled at her sister. 'At least you'll have a bit more room in Stephen's car than you would have had with three of us in Mirabelle. And it probably doesn't leak, either!'

Despite her words, Maddy felt nervous and unsettled as she got into Stephen's car later that evening. She knew that he had told Stella about the girl he'd lost, and that he'd promised he would do no more than offer his friendship at Maddy's own pace, but she still couldn't quite believe in it. The only Stephen she knew was light-hearted, flirtatious and rather feckless; this other Stephen, whom Stella had glimpsed, was outside her experience.

129

'Are you sure you're comfortable?' he asked as they set off, leaving Stella, Felix and Dottie waving by the gate. 'You're not cold? I've got another rug.'

'I'm warm as toast.' She smiled at him tentatively. 'Thank you for coming to my rescue.'

'My pleasure,' he said a little gruffly. 'I didn't think I was going to see you at all this weekend.'

'Stephen–' she began, but he broke in quickly.

'You don't have to say anything. I know you don't feel like being sociable at present. I really do understand that, you know.'

'Yes.' She hesitated. 'Stella told me – about the girl you lost.'

'I'd probably have told you, if we'd ever got to the point where I felt you'd want to know,' he said. 'I probably will one day, anyway. It's not something I talk about much, but it does help me to understand a bit of what it's like for you just now.'

'I just don't know when I'm going to feel like crying,' she said. 'It's little things that set me off, things I don't expect. And when I'm with other people – sometimes I'm not even sure if they know. If they haven't said anything, to let me know that they do – well, I don't know quite how to *be,* somehow. I feel I'm not quite the person they think I am.' She glanced sideways at him. 'Just as you're not quite the person I thought you were – now that I know about her.'

'Yes,' he said. 'And they don't have to say much, do they? Just "I'm sorry". There's not much more anyone can say than that, anyway.'

'And the things they talk about,' she said drearily. 'They all seem so unimportant – so

130

trivial. I know it's terribly selfish to feel like that, but I can't help it. It's not as if I want to talk about Sammy all the time – and yet, somehow I do. He's the only thing in my mind, and he's there all the time.'

'I know,' he said gently, and took his hand from the wheel to touch hers. 'I know.' They were both silent for a few minutes and then he said, 'Talk about him all you like, Maddy. Or don't talk at all – whichever you feel like. You don't have to be polite with me.'

Maddy turned her head and looked at him. He was watching the road ahead, his profile smooth and clean-cut, his fair hair brushed loosely across his forehead. Feeling unexpectedly calmer, she snuggled down into the soft blanket he had wrapped around her.

'D'you mind if I doze off a bit?' she asked, and he smiled and shook his head.

'I don't mind at all, Maddy. Sleep all the way to West Lyme, if that's what you want.'

The sweep of the wide bay was invisible in the darkness as they drew up outside the Archdeacon's house, but as they stepped out of the car they could hear the wash of the sea against the rocks at the foot of the cliff. Above them, stars glittered as brightly as if the sun were still high in the sky and shining through a curtain of old black lace. Maddy stopped and gazed up at them.

'You could hardly put a pin between them,' she said quietly. 'Sammy and I used to watch for shooting stars on nights like this. Sometimes, you can see quite a lot. It's supposed to be lucky to see one.' Her voice quivered suddenly and she turned away abruptly. Stephen laid his hand gently on her arm.

'I'm sorry,' she said. 'I didn't mean ... it's just little things you don't see them coming.'

'I know,' he said. 'It's all right. You can be however you want to be with me. You don't have to be sorry. I'm your friend, remember?'

She smiled up at him, the tears sparkling her eyelashes in the soft glow from the curtained windows. Then, before either could say any more, the front door opened, light spilled over them and Archie rushed out, whimpering with excitement and leaping about them as if he were twenty dogs.

'Archie!' Maddy exclaimed, half laughing, half crying as he stood up against her, his paws on her shoulders, and covered her face with kisses. 'Down! Your manners get worse all the time.'

'He needs a firmer hand than mine, I'm afraid,' the Archdeacon said, coming down the steps. He kissed Maddy and shook Stephen's hand. 'It's good to see you again, my dear. And you too, Stephen. Thank you for bringing her back.'

'It's my pleasure, any time she wants a lift.' Stephen turned back towards his car. 'Don't forget, Maddy. You know where to find me.'

'Oh, you'll come inside, surely,' the Archdeacon protested, but Stephen shook his head.

'I have to be getting back to the station. And Maddy needs to settle in again. Next time, perhaps.' He hesitated, as if not quite sure how to make his farewell, but Maddy stepped forward and stood on tiptoe to kiss his cheek.

'Thank you, Stephen dear. And not just for the lift.' She looked at him for a moment and then turned away, a tear lying like a pearl on her cheek, and Stephen bowed his head slightly and got into the car. As they watched him drive away, the Archdeacon took Maddy's arm in his and drew her closer against his side.

'He's a nice young man. There's something about him – I always thought him a little frivolous, but tonight there's something deeper. I'm not sure what it is...'

'I think I know,' Maddy said. 'But he'll never be able to take Sammy's place. He'll only ever be a friend to me.'

'A good one, though?' the Archdeacon said, and she nodded.

'Yes. A very good one.'

'I do hope she's going to be all right,' Stella said, watching the tail lights recede along the lane.

'I think she will. Uncle Gerald and Aunt Barbara will look after her. They aren't just employers, you know, they're part of her family. Or will be, when we're married,' he added, giving her shoulders a squeeze.

Stella turned and smiled up at him. 'Is that a hint?'

'It could be,' he admitted. 'Look, darling, I've been thinking about it a lot. I know you feel we can't flaunt our own happiness in front of Maddy, but would a wedding just after Christmas really do that? It's nearly ten months away, and surely she can see how we feel every time she looks at us. Getting married isn't going to change that.'

'No, but our wedding, when she knows she'll never have the wedding she wanted for herself, is going to rub salt into her wounds. And don't forget, it was at a New Year wedding that she and Sammy first met again. I really don't see how we can.'

'Let's walk along the lane for a little way and think about it,' Felix said, and Stella went back to close the front door, telling Dottie they were going for a stroll. For a few minutes they walked in silence, then he said, 'I agree with what you say, and I wouldn't hurt Maddy for the world. But is there ever going to be a right time for us? If we put it off again, we'll be talking about spring – and that will be a year since he died, and seem even worse. And that takes us into next summer, and maybe the summer holidays *would* be a good time, but – oh, darling, it's such a long time to wait! Over a year from now, a whole year for me to live on my own in that great vicarage, only able to see you when I can snatch time to come over to Burracombe, or you can come to me. And you know what a vicar's life is like – it's open house, with any of the parishioners likely to pop in at any time with some problem or other. We'll never be able to be sure of time on our own. Not to mention the gossips if you stay late in the evening. It's going to be like living in a goldfish bowl.'

'You're not regretting being a vicar, are you?' she asked, and he shook his head vigorously.

'Not at all! It's what I want to do. But I am regretting that you won't be a vicar's wife for what seems half a lifetime.' He stopped and gripped both her arms, turning her to face him. 'It isn't just that, Stella, I told you. What happened to Sammy – it's scared me.' His voice shook.

Stella stared up, trying to see his face clearly in the darkness. A little breathlessly, she asked, 'Didn't you say a vicar shouldn't be superstitious?'

'Maybe not, but I'm a human being as well, and I'm a human being very much in love and wanting nothing more than to be married to the woman I adore. I can't help it, Stella. I want to be married to you as soon as it can possibly be arranged. I'll wait until Christmas, as long as we can be making plans in the meantime – but please, please don't make me wait any longer.' He pulled her close and wrapped his arms around her so tightly that she gasped. 'Darling, I love you so much. Please say yes.'

Stella quivered against him. She turned up her face and stared at the silhouette of his head against the myriad stars and saw their light blazing in his eyes. Her heart surged and she caught her breath and whispered, 'Yes... Yes, we'll get married, straight after Christmas. The first Saturday after Christmas Day.'

'Oh, darling! D'you really mean it?' He hugged her again until she cried out for mercy. 'Oh, that's wonderful! Wonderful! Just a minute–' he loosened his grip '–which day will that be. Oh...'

'What's the matter?'

'It'll be Boxing Day,' he said doubtfully. 'Christmas Day's on a Friday. Nobody will be able to get here unless they've got a car.'

'Well, could we make it the Monday?'

'Everyone will be back at work. Oh, darling!'

'It'll have to be the next Saturday then,' she said

firmly. 'January the second. I think you're right – Maddy won't want us to wait any longer. And you'll have been in Little Burracombe for eight months by then. That's quite long enough for you to be on your own, without me to keep an eye on you.'

Felix laughed and pulled her close again. 'And just what d'you think I'm going to get up to, hmm?'

'I don't know, but I do know what women can be like when there's a handsome young unmarried vicar on the loose. They can lose all sense of reason. Not that I ever did myself,' she added as he hooted with laughter. 'I just noticed it, that's all. Oh, shut up, Felix, or I won't marry you at all!' she finished, laughing and shaking him by the shoulders.

Felix grew serious again and bent his head to hers. 'Don't say that, darling. Don't ever say that, even in jest. Maybe I'm being superstitious again, but I just don't want to hear it. Tell me again we're getting married straight after Christmas, and then give me a kiss to prove it – quickly.'

'We're getting married straight after Christmas,' Stella said resolutely, and lifted her lips to his. 'But we won't tell Maddy straight away. We'll wait for the right moment.'

A cottage door opened and Val came out with a torch. She shone it on their closely embracing figures and laughed.

'Oh, it's you two! Luke and I were wondering what all the chattering was about. Isn't it a bit chilly for canoodling in the middle of the village street?'

136

'It's never too chilly for canoodling,' Felix said, and Stella turned a radiant face towards her friend.

'We're getting married. Straight after Christmas. You're the first to know – isn't it wonderful?'

'And about time too,' Val said. 'I don't know how you'll wait so long as it is.' Then she grinned and added, 'Yes – it's wonderful. Come in and tell Luke, and we'll have a celebration!'

Chapter Twelve

Minnie Tozer had indeed turned the corner and once she had done so she continued to mend. Jackie sat with her for most of the evening, talking about her new life in Plymouth and asking about the old days on the farm, before her father had been born. The conversation was slow and halting, with many pauses, but by the time Alice came upstairs again Minnie was looking much more her old self, and even had a few roses in her cheeks.

'It's really done her good, having you here,' she said to her daughter. 'Perked her up no end. I reckon she'll be all right now, though it'll be a long job, mind. Her won't be getting about downstairs for a bit.'

'Don't you be too sure,' the old lady said, her voice not much more than a whisper yet with just a hint of its old sturdy tone. 'I'll need to see what you've all been up to while I've been poorly.'

'Well, that's as maybe,' Alice retorted, using a corner of her apron to wipe a tear from her eye. 'We'll see what Dr Latimer says before we lets you put a foot to the floor. You've given us all a fright, and we don't want to take no chances.'

Minnie looked as if she wanted to reply, but before her lips could frame the words her eyes had closed and she was asleep. Alice smiled waveringly and Jackie stood up and slipped her arm round her mother's waist.

'I'm glad I came. I was really worried when that telegram arrived.'

'We were worried when we sent it. It's good to have you home anyway.' They went out on to the landing, closing the door softly behind them. 'What was it you were doing this weekend that was more important than coming to see your family, anyway?'

Jackie flushed a little. 'Nothing, really. I just wanted to be in Plymouth. You know, I've come home every weekend since I went to live with Jennifer, so I've never really had time to myself there. Just going to work every day – well, you don't really feel part of the place.'

'And is that what you want?' Alice looked at her in the dim light. 'To feel part of Plymouth?'

'I want to know what it feels like, yes. Just to have time to wander about, go where I like without having to be back at a certain time – explore a bit. That sort of thing. There's a lot to do there.'

'I suppose there is,' Alice said doubtfully. 'And I dare say it don't matter too much if you do stop there for a day or two extra now and then. But this is your home, Jackie. This is where you belong.'

138

Jackie started to go down the stairs. At the bottom, she opened the door into the kitchen and looked into the big, warm room where her family were gathered. They were all there: Ted in his big chair by the range, his boots off and his feet encased in thick woolly socks, Tom and Luke helping Robin to build a castle with his wooden bricks, Val putting the finishing touches to a cake she had just taken from the oven and Joanna with a baby lying contentedly in each arm. Only Minnie's chair was empty, and the gap seemed less now that they knew the old lady was getting better.

She turned to her mother. 'I know this is my home,' she said quietly. 'It always will be, and I'll always come back. But I'm not sure it's where I'll always belong. There's something else for me – I know there is. And even if it doesn't turn out to be in Plymouth, that's where I've got to start looking for it.'

With Minnie definitely on the mend, the Tozers were able to give more thought to the Coronation celebrations. Ted started to make plans for some extra-special bell-ringing on the day, and Alice began to draw up lists of people who would help with teas in the marquee and a bit more of a spread later on, for the dance.

'We won't be able to ring all day, like I first thought,' he said as they sat on opposite sides of the table with sheets of paper and pencils. 'On account of the service being broadcast in the church. But us'll ring beforehand and straight after, like we planned to begin with, and then through the afternoon. I been talking to Abe Lillicrap, over to Little Burracombe, and he's agreeable to us taking a turn on each others' bells, for a bit of variety. We'll need a bit of practice, mind. I don't want no bad striking when we're over there.'

'We could have the handbells, too,' Alice said, looking up at the shining row hanging on the beam overhead. 'Mother'll be as fit as a flea again come June. She can do some new harmonies, special – it'll keep her sitting quiet for a bit too, once she's downstairs again.' She frowned down at her own list. 'What do you think us ought to do for the evening? We'll be having cakes and scones and sandwiches in the afternoon, so it ought to be something different.'

'If you ask me,' Ted said, as if she hadn't done just that, 'you can't beat a nice ham salad for an evening do. And a trifle for afters. George Sweet'll do us a ham, I dare say. You wants to make sure they womenfolk over to Little Burracombe does their share, though. If the two villages are going to pull together for this lark, us wants to be sure they pulls their weight, and we don't end up doing the whole thing just because it's our side of the river.'

'Oh, is it going to be our side, then?' Alice asked. 'Last I heard, the marquee was going up their side.'

Ted stared at her. 'Never in all your life! 'Tis obvious it makes sense to have it Burracombe side. That field's dead flat – if we tried to pitch it their side, everything would be on a downward slope.'

'It's bigger their side, though,' she said. 'And you needn't look at me like that, I'm only trying to be fair.'

'Being fair's one thing. Being downright foolish

is another. How could us run the kiddies' races and such on a slope? They'd be all tumbling to the bottom. And you can't have them running sideways along it, they'd be falling over and twisting their ankles.'

'It's not that steep,' Alice said. 'You're talking as if it's Mount Everest. Anyway, I'm only telling you what I've heard.'

'Well, whoever you heard it from, you'd better set 'em straight next time you see 'em. The marquee's going up on Burracombe side of the Clam, and that's all there is to it. Why, us'd never hear the end of it if we let them have it. Next thing, they'd be wanting to change their name to Great Burracombe.'

'I wonder why *we* were never called that,' Alice mused. 'You'd think that with one village being called Little, the other one'd want to be called Great, wouldn't you.'

'Just being Burracombe's enough,' he said firmly. 'And none of this is helping me work out a peal for the day. I know we'll be ringing the Queens Peal, that goes without saying, but I'd like to do summat special, summat us've never done before.' He chewed his pencil and stared at the rows of numbers. 'I want to bring in all the best changes – Queens and Whittingtons and Tittums – so folk have got some real bell music to listen to.'

Alice went back to her own calculations. Whichever side of the river the festivities were to be held, she would still need the same amount of cakes and sausage rolls and so on, and an extra-large army of women to prepare them all. I could get our side to do the afternoon food, she thought, and the Little Burracombe folk to do the evening. Or the other way about... There's Freda Lillicrap, she usually takes charge over there and she's a good baker. But that'd mean she'd want to make cakes and such, and I was hoping to do that. And we've got Dottie Friend too, nobody makes a better Victoria sponge than she does. And if we do trifle for the evening, we're going to need a master lot of bowls, and folk always like to make trifle in their own bowl... I'm not sure this is going to work, I'm not sure at all...

Joyce Warren had no doubts at all about her own plans.

'As long as the villagers play their part,' she said to Basil Harvey as she spread the purple cloth over the altar. While taking Holy Communion on the previous Sunday, she had noticed a wine stain on the front and had stayed behind specially to take it home to be washed. Joyce had not, of course, washed it herself; she had given that task to Mabel Purdy, who 'did' for her. But she made sure that the Vicar knew that she had been the one to notice and take it home, and also that he was in the church when she brought it back. Now, she spread it reverently over the ancient stone table, patting it and giving it little tweaks to make sure it was perfectly smooth.

Basil watched politely, thinking of his wife's chagrin at Joyce's officiousness. 'I'd meant to do that myself,' Grace had said crossly. 'I would have done, too, if she hadn't slipped in first, while I was talking to Jessie Friend. You know their Billy's poorly again, don't you? Only a cold, she

142

says, but they always worry about his chest. Oh well, if Mrs Warren wants to give herself extra work, that's up to her, I suppose.'

'I think it was Mrs Purdy who got the extra work,' he'd observed mildly. 'But I dare say Mrs Warren paid her to do it, so maybe all's well that ends well. The Purdys can always do with a little more money.'

Joyce's mind was still on the villagers and the likelihood of their playing their part. 'They're so easy to manage, if you know how,' she continued complacently. 'I can usually win them round, even when they're a little slow to start with.'

Privately, Basil translated this as 'I can usually bully them into submission', but he maintained his usual diplomacy and reflected that it was, after all, six of one and half a dozen of the other. 'Letting the interfering old biddy get away with it' – the villagers' view of the matter – worked out easier, in the end, than thinking up and carrying through their own plans. And between them, given a bit of robust opposition (from Alf Coker and one or two others), and a quiet determination to go their own way and do things as Burracombe had always done them (from Ted Tozer and his bell-ringers), they usually enjoyed a fair measure of success. Things got done, and things happened, and while there would always be a few who grumbled, they were generally pretty successful.

'It certainly seemed as if they all liked the idea of the Monarchs' Procession,' he said.

'Oh, yes. Well, it's the obvious thing to do, isn't it?' She frowned a little, as if wondering if it might not be a little too obvious and that every other village in the county, if not the entire British Isles, might decide to do the same, then shrugged. 'It hardly matters anyway, if everyone does have the same idea. Nobody can attend more than one celebration, after all. And we shall each put our own interpretation on events. Now, once I've finished here, my next task is to visit the school and have a word with Miss Kemp. She and young Stella Simmons are very enthusiastic but they do need a little gentle guidance from time to time. Those Crocker twins, for example – I doubt if it's even occurred to them that they would be ideal for the Princes in the Tower. It's so easy to overlook the obvious, don't you agree?'

Easy to state it, too, Basil thought with another polite nod. Really, he wondered sometimes if God really intended vicars to be quite so hypocritical as he found himself being with Mrs Warren.

'I think you're quite right about the Crocker boys,' he said. That was true enough, at any rate. 'But I wouldn't be at all surprised if the teachers hadn't already thought of it. In fact, I'm sure I heard something about it after the meeting.'

'Oh.' Joyce's tone was slightly affronted. 'Well, I'll mention it anyway. And there's the question of little Shirley Culliford, too.'

'Oh yes,' he said more eagerly. 'She must certainly have a good part.'

'And there, I'm afraid, I do *not* agree. She's had prominent parts in both the pantomime and *A Midsummer Night's Dream*, not to mention the pageant last year. I'm not at all sure it's a good idea to encourage her. That class of person is so quick to take advantage, don't you find?'

'No,' Basil said, conversationally. 'I don't think I do. What do you mean, exactly?'

'Oh, I'm sure you know, Vicar! Look at her father–'

'I wasn't aware we were discussing Arthur Culliford. Unless you have a part in mind for him too. Richard the Lionheart, perhaps?'

Mrs Warren gave him a sharp, suspicious glance and spoke rather stiffly. 'I don't think that's at all suitable, and if you meant it as a joke I don't find it funny either. I simply meant that if you give that type of person an inch, they'll take a mile, and–'

'And *I* mean, that if Shirley Culliford is suited to any particular part, then she should have it, regardless of what her father is likely to take or not take,' he retorted sharply. 'She's a bright and interesting child, and well worth encouraging, in my opinion. Now, if you'll excuse me, Mrs Warren, I do have rather a lot to do and I want to call in and see how Billy Friend is getting along. He's a delicate young man and his sisters do worry about him.' He turned away and marched down the aisle, his cassock flapping around his ankles, aware that he was breathing rather quickly, and already regretting his outburst. And in front of the Lord's table, too! Would he ever learn to control his temper?

In fact, most of his parishioners would have been surprised to learn that he had a temper at all. They saw him as a mild, sometimes slightly panicky little man, more like Alice's White Rabbit than a fighter; not that that lessened their respect for him one iota. Basil Harvey was one of the most loved men in the village.

145

One of the others most loved was Jacob Prout. He could be found on almost any day, working around the lanes and gardens of the village, whistling as he trimmed hedges, cleared ditches or swept the roads, usually accompanied by his little dog, Scruff. He kept the churchyard tidy and dug graves, yet, busy as he was, he never seemed to be in a hurry and always had a moment to spare for a word with passers-by.

He was digging out a ditch near the gates to the Barton when Travis Kellaway came by in his Land Rover. Travis pulled in and stopped the engine, then jumped out and came over to Jacob, who straightened up and leaned on the long handle of his spade, nodding a good-morning.

'Morning, Jacob. You're doing a good job there.'

'Does me best,' Jacob said laconically. The estate manager was still new to the village and while Jacob never believed in being unfriendly, he also believed in taking his time over getting to know newcomers. 'I been looking after things round here for the past fifty years or so,' he added, 'give or take the time when I was away fighting for me country, so I reckon I knows what needs doing and how it oughter be done.'

'You certainly do. There was a chap in my village in Dorset a bit like you, always working at some job around the place. Then he died and gradually the place started to look a bit scruffy and untidy – hedges overgrown, ditches full of sludge, culverts blocked, that sort of thing. And we all started to realise just how much he'd done. Eventually, the parish council had to pay two younger men to do what he'd done.'

'In half the time too, I don't doubt,' Jacob said with a small grin, and Travis laughed.

'They certainly seemed to string it out. Didn't last very long, either. Now they're talking about getting machines to sweep the roads. I know they'll still need a man to operate them, but it won't be the same.'

'Reckon it'll be a while before us gets road-sweeping machines here in Burracombe,' Jacob said. 'And a good thing too – can't be doing with all these noisy contraptions.' He looked reflectively at the other man and decided he wasn't such a bad chap, all things considered. It wasn't his fault he'd been born in Dorset. 'So how be you settling in at the Barton, then?'

'Pretty well, thanks. It's a nice area. I like the moor – Dorset's wonderful for farmland and rolling hills, and the sea of course, but we don't have these wild spaces. And Dartmoor's got a special atmosphere all of its own. I dare say you know any amount of old stories.'

'I do. So you reckon you'll stop here? I saw you in that pantomime the curate got up just before Christmas.'

Travis grinned. 'It was good fun. Pity he's leaving to go over the river. I don't know if it'll be so easy to organise the drama group from there.'

'No, and that's the trouble,' Jacob said darkly. 'If us don't look out, that Mrs Warren'll be taking over again, like her always does. Her wasn't best pleased about him doing the pantomime as it was, always thought it was her pigeon and didn't like it when folk made it clear they were more ready to follow he. I suppose it'll all fall flat again, once he leaves.'

'That'd be a shame,' Travis said thoughtfully. 'But you think people would like it to carry on, do you?'

'Oh, ah, if they could only find the right person to take charge.' Jacob's bright eyes scrutinised the other man's face. 'You wouldn't be thinking of doing it yourself, would you?'

'No,' Travis said, startled, although that was exactly what he had been thinking. 'I know just what all the locals would say if yet another outsider came in and started to take over.'

'It's only when they starts taking over what us is already managing for ourselves that us don't like it,' Jacob said, not entirely accurately. 'When it's summat that might go to the wall, us don't take no exception. What would you be thinking of doing? Another pantomime?'

'Look, I didn't say I was thinking of doing anything,' Travis protested in alarm, but Jacob was scratching his chin thoughtfully.

'Young curate had it in mind to put on two productions a year, as I recall. A play or maybe a revue, as he termed it, in the spring and then pantomime in the winter. He mentioned it to me on account of my Dartmoor songs and stories, asked if I'd be willing to do a few on stage and I said I would. But then, what with him being induced over the river at Easter, and this Coronation being took over by Mrs Warren with her march-past and so on, it got put aside. I reckon us'd be ready for a pantomime, though, and 'tisn't any too soon to start thinking about that.'

148

'It is,' Travis said positively. 'Much too soon. After the Coronation would be quite soon enough – say, the last week of June for a meeting to see who'd be interested, and then start casting in the summer ready to start rehearsals in September. Mind, it would be a good idea to have one or two scripts on hand early on, to see what people would like to do. I could start getting–' He stopped abruptly and gave Jacob a look of exasperation. 'Now, look here. I haven't said–'

'I don't think you needs to say no more,' Jacob said, chuckling. 'I can see the look in your eye. You done a bit of this before, I take it.'

'Well, yes. I did put on a couple of things at home,' Travis admitted. 'But that doesn't mean I want to start doing it here. It's too early. And it's a busy time for me.'

'Any time of year's a busy time for us country folk. But us has always managed to make time for a bit of entertainment as well, specially round Christmas. You think about it, Mr Kellaway. And I'll tell you who wouldn't mind giving you a hand, too, and that's my Jennifer, what lives in Plymouth but comes out to stop with me of a weekend most times. Her was saying last time, her wouldn't mind getting a bit more involved.'

'Was she?' Travis said. 'Well, maybe we ought to meet sometime and have a chat about it.'

'Ah,' Jacob said, nodding. 'Maybe you should. And there ain't no time like the present. Why don't you come in this Friday night and have a bit of supper with us? Won't be nothing special, mind – just a meat pie and some of me own vegetables and maybe some stewed fruit and custard for afters. But you'm welcome to join us.'

'All right,' Travis said, turning back towards the Land Rover. 'I will. And thank you, Jacob.'

Jacob touched his cap and watched as the Land Rover moved off down the lane. Then he turned back to his work.

'That ain't a bad chap,' he said to Scruff, who had been sitting patiently at his feet, waiting for the conversation to end. 'That ain't a bad chap at all.'

Chapter Thirteen

'It seems almost *too* obvious to choose the Crocker twins for the little Princes in the Tower,' Miss Kemp said thoughtfully as she and Stella settled down at her house for cocoa and a chat. 'But since we've got them handed to us on a plate, as it were...'

'I can't see what else they could be,' Stella agreed. 'And Shirley Culliford will do beautifully for the new Queen, as a little girl, with her sister as Princess Margaret. It's a pity there aren't more good parts for the children, but at least they'll need less coaching if they're simply to be part of each monarch's entourage. It means a lot of work on costumes, though.'

'Well, we've plenty of willing helpers,' Miss Kemp said comfortably. 'A lot of the mothers have promised, and we've got Dottie to oversee it all. That woman is a treasure,' she went on,

150

holding up the jug of cocoa enquiringly. Stella nodded, and the headmistress refilled her cup. 'You'll miss her when you go over to Little Burracombe.'

'I know. I've been terribly lucky to live with her – she does far more for me than she ought to. But I've been learning to bake all the cakes and scones and so on that she makes, and I did a lot of cookery at the Home, so Felix won't starve.'

'A vicar never needs to starve,' Miss Kemp said. 'He gets offered tea and cakes wherever he goes. That's why most of them end up looking like barrels.'

'You wouldn't be referring to our own vicar, by any chance?' Stella asked innocently. 'I don't know that he'd like being called a barrel.'

'He shouldn't eat so much cake, then,' the headmistress said unrepentantly. 'He gets fed perfectly well at home. Mind you, I don't think your Felix will ever look like a barrel. He's far too energetic. And what's this you were saying about you two getting married at Christmas?'

'Well, immediately after,' Stella said. 'We just decided we didn't want to wait any longer. We'll have been engaged a year by then. And it's not really good for a vicar to be unmarried. We don't really want it to be common knowledge yet, though.'

'You're not afraid one of those young floozies from Little Burracombe will catch his eye?' Miss Kemp said, amused, and Stella laughed.

'No, not at all! But he needs a wife to help him. And it's going to be quite difficult to see much of each other as it is. I know the two villages are

151

only a mile apart as the crow flies, and it's only a short walk over the Clam, but really he might as well be in Scotland for all the chance he'll get to be out of the village. He'll be at everyone's beck and call as a vicar.'

'And so will you as a vicar's wife. You do realise that, don't you? And I'm going to miss you terribly. We've worked well together. I was hoping you'd take over from me one day.'

'As headmistress?' Stella's eyes widened. 'I never thought...'

'Well, you should have done. You didn't want to remain an assistant teacher all your life, did you?' Miss Kemp's eyes rested on Stella's face and she sighed. 'No, of course you didn't. You wanted to be a vicar's wife.'

'Well, not to begin with,' Stella protested, laughing. 'I didn't know I'd ever be anyone's wife. Yes, I suppose it's true I did think I'd teach for longer than I'm turning out to be doing. And I'm sorry to be leaving so soon. But I can still help out. I'll be able to do supply teaching, even after I'm married.'

'It's ridiculous that women have to leave so many jobs when they marry,' Miss Kemp said. 'Teaching ... the Civil Service ... all manner of good careers. And not everyone has a family immediately, or ever. It's such a waste.'

'I know. But we're always told we're taking jobs away from men, or from unmarried women who need them.'

'So married women work for nothing – as you'll do, helping your husband do his job as a vicar. I sometimes wonder why we educate girls at all.

And then I think of women like myself, who have never married. And it's important for mothers to be educated too. They have the most important job in the world. There's so much difference between children whose mothers have got more in their heads than just washing and ironing, and take some trouble with their children, and those who just leave them to themselves. Look at the Crocker boys, for example. Bright children, annoying though they can be, but their poor mother has probably never sat down to read them a story – I doubt if she's ever had time. While young Henry Bennetts has a quite astonishing breadth of general knowledge. And do you know why? I went to see Mrs Bennetts once and the living room is full of books. Henry himself was lying on the floor reading one of those 'Wonder' books – you know the sort of thing, the *Wonder Book of Wonders* and so on, full of articles about the Northern Lights and birds and animals, and how a telephone works, as well as odd bits of poetry and extracts from classical stories. Absolute goldmines. It's no wonder he's full of information. Not that it stops him getting into plenty of mischief with Micky Coker,' she added ruefully.

Stella laughed. 'I wonder how they'll end up, the pair of them. Micky will be a blacksmith like his father, of course, but Henry might become a doctor or a politician or anything. He might even become a teacher!'

'If he does,' Miss Kemp said, 'the children in his school will never get away with anything. Whatever tricks they get up to, he'll have thought of them first. Well, it's been a productive evening and I

153

think we've got our part in the Royal Pageant reasonably well organised. And just as well, since you're going to be so busy getting ready for Felix's induction. Is he looking forward to it?'

'He's getting a bit nervous,' Stella said. 'He's terrified he'll do something silly, like trip over his robes or something. I tell him it doesn't matter if he does – his new parishioners know him pretty well already, and if they don't they might as well find out now as later. He doesn't seem to think that's much comfort.'

She finished her cocoa and got up to go. Dottie was working at the inn that evening, and although she would have left something out for Stella's supper, they both knew that she was unlikely to need anything after an evening drinking cocoa and eating ginger biscuits at Miss Kemp's. These evenings are another thing I shall miss when I'm married to Felix, she thought, walking back along the starlit street. Talking over school matters, planning the term's work... And I shall miss the children most of all.

It seemed that whatever you did in life, wherever it took you, there would always be losses as well as gains. You just had to balance them with whatever was most important to you. And being with Felix was the most important thing that Stella could imagine.

Plans for the Easter Sunday induction were finally complete. It was to take place immediately following Matins at Little Burracombe, and most of the congregation of Burracombe itself were there to witness it, including Maddy, who had come

154

down from West Lyme for the big day. Dressed in their Sunday best, they walked across the Clam together, filing across the narrow wooden bridge over the tumbling river. The banks were thick with violets and primroses, while above them the leaves were uncurling on the branches of the trees; the oaks a bright, fresh green, the beeches a delicate salmon-pink. A few early hawthorn blossoms showed white, daisy-like faces and there was a constant flurry of birds busy building their nests and, in some cases, already feeding mates sitting on eggs.

Basil Harvey, who had preached a shorter sermon than usual so that their own service could end early, led his congregation into the church and then took his place in the choir stalls. The service was led by the Bishop and there were a good many of Felix's relatives there too, all wearing their best clerical robes. Maddy, who had come with the Archdeacon and his wife, sat in the front pew with Stella.

'It's very grand, isn't it,' she whispered.

'Well, it's an important occasion.' Stella's eyes were misted with tears as she looked at Felix, his face unusually grave as he listened and made his responses. She listened with slight anxiety as he chimed the tenor bell; tradition had it that it would strike once for every year that Felix would remain here as vicar, and he'd been practising surreptitiously at Burracombe, to make sure he didn't miss a stroke too early. To her delight, it struck twelve times before a lighter pull caused the clapper to swing back without touching the sound bow of the bell. Twelve years would do, she thought, before they had to move on.

When his voice rang out at the end of the service, taking charge for the first time in his own church, the tears brimmed over and she brushed them away quickly, hoping that nobody had noticed. Maddy squeezed her hand.

'He looks quite different. So confident and strong. It's hard to imagine him sitting at Dottie's table with jam on his chin.'

'I'm sure he'll do that again,' Stella murmured, smiling a little shakily. 'He's the same Felix underneath.'

'But this is him too.' They watched as he strode down the aisle to greet his new flock at the door, his robes flowing behind him. 'I know I've seen him taking services before, but it was always just Felix. Today, he looks – well, as if he'd grown up, somehow.'

Stella laughed softly and dropped to her knees for her final prayer. Then she got up and followed her sister slowly from the church, the last to take her fiancé's hand.

'Well done, darling,' she said quietly, looking into his eyes. 'It was beautiful. You're going to be such a good vicar.'

'I hope so,' he answered seriously, and then, with a flash of a grin, 'If I'm not, I shall have my whole family to answer to!'

'He certainly will,' the Archdeacon said, standing beside him. 'We shall be watching like hawks to see that he doesn't besmirch the family honour.'

'Well, thank you for that vote of confidence,' Felix said indignantly. 'Hawks? Vultures, more like!'

They laughed and followed the congregation to the village hall, where sandwiches and coffee were being served. The inhabitants of both villages mingled together chatting amiably about farming matters or gossiping about various members of the two communities, until inevitably the talk turned to the Coronation celebrations.

'Have it been decided which side of the river's to have the marquee?' old Abel Prowse, one of the Little Burracombe farmers, asked loudly, and Felix groaned.

'I was hoping we could keep off that subject. But if anyone was likely to bring it up, Abel would.'

'Ssh,' Stella warned him. 'You'll have to be careful what you say about your parishioners now you're vicar.'

He grimaced. 'Is it too late to change my mind? Now look what he's done!'

As soon as Abel had spoken, the buzz of conversation had ceased and all eyes turned towards the new vicar. The Bishop and Archdeacon, standing together in a corner with a cup of coffee and a sandwich each, glanced round in surprise.

Ted Tozer spoke first. 'Like I been saying all along, it only makes sense to have it our side. You start playing ball games or putting up tables at the top of that field over this side, and everything'll end up in the river.'

'And we know what'll happen if you has it your side,' Abel retorted. 'All the best places will go to Burracombe and us'll hardly get a look in.'

'All what best places? As far as I know, there's going to be teas in the marquee, and games and races for the kiddies outside.'

157

'Not just for the kiddies.' Abel's son Joe, a tall, solidly-built man in his thirties, moved to his father's side, looking pugnacious. 'As I heard it, there's going to be a greasy pole and a tug-of-war and one of they things you can test your strength on. 'T'isn't all going to be egg-and-spoon and sack races.'

'I never said it were,' Ted began indignantly, but he was stopped by Alice who gripped his elbow firmly and said, 'That's enough now, the two of you. Us is on church ground–'

'Village hall don't belong to the church,' someone objected, but Alice raised her voice and continued.

'The church is paying for us to be here, so for the minute it counts as church. And you might as well remember why we're here – because it's Easter Sunday and we just handed over our curate to be your vicar, and if you want to know what I think, I think if this is the sort of behaviour he got to look forward to here in Little Burracombe, us might just decide to take him back home with us and done with it!'

She paused for breath and the assembly gazed back at her, half in admiration, half in silent mutiny. 'Coming over here and talking to us like we was a lot of school kids,' someone muttered, but she was nudged sharply by her neighbour, who muttered back, 'Better not behave like 'em, then,' and the rebellious muttering died away. Alice, looking suddenly embarrassed, turned away and Dottie Friend passed her a cup of coffee.

'I dunno what come over me,' Alice murmured. 'Showing myself up like that.'

'It wasn't you that showed yourself up, it was them. But I reckon most of 'em's on your side, Alice. That Abel Prowse and his Joe were always troublemakers, and why they're here I do *not* know. Haven't set foot in the church since VE Day, neither of them. I suppose they just wanted to see how Felix was likely to shape up. They used to give poor Mr Berry a hard time of it, from what I've heard.'

'They needn't think they can bully Felix,' Alice said. 'Hullo – looks like he'm about to say something.'

Felix was holding up his hands and calling for attention.

'First of all, I'd like to say how very good it is to see you all here this morning, and how good it was to see so many in church too. I don't expect such large congregations every Sunday but of course I'll be delighted to see as many of you as can manage it. I know how busy farmers are.' He paused, then went on in a firm voice, 'And since Mr Prowse has brought up the question of the Coronation celebrations, and there are so many of you here from both villages, I'd like to make a suggestion. If we are to work together to make this a real and memorable day, I suggest we start straight away. Let's have a public meeting for both communities, here in this village hall, and discuss the whole thing. I know both villages have had meetings separately – I've been lucky enough to attend both – and we've made certain plans, but now is the time to start serious co-operation. So what do you say? Would this coming Friday be suitable? I don't suppose you'll all be able to

159

manage it, but if as many of you as possible can come along I'll be more than willing to act as chairman. Would seven-thirty be a good time?'

Taken by surprise, nobody could think of an objection. A few murmured that they wouldn't be able to come, but most seemed free to attend. Joyce Warren, looking disconcerted and none too pleased at having her chairmanship whipped away from her, tried to raise an argument, but nobody took any notice and she subsided with a dissatisfied expression. Basil Harvey's lips quivered and he turned away hastily and found himself face to face with the Bishop.

'It looks as if your erstwhile curate is in for an interesting time,' the Bishop remarked. 'How do you think he'll be able to cope?'

It occurred to Basil that this was a question the Bishop might have asked earlier, but he smiled and said, 'Extremely well, I suspect. And he knows most of his new parishioners already, so I don't imagine he'll be in for many surprises.'

The Bishop nodded and looked round with a smile as Felix's father, also a bishop, approached. Basil, feeling slightly overwhelmed, escaped in search of fresh coffee for them all but was distracted by finding Maddy alone in a corner, a plate of untouched sandwiches and a cup of coffee on a small table in front of her.

'My dear,' he said, stopping at once, the Bishop's coffee forgotten. 'Are you all right?'

Maddy looked up and smiled wanly. 'Yes, I suppose so. I just felt a bit shaky for a minute.' Her glance drifted past him and her voice was touched with wistfulness. 'They look so happy, don't they.'

Basil turned and saw Stella and Felix laughing together. Her hand was on his arm and he was smiling down at her with a look of such tenderness that Basil caught his breath. Distressed, he turned back to Maddy.

'My dear girl. It must be so hard for you.'

'It's not really. I'm really pleased to see her – to see them...' Her voice quivered and she leaned forward to pick up her cup, only to put it down again quickly as it shook in her hand. 'I feel so selfish sometimes,' she said in a low voice. 'Stella's my sister. I ought to be happy for her – I *am* happy – but at the same time, I feel hurt and angry and as if everything's been snatched away from me. And I don't know why. What did Sammy or I ever do? What did *he* do? He had such a sad life, Mr Harvey. His mother died when he was just a little boy and he hardly knew his father. He was taken away and sent to live with strangers in a strange place–'

'Strangers who were very kind to him,' Basil interposed quietly. 'Strangers who loved him and who he grew to love. And his father, too – they grew to know and love each other. More than half his life was happy, Maddy.'

'But it was too *short*,' she said rebelliously. 'Why did it have to be taken away from him so soon? Why did he have to lose everything – and leave me with nothing?' she ended in a small, desolate voice.

Basil felt helpless. He knew all the answers he should make – the platitudes, the reassurances. Sammy was in Heaven now, with God, with his mother, he would wait for Maddy to join him, but meanwhile she must live her own life here on earth, as God evidently wished her to do. But he

161

knew that they would do no good. Maddy was in the grip of her anguish and nothing he could say would ease it. He wasn't even sure that such words would have eased his own grief, had he been in her situation.

'Come and see me at the vicarage, my dear,' he said gently, putting his hand on her shoulder. 'Come at any time. It may ease you just to talk about him, and about how you're feeling.'

She looked up at him. 'The Archdeacon says that, too. But I can't – not to order, anyway. It has to come when I feel like it. Anyway, we're going back to West Lyme this evening.'

'Of course.' Basil took a step back, feeling dismissed and chiding himself for forgetting that Maddy lived in the home of a clergyman far senior to himself. How could he have had the temerity to offer help when she had all the counselling she might need there at her hand? Yet I might have said something, he thought, as Dottie came over and he wandered away, almost overwhelmed by a sense of his own inadequacy. I might, just by accident, have said just the right word.

He was back in the vicarage, enjoying a late lunch, when he remembered that he had never fetched the fresh coffee for the Bishops.

Val and Luke walked back to their cottage, next door to Jacob's, and collected a packet of sandwiches she'd made earlier. They put them into Luke's haversack, changed their best clothes for old ones and set off for a walk up the Burra Brook.

'It's far too good a day to spend sitting indoors,' Luke said. 'Let's walk up to the tor. We haven't been there for ages.'

They walked through the village and up the footpath that led through the woods to the charcoal burner's cottage, where Luke had lived when he first came to the village. He and Val had started their married life there, and they paused to look at it. Nobody else had occupied it since they left, and it was beginning to look forlorn and abandoned.

'It's a shame to see it fall to bits,' Luke said. 'It was a cosy little place.'

'Little being the operative word,' Val commented. 'And I'm not sure "cosy" is altogether accurate. But we were very happy here and I agree, it's a pity to see it being unused. I don't know who else would want to live here, though.'

They walked on up the hill and out on to the moor, pausing again at the Standing Stones. These were well known as a meeting place for those who wanted some privacy (so well-known that there was often less privacy there than at any other place in Burracombe) and commanded a view over the whole village.

'I always think it looks as if the cottages are clustered together as if for protection against the moor,' Val said, gazing down fondly. 'Or like a family of children, with the church in the middle like a mother looking after them. And the Barton stands apart, rather aloof, as if it's too grand and important to need protection from anyone.'

'You'd better not let Hilary hear you say that,' Luke observed. 'She doesn't like to be thought of as grand and important.'

'Not her – the Barton itself. I expect the

original Napiers thought they were pretty grand and important. You know, I feel rather sorry for Hilary.'

'Do you? Why?' They turned and continued their climb towards the great mass of granite rocks on top of the hill. 'She seems to have her life pretty well organised now.'

'D'you really think so? I know that's what it looks like, but think about it, Luke? She lost her fiancé in the war and doesn't ever seem to have found anyone else; she had to leave her own war work and come home to look after her mother; then she wanted to go to London and make a life for herself, with a career, but she couldn't because her father had a heart attack and she had to come home and look after *him*. And no sooner did she start to make a success of running the estate, than he went and got a manager in so she nearly lost that, too. Even now, she has to share the responsibility with Travis and it isn't really hers any more.'

'I thought they got on pretty well,' Luke said.

'Oh, they do. They've had to learn to, though she didn't find it easy to start with. But the thing is, she never thought they needed a manager. She knew she could do it herself. It was just Colonel Napier, thinking she ought to be looking for a husband, who insisted on it.'

'I suppose he was right, in a way,' Luke said thoughtfully. 'She wasn't likely to find a husband if she spent all her time working on the estate.'

'And maybe she doesn't want one! Nobody seems to have thought of that. Maybe she knew she'd be happier without one.'

'Goodness me,' Luke said after a moment, 'that was spoken with feeling.'

Val turned and looked at him, startled. Then she stopped and flung her arms around his neck.

'Luke! I didn't mean it that way! I mean, *I* know a husband's the best thing in the world a woman can have – but then, I've got *you*. He's got to be the right one. And I don't think you can go out looking for one, as if you were searching for mushrooms. Husbands don't spring up in the grass overnight. Maybe Hilary doesn't want to be bothered any more. To tell you the truth, I don't think she was really all that much in love with Henry anyway, and she's never met anyone she could really fall in love with.'

'I'm beginning to feel sorry for her myself now,' Luke admitted as they walked on. 'When you look at her life, it seems to be a pretty good one – but if she's lonely...'

'Yes,' Val said thoughtfully, 'I think that's what it is. Deep down, she's lonely because she doesn't have what we have. And–' she stopped suddenly.

'And what?' he asked when it seemed she wasn't going to go on.

'And nothing! Come on – let's get to the top of the tor and have our lunch. I'm starving.'

They shortened their steps as they climbed higher, between gorse bushes that were spread with gold, and with the melodious singing of a skylark sounding high above their heads. The bird was almost impossible to spot against the clear blue sky and it was only when they reached the piled rocks and sank down, breathless, that they were finally able to focus on the minute speck.

'Isn't that wonderful,' Luke said. 'Hardly bigger than a sparrow, and hundreds of feet high, and yet we can still hear his song. I think the skylark must be my very favourite bird.'

'Yes,' Val said. 'Mine too. But listen to me now, Luke. I've got something to tell you...'

Chapter Fourteen

Alice returned to the farm to find Minnie downstairs and sitting in her accustomed chair by the range.

'What in the name of all that's wonderful do you think you're doing?' she demanded, standing with hands on hips even before she began to take off her coat. 'Who said you could come down here?'

'It's the first time anyone's told me I need permission to come into my own kitchen,' Minnie retorted smartly, reminding Alice that the farm had been her home first. 'And I didn't come by myself, so you don't need to look at me like that. I got young Joanna to give me a hand.'

Alice turned accusing eyes on Joanna, who shrugged helplessly.

'You know what she's like. And she does seem a lot better. Dr Latimer said she could start to get up for a while when she felt like it.'

'And I felt like it this morning,' Minnie declared, knowing perfectly well that Alice wouldn't have allowed it for at least another two days. 'It's all right, I'm not going to overdo it. I'll stop down

166

here for my dinner and then you can help me back up the stairs. And I can be a bit of use while I'm here – I've already done the spring greens and I could have made the pastry for the pie if Joanna had let me.'

'No, you couldn't. That would have meant standing up.' Joanna went to the door. 'I'll just go and see what Robin's up to. And the twins are outside, too, in their pram under the apple tree. Heather's been awake nearly all morning, watching the leaves uncurl. The potatoes are just coming to the boil, Mother.'

Alice finished taking off her coat and took it upstairs to hang in the wardrobe. She came down again in her second-best dress and wrapped a pinafore round her.

'I won't say it's not good to see you down here again, Mother,' she said, casting an eye over the dinner preparations. 'But us don't want you poorly again, so just be sensible.'

Minnie waved an impatient hand. 'I already told you I would be. Now, how did the service go? Is young Reverend Copley going to settle in all right over the river? I hope they're going to treat him right.'

'Well, I don't think they're actually barbarians, even if they do live in Little Burracombe,' Alice said, opening the oven door to look at the leg of pork roasting there. She took the pan out and set it on the table. 'I reckon 'tis time to put they potatoes round it now… It was very nice, Mother, and he sounded the bell twelve times, so he should be there for a bit.' She took the pan of potatoes from the hob and drained out the

167

boiling water, then shook them about to roughen the edges and sprinkled a spoonful of mustard powder over them before placing them around the meat. The edges that had been touched by mustard immediately turned golden. 'Us had a nice little do in the village hall afterwards too, with coffee and a few biscuits and sandwiches and such, and Felix asked everyone to a meeting on Friday night to talk about the Coronation.'

'In their hall?'

'Well, of course in their hall. He's their vicar now.'

'You mean he'm taking over all the Coronation celebrations for both villages?' Minnie's voice began to rise. 'I thought better of him!'

'No, I don't think that's what he means at all, and if you start getting yourself worked up, Mother, I'll call Ted in to help me get you back upstairs to bed. He just thought it would be a good idea to get everyone to work it out together, so we'm all in agreement, and the sooner the better.' Alice slid the sizzling pan of meat and potatoes back into the oven and closed the door. 'And I don't think he'd have chosen to say anything at all today if that Abel Prowse hadn't spoke up. He soon sorted *him* out, I can tell you.'

'Oh,' Minnie said, mollified. 'All right, then. I must say, I didn't really think he'd go over there and tell 'em all our best ideas.'

'It's not a competition, Mother,' Alice said firmly. 'It's a celebration, and it's one us wants to be able to look back on with a bit of pride and pleasure, and if young Felix can bring the two villages together to enjoy theirselves in a spirit of

168

common humanity, he'll have done a good job and made a good start as vicar.'

'So long as us can get back to normal afterwards,' Minnie stipulated, and Alice laughed.

'Back to feuding and fighting, you mean! Honestly, Mother, I'll swear you old folk take a pleasure in keeping the old arguments going. Wouldn't be the same if us was all in agreement all the time, would it! Now, what's Joanna done us for afters? She was talking about a rhubarb pie – there were some lovely young pink stems just about ready for picking, I noticed yesterday. I'll make some custard to go with it, and there's a dish of cream as well.'

The rest of the family began to appear in the kitchen, talking cheerfully about their morning. Robin had been collecting eggs and wanted to colour every one, as his own breakfast egg had been coloured with cochineal. It was taking Joanna all her powers of persuasion to convince him that the villagers who bought their eggs wouldn't necessarily want them to be bright red, even at Easter. Jackie came back from the village where she had been to visit Roy Pettifer's mother and Tom, who had been walking the fields with Ted's cousin Norman after finishing the milking, was talking about the progress of the winter wheat they were trying out in one of the more sheltered fields down by the river. Joanna reported that both twins were now fast asleep under the apple tree, with a net stretched over the pram to stop anything dropping on to them or the farm cats deciding it would be a good place to sleep.

Alice watched as they bustled about the kitchen,

talking, washing hands, chatting to Minnie and saying how good it was to have her back with them, and felt a glow of warmth at having her family around her. The only one missing was Val, but she had promised to come in later with Luke, after they'd had a good brisk walk on the moor. They'd stay to tea then, and Alice already had a simnel cake and a sponge in the larder, along with a trifle and some ham for a salad.

Now that Minnie was better, and the Easter weather was mild with promise of a good summer, life seemed suddenly to have taken on an altogether brighter and more optimistic turn. The winter's behind us now, she thought, and better times are surely ahead.

'Are you pleased?' Val asked, snuggling into Luke's arms. 'Really pleased, I mean?'

Luke laughed at her. 'Haven't I just said so? Can you really doubt it? Of course I'm pleased.'

'I just want to hear you say it,' she said. 'It helps me to realise it's true.'

'I'm pleased. I'd delighted, thrilled, over the moon.' He gave her a smacking kiss. 'Will that do? Do you believe it's true? We're having a baby, Val. A *baby*.'

She smiled at him. 'A baby.'

They were quiet for a moment, each thinking of the miracle that had come to them. For so long, they'd feared it would never happen again, that Val, who had lost their first baby at sea, would not be able to conceive. Even now, they knew there was a long way to go before they could be certain, could hold their child in their arms and know it was strong and healthy. But the first step had been taken; the journey had begun.

'When?' Luke asked at last.

'October. About the middle of the month, I think.'

'October? That's months away!'

She giggled. 'It usually does take months. Nine, to be exact. But we've only got to wait six from here.'

'It's still half a year.'

'And then the rest of our lives to love him. Or her. Oh Luke, we're going to be a real family. Isn't it wonderful?'

'Yes, it is.' He kissed her again, then looked anxious. 'But why did you wait till we got all the way up here to tell me? Should you be doing this anyway – going for long walks, climbing about on rocks? Aren't you supposed to put your feet up in the afternoons?'

'I will, I expect, later on. And I have been resting a bit more than usual just lately, when I get the chance. It's surprising how tired it makes you feel. But there's no reason why I can't go for walks – exercise is good for expectant mothers.'

'Mothers,' he said wonderingly. 'You're going to be a mother. And – oh, my lord – I'm going to be a *father!*'

'It seems quite likely,' she said gravely, and then burst into laughter. 'Honestly, Luke, you're be-having like that man in the film we saw the other week. People do have babies, you know, and it usually means they're going to be mothers and fathers. It sort of goes with the job.'

'All right, you can mock. But it's never happened to me before.' He met her eyes. 'Well – not knowingly. Oh, Val – I'm so sorry you had to go through all this on your own last time. And it must be reminding you of Johnny.'

'Yes,' she said quietly. 'It is, rather. But I've got to get over that. Johnny's in the past. I'll never forget him, but this is a new baby – a new life. And this time, everything will be all right.'

'I hope so.'

'It will be. Remember, I was on my own – I mean, I had friends, but I didn't have you, I didn't have a husband – and I was on that crowded ship coming home from Egypt, expecting to be bombed or torpedoed at any minute. It's no wonder I lost him. And probably – well, probably it's just as well. At least he was spared anything worse. He never even breathed, Luke. He never knew anything – no pain, no suffering, nothing.'

'And no joy either.'

'We can't think like that,' she said with sudden energy. 'We've got to look forward now, not back. This baby will know all the joy we can give him, and all the love.' She started to pack away the lunch things. 'Let's go back now. I want to tell the family – that's if you don't mind. I don't want to keep it a secret a minute longer than we have to.'

'Nor do I.' He helped her up and swung the haversack on to his back. 'I want to shout it from the rooftops! Oh.' He stopped. 'I've just had a thought.'

'What?'

'We'll need my studio for a nursery.'

'Yes,' she said. 'I know. It's been worrying me a bit, to be honest. I suppose we'll have to start

172

looking for somewhere else to live.'

Luke began to walk down the hill, his brow creased in thought. Then he stopped and turned to her, a grin breaking out over his face.

'Not necessarily. Not yet, anyway. Because there's somewhere not too far from here that would be ideal for me to use as a studio.'

'Is there? Where?'

'The charcoal-burner's cottage, of course! Come on – let's go and have a proper look at it. And then we'll go straight to the farm and tell the family.'

Sunday dinner was over, the dishes cleared away and the oven cleaned. Jackie had gone out for a walk with some of her old friends, Ted was asleep in his chair and Minnie had been persuaded to go back to bed for an hour or two. 'Otherwise you won't be fit to sit up for tea with our Val when her and Luke gets here,' Alice had warned her, and Minnie had departed with unaccustomed meekness.

'She's more tired than she lets on,' Alice said to Joanna. 'Us'll have to keep a sharp eye on her to make sure she don't overdo it. She could slip back as easy as winking.'

'We'll all take care of her,' Joanna said, giving the range a last wipe. 'I want my little ones to have their great-granny for as long as they can. I never even had a granny myself. Or a granddad really – the only one still alive when I was born died before I was a year old. I've always wished I could remember him.'

The twins had been fed and were back out in their pram, beneath the apple tree. Robin had also been put to bed for a nap, and the two women passed a quiet hour or so in the garden, Joanna tidying the flower-beds and Alice sowing a few rows of peas, before he woke up and was brought downstairs, bunching his fists into his eyes and grizzling a little, as he usually did after his afternoon sleep. He cheered up when Joanna produced a glass of lemonade and then demanded to be taken to find his father, who was in the stable looking over the two carthorses and their tack.

Left alone, Alice peeped at the twins, fast asleep now, and then sat on the old garden seat. After a while Ted came out to join her, bringing two cups of tea and some home-made biscuits on a tray. This was his Sunday tradition, begun when they were newly-weds and he'd remarked that Alice waited on him all week and the least he could do was bring her a cup of tea on a Sunday. Tom had kept it up too, taking Joanna tea in bed on Sundays and Robin now joined in by bringing her a biscuit, although he usually ate that himself.

'It ain't a bad life, when all's said and done,' Ted remarked as they sat there. 'Now that Mother's on the mend, us ain't got a lot to complain about.'

'We're luckier than a lot of folk,' Alice agreed. 'A good family round us, and more to come if I'm not mistaken. Our Val's got a look about her these days... And these three little ones Tom and Joanna have given us, they're a real blessing. The only one I worry about is our Jackie.'

'Ah – Jackie. I has to admit I dunno what goes on in that girl's head. I mean, when she's at home she seems happy enough, but you can see she's itching to get back to Plymouth. What she can see in a place that's nothing but shops, I just don't understand.'

'I think that's just what she do see,' Alice said, smiling. 'Shops! And streets with pavements, and people, and the pictures, and plenty going on.'

'There's plenty going on here. What with whist drives and country dancing and the drama club, and all the preparations for the beanfeast on Coronation Day, us hardly has time to go to bed. And what's all this about pavements? You only needs pavements when there's too much traffic for a chap to be able to walk without getting run down by a car or a bus. It'll be a sad day if us ever has to have pavements in Burracombe.'

'I know, love,' Alice said, laying her hand on his arm. 'I feel just the same. But our Jackie's different, and young people are different now, the whole world's different, and it don't seem as if there's much us can do about it. We must just hope she don't do anything silly. And Jennifer Tucker's a sensible body, she's looking after her all right.'

Ted grunted. They'd had this conversation before and always ended up sighing and hoping for the best. 'What I wants to know,' he said, 'is what sort of a chap is she going to take up with, working in a hotel. You don't know who stays in a place like that.'

'Oh, Ted! The Duke of Cornwall's the best hotel in Plymouth.'

'So it may be, but that don't mean you don't get no funny types staying there. They don't go into their family history when a man books in – it's the money they're interested in. As long as you can pay, you can stay. Here,' he added,

175

momentarily diverted, 'that's poetry!'

'I don't think it's enough to earn you a living,' Alice said drily. 'And don't think I don't worry about that too, Ted. But there's nothing we can do about it. We've brought Jackie up the best way we could and taught her right from wrong, and now it's up to her.'

'Yes, but it *shouldn't* be!' he exclaimed. 'She's not twenty-one for another two years and she ought to be under my eye, where I can see what she's doing and who she's meeting. That's what I don't like about it, Alice. She can get up to whatever she likes down there in Plymouth and we wouldn't know anything about it.'

Alice agreed, but she didn't want this lovely afternoon spoiled. Placatingly, she said, 'Well, she's done nothing silly yet so let's just make the most of our good fortune. It was you that started all this off by saying what a good life we got here.'

'Yes, it was,' he admitted. 'And we have. I'm sorry, love. I didn't mean to get on my high horse. I'll go in and fetch another cup of tea.'

Beyond the garden, Alice could see the rise of the fields towards the moor. This was the first Sunday since the clocks had gone on for summertime, and the sun was still high. The gorse was a golden coverlet flung over the slopes, and the Standing Stones were silhouetted against the blue sky. She could see two figures making their way down the hill and guessed it was Val and Luke, on their way back from their walk. She turned as Ted emerged with the tea.

'It's turning a bit cooler,' Alice said. 'I don't reckon I'll sit here much longer.'

'I'll have to start afternoon milking soon, anyway,' he said. 'Norman's coming up and bringing his boy, so it shouldn't take too long. Turning into a useful milker, that little tacker is, for all he's so small.'

'Well, Norman's not exactly a giant.' Alice shaded her eyes. 'That's our Val and Luke up there, see? Just going into the woods. They'll be here in about ten minutes. I'll just drink this and then go indoors and start getting tea ready. There's a nice piece of ham, and Joanna made a fruit cake in the week, it'll be just right now.'

'How about the little uns?' he asked, glancing towards the pram.

'I just looked at them. Wrapped up as warm as toast, they be, and snoring their little heads off. They'll be all right till Joanna comes back, she can bring them in then.' Alice got up and dusted down her pinafore. 'Well, it was good to sit there counting our blessings. Let's hope we've got a good week ahead of us. I'm looking forward to the Easter Monday picnic tomorrow.'

She went indoors and Ted strolled out of the garden and across the yard to the milking-parlour. Norman and his young son Colin were already bringing the cows in from the field. They all went inside together, and for a few minutes the farmyard was quiet.

From the kitchen window, Alice saw Val and Luke coming across the road and up the track. Minnie had come downstairs and was in her chair, sipping a fresh cup of tea. Joanna came in with Robin and began to wash his face and hands at the sink.

Alice watched Val pause and peep at her little nieces. Looking at her daughter's stance, Alice was more sure than ever that she had good news for them. There was something in the way she leaned across the pram, something in the softening of her expression...

And then, as Alice turned away to take a batch of fresh scones from the oven, she heard a cry of horror.

'*What*–?'

Joanna had dropped the flannel and was at the back door. Before she could touch it, it was thrust open almost into her face and Val stood there, her face ashen, her eyes huge. The women stared at her and Joanna pushed her aside and rushed out into the yard.

'Val – what is it? What's happened?'

'It's the baby...' Val gasped. 'Suzanne ... I just looked in at them and she – she – oh, *Mum*...' There was a long pause while Val fought for words and everyone stared at her, and then she said, in a whisper, 'I think she's died...'

Chapter Fifteen

Nobody could believe what Val had just said. Alice stared at her in stupefaction and Minnie half rose from her chair and then sank back, her face as white as Val's. For a second or two, it was as if time had frozen and nobody could move. Then Robin, abandoned at the sink with soap on

178

his face, started to cry and it was as if the sound had set them all in motion again.

'Val! What are you saying?' Alice, too, pushed past her and ran out to the garden where Joanna was bending over the pram. Val was close behind her as they reached it, and Joanna lifted a small, white-wrapped bundle from the pram, holding it close against her rocking body and stared at them with a face distorted with grief and rage.

'She won't wake up! My baby won't wake up!' She turned anguished eyes on Val. 'What did you do to her? *What did you do to my baby?*'

'I didn't do anything!' Val reached out, but Joanna turned swiftly away. 'Jo, let me see – there may be something we can do...'

'*No!* Don't touch her! I won't let you touch her!'

'Joanna, dear, let our Val have a look. She's a nurse, she knows what to do. She won't hurt her, she'd never hurt a hair of your babbies' heads...' Alice was aware that she was babbling, but the words seemed to well up like the tears that were already running down her cheeks. Like Val, she reached out her arms, but again Joanna twisted away. 'Let's look at her. You've got to let us look.'

'If there's anything we can do, it has to be done quickly,' Val urged. 'Please, Jo.'

There was a moment's silence, then Joanna turned back and, reluctantly, parted the shawls that almost covered the baby's face. The other two women came closer and looked down fearfully, and Alice drew in her breath.

The small cheeks, that had been like downy peaches, were grey, and there was a blue tinge about the tiny, pursed lips. As Joanna shifted her hold, Alice could see that there was no resilience in the small body; it was as limp as a rag doll. And when she touched the skin with a gentle, tentative finger, it was already cooling.

'I'm afraid she's gone, Jo,' Val said after a second or two.

'But *why?*' Joanna's anger had been displaced by anguish and bewilderment. *'Why?* She was all right a little while ago. I looked at her – I looked at them both. I didn't think they were cold or anything.'

At the word 'both' Alice turned quickly to the pram. 'What about Heather? Is she...?' She reached in and felt the second baby, who stirred and let out a small cry. They all gave a sigh of relief. 'No, she's all right. And she's not cold, Jo. I don't think either of them was cold.'

'Bring her in.' Joanna was already on her way indoors, followed by Robin, who was still crying and tugging at her skirt. 'Bring her indoors. And for God's sake, someone get the doctor.'

'Luke's already gone. I sent him off the minute I realised.'

'Why not phone?' Joanna demanded savagely. 'Why doesn't anybody ever think to use the telephone in this house?'

'Because we noticed him and Mrs Latimer in their garden as we were coming down the hill. We didn't think they'd hear the bell.' The sound of a car turning into the yard interrupted her, and they turned to see Dr Latimer and Luke leap out and run towards the back door. Ted appeared at the door to the milking-parlour, curious to see who was visiting the farm in a car, and as he recognised the doctor he too came running across the yard.

'What's happened? Is it Mother?'

'Let me see her,' Charles Latimer commanded crisply as he set his bag on the kitchen table. Joanna was standing by the range, still holding the small bundle close to her breast, her head protectively bent. The doctor reached out and gently took the baby away, laying her on the table which Alice had hastily cleared of her tray of scones, and parting the clothes. He laid his stethoscope on the tiny chest and listened, and with one finger he felt behind the baby's ear. At last, conscious of the ring of anxious faces, he looked up, his face grave.

'She's gone, I'm afraid,' he said, echoing Val's words. 'There's nothing we can do.'

Joanna let out a scream that startled them all and set both Robin and Heather crying as well. Alice turned swiftly and Val said, 'I'll take him out for a minute or two,' and steered Robin by his shoulders towards the back door.

'Fetch Tom,' Joanna sobbed. 'I want Tom.'

'I will. Come on, Robin, let's go and find Daddy and then you can help Uncle Norman and Colin milk the cows.'

'I'll come too,' Luke said, and followed her into the yard. 'Val, what on earth d'you think happened?'

'I don't know. I've heard of it – babies dying in their cots when they seemed perfectly all right – but I don't think anyone knows what causes it.' She glanced down at Robin, hoping he had not heard her murmured words. 'Look, we've got to

181

get Tom out of there – you take Robin, will you, and I'll help with the milking.'

She went into the big shed and found Tom on his stool, his head pressed against a warm, brown flank. 'Tom – stop a minute. They need you indoors.'

He looked up at her, surprised. 'But I'm in the middle of milking. What on earth's happened?' He saw her face and his tone sharpened. 'Val?'

'It's one of the babies,' Val said quietly, knowing that there was no easy way to break this news. 'I'm afraid it's not good. Tom, I'm most dreadfully sorry, but little Suzanne has died.'

'*What?*' He leaped up, kicking his stool to one side, and the cow let out a surprised moo. 'She *can't* have done.'

'I'm afraid she has.' Val laid her hand on his arm. 'Oh Tom, I'm so sorry.'

He stared at her, unable for a moment to take in what she had said, then he shook his head slowly, his face creased. 'But they were doing so well...'

'I know. Nobody can understand it. Tom, go indoors. Jo needs you.'

'But...' He looked helplessly round the barn. Norman, was on his feet too now, while Colin stared from his stool with all the fearful embarrassment of a young boy faced with a situation he's not ready to deal with. 'There's all these cows...'

'I'll help Norman. You go in.' She pushed him gently towards the door. 'Please, Tom.'

He turned and looked at her again. 'You say she's dead? Our little Suzanne? You did say *dead?*'

'Yes,' Val said sorrowfully, and felt the tears brim up and run down her face. 'Yes, I did.'

182

'Dead,' he said, almost to himself, as if tasting the word. 'Our baby's *dead*.' And then he seemed at last to understand what he had been told and his own distress broke through. 'Oh, my *God*...'

He blundered past the cows and out of the door, and slammed it behind him, and they heard his faint cry as he ran across the yard. '*Jo*...'

Val turned back and met Norman's eyes. He came over and put his arm awkwardly around her shoulders and she collapsed against him, sobbing as the shock of her discovery and the need to put Joanna's feelings before hers gave way to her own welling feelings. He held her, patting her back and murmuring the soothing 'there, there' sounds that everyone seems to employ at such times, that Val herself had employed often enough, and after a while she drew in a deep breath and lifted her face away from his shoulder.

'Thanks,' she said shakily. 'I'll be all right now. Let's get on with the milking.'

The door opened and Ted came in. 'I'll do that,' he said gruffly. 'Reckon they needs you indoors more than me just now. Me and Norm and young Colin'll get on here – you go back and give the doctor and our Joanna a hand. God knows, that poor girl's going to need all the comfort she can get after this do.'

Val nodded and turned away. She let herself out of the milking parlour and stood for a moment looking across the farmyard at the house, looking so deceptively serene, and beyond at the hills and moors where she and Luke had spent such a happy day. The scene was as beautiful and as peaceful as it had ever been, as it had been only

183

half an hour before, and yet it now seemed tainted, touched with anguish and despair.

How could the whole world turn upside down in such a short space of time? She remembered the night the babies had been born, earlier than expected, and how shocked and delighted everyone had been to discover that there was not one, but two. And now there was, heartbreakingly, just one again. That second baby, unanticipated but welcomed with so much love, had gone as swiftly and unexpectedly as she had arrived, and the grief she would leave behind her had only just begun to be felt.

Life at Tozer's farm had indeed been turned upside down.

The happy family tea was forgotten in the turmoil. Tea itself was made and drunk or left to get cold, sandwiches and scones and slices of cake were eaten without being noticed, or left to go stale on plates scattered all over the kitchen. Alice was finding them for days afterwards. And nobody seemed to know what to do. If it had not been for Charles Latimer's presence, Alice dreaded to think what might have happened.

'What's going on?' Tom had burst in, his face white, and gone straight to his wife. 'Jo, what's all this our Val's saying about Suzanne? It can't be true!'

'I know,' she wailed, putting up one arm to cling to him while with the other she clutched the dead baby to her breast. 'I know it can't! But the doctor says it is, and Val, she found her, and Mum, and— Oh Tom, Tom, I can't bear it! I can't bear it!'

184

He dropped to his knees beside her. 'Let me see.'

Charles Latimer was behind him, his hand on the young man's shoulder. 'I'm afraid it is true, Tom,' he said gently. 'I'm most terribly sorry.'

'But why? What happened, for God's sake? She was all right when I went over to start the milking – I looked at her then, I looked at them both, they were both all right. How could...?' He looked down at the waxy face and a great, shuddering sob tore through his body. 'What in God's name *happened?*'

'We don't know. We may never know. But we'll try to find out.' The doctor looked uncomfortably around the ring of shocked faces. 'Val, will you telephone for the nurse? And I'll have to go home and make some calls myself. I'll come back as soon as the arrangements have been made.'

'What arrangements? And what good's the nurse going to be now? You've already said there's nothing to be done.' Tom's voice was sharp, almost belligerent and he half rose from his crouching position.

'Not for this little soul, no,' the doctor said kindly. 'But I'm afraid there are a number of things we do have to do. I have to inform the coroner, for a start–'

'The *coroner?*'

'It's a sudden death,' he explained. 'And since we don't know why little Suzanne died, there may have to be a post-mortem and an inquest.'

'An *inquest?*' Joanna stared at him. 'You mean they might think I ... they might think we ... they might think...' Her voice broke into sobs and

185

Tom came angrily to his feet and there was an instant babble of voices.

'Nobody here hurt our baby, nobody'd even think of it.'

'Shame on you, Doctor, for even thinking for one moment—'

'I'd have thought you knowed us better than that—'

Charles Latimer raised his hands in distress. 'No, no, of course I don't mean that. It's just that it's the law, and we have to do it. I have no choice.'

There was a silence while they took this in. Then Alice said, 'But why d'you want Val to phone for the nurse? I can't see what she can do now. And anyway, our Val's a nurse. If there's anything to be done, she can do it.'

'Yes, but the body has to be laid out,' he explained. 'It has to be prepared in case a post-mortem is ordered. Which I very much suspect it will be.'

Joanna cried out again and buried her face against the soft shawls still wrapping her baby's body. 'A post-mortem! That means cutting her up! My baby – oh, my poor little baby! I won't let them do it, I won't.'

'Does it have to be right away?' Alice asked the doctor. 'Can't the poor girl be left with her little one for a while? It's all too quick – too sudden. Us haven't had any chance to take it in.'

He hesitated, then nodded. 'I don't see why not. All those other things will take time anyway. There really isn't any need to rush.' He turned back to Tom and Joanna. 'Take your baby upstairs. Take both of them, and spend some

186

time together before we have to do what must be done. I'm so terribly sorry,' he added, turning back to Alice and the others. 'So very, very sorry.'

'It's such a shock,' she said, her eyes lost and bewildered. 'After all we been through with them, and they were doing so well – and then this. And what about little Heather? Is she going to be all right? Won't you have a look at her, doctor, to make sure?'

'Yes, of course I will. And you too,' he said, looking at Minnie. 'This has been a shock for you and you'll very probably feel a setback for a day or two. Why don't you go back to bed and have a sleep now?'

'Yes,' the old lady said, her voice feebler than anyone had ever heard it. 'Yes, I think I will. I do feel a bit leery. Val, if you'll give me a hand up the stairs...'

Val helped her from her chair and supported her over to the staircase. As they disappeared up the stairs, Ted said uncomfortably, 'I might as well go out again and help Norm finish the milking. Sooner it's done with, the better.' He went out and Alice looked again at the doctor.

'I don't understand any of this. How can a little baby die, just like that? I'd looked at them not quarter of an hour before, and there was no sign of anything wrong.'

He heaved a sigh. 'I don't know, Alice. I just don't know. All I know is that it does happen sometimes, to the strongest and healthiest of babies, and nobody's been able to find out why. It's nature's cruellest trick.'

'On Easter Day, too,' Alice said bitterly. 'Of all

the days in the year, when us is all celebrating new life. I don't reckon it could come much more cruel than that.'

The door opened and Jackie stood there, her eyes like dark holes in the paper-white of her face.

'I just met Luke with Robin. He says something terrible's happened. He says Suzanne is dead.' She came into the kitchen, her gaze going from one to the other, and shook her mother's arm. 'Tell me it's not true, Mum. Please tell me it's not true.'

Chapter Sixteen

Nobody wanted to believe it was true. Charles Latimer was as distressed as any of them. He had delivered Suzanne and her sister Heather in this very house, not three months ago, and seen the babies through those first anxious weeks while Minnie and Joanna had fed them with eye-droppers and tiny teats with the milk Joanna had drawn from her own breasts, when their mouths had been too small and their muscles too weak to suckle. The entire village had been on tenterhooks, the gloomier souls predicting that neither would survive while stouter folk kept a sturdy faith that both would live. And it had seemed that their confidence had been justified – until now.

'She seemed to be getting on so well,' Alice kept saying in a bewildered voice. 'They both did. But maybe us was all wrong, and they were just too early, poor little flowers.'

'I don't think it was anything to do with their being premature,' Charles said. 'I'd have said they were as fit as any three-month-old baby. They were smaller, it's true, but they were catching up fast and their hearts seemed strong. It's a mystery why it happens, Alice, and there's nothing more I can say.'

'So what's the use of a post-mortem, then?' she burst out. 'Why cut the poor little dear up? I can't bear to think of it, and as for Joanna – her's going through torment, poor maid.'

'I know. I don't like it either. But they'll be as gentle as possible.' The doctor felt a twinge of guilt as he spoke; he knew all too well what happened during a post-mortem. 'And there'll be nothing to see afterwards.'

'It don't bear thinking of,' Alice repeated. 'Poor little soul. Taken from us so soon – it don't seem fair.'

The door opened and Basil Harvey came in, his round face grave. 'Luke came over to tell me the news. He had Jackie and Robin with him. Alice, I'm *so* sorry.'

Alice burst into tears again. It seemed that every new face that appeared was a trigger for more tears. She held out her hand, and Basil took it and held it between both of his. 'Where's Joanna?'

'Upstairs with Tom and the little uns, both of 'em. She don't seem able to let them go. Won't let poor little Suzanne out of her arms.'

'It's natural. It will take her a while to believe it.' He looked at Charles. 'What caused it, do you know?'

The doctor shook his head. 'It's one of those mysteries, I'm afraid. They both seemed perfectly healthy a few minutes earlier.'

'Quarter of an hour, it was,' Alice said dully. 'I looked at them meself and they were as peaceful as could be. Oh, it's not fair, it's just *not fair!*'

Basil stroked her hand. 'Grace asked me to tell you that Jackie and Robin are welcome to stay with us tonight. This is no place for that little boy just now.'

'Jackie!' Alice looked up. 'She's meant to be going back to Plymouth – on early turn to-morrow, she told me.'

He shook his head. 'She's not going back. She's going down to Jacob's to tell Jennifer she won't be catching the bus with her, and she was tele-phoning to the hotel as I left. She'll stay to look after Robin, and I'm to take night things back for them both.'

'It's good of you, Vicar, but it's too much trouble. And they ought to be with their family.'

'Not tonight,' he said firmly, and the doctor nodded his head in agreement.

'There'll be a lot of coming and going, and with everyone so upset it will be bad for the little boy. He'll have Jackie with him. And Joanna needs all her strength.' He picked up his bag. 'I'll go up and see them now and I'll give Joanna something to help her sleep.'

'May I come with you?' Basil asked, and the two men went up the stairs.

'Sleep!' Alice said bitterly. 'There'll be no sleep for anyone in this house tonight.'

Luke came in. 'I just looked in at the milking-

parlour. They've almost finished. Is there anything I can do?'

'You could make a fresh pot of tea. And there's
all that ham we were going to have for tea, with a
bit of salad. Nobody's had anything to eat yet,
and I can't say I feel like it meself, but 'tis no
good starving ourselves.'

'I'll make sandwiches,' Luke said, and began to
cut bread. The kettle came to the boil and he
spooned tea into the big brown teapot and poured
in water. Alice watched him, feeling that this was
something she ought to be doing herself, yet
somehow unable to move. It was as if her limbs
were too heavy to lift. Her thoughts were upstairs
with her son and daughter-in-law and her grandchildren, and physical activity seemed impossible.

'Oh, Luke,' she said in a broken voice, 'why did
this have to happen?'

'I don't know, Mother. It's the worst thing in
the world when babies die.' He thought of Val,
who had lost her own baby – and his, although he
hadn't known it – on the voyage back from
Egypt. Johnny hadn't even been ready to be
born, had never lain in his mother's arms and
gazed into her face and suckled at her breast, yet
Luke knew that the pain had been just as acute.
What was Val feeling now, he wondered, seeing
the anguish that Joanna was suffering, knowing it
for herself, yet forced to hide her knowledge. She
must be going through it all again, he thought,
and this is the worst possible time for her.

Charles and Basil came downstairs at last, both
looking very grave, and drank a cup of tea each
before setting out into the darkness. Night seemed

to have fallen almost without being noticed. Ted had come in, saying that the cows were all done and Norman and his boy had gone home, and he'd fed the hens and geese and shut them up for the night.

'The birds!' Alice exclaimed. 'I never gave them a thought. This business has left us all at sixes and sevens, Ted. I don't know whether I'm on my head or my heels.'

'It's not surprising, love. It's a bad do.' He poured himself a cup of tea and piled a few sandwiches on to a plate. 'It's set us all back on our heels. I dunno how young Joanna's ever going to get over it.'

'The others will help her, won't they?' Luke asked. He was sitting in a corner, unable to settle. Since marrying Val, he had grown to know the ways of the farm and helped out from time to time, but it wasn't in his blood as it was in the Tozers' and he didn't feel confident to take on jobs without asking. 'I could have done the birds,' he added apologetically. 'I didn't think about it. You must tell me if there's anything I can do.'

'It's all right,' Ted said. 'Us'll do that soon enough. It's just that we've been taken by surprise.' He turned to his wife. 'What's going to happen next, love?'

'Doctor says we can keep the dear little soul here for tonight, but the nurse will come first thing in the morning. And he's going to let the coroner know. It's Mr Penrose, in Tavistock. Vicar's going to arrange for her to be taken away decent – just because she's a tiny babby don't mean she won't be treated right. And he said he'd get Ernie Littlejohn to come over later on tomorrow and have a word.'

Ted nodded. 'Ernie's a good chap. I've knowed he all my life,' he told Luke. 'Went to school together, us did. His dad was undertaker to the whole village and Ernie took over from him. He'll do a good job, and he knows how to talk to people.'

'I don't suppose he talks to many people going through what Tom and Joanna are going through,' Alice said, her eyes welling again.

'I dunno, love. There's been plenty of people lost little uns. Look at old Mortimer Bray, over at Stalleybrook, his little tacker went under a horse's hooves, and then there was that little feller from out Horndon who got drowned at the Clam a few years back. And...'

'Yes, so there might have been but I don't want to hear about them now,' Alice said sharply, and Ted subsided. ''Tis enough to be going on with, knowing we've lost our little Suzanne. Oh, why do such things have to happen?' she broke out again. 'There weren't nothing *wrong* with her. Why?'

But nobody could answer her. And as they heard fresh sobs break out in the room upstairs, they knew that the same question was being asked there, and that it would be asked again and again in the coming days, weeks and months. And still there would be no answer.

The news was a shock to the entire village. Jacob Prout was one of the first to hear, when Jackie went to his cottage to tell Jennifer she wouldn't be going back to Plymouth with her that evening.

193

Jacob wasn't one to gossip, but he was seriously upset and went round to Dottie Friend to ask if she'd heard about it.

'Never!' Dottie exclaimed in amazement. 'One of they twins, found dead in her pram? Jacob, are you sure you've got it right?'

'Jackie Tozer told me herself. She's stopping up at the vicarage with young Robin – they thought he'd be better off out of the way. Jackie's in a rare state about it. Says the vicar's up at the farm, and the doctor too, and the whole family's in turmoil. I wondered if you knew anything more.'

'I didn't even know that much.' Dottie went back into her living room and sat down heavily, and Jacob followed her. 'Sit down, Jacob, do, I can't abide people looming over me... One of they little twins! I can't believe it.'

'Nor could I. They seemed to be doing all right, from all accounts. Jackie says the doctor didn't think there was a thing wrong with either of 'em.'

Dottie stared at him. 'Jacob – what about t'other one? Is she all right? Which one was it anyway?'

'Suzanne – she was the youngest one, wasn't she? Bit smaller than her sister, if I remember right. As for t'other, it seems she's all right, as far as anyone can tell. But Jackie said her mother looked in at them only a quarter of an hour or so before, and they was both all right then, so who can tell? Anything could happen.'

'That poor young woman,' Dottie said, beginning to cry. 'Oh Jacob, that poor, poor young woman. Losing her baby like that. And she'll be frightened to let the other little soul out of her sight. Oh, 'tis terrible.'

194

'I know,' Jacob said, and turned as Stella and Felix came through the door, surprised by the scene that met their eyes. 'Have you heard the news, maid?'

'No – what's happened?' Stella listened in dismay as Jacob told her, and turned to Felix, whose face was equally shocked. 'But that's awful! Those twins were so lovely, and doing so well, too. I thought they were going to be all right now.'

'Everyone thought that,' Dottie said. 'Mind you, the first few months can be difficult, but there didn't seem to be nothing the matter with them. They were feeding well, putting on weight, and as rosy as little apples. Whatever can have happened?'

Stella sat down. 'What a terrible end to the day,' she said sadly. 'I felt so happy, coming back from Little Burracombe. Felix and I walked across the Clam and up the footpath, and there's a beautiful full moon, and it all seemed perfect. And then this. It's just terrible.'

'Perhaps I ought to go and see the Tozers,' Felix said, but Jacob shook his head. 'Vicar's up there now. He'll look after 'em. You'd best get back to your own parish – no offence, but that's where your place be now.'

'I think he can have a cup of cocoa before he sets off, all the same,' Dottie said, getting up. 'Little Burracombe vicar he might be, but he'm still a friend and he'm still our Stella's fiancé and welcome here any time.'

'I didn't mean...' Jacob began, but Felix raised a hand, smiling.

'I know you didn't, Jacob, and you were quite

195

right. It's not my place to go to the Tozers now, though I certainly shall in the next day or so. As Dottie says, I feel that most of Burracombe are my friends now. But Mr Harvey will do all that's needed tonight.' He shook his head. 'It's hard to understand, I know – but if you'd like me to say a short prayer for the baby and her family...?'

'I'd like that,' Dottie said, and Jacob murmured his agreement. They bent their heads and Felix murmured a few words about the passing of a little soul and the love and support needed by the family left behind. Then Dottie went to make the cocoa and the other three sat quietly together, looking into the fireplace and trying to come to terms with an event that was one of the saddest any of them could remember.

After a while, Felix got up and left to go back to his vicarage for the first time. He and Stella stood at the gate, reluctant to part.

'I feel even more now that I want to be with you all the time,' she said. 'First Sammy, and now little Suzanne... We just don't know what's going to happen to us, do we? I feel we must make the most of every day we have.'

'I know,' he said. 'And if I had my way, we'd be married tomorrow. But you were right – we can't make it any sooner than Christmas. We must just hope and pray that nothing happens to part us before then.'

'Oh, Felix!' she cried in sudden terror. 'Don't even say such things! Don't! Maddy and I have lost so much in our lives – I can't bear to think I might lose you as well.'

'You won't,' he said, bending his head to kiss

her. 'You won't lose me. We're going to live for fifty or sixty years together, Stella, and nothing is ever going to come between us.'

But as he turned and walked away through the darkened village, with only the moon to guide his steps across the narrow footbridge of the Clam, he felt that his confidence, which had never wavered before, was badly shaken. A tiny baby, taken as she lay sleeping in her pram, leaving such terrible grief and anguish behind her. Where was the purpose in that? And how could anyone make plans when life turned out to be so fragile, so vulnerable, so easily snatched away?

Chapter Seventeen

Next morning, because it was Easter Monday, no shops were open, but the news went quickly from door to door and soon there was a cluster of people gathered on the village green under the ancient oak tree, their faces shocked and their voices lowered. Almost all the women were in tears, and the men were clearing their throats.

'Poor little scrap,' Jessie Friend said, wiping her eyes. 'It don't seem fair. And that poor young woman, her must be heartbroken.'

'Her's still got the other one,' George Sweet pointed out. 'And young Robin.'

'But her ain't got little Suzanne, have her!' Jessie flashed. 'Wouldn't matter if her had twenty other children, her'd still miss the one she've lost.

And a mother never gets over losing a child, never. 'Tis the worst thing that can happen.'

'I'm amazed you know so much about it, since you never had no children of your own,' George said, nettled, and Jessie flushed crimson and turned her back.

'Leave it, George,' Alf Coker said in a low voice. 'Jessie's right, and you don't have to have had your own to know it must feel like the end of the world to lose one. You'll upset people, going on like that, and this ain't the time for it.'

George shrugged and said no more. He drifted to the edge of the group.

'I tell you what,' Mabel Purdy, the school cleaner said in a gloomy tone, 'they'll have to watch that other twin like hawks. You know what they say – if one goes, it's sure as God made little green apples the other will as well. Can't live without each other, see.'

'Oh, here she goes again,' Mrs Dawe, the school cook, groaned. 'Us went through all this when they was born. I said then, you only got to look at old Abraham Bellamy, from over Lovaton. Nearly seventy-five he is, and his twin died when he was only four, so my old mum used to tell me. If Abe's going to die of a broken heart, he's taking his time about it.'

'That's right,' Edie Pettifer joined in. 'Lot of nonsense. And it don't help no one to drag up all these old wives' tales. I hope nobody'll go repeating it to young Joanna.'

'Well, I've heard of it happening plenty of times,' Mrs Purdy said obstinately.

'Seems to me,' Alf Coker declared, 'that us'd be

better thinking what us can do to help out up at the farm than standing here chewing the rag over it. Old Minnie Tozer ain't out of the woods yet, and now they got this new trouble they'm bound to be all at sixes and sevens up there, and half the work not getting done.'

'Handy about the place was she, then, the babby?' George Sweet enquired, and they all turned on him.

'If that's meant to be a joke, it's not funny!'

'You ought to be ashamed of yourself, George Sweet, and if you can't think of anything better to do than make stupid remarks you might as well go home. It stands to reason there's a lot to be done, and that poor young woman's going to need her man beside her for a few days. Her must be almost out of her mind with the sorrow of it.'

George scowled but said no more, and they were pleased to see that he did look somewhat discomfited. They turned their backs on him and went on with the conversation.

'I've just thought,' Bert Foster said. 'There'll have to be a funeral. Look, there's Jacob Prout – I wonder if he knows anything.'

Jacob approached the group and confirmed that he had heard the news, but shook his head when asked about the funeral. 'I ain't been asked about that yet, but I daresay I'll be digging the grave for the poor little mite. I tell you what, though, there's going to have to be an inquest. Sudden death, see. It don't mean there's anything suspicious about it,' he added quickly, seeing Mabel Purdy's mouth open. 'They always has to look into a sudden death because – well, just in case, I suppose,' he finished rather un-certainly. 'Anyway, I suppose it'll hold things up a bit for the funeral.'

'Well, I still think someone ought to go up and offer a bit of a hand,' Alf Coker said. 'The forge is closed today so I'm willing.'

'I'll come,' Bert said, and George Sweet nodded. 'So will I. And I'm sorry about what I said – didn't mean no offence.'

'I've got a fruit cake us didn't start yesterday,' Mrs Dawe said. 'Not that Alice Tozer's ever short of a bit of cake in the tin, but that's a big family and I daresay they gets through quite a bit.'

Edie Pettifer nodded. 'It's always handy to have some extra food around at a time like this. I expect they'll be getting Joanna's mother and father down too. Bert, if you'll open up your big fridge and get me out some beef, I'll make them a casserole. I've got enough points in my book.'

'They can have my ration too,' Jessie promised, and two or three other women offered theirs as well. The gathering broke up then, with several of the men making their way up to the farm and most of the women going home to review their larders and bake some contribution for the Tozer family. As Mrs Dawe remarked, it wasn't so much that you thought they'd actually need it, as to show that folk were thinking of them and ready to give a hand, and there were bound to be visitors in and out.

Charles Latimer's car was standing in the farmyard when they arrived but Ted was still in the milking parlour, finishing the morning milking. He opened the door and looked at his friends, unable to think of anything to say.

'We heard the news, Ted,' Alf Coker said. 'Us just wanted to offer our condolences, and ask if there be anything us can do.'

'Well – I dunno...' He scratched his head. 'I'm not sure I'm thinking all that straight this morning, to be honest.'

'That ain't surprising. But you just tell us what needs to be done and us'll get on with it. We'm all on holiday today, and there's not much else doing.' In fact, a lot of them had planned picnics and outings with their own families, but they could be set aside for an hour or two. 'How about a couple of us washing down the milking parlour, for a start?'

'Well, me and Norm–'

'You let me and George do it,' Alf commanded, 'and then you and Norman can get on with the jobs we can't do. We'm here to help out, so don't pass up the chance of a bit of free labour!'

Ted grinned faintly. 'All right. And thanks.' He pointed out the brooms and buckets and the two men went inside. Then he gave the others a few tasks to do and went into the farmhouse, where Alice and Val were talking to the doctor.

'Oh Ted, there you are. Doctor's come to tell us about what's going to happen. We were just going to fetch Tom and Joanna down.'

'I'll go now,' Val said, starting up the stairs.

'How is she this morning?' Ted asked. He'd gone out early, before anyone else was up, Tom having been told to stay with his wife and not to worry about the farm work. 'Did her get any sleep?'

'Not much, I don't think.' Alice looked at the

doctor. 'Tom came down to get a bit of breakfast together an hour or so ago and he said she wouldn't take those pills you left, said she was frightened to go to sleep in case little Heather – well, in case she needed her mother in the night. And she's fretting about Robin too, and what he's making of it all, being sent off to stop at the vicarage.'

'She don't have to worry about him,' Ted said. 'He's with our Jackie and I daresay he thinks it's a bit of a holiday. Mrs Harvey'll be spoiling him to dea–' He stopped abruptly and cleared his throat. 'Is there any tea in the pot, love?'

'Oh – yes.' Hastily, she got up and poured cups for all of them. 'I've only just made it. Here come the others now.'

Val, Tom and Joanna came down the stairs and into the kitchen. Joanna was looking pale, her eyes red and swollen, and she was carrying baby Heather as if she was as fragile as spun glass. She sat down in Minnie's chair, and Tom pulled up a stool to sit beside her. Val passed the tea around and then sat down herself on one of the chairs around the table.

Everyone looked at each other and then away again. Dr Latimer cleared his throat.

'I know you're all wondering what's going to happen, and I'm very sorry that circumstances force us to do certain things you'd rather we didn't. But it can't be helped, I'm afraid.' He glanced down for a moment before continuing. 'I've talked to Mr Penrose, the coroner, and he tells me that there will have to be an inquiry into little Suzanne's death. It's not that anyone

202

believes there was anything suspicious about it, but the law decrees that this has to be done, because in some cases – very few, I'm glad to say – there *are* suspicious circumstances, and nobody wants such an event to go unnoticed. It won't be anything too painful – not more painful than it has to be, anyway – and its main purpose is to find out just why Suzanne died. I'll be asked as many questions as anyone else, because I'm her doctor and the fault could be mine.'

'Well, that can't be true for a start,' Alice broke in. 'Nobody could want for a better doctor than you.'

Charles smiled. 'It's good of you to say so, but Mr Penrose doesn't know that, so he has to ask the questions.'

'Mr Roger Penrose, you mean?' Ted asked. 'Him that lives in that big house up on Kilworthy Hill? Surely to goodness he knows you.'

'Yes, he does, but in the eyes of the law he can't be sure. He has to ask. And I'm afraid there does have to be a post-mortem examination.' He gave Tom and Joanna an apologetic look. 'I know this is something you don't want to think about, and to be honest it's best if you *don't* think about it. Just let me take her away, in her little crib, as if she were just going to the undertaker and–'

'Just going to the undertaker?' Joanna cried. 'You talk as if she were going to a party!'

He bit his lip. 'I'm sorry. There's really no easy way to say these things.' He paused while Tom rubbed his wife's shoulder and Joanna regained her control. 'And you will also have to think about the funeral.'

'Well, when can us have that, if there's got to be a post-mortem and all these questions?' Alice asked. 'We all know how long it takes to get things done these days.'

'It won't take longer than anyone can help. I called in at the vicarage on my way here–'

'Did you see my Robin? How is he?' Joanna broke in again, and the doctor smiled, relieved to be able to impart better news.

'He's having the time of his life. He was having his breakfast when I saw him – a boiled egg with toast soldiers – and Basil Harvey was talking about getting out his old railway set and laying it out on the drawing-room floor. I really don't think you need worry about Robin.'

'He'll have to come home soon,' Joanna said fretfully, but Alice leaned across and laid a hand on her knee.

'Let him bide there a bit longer, if Mrs Harvey don't mind. I'll call over later and see how things are, and find out when Jackie's going back to Plymouth.'

'Not yet, I hope,' Ted said. 'Her place is here with her family when there's trouble.'

'And she knows that well enough, Ted, or she wouldn't have stayed. But she can't stay for ever – she's got a job to go to.'

'And you know what I thinks about that.'

'Ted,' Alice said firmly, 'this isn't the time. Jackie's a good girl and she's helping out now, and that's all that needs to be said. Now, Doctor, I think you were going to tell us what Mr Harvey had to say.'

'Indeed.' He gave Alice an understanding smile.

204

Emotions were bound to be raw at a time like this, and tempers liable to flare over things that were quite irrelevant. It was often a safety valve, but could lead dangerously into other waters. 'He says that he'll be here himself sometime this morning, but he wants you to know that you can have the funeral at any time you choose and everything will be done exactly as you wish. Mr Littlejohn will help you to go through it all. You just have to let him know when you're ready.'

'I don't think I'll ever be ready,' Joanna said in a wobbly voice, and the doctor looked at her gravely.

'I really think you should take the sedative I gave you, Joanna. You desperately need your rest, and there are plenty of people here to look after Heather. Why not go back to bed now and have a good long sleep?'

'It's nearly time for her ten o'clock feed. And she'll need feeding again at two.'

'Draw some milk off for her now, and let your mother-in-law or Tom give her the two o'clock feed. If you don't rest, you'll lose your milk anyway.'

'Oh, I've got plenty of milk, Doctor,' she said bitterly. 'I've been feeding two, remember?'

'Of course. But it wouldn't hurt for her to have a bottle-feed now and then,' he said. He looked at the others. 'Does anyone have any questions?' They shook their heads and he got up. 'I'll be off then. And remember what I said about getting some rest, Joanna. It really is important for this little one.' He bent over the sleeping baby. 'I'd like to have another look at her too – just to check that she's still all right.'

'Why?' Joanna was instantly alarmed. 'You don't think it was catching, do you, whatever Suzanne had? I know what people say about twins.'

'So do I, and it's nonsense. No, I don't suppose for a moment that whatever happened to Suzanne is going to happen to Heather, but I'd be neglecting my duty if I didn't make sure she's well.' He examined her, listening to her heart and feeling her body with gentle hands. 'She's perfectly sound. I really don't think you have anything to worry about.'

'We didn't think we had anything to worry about before,' Joanna said drearily.

'I'll look in again soon. And the nurse will be along shortly to do whatever is necessary for Suzanne. Would you like me to take her to the hospital, or would you prefer to do that yourselves?'

'I'll take her,' Tom said gruffly. 'Seems to me 'tis the last thing we can do for her.'

'Very well. And while I'm here, perhaps I should take another look at old Mrs Tozer. This must have been a terrible shock for her.'

'It was. We managed to get her to stop in bed this morning but I don't doubt her'll want to be up and about soon.' Alice led him to the staircase. 'You know which room it is, Doctor.'

He came down soon enough, saying that Minnie was pretty well her old self and could get up after lunch but must not be allowed to do more than sit in her chair. 'She can direct operations from there, I'm sure,' he said with a little smile, and went out into the yard.

'He's a good man,' Alice said. 'We're lucky to

have a good doctor in this village, and a good vicar as well. I don't reckon we got anything to fear from this inquest, Joanna. Whatever took our dear little Suzanne away from us, 'twas nobody's fault.'

'It was,' the younger woman said dully. 'It was mine. I should have looked after them better. I shouldn't have left them in their pram all afternoon. I should have been *there*.'

Chapter Eighteen

For the rest of that week, the village was unusually quiet. The bells didn't sound for their usual practice, when people greeted each other in the street or on the green their voices were subdued, and even the children didn't fill the air with their shouts and laughter as they normally did during the holidays. Some of the mothers got together and took groups of them off for picnics, up to the Standing Stones or by the reservoir. Henry Bennetts' mother came up to the farm and invited Robin to go along, but Alice shook her head.

'His mother wants him to stop at home. You can understand it – I know he'd be safe with you, and it'd be good for him to get away, but she don't want him out of her sight just now. She seems afraid to take her eyes off either of them – him or little Heather.'

Sheila Bennetts sighed. 'I thought you might say that, but I had to ask. Poor soul – she must be at her wits' end with it all. I can't imagine anything worse than finding my baby dead in its pram. I don't know how you'd ever get over it.'

'I don't, either,' Alice said soberly, and Mrs Bennetts departed, saying that Robin was welcome to come down and play with her little ones the minute Joanna wanted him to. Henry was too old to be much interested in his smaller brothers and sister now, but her Davey often played with Robin and they were good friends.

To everyone's relief, the coroner was satisfied with the answers to his questions, although the post-mortem had shown no results. Why the baby had died so suddenly, when she had seemed as healthy as her sister, remained a mystery. And a cruel one, as Alice observed when Charles Latimer came to tell them.

'It would be better if us did know. Then we'd know whether it was likely to happen to Heather as well. But this way, we're going to be on tenterhooks for ever more.'

'Well, I've examined Heather every day and she shows no signs of any kind of illness,' he said. 'Not that that's any great reassurance in this situation, I know, but we must take what comfort we can. As far as I can see, she's thriving and has suffered no ill-effects.'

'She must be missing her sister, though,' Joanna said. 'They've been together ever since they were born – *before* they were born. They've slept together in their cot and their pram and I fed them together. She must feel as though her other half has been taken away.' Tears began to fall on the bundle that was rarely out of her arms now, as the pain struck her once again. 'I don't see how you can say it hasn't affected her.'

'No, I can't,' he agreed. 'Not really. But I can only say what I see as a doctor, Joanna. Nobody knows what's going on in little Heather's head, and it may be that she doesn't miss her as much as we think. We must hope so, anyway.'

'And what about twins not being able to live without each other?' she asked. 'People don't say it to me, but I know it's what they're thinking. And every time I look at her in her cot, I'm afraid she's died too. I don't know how I'm going to stand it, Doctor, going on like this all the time.'

'Are you taking the pills I gave you?' he asked, and she shook her head.

'They'll make me sleep too much. Suppose she started to cry and I didn't hear her.'

'I'd wake up,' said Tom, who had come in from the yard when he saw the doctor's car. 'I could feed her then too, if you'd only do a bottle for her, like the doctor said the other day. You've got to get your sleep, love.'

But Joanna could not be convinced, and they knew that it would take time before she could relax enough to let someone else take charge of her baby, even for a little while.

'So can us arrange the funeral now, doctor?' Alice asked. 'Ernie Littlejohn said to let him know and he'll come round and have a talk about it.'

'Yes, you can go ahead with that now.' The doctor rose to his feet. 'I must be on my way. I'll call in again tomorrow, and of course you will call me if you're the slightest bit worried.'

Alice followed him. 'I just wanted to ask you, Doctor, what you really think about Joanna. I know 'tis early days and her's had a terrible shock, but it can't be good for the baby to be fussed over as much as she's doing now, can it? Joanna hardly ever puts her down. She seems frightened to take her eyes off the dear little mite. And it's not good for Joanna either – she's not getting the rest she ought to be. Next thing, her'll be losing her milk altogether.'

'I know. Don't worry, I'm keeping my eye on her. And Tom's ready to help all he can. It's going to take her a long time to come to terms with this, and the trouble is that the rest of you are grieving too. It's hard for all of you to give each other the support you need.'

'I don't know about the rest of us,' Alice said. ''Tis Joanna and Tom that needs it most. Not that we aren't feeling it too. There's nothing worse than a baby being took.'

'How about Jackie?' he asked. 'Has she gone back to Plymouth?'

'Went yesterday. She hardly knew what to do, poor maid – you could see she wanted to get back to Plymouth and her job, and be away from it all, but at the same time she didn't feel as she ought to be leaving at such a time. I walked along to the bus stop with her, and she was in tears the whole way.'

He nodded. 'It's hard for a young girl like Jackie, and coming so soon after all your anxiety over old Mrs Tozer too. It's probably good for her to be back at her job, though.' He sighed and put on his hat. 'I'll be in again tomorrow but remember, if you're at all concerned, about Heather or Joanna or any of you, you're to call me at once.'

Alice closed the door behind him and went back into the kitchen. She looked at her mother-in-law and then sank into her chair on the other side of the range.

'It's a bad job, this. I can't see us ever getting back to the way we were before.'

'We won't,' Minnie said. 'But us'll find a new way, and it won't be all that different. Poor Joanna won't never forget her baby, but her'll learn to smile again, and so will the rest of us, and the family will go on. 'Tis the way of the world, my dear; it has to keep on turning and us can't stay grieving for ever. I dare say you all thought 'twas me you'd be grieving for.' She sighed and shook her head as Alice began to protest. 'Don't try to pretend. I'm an old woman and it must be my time soon. I just wish the good Lord had come for me now, instead of taking that poor little babby.'

'I didn't want him to come for anyone,' Alice said, wiping her eyes. 'I know they say God moves in mysterious ways, his wonders to perform, but I can't see anything wonderful coming out of this. But you're right, Mother – life has to go on, and once the funeral's over us'll have to try to get back to normal, one way or another. And help poor Joanna and our Tom, for they've a harder furrow to plough than any of the rest of us.'

Val too felt she had a hard furrow to plough.

She had spent as much time as she could at the farm, sitting with Joanna and helping her to care for her remaining baby and little son, but it had not been easy. Although she knew that Joanna could not really blame her for the baby's death,

211

and that her accusation had come from fear and shock, she couldn't quite forget the scream of pain and anger that had been directed at her. She could see from Joanna's eyes that she remembered it too, and she had an uneasy feeling that there was still some doubt there.

'Why did it happen?' Joanna asked over and over again. 'Why? They were doing so well, both of them. There was nothing wrong. How can a baby die, just like that?'

'I don't know,' Val said wretchedly. 'It just does happen, and nobody can explain it. It's nothing to do with the way they're looked after, or because they were twins, or anything like that. It just happens.'

'And how do I know it won't happen to Heather as well?' Joanna went on, holding her baby close against her. 'How do I know I won't look into her cot one day and find her dead, too?'

'Jo, you mustn't feel like that. It won't happen.'

'How do you know? It happened to Suzanne. Why shouldn't it happen to Heather as well? Why?'

'God couldn't be so cruel—' Val began, not knowing what else to say, but Joanna broke in angrily.

'He was cruel enough to take Suzanne away. And after we had them both baptised as well, when they'd just been born. That was meant to keep them safe, wasn't it? Or did He think it was a good chance to get a new little soul? Well, He's not having another one.' She clutched the baby even closer, so that Heather let out a small cry of protest. 'I won't put her into her cot ever again, and then He *can't* take her away!'

Val felt helpless. She laid her hand on Joanna's arm but it was shaken off and the eyes that the anguished young mother turned on her were filled with resentment.

'Go away, Val. You're not doing any good. I know you mean well and I know you didn't do anything to make it happen, but I can't help remembering – every time I look at you, I remember you coming in to tell us. I'm sorry, I can't help it, but I just can't bear having you around me. Please – just go *away!*'

She bent her head over the baby, her tears falling on the shawl Minnie had knitted, and Val stared at her in dismay.

'Jo – I can't leave you like this.'

'You can. I want you to. Don't you understand? I don't want to see you any more. Not now, anyway. I want you to go.'

Uncertainly, Val stood up. Tears were sliding down her own cheeks now, but she could see that there was nothing more she could do. Reluctantly, she turned towards the door and opened it, glancing back over her shoulder in the hope that Joanna might call her back. But Joanna had turned away and in the moment that followed, she lifted her shoulders as if shrinking from Val's presence. There could be no clearer dismissal.

Val went down to the kitchen. She told her mother what had happened and Alice stared at her, horrified.

'She don't mean it, love. She's all upset.'

'I know she is. But she means it for now. I'll have to go, Mum, and I don't know when I'll be able to come back.' Val was crying now. 'It's as if

213

she just can't bear to look at me. It's awful – we've always been such good friends.'

'And you will be again,' Minnie said. 'This is just part of the poor maid's shock. She'll come to, soon enough, and she'll need to find you here waiting. It's for you to keep the door open, Val, so her doesn't have to push too hard against it.'

Val nodded and put on her coat to go. But the tears were in her eyes all the way back through the village to Jed's Cottage, and when she got indoors Luke took one look at her and took her in his arms.

'Your gran's right,' he said when Val had told him what had happened. 'Joanna doesn't mean it. She hardly knows what she's saying, poor girl.'

'It's not just that,' Val wept, leaning against him. 'It's our baby too, Luke. We were going to tell the family on Sunday. But how are we ever going to be able to tell them now? How can I look at Joanna and tell her that I'm having a baby?'

Chapter Nineteen

The postponed meeting about the Coronation festivities was held at last, a week after it had been intended. The villagers from Burracombe went across the Clam in a long, straggling group, grumbling a bit about having to go all that way when they had a perfectly good village hall of their own. Joyce Warren was the most vociferous.

'I'm not at all sure this is a good idea. It seems

214

to me that our celebrations are being taken over.'

'Us agreed to pull together,' Ted Tozer reminded her. 'And if us can't do that for an occasion like our Queen's coronation, 'tis a bad job.'

'Yes, of course, but all the same...' Her voice faded as Ted quickened his step to catch up with Jacob Prout, who was just ahead with Travis Kellaway.

'Glad to see you fitting in so well with the village,' he said to Travis. 'Reckon you'll take on a part in this pageant if it comes off?'

'Oh yes,' the estate manager said. 'I think we all need to pull together to make it a good day for both villages. I was very sorry to hear about your trouble,' he added.

'Ah, 'twas a bad business,' Ted agreed. 'But now the funeral's done, us have got to try to get on with things. It's going to take our Tom and Joanna a while, mind. Knocked 'em for six, it did.'

'I saw your Tom yesterday,' Jacob said. 'Always had a grin on his face and a joke on his lips, but all that's gone now. Not surprising, I suppose, but 'tis a pity. I don't suppose he's coming over tonight, is he?'

Ted shook his head. 'Can't bring his mind to it, and I don't think Joanna would want him to anyway. She seems to need him and the babbies in her sight all the time. My Alice is proper worried about her.'

'It takes time to get over anything like that,' Jacob said soberly. 'But you know what they say. Time's a great healer.'

'And how's your Jennifer getting along?' Ted enquired. 'We hear a bit from Jackie when she

215

deigns to pay us a visit, but me and Alice have been wondering if she's likely to settle in the village. She's got that cottage of hers after all, and she seems to like it out here in Burracombe.'

'She's said nothing more to me. I'd like nothing better than to have her there, as you know, but it don't seem too likely yet awhile. Got to earn her living, after all, and that means going to Plymouth every day if she moves out here, so I guess she thinks it's as well to stop there for the time being. And there's always a bed for her at my place, weekends.' He glanced over his shoulder at Travis Kellaway. 'She's getting a bit more involved with things, mind – her and Mr Kellaway here are putting their heads together about the next pantomime.'

'Are they?' Ted looked round in surprise. 'Why's that, then?'

'Well, stands to reason young Mr Copley won't be able to take it on, not now he's not in the village any more, and us don't want *you-know-who* to try and take over again. And it turns out our friend here got a bit of experience back in his own village, and my Jennifer's been mixed up with the Dockyard Players in one or two of their productions, down in Devonport, so I thought it might be an idea to start the ball rolling early. They been at my cottage a couple of times now, having a chinwag about it – haven't you, Mr Kellaway?'

'I told you, it's Travis,' the younger man said, catching up with them on the narrow path. 'I can't sit with my feet under your table, eating your cottage pie and have you calling me Mr Kellaway. Yes, that's right,' he added to Ted. 'Jennifer and I are

216

getting a few ideas together. We won't decide anything before we've had a meeting with the whole group, of course – it's not for us to make decisions. But we thought probably Mrs Warren would be glad of a hand, as she's so busy with the pageant.'

His voice was solemn and Ted couldn't see his face in the darkness, so was unable to decide if he were being ironic or not. As they were now coming into Little Burracombe and approaching the village hall, he decided to say no more. But the idea of Joyce Warren being 'glad of a hand' when it sounded more as if the decisions were (whatever Travis said) being taken *out* of her hands, made him chuckle.

It was the first chuckle Ted had enjoyed for some time. Even in the midst of sorrow, there were generally still things to make you smile, but the tragedy his family had suffered seemed beyond that. Even at the gathering after the funeral, when people generally did relax a bit and start to look forward, there had been only sad faces and quiet voices. Nobody could rid their minds of the sight of that tiny white coffin being carried into the church and then placed into the grave Jacob Prout had dug ('and a worse job than that I never wish to have,' he'd told Ted later), nor of the sound of Joanna's heartbroken sobs or the look of anguish on her face.

If it hadn't been for little Heather Mary, who could make them all smile with a wave of her tiny fists and her infectious baby laugh, and Robin, who had to be protected from the family's grief, Ted didn't know how his son and daughter-in-law would have managed. But you couldn't look at the surviving baby without feeling the warmth of love, even though you also felt the sadness of her loss as well as your own. She would grow up never knowing her twin, he thought, and always wondering just what was missing from her life.

But that was the way it was – one of life's cruelties that just had to be accepted and lived with. And meanwhile, the rest of life had to go on, whether it be the day-to-day pleasures and anxieties of the farm and family, or the rarer excitement of a coronation.

The straggle of people formed into a group as they left the narrow path and reached the road leading to Little Burracombe village hall. This was an old building, not much more than a tin-roofed shed, put up after the Great War of 1914–18, and out of politeness they tried to mask their expressions of disdain. Burracombe's own village hall had been donated by Constance Bellamy, in memory of her father, on the occasion of King George the Sixth's coronation, and was modern in comparison.

'I hope they aren't going to suggest holding any of the festivities here,' Mrs Warren said, in a loud whisper.

'Well, that's what we come to discuss, isn't it,' Alf Coker said in an annoyed tone. 'And if you wants my opinion, it'll go best if we remembers our manners.'

Joyce opened her mouth indignantly but Felix, who was waiting with some of his new parishioners, came towards them then, holding out his hands. 'Welcome, everybody. We're so pleased to see you. Hope you didn't encounter too many

218

dangers on the way!'

'Well, 'tis a bit like venturing into uncharted territory,' Ted said, shaking his hand. 'Good to see you, Felix, or should I be polite and call you Vicar now?'

'Felix will do very well. I'm trying to train my new flock to call me that, and your example may help. They're finding it rather difficult so far.'

'Well, you ought to be given your proper title. You earned it, after all, and people ought to be showing you proper respect. 'Tis all right for us that considers ourselves friends,' Alf Coker said. 'I think us had better stick to Vicar as well, since this is a meeting.'

Stella, who was standing beside Felix, smiled. 'It's no good trying to bring your city-slicker ways here. You ought to know that by now.'

'I thought it was worth a try,' he said with a sigh. 'Never mind. The real question is, are there enough chairs?'

There weren't, so a lot of people remained standing, either at the back or around the sides of the tiny hall. Felix, who would have given up his chair if it had been possible, rapped on the rickety table for attention and then caught it as it threatened to topple over.

'Good evening everyone, and thank you for coming. It's good to welcome both my new parishioners and my old friends from Burracombe. I hope this is only the first of many occasions when the two villages will work together for the common good.'

'Here, nobody told me this were a Commoners' meeting,' one of the Little Burracombe villagers

219

said suspiciously.

'I'm sorry – I didn't mean that. I just meant...' Felix decided that explanations would be too cumbersome and continued swiftly. 'Anyway, we're here tonight to discuss the Coronation celebrations. We're all agreed that this is something we should celebrate together, to make it a really memorable occasion, aren't we?' He looked at the little crowd in front of him and took their murmurs for assent. 'Then let's have some ideas to start the ball rolling.'

There was a moment of silence and then Ted Tozer spoke up. 'How about someone from each village going through a sort of list of what they've thought of so far? Then us can get down to the nuts and bolts of it all.'

'A good idea,' Felix approved. 'Perhaps you'd like to be spokesman for Burracombe, Mr Tozer.'

Joyce Warren opened her mouth again, then closed it, looking annoyed. Ted, who was one of those standing, looked nonplussed for a moment, then gathered his thoughts and outlined the suggestions that had already been made. At some of them the Little Burracombe villagers could be seen shaking their heads, but others seemed to meet with their approval and when he stopped there was a spattering of applause.

'Thank you, Ted,' Felix said, forgetting that he'd intended to maintain the formality the villagers seemed to prefer. 'Now, who would like to speak for those this side of the river?'

'I will,' said a large lady in tweeds, who was sitting in the front row. She stood up and turned to face the assembly and Hilary, who was standing next to Travis, stifled a giggle. 'She's Little Burracombe's version of Joyce Warren,' she murmured in his ear. 'President of the WI, Mothers' Union and leading light of Tavistock WVS. Finger in every pie ever baked. If she and Joyce come up against each other, it'll be a battle of the Titans.'

'Or the Amazons,' he replied. 'Which of them do you suggest for Boadicea?'

'I thought you had me down for that part,' she said. 'And what's this I hear about you and Jennifer Tucker taking over the pantomime?'

'We're not taking it over,' he began, but Felix rapped on the table again and his glass of water slid dangerously close to the edge and was caught by Stella.

'Let's have some quiet for Mrs Barnicoat, shall we?' he suggested, and the tweedy woman inclined her head graciously and began in commanding, cut-glass accents to list the smaller village's proposals.

'Well, that don't sound too bad,' Alf Coker commented when she had finished. 'Apart from the dancing in the evening it all fits in pretty well with what we been thinking of doing. But I can't see all our lot coming over the Clam to spend the rest of the evening here, and this place ain't big enough to hold everyone anyway.' He glanced dismissively round the small room. 'Not much bigger than a garden shed, this be.'

There was a murmur of indignation from the 'Littlers' as Burracombe folk termed them, and Felix rapped the table again, more carefully this time.

'What Alf says is quite true. We couldn't hold a

221

dance for both villages here. As I see it, we have three options. One, to hold a dance for both villages at Burracombe, which does have a bigger hall but would mean everyone from here having to go back late, across the Clam, and we don't want any accidents. Two, to hold separate dances, which might be the best answer, although it does seem a shame to split up after having enjoyed afternoon games by the river and a picnic tea. And three, to use the marquee for the dance, as Ted suggested. I must say, it seems sensible to me.'

'But that still means us has got to cross the Clam to go back,' someone from Little Burracombe protested. 'It's only narrow and it do get slippery in wet weather.'

'Well, you can all go together and look after each other, can't you?' Alf demanded. 'Or d'you want us to hold your hands till you'm safely across?'

Felix called for order again. Really, he thought, Stella ought to be doing this, she's far more used to dealing with bickering infants than I am. But he sensed that the tone of the meeting was basically in agreement and that any objections were made more for form's sake than because anyone was really opposed. The two villages had to maintain their independence, even when they were co-operating. 'So is that agreed, then? We hold the dance in the marquee, and it's open to all – old and young alike.'

The rest of the evening was spent in appointing committees to deal with various aspects of the day. Joyce Warren found herself, to her satisfaction, in charge of the Procession of Monarchs, while in Little Burracombe Mrs Barnicoat took over the organisation of the dance, from booking a band to arranging the refreshments. Alice Tozer, who hadn't wanted to leave Joanna, had given Ted permission to volunteer her services for the tea and Alf Coker had offered to get a team together to set up the marquee. Ted Tozer announced his plans for bell-ringing and Brian Standing, his opposite number in Little Burracombe, said he was training up some youngsters and hoped to have them ringing on the day. Travis and Luke said they would see to the games for the adults and Stella took on the job of arranging egg-and-spoon, sack and three-legged races for the children. There would be rounders in another part of the field and if they could get enough young men together they could have a football match and a tug-of-war. One of the Littlers, a big, brawny, fair-haired young man by the name of Abel Lock, more commonly known as Curly, offered to see to the greasy pole. Having said this, he blushed scarlet and fell silent for the rest of the evening.

'He's a forester,' Hilary murmured to Travis. 'He'll find a good straight pole. He's terribly shy, poor boy – I'm surprised he could bring himself to speak at all.'

Felix brought the gathering to an end with two announcements.

'It's been a real pleasure to hold this meeting and to see so many old friends here, together with the new ones I'm making every day. Now, some of our ladies have kindly supplied refreshments at the back of the hall and I hope you'll all partake before you go. But there's just one more thing.' He paused and smiled around at them. 'I know a few

223

of you have been a little – shall we say dismissive? – of our facilities here in Little Burracombe.' There was a shuffling of feet and a hasty murmur of denial from the visitors. 'And you're quite right, this hall is very small – not much more than a garden shed, did I hear someone say? – and probably due to fall down around our ears at any time. As you know, it was built to commemorate the Great War, when there wasn't much money about, and it's served faithfully for the past thirty years or more. But now we've decided it's time to build another one, and what better dedication than to the event we're here to discuss tonight – the Coronation? So as soon as the festivities are over, we shall set about raising money for our own, brand new Coronation Hall. And we hope you will all help us by coming over the Clam, now that you've found the way–' there was a ripple of laughter '–to all the events we're going to organise for enjoyment and fund-raising. And I'm proud to say that we've been donated a very generous sum by a local benefactor, Colonel Napier himself, which will enable us to start making plans straight away. By this time next year, we may be welcoming you to our inauguration.'

Amidst the excited babble of chatter that broke out as he finished his announcement, Hilary and Travis turned and stared at each other in amazement.

'Did you know anything about this?' she demanded, and he shook his head.

'Not a thing. And obviously you didn't, either. But you're going to have a job persuading the villagers of that.' Already, people were beginning

224

to crowd around Hilary, thanking her and asking questions she couldn't answer. She shook her head and warded them off, saying that the details hadn't been fully worked out yet, but inside she was seething. How could her father have done this, making gifts to the other village and not giving her so much as a hint? He must have known that the people of Burracombe itself would feel slighted and that she would have to face them. Whatever was he thinking?

It's not just that, she thought, pinning a smile firmly to her face and helping herself to tea and a buttered scone because to turn and walk out, as she would much have preferred to do, would have been rude. We're supposed to be business partners. He *ought* to discuss it with me before he makes generous gifts. But once again, he's shown me that he simply doesn't take me seriously as a partner. Once again, he's done his best to put me firmly in my place.

Chapter Twenty

'Why didn't you tell me you were thinking about this?' Hilary demanded. She had come home to find her father already in bed and had spent the night simmering with resentment, so that by breakfast time she was ready to boil over. 'I thought I was supposed to be a partner in the estate. We're supposed to consult each other on expenditure.'

Gilbert Napier looked up from his eggs and bacon. His white hair looked even more like a lion's mane today, and his blue eyes were fierce. Hilary had a momentary pang of guilt, remembering Charles Latimer's warnings that her father's temper should not be provoked, in case it led to another heart attack. But that doesn't mean I can never question anything he does, she thought defensively. Life would be impossible.

'May I remind you, Hilary,' he began in a dangerously quiet voice, 'that not all the money belongs to the estate. I do have some of my own, and I do still have the right to dispose of it as I see fit. Or at least, I thought I did.'

She stared at him. 'But–'

'Perhaps you'd like me to account for it,' he went on, holding up one hand and ticking off the fingers as he spoke. 'There's my Army pension. I think you'll agree I earned that? There's my "salary" if you wish to call it that, from the estate – you're paid yours too, as is Kellaway, and I imagine you consider you have the right to spend it as you wish. There's income from investments I've made over the years from *my own money*, and there's income from the money left to me by your mother. Again, you have your own similar income, which again I presume you consider you may spend as you wish. And from all these sources I have savings. Now, a good deal of this has been put back into the estate over the years and naturally I don't begrudge that, but now and then, just occasionally, I feel I'd like to do something else with it. Something for the village. And as you know, the estate has interests in Little

Burracombe as well as Burracombe itself, so why not do something for them for a change? I've been looking around for some time and it seemed to me that if nothing is done soon about that apology for a hall, it's either going to collapse or be blown away in the next gale. And, as young Copley agrees, what better time to start a fund than to celebrate the Coronation of our new young Queen? I'll tell you another thing – John Berry himself had it in mind to do it in *time* for the Coronation, and if he hadn't been so ill for the past few years he'd have done it, too. And I'd have been happy to contribute.' He returned to his eggs and bacon.

Hilary sat down. Her cheeks were burning and she felt foolish and wrong-footed. Everything her father had said was true, and she knew that she had been too hasty. She tried to retrieve a fragment of composure.

'I still think you could have mentioned it to me. I felt such a fool, hearing Felix announce it and not knowing a thing about it. People were asking me – saying how pleased they were. It was embarrassing.'

'I don't see why. You should have accepted their thanks graciously. No need to do anything more than that, and no need to let them know you hadn't been told.'

'I'm afraid I haven't your arrogance, Father,' she said, a little too sharply, and his head came up again.

'And that's enough of that! There's nothing arrogant about knowing your place in the world. Your trouble, Hilary, is that you don't *have* a proper place and, whatever you may say, it makes a difference and you're aware of it. You don't know how to conduct yourself with the village people.'

'That's ridiculous! They're my friends.'

'Well, they shouldn't be. Oh yes, Charles and Basil and Constance Bellamy – they're our sort. But treating people like Jacob Prout and Coker and even the Tozers as friends – well, it's not in the natural order of things. They don't expect it. They're uncomfortable with it, and so are you, if you're honest.'

'You're living in the past, Father. There's been a war–'

'I know that! I fought in it, if you remember.'

'–and attitudes have changed. People mix more now – class isn't so important. And I *do* consider the Tozers my friends – Val in particular. We've been friends all our lives.'

'So you might have been. It still doesn't give you the right to know what I intend to do with my own money, and if you find yourself included in their gratitude for my generosity, you should at least have the courtesy to accept it with good grace. You'll have plenty of say in what happens to it after I'm dead, but until then you'll mind your own business!'

He stood up. Hilary, scarlet and almost in tears, could find nothing to say and after a moment he turned on his heel and marched out of the room.

Hilary sat quite still, staring at her plate. The food looked congealed and unappetising and she pushed the plate away. A tear crept out of one eye and she scrubbed it away furiously with her napkin.

He would have told Baden, she thought. He discussed everything with Baden, even before Baden was doing any work on the estate, even when he was still at Oxford. Even if it wasn't estate business, he'd have talked it over with Baden and they'd have planned it together. But I'm just Hilary – a daughter, who he's had to accept as part of the business, but still doesn't trust enough to take wholly into his confidence.

It wasn't that she resented his gift, nor that she thought it had gone to the wrong village. Little Burracombe badly needed a new hall and, from what Felix had said to her afterwards, the gift would go a long way towards providing it. And the Napiers did have an obligation to both villages, since they owned so much of the land.

As she sat there, Hilary had to admit that much of what her father had said was right; it was his money and his right to spend or give it as he chose. What really hurt her was that he had let her go to the meeting unaware, knowing that Felix was likely to announce it there. It was as if he were telling her that she was of no account; that she might be his daughter, even his business partner, but she was not, as Baden had been, his friend.

Once again, she wondered how long she could continue with this life. For a long time everything had seemed to be working out well, but no sooner did she begin to feel that she had been accepted than he did something to knock her back. First Travis and now this.

If only Baden had had time to marry and have a son, she thought. Or if Stephen had been interested enough to take over, setting her free to live her own life. But neither of those things had happened and she had found an unexpected talent for running the estate. She would have been happy to take over completely – if only her father would retire and let her do it. Or at least treat her as an equal.

It didn't seem likely, though, that either of these things would happen for a long time, and she sighed and got up from the table to go and start the day's work.

Stephen Napier felt himself well out of the affairs of the estate.

He had never been as interested as his brother and sister in the life of a country gentleman, and when Baden had been killed his one dread had been that he would be expected to take over. Indeed, his father had assumed that this would be the case and it had taken Stephen a long time and a lot of argument before Gilbert finally, and reluctantly, accepted that it wouldn't. Even now, he was inclined to harp on the subject when Stephen came home on leave from the RAF.

National Service had been Stephen's escape. Refusing his father's attempts to get him into his own Army regiment, he had been delighted to find himself in the Royal Air Force and worked hard to achieve his present rank of Squadron Leader. He had now signed on for five years and his ambition, when he was discharged, was to set up his own flying business in Canada. If he had known about his father's gift of money for a village hall at Little Burracombe, he would simply have shrugged his shoulders, and he certainly wouldn't have been bothered by not having been consulted.

The only fly in Stephen's pot of ointment was his increasing feeling for Maddy Forsyth. For a while it had been no more than a flirtation with a pretty girl, but he had soon found himself thinking of her more and more, even when he was out with other pretty girls. He had been put out to find young Sammy Hodges as his main rival, but confident that he had more to offer than the young son of a blacksmith. But then she had made it clear that she was in love with Sammy. If Sammy hadn't died, there might still have been a chance – but Stephen knew that it was impossible to fight a dead man. Maddy would have to be given time to recover, and might never turn back to him.

I wish I'd realised earlier that I was really in love with her and it wasn't just a game, he thought as he drove down to West Lyme the following weekend. He'd telephoned earlier to say he was going to Burracombe for a late Easter leave and asking if Maddy would like to go with him. She had hesitated and then agreed, but declined his offer of hospitality at the Barton. 'I'll stay with Stella,' she'd said. 'Or over the road at Mrs Madge's – I don't like turning Dottie out.' He'd wanted to argue, but remembered his resolve to tread very carefully and stayed silent. At least she was coming!

Maddy was ready and waiting, but invited him in for a few minutes first and the Archdeacon offered him a drink. Stephen shook his head.

'Thank you, but I'd like to get on our way and do most of the driving in daylight, and Hilary's expecting me for supper.'

231

'Off you go then.' The Archdeacon came out to the car with them, followed by Archie, who was wagging his tail but looked dispirited when he realised they were going without him. He settled Maddy into the passenger seat, wrapping her in a woollen tartan rug. 'That should keep the draughts out. Take care of her, won't you, Stephen?'

'I will. And we'll be back on Sunday evening.'

'Come for supper,' the Archdeacon invited, and Stephen nodded and started the car. He spun it round on the gravel and they roared off up the drive.

'A nice young man,' the Archdeacon said to his dog as they watched the car disappear. 'And good value. It's a pity he was involved in Maddy's life at the same time as Sammy. It will make it all the more difficult for him to make progress.'

The labrador thumped his thick tail and gazed up at his master with soulful eyes, and the Archdeacon laughed.

'All right, you rascal! I'll take you for a walk, since she's not here to do it. Where shall it be? The beach?'

Archie bounded ahead, barking with excitement, and the man followed more slowly, thinking how uncomplicated life was for dogs. If I believed in reincarnation, he thought, I'd apply to be a dog next time round. A dog like Archie, full of joy just for being alive, and never worrying what might be round the corner because he doesn't even know there are corners.

But I don't believe in it, he rebuked himself, and I shouldn't even be thinking this way. I'll just envy Archie his carefree life – or I would, if envy weren't a sin!

Sometimes life was difficult for Archdeacons.

'I'm glad you agreed to come with me,' Stephen said after they'd driven for a while in silence. 'But you know, you'd be welcome to stay at the Barton. Hilary would be pleased to see you and Dad's very fond of you.'

'I know.' During the war, Maddy had lived at the Barton which was being used as a children's home. After Fenella Forsyth, who had been a great friend of Isobel Napier, had adopted her, and before she had gone to live with Dottie Friend, they had often stayed at the estate manager's house in the woods where the Napiers had lived for the duration. She had never met Baden, who had been killed early in the war, and hadn't seen much of Hilary or Colonel Napier, but the visits had continued after the war and then she had come to know them well. 'But now that Stella's in Burracombe I really like to see as much of her as possible. We missed so much when we were separated during the war.'

'Well, come for a meal anyway. Come to lunch on Sunday. Bring Stella as well – and Felix if you like. He and Hilary were friends when he first came to the village.'

'I'll ask them if they'd like to come.'

'And I thought we might go into Tavistock tomorrow,' he went on. 'There's a special market on, and we could have a coffee at the Bedford and maybe some lunch there – what d'you think?'

'I'll see what Stella wants to do. Felix is usually

233

busy on Saturdays, so she might like that.'

Stephen hadn't meant the invitation to include Stella, but he said nothing. It was clear that Maddy intended to keep him at a distance, and that this lift to Burracombe was no more than that – a lift. Spending the weekend with him had not been part of her plan.

He sighed and shrugged. It was still very early days, and he was determined to stick to his agreement to be no more than a friend. But it wasn't going to be easy, now that he had finally recognised his true feelings for her. And suppose he had got no further when he came to leave the RAF and carry out his plan to emigrate to Canada? How could he ever bear to leave her behind?

You may have no choice, he told himself. You can't force her to love you. She's already turned you down once for another man, and there's no reason why she should turn back to you now.

Maddy, glancing sideways at his profile, thought he looked grave and withdrawn. She sighed in her turn, aware that he still had feelings for her, although how strong they were or how lasting, she had no idea. I just hope he'll get over them and find someone else, she thought, because I'll never be able to love him as he'd like. Sammy took my heart, and it was broken that night on the bridge, and I don't think it will ever really mend.

She felt the tears begin to sting her eyes and turned away quickly, looking over the rolling Dorset hills towards the sea.

Chapter Twenty-One

'We got a lot sorted out at the meeting,' Ted said at breakfast next morning. 'Looks like it'll be a good day, and I reckon 'tis a good idea for both villages to pull together. Those fields down by the river are just the job.'

'What about the bells?' Tom asked. He had managed to persuade Joanna to come down to breakfast and she sat silently beside him, toying with her plate of bacon and eggs. 'Have Little Burracombe got a decent team?'

'I reckon so, and they're training up a few boys. You know, Tom, we ought to be thinking about that too. I know we've got a pretty good band, but you always need new youngsters coming along. They won't be ready in time for the Coronation, of course, but it's not a bad time to be looking around.'

'Good idea,' Tom said. 'There's a few handy youngsters I can think of straight off – Micky Coker, for a start, and that young feller he's always knocking about with – Henry Bennetts, isn't it? I'll have a word with them.'

'You're not thinking of doing it yourself, surely?' Joanna asked, with an edge to her voice. 'When are you going to find the time?'

'Well, it'll only be an hour or two a week. We could tie the bells and have a silent practice on Mondays – I don't do anything then. You wouldn't

235

mind that, would you?'

'You ought to be at home,' she said. 'With your own family. We don't see all that much of you as it is.'

'I'm in and out all day,' he began, and then caught the expression on her face and stopped. There was a moment of awkward silence and then Ted said, 'Well, it seems a good idea to me. Us got to keep the bells ringing, after all, and if we got some young chaps ready to take it up, now's the time to catch 'em before they gets interested in other things. You wouldn't begrudge an hour of a Monday evening, Joanna, surely.'

'It's not a matter of begrudging,' she began, and then laid down her knife and fork with a clatter. 'Oh, never mind me. I don't matter round here, I know. You just go ahead and enjoy your-selves.' And she pushed back her chair violently and ran quickly up the stairs.

The others looked at each other and Tom, his face grim, rose and followed her.

'I dunno what I said then,' Ted said, looking bewildered. 'Why did us talking about the bells upset her?'

'Don't be so daft,' Alice said sharply. 'The poor maid's grieving. Anything can upset her, anything at all. We've got to be patient with her.'

'I know she's grieving and I don't mind being patient,' he said. 'I'd just like to know what I *can* say without sending her in to a tizzy. I don't want to upset her, Alice. I'm upset enough myself.'

'I know you are. We all are. And I don't think there's any way of knowing what's going to touch her on the raw. It's a bad time, and us just got to get through it somehow and help her get through it, that's all.'

'It's right what the vicar said,' Minnie put in. She had been sitting quietly in her chair, still small and shrunken but looking a good deal better than she had looked a few weeks previously. 'Time's a great healer. She'll start to feel better in time.'

'I hope so,' Alice said. 'But I don't really know how a mother can ever get over losing her little one. Especially when the little mite wasn't even ill. It's so cruel. And it's not a bit of use Mr Harvey telling me there's a purpose in all things. I can't see no purpose in taking away a little baby, none at all.'

Upstairs, Tom was trying to comfort his wife.

'Of course I want to be here with you, love. But life's got to go on. You don't really grudge me an hour or so of a Monday evening, do you?'

'I don't grudge you anything,' Joanna said wearily. 'I just don't see how you can be so cheerful and talk about things like bell-ringing when our baby's hardly cold in her grave. And don't tell me again that "life's got to go on". I know it has. I just wish it didn't, that's all. I wish we could all just stop, like my little Suzanne did, and have done with it.'

'Jo! You don't mean that!'

'I do. I *do*. What's the *point* of it all, Tom?' she cried, turning to him with tears streaming down her face. 'We go through all the hard work of bringing up a family and working all the hours there are to keep them warm and fed, and work the farm for a living to pay for it all – and then this happens. And why? Why can't anyone tell us

237

why? The doctors don't know, the vicar doesn't know, nobody knows. It doesn't make sense.'

'I know it doesn't. But Jo, people die all the time. *Babies* die. It's just part of life–'

'Part of *life?* It's death, Tom – *death*. And it was *our* baby. Not anyone else's, not a baby we didn't know and would never hear about anyway. It was *our* baby.'

'That doesn't mean it can't happen to us,' he said quietly. 'We aren't special people, that bad things don't happen to. You know that.'

'So maybe we're being punished for something,' she said. 'But what have we done that was so bad that we needed this to happen? What could little Suzanne have ever done, to deserve to be taken away from us?'

'I don't know,' he said helplessly. 'I don't think anybody knows the answers to those questions, Jo.'

'I still can't help asking them,' she said, and her head drooped.

Tom sat on the bed, gazing at her. He felt completely powerless. He longed to be able to comfort her, but he knew that when she was in this state almost anything he did would be wrong.

'Jo, why are you so upset about the bell-ringing?' he asked at last, and her head came up.

'Why? Why do you *think?* Our baby has just died and you can talk about bell-ringing and fairs and greasy poles and ... and all those things, as if you don't even *care!* Of course I'm upset. I feel as if I'm the only one who's grieving. You're all getting over it and I'm the only one who really cares, the only one who really loved her.'

'Jo, that's a terrible thing to say!'

'Is it? So if you loved her, if you're really upset at losing her, how is it you can think of all those other things? *I* can't, so how can you?'

'I can't, not all the time. There's a lot of times when I don't want to think about anything at all, when I feel just as bad as you. But there are other times when I feel a bit better. I can't help it, Jo. It just happens, and maybe it's the way we start to get over it.'

'I haven't,' she said dully. 'I don't think I ever will.'

'You will, in time—' he began, but she cut in again,

'But what if I don't want to? What if I feel that getting over it is betraying her? It's the first step to forgetting about her, isn't it? And I don't *want* to forget her, Tom. I don't *want* to feel better. It wouldn't be right.'

He sighed and sought for the right words. 'It would be right, Jo. It's the way things are. And we've got two other children.'

'You don't have to tell me that,' she said bitterly. 'I know we've got two other children, and I mean to keep them, too.' He moved to put his arms around her, and she pushed him away. 'You go and talk to your father about bell-ringing. Leave me here to do all the grieving for both of us. Go away,' she said when he didn't move. 'I don't want you here. You're just making me feel worse.'

Tom stared at her. He felt as if she had driven a knife into his heart and was now turning it slowly in the wound. She turned her back and he reached out, tentatively, to touch her shoulder. Sensing his movement, she shrugged him impatiently away and he let his hand drop. He waited a moment or two then got up and moved hesitantly towards the door.

'Jo?' he said, unwilling to leave her, but she shrugged again and he opened the door and went out, closing it quietly behind him, then went slowly down the stairs.

The rest of the family had finished their breakfast. He shook his head when Alice offered to warm his up, and went out into the yard and across to the cowshed to help Norman with the milking. Sometimes, he felt that only the cows understood.

When Jennifer got off the bus at the main road, she found Travis there in the Land Rover.

'Hullo,' she said in surprise as he climbed out and held open the passenger door. 'You didn't come specially to meet me, did you?'

'Why not? Jacob told me you were coming out for a few days, so I thought you might have luggage to carry.' He took her small suitcase and slung it on to the back seat. 'You didn't tell me you were coming.'

'I didn't think you'd be interested. It's just to use up the last of my holiday allowance, that's all, and Burracombe is lovely in the spring. It's good to get out into the fresh air when you live in Plymouth.'

He glanced at her as he started the engine. 'Don't you ever think of moving out here permanently?'

'Yes, of course I do. I'd love it. But I have to work for my living, so if I did I'd have to travel into Plymouth every day – I wouldn't see much more of the village than I do now. And I've got Jackie Tozer staying with me too. I couldn't really abandon her until she gets a live-in job at the hotel.'

'She's not really your responsibility, though. And what about your cottage in Burracombe?'

'You know Val and Luke live there. I couldn't throw them out. No, I'm sure I'll move out to Burracombe some day but for the time being it suits me to go on as I am. I can stay with Jacob any time I want, and he's always pleased to have me.'

'I've never really understood about you and Jacob,' Travis observed. 'He's not really a relative, is he?'

'No, but he thinks he ought to have been my father. He and my mother were sweethearts, you know, when they were young, but things didn't work out and he went off to war – the First World War – and my real father, Jed, who was always his rival, came between them. It's a long story.' She stopped.

'Maybe you'll tell me one day,' he suggested after a moment, and she turned and smiled at him.

'Maybe I will.'

They drove in silence for a while, Travis thinking what a pleasant person she was. Not especially pretty, but with warm brown eyes and a smile that lit her whole face. He felt comfortable and at ease with her, too, and since their talks over the pantomime in Jacob's cottage he had begun to think of her as a friend. He liked being with her.

'I wonder if you'd like a day out while you're here,' he said. 'I have to go over to Widecombe tomorrow. You could come with me for the ride and have a look around the village. There's a café by the green – we could have a bite of lunch. Maybe have a walk as well. What do you think?'

'I'd like that. Thank you. I've never been to Widecombe.'

'You know all about it from the song, I expect,' he said, and she laughed. 'Oh yes! "All along, down along, out along lee" – we learned that in school. I should think everyone does.'

'We'll sing it on the way,' he said. 'We might even bring it into the pantomime.'

'And who,' she asked, 'are you going to ask to play the grey mare?'

They passed the rest of the short drive by casting various villagers for the parts in the song and decided that Jacob Prout should be Uncle Tom Cobley, and Alf Coker, George Sweet, Bert Foster, Basil Harvey, Henry Warren and Dr Latimer should play the rest. 'That still leaves two parts,' Jennifer said. 'Tom Pearce and "I".'

'Tom Pearce and you? What do you mean?'

'No, not me. *"I"*. The one who actually sings the song and asks for the grey mare. You never know his name. He just says "I want to go to Widecombe Fair, with..."'

'Bill Brewer, Jan Stewer, Peter Gurney, Peter Davey, Dan'l Whiddon, 'Arry 'Awk, Old Uncle Tom Cobley and all,' Travis finished. 'You're right. There *is* another man. And what about "all"? How many of them do you think there really were, Jennifer?'

'I don't know,' she said as they drew up beside Jacob's cottage and she opened the door. 'But it's

242

no wonder the poor mare died! Thanks for the lift, Travis, and thank you very much for coming to meet me. What time do you want me to be ready tomorrow?'

'About ten,' he said. 'I've got this man to see at a farm near Widecombe, but after that my time's my own. The weather looks set fair so we'll make a good long day of it.'

She smiled at him and went through the garden gate. Jacob already had the front door open in welcome, and they both waved as Travis turned the Land Rover and went back towards the Barton.

He was still smiling as he drew up in the yard and went into the estate office.

Ted lost no time in getting his new ringers organised.

'I thought about my Micky a while back,' Alf Coker said when Ted went to see him at the forge. 'He's a bright nipper, picks things up in no time and I reckon if he come along young Henry'd come too. Eleven or twelve is a good age to start, too.'

'They won't be able to ring for the Coronation, mind,' Ted warned him. 'It'll be a good while before they'm ready to join the band, but they'm welcome to come along and watch at the practices.'

'I'll tell you another thing,' Alf said, resting his bellows on a bench. 'That new estate bloke let slip he used to do a bit of ringing up in Dorset. You might want to ask him along some night.'

'Kellaway?' Ted stared at him. 'He's never said a word to me about it.'

243

'No, he never said anything to anyone till the other day when he dropped in with Miss Hilary's horse to be shod. We just got talking and I asked if he was interested in coming along, and he said he'd rung regular at his old place.'

'Did he now?' A thought struck Ted. 'Here, but didn't he come from up-country somewhere? Dorset, wasn't it? Well, he'll have rung scientific then. Won't be interested in our sort of ringing.'

'I thought that too, but he says he can ring call-changes as well.'

'Not the same as us,' Ted said positively. 'You know what they scientific ringers are like. Changing every half-pull – stands to reason they can't give the same concentration to their striking. I've heard it a time or two, when I've been away, out of the county, and 'tis rubbish – jangling away all over the place, you can't make no sense out if it at all. It won't be no good him joining us if he can't do better than that.'

'And I daresay that's why he's never mentioned it,' Alf said, and picked up his bellows. 'If you'm serious about getting a few more ringers in the team, you didn't ought to be too ready to pass up someone who can already handle a bell. It struck me he missed it a bit, and he's the sort who'd fit in with our ways and not try and take over.'

'Hm,' Ted said, unwilling to concede the point too readily. 'Maybe we'll try him out. I got to admit, he do seemed to have fitted into the village quite well for an outsider, being in last year's pantomime and coming to the Coronation meeting and generally making himself friendly around the place. All the same, the sort of ringing

244

they do up-country's a bit different from our ways. To my mind, there's nothing better than proper Devon call-changes, with only two bells at a time changing places. You got time to pay attention to your striking then. That "scientific", ringing such they do up the line, where every ringer got to make his own change, at every pull, with no help from a conductor – well, it stands to reason it can't sound so good, with all the bells crashing about together like so many tin pans.'

'I know,' Alf agreed. 'Method-ringing, that chap from upcountry – Sussex, or somewhere – told me they called it, when he come here on holiday last year. All sorts of different patterns and permutations – I couldn't make head nor tail of it. And it's not just one method, neither! There's any amount, with outlandish names, I can't remember what they were. Grandfather's triplets, or summat.'

'Grandsire Triples,' Ted said. 'I remember that. And Plain Bob, whoever Bob was. Mind you, there's some quite pretty names – Canterbury Pleasure, I remember. And April Day, I quite liked the sound of that.'

'Place names, too,' Alf said, screwing up his face in thought. 'Didn't he say something about Oxford and Cambridge?' He laughed suddenly. 'Here, d'you suppose there might be one called Burracombe?'

'Shouldn't think so. They'd have to ask our permission, wouldn't they? Anyway,' he said firmly, 'to get back to Mr Kellaway, I don't mind him coming along but he needn't think he's going to get us ringing scientific. Not while I'm captain, anyway.'

Chapter Twenty-Two

'I just don't know what to do,' Tom said miserably. He had met Luke as he walked slowly through the woods towards the Standing Stones. It was the spot everyone in Burracombe was drawn to when they needed to have a think, a place where they could look out over the clustered cottages and beyond to the distant moors, a place that had been for centuries a guardian over the village, secret yet benign.

Luke was standing outside the charcoal-burner's cottage. He was holding a sketch-pad and pencil, and drawing with quick strokes.

'I'd have thought you'd seen enough of this place,' Tom observed, pausing beside him. 'It's a bit primitive, isn't it?'

'It's fine as long as you don't mind collecting water from the stream,' Luke said with a grin. 'And there are still plenty of people using wells. You've got a pump, but not everyone in the village has.'

'That's true. Still, I know Dad was glad when you moved down to Jed's Cottage.' He regarded the shack thoughtfully. 'I wonder if anyone will ever live here again.'

'Well, not yet,' Luke said. 'I'm going to use it as a studio. It'll make room for—' He stopped abruptly, then went on, 'Oh well, you may as well know. We were going to tell the family the day ...

well, on Easter Day.'

Tom turned enquiringly. 'Tell us what?'

'About the baby,' Luke said wretchedly. 'Our baby. Val's going to have a baby.'

There was a long silence. Tom stared at him, then looked away. Luke waited, wishing that he had held his tongue. But the family had to know sometime, and maybe it was better that Tom and Joanna knew first, privately, now that it was impossible to break the news joyously, as they had hoped.

'You're having a baby,' Tom said at last, turning back, and Luke nodded. 'Well, that's good news. You must be very pleased.' His voice was curiously flat.

'We are. But it's been difficult. Val's been really upset, you know – about Suzanne, of course, and about you and Jo. And we just didn't know what to do about telling you all. It seemed like rubbing salt into the wound.'

Tom nodded. 'I can see that.' He fell silent again and Luke waited, wondering what thoughts were going through the other man's mind. He couldn't really imagine what it felt like to lose a child. Johnny, the baby Val had lost before he was even born, was a sadness to Luke, but it couldn't be at all the same – he hadn't even known about him for years and his sadness was mostly for Val herself. But Suzanne had been living and breathing, kicking in her cot, just beginning to smile and laugh... The anguish of losing a child like that must be almost unbearable.

'I'm sorry,' he said awkwardly. 'We've been racking our brains to know what to do. It's not

247

something we could keep quiet about for long.'

Tom's mouth twisted a little. 'No, I think we'd have noticed. It's all right, Luke. It's not as if you've done anything wrong, after all.'

'No, but you know how Val is. She hates upsetting anyone, and she knows it wouldn't be easy for Jo. And it makes it worse that she was the one who found Suzanne. She feels as if Joanna blames her in some way – says Jo doesn't even want to see her now.'

'It's not just Val she doesn't want to see,' Tom said sombrely. 'She's sent me packing too.'

Luke turned in surprise. 'What – not for good?'

'No – well, I hope not. No, she just can't seem to bear having me near her. She says I'm making it worse. And if I laugh at something – not that there's much to laugh at these days, the house is like a morgue – or make any sort of joke, she looks at me as if I'd betrayed her. She makes me feel like something that's crawled out from under a stone.'

'But she must know you're as upset as she is.'

Nobody is as upset as Jo is,' Tom said heavily. 'If they are, she tells them they can't be because she was Suzanne's mother, but if they're not she doesn't like that either. I just don't know what to do, Luke, and that's the truth of it.'

'It'll get better in time, surely,' Luke said. 'It must do.'

'That's what people say, isn't it. But it doesn't always work that way, Luke. There was a woman over to Sourton a few years back – she lost a child, and she took to her bed and never got out of it again. She died the year before last.'

'That won't happen to Joanna. She's got

Heather and Robin to think about – and all the family around her.'

'I hope you're right,' Tom said, without much conviction, and they were silent again.

'Are you all right yourself?' Luke asked after a minute or so. 'I mean, do you think you're getting over it?'

'Oh, I don't know. It's too soon, isn't it. There are days when I do feel a bit better – when I can look around and take a bit of pleasure in things. But then I feel guilty, as if I'm getting over it too soon, as if I didn't care properly. And Joanna certainly thinks that. That's why she gets so angry with me, and that makes me feel bad again, and before we know it we're both down in the dumps again. It wouldn't be so bad if we could both be miserable at the same rate, at the same time. But it's like a see-saw – if one of us is up, the other's got to be down. I don't see any end to it. And it makes you feel nothing's safe. You can't take anything for granted any more.'

'No... There *will* be an end, though,' Luke said, picking his words carefully. 'Nothing stays the same for ever. Things do change, even if it seems so slow they never will. You *will* both start to feel a bit better, and the children will help you. They're growing, and doing different things, and they need their mum and dad. And Heather won't even remember. Honestly, Luke, you won't ever forget little Suzie but you will be able to live again.'

Tom nodded. He stared at the ground for a while, then said in a difficult voice, 'So what are you going to do about your baby, Luke? I wouldn't be surprised if Mum and Gran hadn't noticed already – you know what they are. Do you want me to tell Joanna?'

'Is that going to make things worse for you?' Luke asked, and Tom shrugged.

'Can't tell. But it doesn't sound as if Val can do it. I reckon it had better be me.' He put out his hand suddenly and Luke took it, surprised and touched. They shook hands firmly, and then Tom turned away.

'I came out to walk up to the Stones. Reckon I'll go back now. Reckon Jo might be feeling a bit more like a talk. We don't like being at loggerheads, you know. But I'll remember what you said.'

'Just hold tight,' Luke said. 'You and Joanna have got a good marriage. Things are pretty rocky for you at the moment, but you'll be all right, if you just hold on. Well, that's what I think, anyway.'

'It's what I think too,' Tom said, and turned to walk back down through the woods.

Luke watched him go and sighed. Then he turned back and gazed again at the shack he meant to turn into a studio.

Maybe Tom was right, and it wasn't a good idea to take too much for granted, he thought. Maybe it would be best to wait until the baby was safely born.

'So what do I do now?' Val asked when he told her about the conversation later. 'He's probably right about Mum and Gran. They're probably waiting for me to tell them.'

'Maybe you'd better just do that, quietly,' Luke

suggested. Then the whole family will know, without making a big thing of it. It's disappointing, I know – we wanted everyone to be as pleased as we were. But...'

'Yes, I know. It's a pity, but it can't be helped. And they *will* be pleased. Even Joanna might be, once it's born, and there are a few months to go yet. Anyway, there it is, there's nothing anyone can do about it. It's just bad timing.'

'Not for us,' Luke said. 'It's exactly the right time for us. And we can't not start our family because of what's happened to Joanna.' He hugged her. 'You can't put other people first all the time, you know.'

'I just feel so sorry for her. And I don't want her any more upset than she already is. Oh Luke, why is life so unfair sometimes?'

'It just *is*, and none of us has the right to expect things to go all our own way. Things were fine for Tom and Joanna for quite a while, and now they're not. But good times will come back for them, in the end. And we've had our troubles too, you know.'

'So does that mean we can feel safe now?' Val asked, and he shook his head ruefully.

'I don't think anyone can really be sure nothing bad is ever going to happen to them again. We just have to take what life gives us, good or bad, and make the best we can of it. Talking of which, are we having any dinner today or are we just not going to bother?'

Val stared at him and then laughed. 'Of course we are! There's a casserole in the oven – can't you smell it?'

251

'I can,' he said, 'but I thought it was a mirage. Come on, Val, turn the radio on and let's see if there's anything cheerful to listen to. I'll lay the table.'

Val punched his arm and went off to the kitchen. She heard him whistling as he spread the gingham tablecloth over the table and set out the cutlery. He was right, she thought. You had to live your life the best way you could, and take it as it came. And she would go up to the farm tomorrow and tell her mother the news about her baby.

'I thought you might be,' Alice said when Val, having made sure that Joanna was out of the way, broke her news. 'Me and your Gran were talking about it the other day. You got that look about you.'

'I don't know what look that is,' Val said, slightly nettled that she hadn't been able to break it as a surprise. 'I hope Joanna hasn't noticed – or maybe she has, and that's why she's being so off with me.'

'No, love, she's not in a mood to notice anything about anyone else just now,' Alice said with a sigh. 'Too wrapped up in her own misery. Not that anyone can blame her – what she's going through is something no mother wants and every mother dreads.'

'Tom's going to tell her, when he finds the right moment,' Val said. 'He had a long talk with Luke yesterday. Poor Tom – I feel so sorry for him. I feel sorry for them both. But he says Joanna won't have anything to do with him half the time, and he just doesn't seem to know which way to turn.'

'Poor maid's half crazed with it,' Minnie said. 'There's nothing anyone can for her, not while she's like that. We just got to be ready to look after her, whenever her needs it.'

'I know,' Val said. 'I can understand it. I think we all can – but she won't let us. She says nobody else can know how she feels.'

Alice poured tea into a cup and set it by Val's elbow. 'Well, maybe we can't. We *think* we can, because we know how much we love our own little uns, but until us goes through it, we don't really know for certain. Joanna feels as if losing her babby makes her different from the rest of us, and she can't seem to get back to where she was before. Anyway, you didn't come here to talk about that. It's your babby we got to think about now. And you – how are you keeping? Have you had any morning sickness?'

'Not much,' Val said, smiling gratefully at the change of subject. It seemed so difficult to keep off Joanna and her loss, and she did want to be able to share her own happiness. 'I'm really well. I went to see Dr Latimer and he says I'm a model mother-to-be.' She felt her colour rise, remembering that she had had to confess to the doctor that she had been pregnant before. To her relief, he had taken the news calmly, without appearing to judge her at all, and she knew it would go no further.

'And when is it due?'

'The middle of October.'

'That's nice,' Minnie said. 'He'll be smiling for Christmas!'

Val laughed. 'And how d'you know it'll be a

253

boy, Gran?'

'Oh, I just do. I can always tell. But we'll do the wedding-ring test to make sure.'

'How often has it really worked?' Val asked curiously.

'To tell you the truth, my lover, I'm not sure. As often as not, we've forgotten what it said by the time the little one's born. But I tell you what we'll do, we'll write it down on a bit of paper and put it behind the clock. You lay back in your father's chair, now. We'll use my ring, I know you won't want to take yours off.'

'Don't forget the hair,' Alice said. 'To work properly, it ought to be on a hair from the mother's head.'

'Ouch,' Val said, pulling out a long hair. 'This had better work first time, I'm not pulling out any more.'

Minnie took off her wedding ring and threaded the hair through it. 'Lay back, now.'

Smiling, Val did as she was told and Minnie stood beside her and held the ring above her stomach like a pendulum. They watched as it swung to and fro.

'You don't think it's a bit early, do you?' Alice asked. 'I mean, she's only three months gone, it might not have decided which it's to be yet.'

'Oh yes,' Val said before she could stop herself, and remembering Johnny, 'you can tell at that age.' She stopped, feeling her face flood with colour, then added hastily, 'Or so we were told in our training.'

The ring had settled from its original swing now and seemed to be hesitating, as if unsure whether to continue or to go round in circles instead. The three women held their breath. For a moment or two it hung perfectly still and then it began, slowly but quite positively, to swing backwards and forwards.

'A boy!' Alice cried in excitement. 'Oh, Val, it's a little boy!'

'But I thought–' Val began, and stopped as the back door opened. Joanna, carrying the baby and with Robin close behind her, came in and stopped short. She stared at them and her eyes went to the wedding ring, still suspended on its hair above Val's stomach.

'What's going on?' she asked in a hard little voice. 'What are you doing?'

Val looked helplessly at her mother, and then at Minnie. They gazed back, equally disconcerted, but Joanna needed no answer. She knew very well what they were doing, and she turned her eyes almost accusingly on Val.

'You're expecting, aren't you?'

'Yes,' Val whispered guiltily. 'Jo – I'm sorry, I wanted to tell you – Tom was going to tell you...'

'*Tom* knows? And he's never told me? How long has he known?'

'Hardly any time – I don't suppose he's had a chance yet.'

Joanna gave a short, bitter laugh. 'Oh, I think he has. He's just afraid to, that's what it is, like the rest of you are afraid to. All laughing and happy – oh yes, I heard you, as I came over the yard – and playing about with wedding rings. None of you wanted to tell me because you thought I'd be upset. That's what it is, isn't it?'

'Well, yes, it is,' Val said unhappily. 'We did think it would upset you. And – well, we were right, weren't we?'

Joanna stared at her. Robin, bewildered and disturbed, crept closer to her and held her skirt in one fist, his other thumb jammed into his mouth. The baby, clasped against her breast, began to whimper.

'Yes, you are right,' Joanna said flatly. 'But then, you always are, aren't you? Val, the little saint, who can do no wrong. Well, I hope that what's happened to me doesn't happen to you, that's all. I wouldn't wish it on my worst enemy.'

She turned and marched out of the room.

They looked at each other and Alice sighed.

'Oh dear. I wouldn't have had that happen for the world.'

'Nor me,' Val said despondently. 'Poor Joanna. We've made everything even worse. But it does seem unfair that I can't be happy over my own baby.'

'And so 'tis,' Minnie said stoutly. She picked up an envelope from the dresser, where letters and bills were kept, and began to write on it. 'Don't let this worry you, Val. We all know Joanna's not herself, and when her feels better her'll be sorry. Just ride over it, and don't hold it against her.' She finished writing and got up to put the scrap of paper on the mantelpiece, behind the clock. 'Here, what's this?'

'Looks like a bit of paper to me,' Alice said. 'What do it say?

Minnie unfolded the second piece of paper and stared at it. 'We'll, I'll go to sea! I must have done this when Joanna was expecting the twins. I forgot all about it in the excitement when they were born.'

Val sat up straight. 'What does it say?'

'It says a girl.' Minnie said. 'A girl. So 'twas right that time. The only thing it didn't tell us, was that there'd be two.'

Joanna sat on her bed, feeding Heather. The baby had fallen asleep and she gently removed her mouth from the nipple, dried the milky lips with a muslin square and cradled her in her arms. She knew she ought to put her back into the cot now and tidy the room, but she couldn't bear to let the warm body go. She sat gazing down at the tiny face, trying as she did every day to memorise the smooth features, the peach-like downy bloom of the skin, the button nose with its minute nostrils, the almost transparent blue of the eyelids.

'Oh Heather, Heather my precious darling,' she whispered. 'Don't ever leave me. Please, don't go away, like your sister did. Stay here with me ... please...'

She thought of the scene downstairs – the shock of coming in and finding the three of them laughing and excited, her grandmother swinging that ridiculous pendulum over Val's stomach. She had known instantly what it was all about – she remembered the day when she had been the one lying back, with Minnie standing over her in just then same way. 'A girl,' she had announced in satisfied tones, and written it down on a piece of paper which she put behind the clock.

Was that piece of paper still there? Joanna knew

that she had never looked for it – never given it a thought. And which of the twins had the ring sensed, as it swung in its circle over her stomach? Had it meant Heather – or Suzanne?

It's all rubbish anyway, she thought impatiently, and I'm surprised at Val for letting them do it. She's a nurse, she ought to know better. And now she's expecting her own baby.

I ought to be happy for her, she thought. I ought to have been pleased and excited and given her a kiss. But I just couldn't. I had to be horrible instead, even though I hated myself for it. I just couldn't help it.

What must Val think of me? What must any of them think of me?

Maybe they couldn't think any worse of me than they do already, she thought hopelessly. Whatever they say – however much they try to pretend they don't blame me – they must think it was my fault. They must think I did something wrong, to let my baby die.

She looked again at Heather, and the grief of her loss flooded over her again. The skin of her face felt drawn tight with misery; her throat and chest and eyes ached with tears waiting to be shed. She let them fall, drawing the shawl over Heather's face to protect her from them and holding the muslin square to her cheeks to mop them up as they streamed from her eyes. A whimper of anguish escaped from her throat, and rose first to a keening moan and then a wail; and then, weeping now without restraint, she got up, laid the baby in her cot, and threw herself on the bed, crying her heart out for Suzanne, the child she had lost, the child whose smile she would never know; the child whose life had been taken away before she had had a chance to know what life could be.

Oh Suzanne, she wept, burying her face in her pillow to stifle the sounds. Oh my *baby* ... my dear, precious little *baby*...

Chapter Twenty-Three

'Now then,' Ted Tozer said. 'You hold the rope's end in both your hands, see, like this, with your right hand over your left one – no, not over it like that, above it on the rope. And then you put both hands on the fillet – that's the fluffy striped bit – and you pull the whole thing down together, let go of the fillet so that it can go up through the ceiling, and let your arms go up with the end. And then you pull that down and catch the fillet. Got it?'

'Easy,' Micky Coker said confidently. 'Can I have a go now?'

'No, you can't. It takes a long time to learn to ring a bell properly, and you're not going to ring like that to start with anyway. You're going to start by pulling it up.'

Henry and Micky gazed at him. They were the only two boys in the tower and had come along for an evening of special tuition, since normal practice nights were given over to the regular ringers, who were perfecting their own technique for Coronation day. Alf Coker had said he would come along too, but he'd been extra busy that day and was working late. He'd told Micky to pass on the message that Travis Kellaway might look in.

'How can we pull it up?' Henry asked. 'The bells are all fixed in those big frames you showed us just now.'

Ted had taken the boys up the tower to see the bells, hung silent and mouth downwards in the frame, with their wheels motionless beside them. He had allowed them to touch the bells but had warned them never, ever, to go up there alone or if the bells were 'up'. Neither of them had understood this but they'd said nothing at the time, just looked at each other, raised their eyebrows and shrugged.

Ted, who had known about bells ever since he was even younger than these two, and hadn't even realised they didn't understand, tried to explain.

'When you saw the bells just now they were "down". That means they were hanging downwards and you can only chime them.' He tugged on the rope of the nearest bell and it gave out a faint chiming sound. 'It moves the bell a bit, see, and the clapper just touches the rim of the bell. And the rope doesn't go up so it's safe for anyone to pull. Here, have a go.' He let both boys have a turn and they grinned to hear the bell respond. 'Now, when the bell's "up" it means it's the other way up, and it's balanced on the headstock and on that wooden stay I showed you – the piece of wood that's fixed on the headstock,' he added, seeing Henry's blank face. 'You can balance it up there then, and the stay prevents it from going all the way over. So you can pull it again, then, see,

260

and it swings over the other way and rings again. That's once on the fillet and once on the rope's end. But before you can ring it like that, you've got to get it balanced up.'

'How d'you do that?' Micky asked. 'Lift it?'

Ted grinned. 'No, you *ring* it up, like I said. You start off by coiling the rope up in your hands, right up to the fillet, and then keep pulling hard until it swings right up on to the balance. Only you got to be careful not to pull too hard, or you'll break the stay, and then the rope'll wind itself right round the wheel in a flash and you'll get pulled right up to the ceiling.'

The boys looked up at the ceiling of the ringing chamber, high above. Henry said nervously, 'What happens then?'

'Well, you let go as quick as you can. It's a long way to fall.' Ted took pity on them. 'It don't happen very often. I've only seen it twice in the whole of my life, and both time the ringer let go real quick and no harm done. But that's the only time you let go, mind. You never lets the rope out of your hand unless the captain tells you to.' He handed the rope's end to Micky. 'Now, you take in your coils and we'll make a start.'

Micky gathered in the rope and put both hands on the fillet. He gave a tentative pull.

'My stars, us'll be here all night if you don't give it a bit more than that,' Ted exclaimed, and pulled with him. 'That's better. And let your coils out gradual, see, and leave the fillet to itself, or you'll be pulled off your feet. The trick is to ring the bell, not let the bell ring you.'

'I thought you said bell-ringing wasn't hard

261

work,' Micky panted, heaving away at the rope.

'It's not, once you've got the bell up. Some are so heavy they need two strong men to get 'em up but once they're there, anyone can handle 'em. Almost anyone, anyway,' he added quickly. 'The tenor in Tavistock weighs twenty-four hundredweight.'

'That's over a ton!' Henry exclaimed. 'Do you mean to say one man can ring that all on his own?'

'Oh yes. Rung it myself,' Ted said proudly. 'But our tenor here, she's only just over twelve. Just a nice size for a ring of six.' He turned his attention back to Micky, who was now red-faced with exertion. 'Come on, tacker, you're doing handsome, but you don't want to let her swing so much. Check her in a bit – like this, see.' He put his hand on the rope again and gave it a tug. 'Let out a bit more rope now. Not too much or she'll be loose and fly all over the place. About an inch at a time, that's the ticket.' He kept pulling with Micky until the fillet began to bob gently. 'Now, I'll look after she – you just keep pulling on the end. Don't try to catch, because you won't be quick enough to let go. That's where the skill comes in. She's almost up now. Let the rope take your arms right up ... now pull down, steady, not jerking it like that or she'll bounce on the stay next time. That's when they get broken, see, when someone pulls too hard. Now, she's all the way up and I'm going to stand her, so don't pull any more.'

'Stand?' Micky asked doubtfully as Ted seemed to stop the fillet in mid-air and the rope stopped moving. 'What does that mean? Why has it stopped? Can we do it again?' He began to gather

262

in the coils.

'No! She's up now – if you try pulling with coils, she'll have you up to the roof in a flash of an eyelid, and a broken stay into the bargain. You must never, never touch a rope when the bell's up,' Ted said seriously. 'Not till you know what you'm doing. That's when they're dangerous. Remember what I told you about the stay. Take that away or break it, and she'll swing over and the rope'll go straight up through the ceiling.'

Micky stepped back a little fearfully. 'But it must be really hard to break a stay, surely.'

'Not that hard. It's made of ash, see. Ash breaks easier than oak.'

'Why not use oak, then?'

'Because if you bump the bell that hard, you *want* the stay to break,' Ted explained. 'If it didn't summat worse might happen. The bell might come right out of its bearings.'

'Coo,' Micky said, looking up again. 'Could it fall right down on the ringers?'

'Well, it might. So you got to be careful, like I said. Ringing's good, but you got to respect what you're doing and not treat it as a game. Now, how about young Henry having a pull? I'll lower the bell first and he can start same as Micky.'

He began to ring the bell, gradually gathering the rope into coils and explaining that he was now returning the bell to its safe 'down' position. Then he gave Henry the end and Henry, having watched Micky, took in his coils as if he'd been doing it all his life.

While he was heaving on the end, with Ted encouraging him, the church door opened and

Travis came in. He waited at the door to the ringing chamber, watching, and when Ted stood the bell he came in.

'Evening, Ted. I hope you don't mind me looking in.'

'You'm welcome,' Ted said graciously. 'I hear you done some ringing up-country.'

'Yes, I learned when I was about the age of these two here. I didn't come along straight away because I know you Devon chaps are very particular.'

'I suppose we are, a bit. Us likes our call-changes and us likes 'em rung proper. I take it you're a scientific ringer – method and that.'

Travis smiled. 'Well, yes, but I'm very happy to ring call-changes too and we care about our striking as well. I'd like to join you, if you've got room for an extra.'

'I dare say we could do with another ringer,' Ted admitted. 'That's why we're teaching these nippers.'

'I could give you a hand with that, if you like,' Travis offered, but Ted looked doubtful.

'I won't say that wouldn't be useful – Alf Coker was supposed to be here but he's got some extra work on – but you'd better come along of a practice night before we think about that. Your ways might be different, see.'

'Yes, they would be,' Travis said. 'We don't teach pulling up and down first, for a start – we teach learners to ring the bell while it's up, before we go on to raising and lowering. And we call the "fillet" a "sally",' he added with a grin. 'But I'd be willing to do whatever you want. You're the captain.'

Ted nodded. 'I'll lower this bell again,' he said. 'The boys ought to have a few goes, to get them in the way of it. Then maybe we'll go along to the Bell and have a pint, and you can tell me about your ringing. There's quite a few differences to get sorted out before you comes for a pull with our band, I reckon.'

'So is Ted going to let you join the band?' Jennifer asked when Travis told her about his visit to the tower. It was a bright, sunny morning and they had decided to walk from Sampford Spiney to Merrivale, have a drink at the inn there and then walk back by Vixen Tor. Travis said he had seen ring ouzels around the tor – 'like blackbirds in evening dress,' he'd told her – and Jennifer, who knew very little about birds, was keen to see one for herself.

Since their day in Widecombe, they had enjoyed several small outings together, mostly exploring the Dartmoor countryside which neither knew well and once or twice going down to the coast to walk by the sea, either along the broad stretching sands of Whitsand Bay or the cliffs and villages of Newton Ferrers and Noss Mayo. So far, they had kept their friendship quite discreet and not made it obvious in the village, although neither had any reason to hide it. But both preferred to take their growing friendship slowly, enjoying getting to know each other without having to run the gauntlet of interested eyes and gossip.

Travis had been telling Jennifer about his visit to the church tower and his drink with Ted in the pub afterwards. 'It was as bad as being interviewed for a job,' he said with a grin. 'I had to tell him how long I'd been ringing, what sort of ringing I did, where I'd been, what our bells were like – I felt as if I'd been through a wringer afterwards!'

'That sounds appropriate,' Jennifer commented, and he realised what he'd said and laughed.

'A thresher, then. I'd been chewed up and spat out. All I have to do now is go along on practice night – if I dare! – and show what I can actually do.'

'And will you be allowed to help teach the boys?'

'Oh, I doubt it. I learned by a different method, you see, and Ted wouldn't want me doing it that way. I'll give a hand if he wants it but I expect I'll have to do a thorough apprenticeship before I'm really accepted.'

'Don't women and girls ever ring?' Jennifer asked.

'I don't think they do much in Devon, though I dare say that will change as time goes on. There's really no reason why they shouldn't. I've known quite a few, and very good ringers they are too. There's even a Ladies' Guild – it started before the First World War, so there must have been some for a while before that. I think they had a bit of a struggle to be accepted, though.'

'Do you think Ted would let me learn?' Jennifer asked mischievously, and he laughed again.

'I don't think we'd better give him too many shocks! He's already half suspecting me of some sort of evil black magic because I'm a method ringer.'

'A *what?*' she asked, and Travis took her arm.

'It would take too long to explain now. We'll

266

leave it for a long winter evening when there's nothing else to do. Let's enjoy the walk – look at that view of Vixen Tor, with the gorse in flower all around it. The rocks look like an old man with a flat cap on.'

'They do. And just look at the white blossom on that blackthorn. And the primroses all along the path. It really is a beautiful walk, Travis. How did you know about it?'

'Why, Jacob told me,' he said in surprise. 'Didn't you realise? He told me it was where he used to walk with your mother.'

'He told you that?' They stopped and looked at each other. 'I wonder why.'

'I'm not sure,' Travis said quietly, 'but I think he may have wanted me to take you somewhere that meant something special to me – a place where he'd been happy.'

Their eyes met. Jennifer felt her colour rise and she looked down at her feet. Travis took her hand and she looked up again.

'I think Jacob has an idea how I'm beginning to feel about you,' he said.

Jennifer could find nothing to say. She searched wildly for words and mumbled, 'I – I don't–'

'You know too, don't you,' he said. 'Don't try to pretend, Jennifer. You know I'm falling in love with you.'

'Travis...'

'I am,' he said, 'and you know it. I'm even beginning to hope that you might feel the same way about me. Do you? Do you think you might?' He waited for a moment. 'Please, Jennifer ... say something.'

'Yes,' she whispered at last. 'Yes, I was beginning to realise – to think perhaps...'

'And how do you feel about that?' he asked. He still had a close hold on her hand. 'You're not upset that I'm in love with you?'

'Upset? No ... no, I'm not upset. But, Travis...'

'What?'

'I don't know,' she said helplessly. 'I don't know what to say.'

He looked at her. Her face was a deep pink, and her eyes bright, almost as if they were full of tears. He put both his hands gently on her shoulders and said, 'You don't have to say anything if you don't want to. You don't even have to think about it. Forget I mentioned it.'

'I can't do that. You've said it – you can't unsay it.'

'No, I can't, and I wouldn't anyway, because I meant it. But if you're not ready to think that way, we won't talk about it any more. I won't pester you, Jennifer, I promise.'

'It doesn't seem fair,' she said in a small voice.

'Nobody's talking about "fair". And I don't want it to spoil our friendship – that means more than anything to me.' He put one finger under her chin and tilted her face so that she looked into his eyes. 'We *are* still friends, aren't we?'

'Yes. Oh yes.'

'That's all right, then.' He bent his head and kissed her lightly on the lips. 'There. That's a kiss of friendship – nothing more. Now let's go on with our walk.'

They strolled on along the path, a little uncomfortable with each other at first, but before long their customary ease returned and they began to chat and point things out as before. But as they sat in the Dartmoor Inn a little later, enjoying their drinks, the memory of the moment drifted back into both their minds.

I wonder what's happened to Jennifer to make her so unsure of herself, Travis reflected, sipping his beer.

And Jennifer looked into her glass of lemon squash and thought: I wonder if I should tell him...

Chapter Twenty-Four

Maddy's plaster came off at the beginning of May, much to her relief, and she was able to feel normal at last. She celebrated by going to Burracombe for the weekend, by herself on the train. Stella and Felix met her at Tavistock.

'Just like old times,' Felix declared, hugging her. 'Remember when I came to meet you that first time and we couldn't get all your luggage into Mirabelle? I had to make two trips.'

'Ouch,' Maddy responded. 'I know I haven't got a plaster on any more, but I'm still a bit tender. And you'll be glad to hear I haven't got all my strength back yet so I couldn't bring much luggage this time.'

'You're only coming for a weekend anyway,' Stella said, ignoring Felix's murmur of 'That won't stop her.' She lifted Maddy's small case.

'Wasn't Stephen able to come this weekend?'

'I've no idea.' Maddy caught her sister's enquiring glance. 'You needn't look like that. We haven't quarrelled or anything. I just don't want him to think I can't go anywhere without him. I don't *have* to tell him every time I come to Burracombe.'

'No, of course not,' Stella said, with a glance at Felix this time.

Maddy walked along beside them both and handed her ticket to the collector. 'It's just that he seems to think he owns me. I've told him there can't be anything between us, and he agrees, but if I say I'm doing something without him he gets all hurt. So it's best not to tell him.'

'Yes, of course,' Stella agreed.

'And you don't have to agree with me all the time,' Maddy said crossly. 'I'm not made of spun glass. I quite understand that other people are entitled to hold their own opinions.'

'How very gracious of you,' Felix observed solemnly, and Maddy gave him an indignant glance, then laughed.

'All right, I was being pompous. It's probably the effect of living with a male Copley. You'll have to be very careful when you marry this man,' she told her sister. 'There are far too many clergymen in the family, in my opinion.'

'Which, of course, you are quite entitled to hold,' Felix said gravely, and they all walked out to the car, laughing.

'So how is everyone in the village? Getting excited about the Coronation? Are all the plans going well?'

'On the whole,' Stella said. 'There's some

270

trouble with Boadicea's chariot, though. Hilary can't find enough matching knives for the wheels. Miss Kemp says we could make cardboard ones and cover them with silver paper, but the children are all saving their chocolate wrappers for blind dogs.'

'Does it matter if it's silver?' Felix enquired. 'After all, if the dogs are blind they won't be able to see– Ouch. That hurt.'

'It was meant to,' his fiancée told him. 'You know perfectly well what I mean. Honestly, being a vicar doesn't seem to have improved you at all.'

'My parishioners are very fond of me,' he said with dignity.

'They haven't got to know you yet, then,' she said. They reached the little sports car and wedged Maddy's cases into the dickey seat, with Maddy between them. 'Are you all right there, Maddy?'

'Yes, but don't stop suddenly or I'll pop out like a cork.'

Felix started the car and they drove down the hill. The tall tower of St Eustachius, the only remaining building of the ancient Abbey that had once covered what was now Bedford Square, rose into the sky from a froth of salmon-pink leaves emerging on the beech trees that surrounded it. Across the square, the river Tavy, the colour of peat after a downpour the day before, surged under the bridge and across the weir, its rocky pools thronged with ducks, while oaks and beeches were bursting into leaf all along the left bank and people strolled along the path to the Meadows on the other side.

'I love Tavistock,' Maddy said. 'It's so full of

trees, it always looks beautiful whatever the time of year, and the river's lovely.'

'I like it when the salmon come up to spawn,' Stella said. 'It's such a wonderful sight to see all those silver bodies leaping over the weir, shimmering in the sunlight and making little rainbows.'

'Goodness me, you are turning poetic,' Maddy said.

'It's being engaged to me that does it,' Felix said smugly, and then sighed with annoyance at himself. 'Oh, Maddy, I'm sorry! Putting my foot in it as usual.'

'It's all right. I can't expect people to watch their words all the time.' She was silent for a moment, then asked, 'How's Joanna Tozer?'

'Still very low,' Stella said soberly. 'Some days she seems to be getting over it, but you've only got to say one wrong word and she's just as upset as ever. And you don't even know what the word's going to be. It's right one day, and wrong the next. If you're sympathetic, she says you can't possibly know how it feels for her, and if you don't say anything she seems to think you don't care. Everyone's terribly sorry for her, but it really is difficult.'

'I dropped in the other day,' Felix said. 'She's not one of my parishioners now, of course, so it was just a friendly visit, and after a minute or two she made an excuse and went upstairs. Alice told me she does that all the time. Apart from Robin and the baby, she doesn't seem to want to be bothered with anyone, even her own family.'

'And she's terribly protective of them,' Stella added. 'She hardly lets them out of her sight.'

'What about Tom? He was always so cheerful and happy.'

'Oh, he's doing his best, but I think he feels guilty if he makes a joke these days. It's a terrible situation. I can't think of anything worse than losing a baby like that.'

Again they were silent, Stella fearing that she'd said the wrong thing for Maddy. She stole a glance at her sister, but although Maddy's face was sad she didn't seem to be relating Stella's remark to her own loss. She looked thoughtful, and after a few minutes she changed the subject.

'Have you two set a wedding date yet? You were talking about Christmas the last time I heard.'

'Yes, we have.' Although they'd let it be known that they were thinking of Christmas, only Val and Luke knew the exact date, for Stella and Felix had agreed to wait until they felt Maddy was ready before announcing it to everyone else.

It looked now as if the moment had come, so Stella gave Felix a quick glance and said, 'We thought January the second. You will be able to come, won't you? I want you as my bridesmaid.'

'Yes, of course.' There was a tight, determined note to Maddy's voice but she smiled brightly. 'What about your dress? And mine too – what colour do you want me to wear?'

'Goodness, I haven't even thought about it!' Stella said with a laugh. 'I think you could choose that for yourself.'

'How many bridesmaids are you having? You don't want just one, surely. You'll want at least two little ones, so if you have a bigger one to go with me that means four to start with.'

'Four! But who could they be? We don't have any little girl relatives.'

'I do,' Felix said gloomily. 'Millions of them. Mostly cousins.'

'Well, I don't want millions of bridesmaids! And I really ought to have at least one from school, though how I'm to choose her without making everyone else jealous... Oh dear.' She sighed. 'It's starting to seem rather difficult.'

'Of course it's not,' Maddy said. 'Anyway, weddings are supposed to be difficult. Look, why don't you have the Budds' youngest girl – Maureen. They asked us to Rose's wedding, after all, and Jess Budd is a wonderful dressmaker, so there'll be no problem with her dress.'

'I'd like that,' Stella said thoughtfully. 'It would be a sort of thank you for all their kindness to us when we were little. But Maureen must be about fourteen years old now – she's not little.'

'All right, so you need someone to go with her, someone for me and two small ones. That's six–'

'*Six!*'

'–which is very fitting. You're marrying an important man, don't forget. Oh, I know it's only Felix really–'

'Thank you,' Felix said.

'–but he *is* a vicar, after all, and you're the village schoolmistress, so it will be a big event for the village. You've got to give them something to enjoy and remember. I don't think six is at all too many. In fact–'

'I'm not having any more than six,' Stella said firmly. 'I think four would be quite enough. It's just a problem deciding who to ask.'

'Well, who's your best friend in the village? Val or Hilary, I should think.'

'Val.'

'Then you must ask her. And—'

'But she's having a baby.'

'*Is* she?' Maddy said, instantly interested. 'How lovely. When?'

'The middle of October.'

'That's all right, then – she'll have got her figure back by January. So that's me and Hilary, Maureen Budd and someone about her size – one of Felix's cousins, you'll have to decide that, Felix. And then two little ones because they always look so pretty and everyone loves little bridesmaids. More cousins, or someone from school?'

'I don't know,' Stella said helplessly. 'I can't make these decisions all at once. I'll have to think about it.'

'And I'll tell you what else,' Maddy said, completely carried away by her own enthusiasm. 'You could have a rainbow wedding – everyone in different colours. Then everyone has a colour that suits them, and it would look so lovely, especially in winter.'

'It's too gaudy,' Stella objected, but Maddy overrode her.

'It's not at all gaudy. Rainbows aren't gaudy. It would brighten everything up. Which church are you having it in? I suppose it ought to be Little Burracombe, since Felix is vicar there now, but our church is so much nicer.'

'And I am a spinster of Burracombe parish, so it will have to be there,' Stella said firmly, then turned to Felix and added doubtfully, 'Unless

275

you'd rather it was in your own church?'

'I'd rather we sat down and talked about it when I can concentrate properly,' Felix said, manoeuvring the car tightly against the bank to let a pony and trap go by. 'These lanes are too narrow for important decisions.'

'Anyway, we're nearly there now,' Stella said, and a few moments later they pulled up outside Dottie's cottage. Dottie was at the door, with her usual beaming smile of welcome, and Maddy jumped out and ran up the path to hug her.

Stella and Felix turned to each other.

'Well!' she exclaimed. 'That went a lot better than I was expecting.'

'She certainly seems more like her old self,' he said. 'You know, I think we ought to let her have her head a bit over this. I know it's our wedding, but if she feels like helping arrange it all, it could do her a lot of good – and she won't really go over the top. She's got good taste.'

'Well, all right,' Stella said doubtfully. 'But – *six* bridesmaids! I was thinking of just having Maddy.'

'And nobody would have let you get away with that,' he grinned. 'This is going to be the wedding of the year in Burracombe!'

'Yes,' Stella said ruefully, visualising herself walking up the aisle at the head of half a dozen girls dressed in a rainbow of different colours. 'I think it will, if Maddy has anything to do with it.'

Maddy went up to her room and sat at the window, looking out at the village street. Dottie, waving aside all her protests, had arranged to sleep at

276

Aggie Madge's again, but just now she was busy downstairs, putting on the kettle and taking a batch of fresh saffron buns from the oven. In a few minutes, Maddy would have to go down and join the others for one of Dottie's lavish teas.

The news of Stella's wedding date hadn't exactly come as a shock, as she'd known they were thinking of Christmas time, but it had struck at her heart all the same. It would be almost exactly a year since she had first met Sammy, after all those years apart after their childhood together. And still not quite a year since he had died. It ought to have been her own wedding she was arranging, but now that wedding would never happen.

Oh Sammy, she thought, leaning her head on the side of the window. Sammy, Sammy, Sammy...

'You really have got the bit between your teeth, haven't you,' Stella said a little later. 'You won't mind if I make a suggestion now and then, will you?'

Maddy laughed and then looked a little guilty. 'I'm not taking over, am I?'

'Oh, I wouldn't say that. No, not at all.'

'All right, you've made your point. But it is fun, arranging a wedding.' Maddy stopped abruptly, then took a breath and went on in a bright voice, 'You will think about a rainbow wedding, won't you? It'll be so pretty. Let's see, what colours could we have? What *are* the colours of the rainbow?'

'Red, orange, yellow, green, blue, indigo, violet. And I'm definitely not having seven, so we'll have to leave one out.'

'Either orange or indigo, I think,' Maddy said

277

thoughtfully. 'Orange would be a nice warm colour for January, but not everyone can wear it. We'll have to consider which bridesmaid is to wear which one.'

'And before that, we need to know who the bridesmaids are. And who is going to make all these dresses? Jess will make Maureen's, but she can't do any more because they live miles away, in Portsmouth.'

'I could make Val's,' Dottie said. 'I'll be doing your dress anyway, my flower.'

'What about your cousins, Felix? Will they be able to get them made?'

'I'm sure they will,' he said, with the easy confidence of one who has no idea what is involved. 'So that just leaves the two from school. Their mothers might be able to do it, or...' He put on his winning smile and looked at Dottie.

'No,' Stella said at once. 'Dottie's already doing mine and Val's. And what about yours, Maddy? Are you going to ask Dottie to make that as well?'

'Only if she wants to,' Maddy said meekly. 'But I'm sure I can find someone at West Lyme to make it, and it'll be easier for fittings.'

'Well, we'll have to see who we choose. And how am I to do that?' Stella asked with a note of desperation in her voice. 'All those children wanting to be chosen! It's a nightmare.'

'No, it isn't,' Felix said. 'Look, there are two ways – you could either draw the names out of a hat or you could get the children themselves to choose. Ask them to vote for who they think should be your bridesmaids. Then you can't possibly be accused of favouritism.'

278

'They'll all vote for themselves,' Dottie said. 'You know what little 'uns are.'

'No, they won't. Well, some might, but that's only one vote. And you can put them on their honour not to do that. It's the fairest way.'

'She'll get the ugliest girls in the school,' Maddy said gloomily.

'I don't think *any* of them are ugly,' Stella said at once. 'Anyway, nobody chooses bridesmaids for their looks. They choose them because they're their friends or sisters or cousins, and they always look nice in their pretty dresses. I'd have all the children if I could, but since I can't I think Felix's idea is the best.'

'See?' Felix said, putting out his tongue at Maddy, who screwed up her face in return.

'I'm not going to think any more about it now,' Stella declared. 'It's months away and we've got the Coronation in less than a month, and we're not half ready for that. Everything else will have to wait until that's over.'

'You won't be able to stop thinking about it,' Maddy told her. 'And you can't fool me, anyway – I saw that magazine with pictures of wedding dresses on your chest of drawers. I liked the one with the sweetheart neckline myself,' she added a little wistfully.

'If that's the one with no sleeves, it's more suitable for a summer wedding, to my mind,' Dottie objected. 'You'll want something a bit warmer for January – something with sleeves – and you don't want a low neckline or everyone will see your vest.'

Maddy giggled, and Stella held up both hands.

'Stop it, both of you. I shall decide for myself,

when I've had a chance to think about it properly. *Which won't be yet*,' she added with emphasis. 'And now I've got to go round to the Barton and see if Hilary's had any more ideas about the knives for Boadicea's chariot. Are you coming with me, Maddy?'

'No, I think I'll go for a walk to celebrate having my plaster off. What's Felix going to do?'

'Go back to my lonely vicarage,' he said pathetically. 'Where I shall spend the evening lighting candles to see my way round the cavernous rooms and endless corridors, and starting at sudden noises...'

'Oh, shut up,' Stella said. 'You can give me a lift to the gates of the Barton. And don't forget we're all coming to lunch with you on Sunday, after church. I'll pop over tomorrow to prepare the vegetables.'

'That's the kind of romantic tryst we have these days,' Felix told Maddy soulfully. 'Peeling carrots and chopping up cabbage in the vicarage kitchen. But it's the nearest to domesticity I'll get until next Christmas.'

Maddy laughed and accompanied them to the gate. She watched the little sports car disappear along the road and then turned towards the river for her own walk.

It wasn't really a celebration, though. Even the plaster on her broken arm had been a kind of memento of Sammy and the last day they had spent together. In a strange sort of way, she missed it.

Chapter Twenty-Five

'Why don't you go for a walk?' Alice suggested. 'It's been a lovely afternoon and you've been cooped up indoors all day. It'll do you good.'

'You can leave the little uns safe with us,' Minnie added. 'Robin's playing with his bricks and Heather's fast asleep in her cradle right here beside me. We'll take care of them.'

Joanna hesitated. She still felt deeply reluctant to leave either of her children but Dr Latimer had told her that she ought to get out of the house each day for a walk, either by herself or with Tom or one of her friends. So far, she hadn't taken his advice but this afternoon she could think of no excuse.

'Go on, maid,' Alice urged, taking advantage of her hesitation. 'You'll feel all the better for it.'

'I don't know...'

'Just down to the bridge and back. Maybe along the river for a little way. See if you can bring back a few primroses and violets.'

There were plenty of primroses and violets along the hedges on the farm, but Joanna smiled faintly and nodded and turned to take her jacket off the hook. 'All right. I won't be long.'

'You take as long as you like, my blossom. The little uns'll be all right along of us.'

Joanna left the house and walked across the fields towards the river, avoiding the main village street. She still didn't feel comfortable about meeting people and having to stop and chat. They never knew what to say, and therefore neither did she. There wasn't anything anyone could say anyway – a simple 'I'm sorry, maid' and a touch on the arm were all that she needed and, for those who realised this, it seemed to set them off on the right foot, for Joanna felt that she was a different person these days and needed it to be acknowledged. Some people said too much, and either embarrassed her or reduced her to tears or, worse, anger; others said nothing at all, and that was just as bad because she hadn't had the acknowledgement she needed, to help move them forward. All in all, it seemed better to keep out of people's way.

She reached the little humpback bridge and leaned over it, staring at the narrow river as it scrambled over the rocks beneath her. It was so fast, and although it always looked the same, it was always slightly different. That smooth curve of water there, flowing endlessly over a rock rounded by years and years of washing, and then breaking into a million droplets of spray. At a brief glance it looked as if it did exactly the same with every passing second, yet if you stared at it you could see that it was changing endlessly. Like life, she thought. It changes all the time; nothing ever stays the same.

If only she had someone to talk to who really understood. But nobody in the village had lost a baby for years; even her grandmother couldn't remember such an event. There were two or three pathetic little gravestones in the churchyard, dating from the 1830s, referring to children of a year or eighteen months old, and Mr Harvey had told her that these had probably died during an outbreak of cholera. And there was a sad little memorial to a boy of four who had been trampled beneath a horse's hooves in 1927, as well as the headstone for the father and son from Little Burracombe who had drowned in a whirlpool in the Clam not long after the war – Joanna herself could remember that. But there didn't seem to be any babies who had died for no reason at all.

Nobody, Joanna thought, who had not lost a child in just this way, could have any idea how she felt. There was nobody to whom she could pour out her heart. Nobody to share her grief.

Well ... there was Tom. But they seemed so far apart these days. It was as if their loss had driven a wedge between them instead of bringing them closer. It seemed so cruel, and Joanna knew she herself was being cruel, that they could not turn and find all the comfort they needed in each other, but it just didn't happen. And yet, I still love him, Joanna thought. I *want* to be able to comfort him – I want him to comfort me. I just can't reach him. It's as if there's a glass barrier between us.

She heard a sound along the road and looked up to see Maddy Forsyth coming towards her. The other girl was walking slowly, her head bent, deep in thought, and hadn't noticed her. Joanna hesitated, then turned and began to walk quickly in the other direction, along the river bank and into the woods.

The movement caught Maddy's eye and she glanced up in time to see Joanna walking away from her. For a second or two she paused, wondering whether to follow her, but from Joanna's hurrying steps it seemed clear that she had seen Maddy and deliberately turned away. Obviously, she wanted to be alone.

As she hesitated, Joanna turned her head, looked as if she were about to walk even faster, then tripped over a root and stumbled. Maddy ran along the path and caught her arm.

'Sorry – I didn't mean to startle you.'

'It's all right.' Joanna disengaged her arm. 'I just looked round at the wrong moment.'

'Are you going for a walk?' Maddy asked, following her along the narrow path.

'It looks like it, doesn't it.'

Maddy bit her lip. It had been a silly question, but Joanna's tone was downright rude. She remembered what Stella and Felix had said, and felt a pang of sympathy.

Joanna was several years older than Maddy and although they had known each other by sight ever since the war, their paths had never really crossed much. Maddy had lived either with Dottie or at the Barton when it had been a children's home, and later had paid visits to the Napiers with Fenella Forsyth, while Joanna had come to the village as a Land Girl and worked on the Tozers' farm, living with the family. Still, they were acquainted and it would have been quite usual for two people going the same way to walk together, and Maddy felt sorry for Joanna and wanted to offer her sympathy.

'I heard about your baby,' she said after a moment or two. 'I'm so sorry.'

Joanna had been wanting someone to say those words to her, but the fact that it was Maddy, who was so much younger and had no children of her own, annoyed her even more. She spoke abruptly.

'Thanks, but I don't really want to talk about it.'

'It's all right. I'm not going to ask questions.' Maddy paused, then added quietly, 'I do understand a bit how you feel.'

Joanna stopped and faced her angrily. 'No, you don't! You've never had children – you've never even been married. You're young and pretty, you've got everything in front of you. How do you dare to say you understand?'

'And how do you dare to tell me I don't?' Maddy demanded, forgetting all her sympathetic resolve. 'Do you really think you're the only one who's ever lost someone? D'you think you're the only one in the world who has a right to be unhappy?'

'I've lost a *baby*,' Joanna said furiously. 'A *baby*. You *can't* know what it feels like – you just can't. *Nobody* can.' As Maddy, already sorry for her outburst, tried to touch her arm, she shook her away. 'Leave me alone. Go away and leave me alone.' She turned and began to walk away again.

Maddy ran after her. 'No, Joanna. Don't go like that. I'm sorry for what I said. You're right – I don't know what it's like to lose a baby. But I do know what it's like to lose someone I loved very much.' She drew a deep breath. All her loss and grief seemed to well up inside her and she couldn't prevent the tremor in her voice as she said, 'Sammy and I only got as far as being engaged, and we only had that for a few hours. I don't know what it would have been like to be loved by him properly, as man and wife, and I never will know.' Her voice broke. 'I'll never hold his baby in my

285

arms, for even a minute or two, and I don't know whether I'll ever have a baby at all. I can't even imagine wanting to marry anyone else.'

Momentarily overcome, she turned away and then, as Joanna began to speak, she wheeled back. 'But you *have* had them. You've had years of being married and you've still got your husband. You've lost your baby, and that's terrible and I really am desperately sorry about it...' She reached out again and this time when she touched her arm, Joanna didn't break away. 'But you do still have Heather, and you do still have your little boy. I know they'll never replace the little girl you lost, but you do *have* them. So ... so don't you think you've had more than me? And don't you think that seeing my Sammy run down and killed before my own eyes gives me some right – just a little bit – to say that I *do* understand what it's like for you?' She searched Joanna's face, then added in a wounded voice, 'And does *any* of it give you the right to be rude to me when I try to understand – to me and to all the other people who love you and are trying to help you?'

By the time she finished, tears were streaming down her face. Through the blur, she saw Joanna staring at her, her face white with shock. Maddy felt a pang of remorse and said brokenly, 'I'm sorry. I shouldn't have said any of that. I'm just making things worse. I'll go.'

'No,' Joanna said, putting out a hand. 'No, don't go. It's just that – nobody's ever talked to me like that before.'

Maddy felt for her handkerchief. 'I said I was sorry.'

'You don't have to be. I – I think maybe they should have done. Someone should have told me what a selfish bitch I was being.'

'No!' Maddy cried, her eyes brimming with tears again. 'No, you're not at all. *Nobody* thinks that. I'm the selfish one. You're right – I *can't* know what it's like to lose a baby. I shouldn't have said anything, and I really am sorry.'

There was a long silence. Maddy mopped her face and sniffed and blew her nose. Joanna looked at her and then, rather diffidently, reached out and touched her arm.

'You don't have to be sorry. I'm the one who should be apologising. I've been a beast to everyone, but – oh, it's all been so hard and I couldn't ... I couldn't ... oh, *Maddy!*' Her trembling voice gave way and her own tears, always so near the surface, began to flow. The two looked at each other, and without another word being said they each took a step nearer, and a moment later were in each other's arms, crying out all their heartbreak together as they had not been able to cry to anyone else in the world.

After a while, they drew apart and smiled a little shakily at each other. Maddy mopped her face and Joanna found her own hanky and did likewise. They began to walk on along the path.

'I've been horrible to everyone,' Joanna said at last. 'Even Tom, and I know he must feel just as bad as me. He doesn't seem able to show it, though.'

'It's because he's a man,' Maddy said. 'Men feel things differently. Ruth says the same about Dan.'

'Ruth and Dan? Who are they?'

287

'Sammy's parents. Well, Ruth's his stepmother really – he lived with her when he was evacuated and he always called her Auntie Ruth.'

'So *they* lost a child as well,' Joanna said.

'He was grown up, though. He was twenty-one...' Maddy stopped, swallowed and then went on, 'He was twenty-one the day he died.'

'Oh, *Maddy.*' Joanna stopped again and put her arms round the other girl's shoulders as the tears began again. 'That's dreadful. And dreadful for them. I don't think it matters when you lose a child, really – whether it's a baby or a grown-up it must be every bit as bad.'

'Well, he did have some life,' Maddy said. 'Not like your little one.'

They walked on again, slowly. 'I don't know,' Joanna said at last. 'I don't know if we can really say which is worse. It's just awful, whichever way it happens.' They were quiet again for a while. 'Have you been to see them – his parents?'

'Yes. I went last weekend. I've been several times. They seem to like me going.'

'And how are they managing? Are they getting over it?'

'I don't think they'll ever really *get over* it,' Maddy said thoughtfully. 'I don't see how you ever can. But they're gradually finding things to enjoy and be happy about. And they've got Linnet.'

'Linnet? A bird?'

Maddy laughed. 'No, although they do have a parrot called Silver and nobody can be really miserable with him about. But Linnet's their little girl – Sammy's sister.'

'He had a little sister?'

'Yes. She's about six or seven now. She absolutely idolised Sammy.'

'Oh dear,' Joanna said in a wobbly voice. 'It gets worse, doesn't it. Poor little girl.'

'Yes,' Maddy said, 'I feel very sorry for Linnet. She's such a sweet little thing. In fact–' She stopped and Joanna looked at her enquiringly. 'It's all right – just an idea I had. It's nothing to do with what we're talking about.'

Joanna nodded and they walked on. It was strange, Joanna thought, how at ease they were together now. She scarcely knew Maddy and had been fiercely hostile at first, and if anyone else had spoken to her as Maddy had she would have been furious. Yet, knowing that the younger girl had suffered her own loss and in such a brutal way had held her back from the savage retort that had sprung to her lips and, as Maddy had continued, her words had hit home. I've just been thinking about myself, she thought. Other people are suffering too, and for some it's even worse than for me. Maddy saw her sweetheart killed, and who knows what he suffered in those last moments. My baby just fell asleep in her pram and didn't wake up, and she never suffered at all.

She and Maddy had shared their grief and, at the same time, had forged a bond that she knew would never be severed. And now she had to start feeling her way back to her place in the family who loved her. She had to find her way back to Tom.

I still don't think I'm ready to forgive Val, though, she thought. Not that she's done anything wrong – but she was the one who found Suzanne, and I can't forget that. Not just yet.

Chapter Twenty-Six

'I don't see why us can't have a practice on our own,' Micky Coker said to Henry as they kicked their heels in the churchyard. They had arrived early, keen to start their next bell-ringing lesson, only to find a note on the door to say that Mr Tozer was up on the moor looking at the Dartmoor ponies he grazed there and was going to be late. 'We can both ring all right now.'

The boys had indeed learned quickly and were each able to ring their bell up, keep more or less in time with each other for a few rounds and then ring down again. Travis Kellaway had given Ted and Tom a hand, and one or two of the other ringers had come along too, including Micky's father. Tonight, however, only Ted was due to be there and he was late.

'I don't suppose us can get in,' Henry said. 'He keeps the ringing door locked.'

'Yes, but it's only like a railing fence. We could climb over that, easy.'

'I dunno. Mr Tozer did say we weren't never to touch the ropes unless he says so.'

'That was before we could ring,' Micky said impatiently. 'We know what we'm doing now. I bet he'd be pleased to think we were keen enough to want to practise on our own. I bet he'd want us to.'

'He'd have said.'

'He never thought of it,' Micky said triumphantly. 'He was in a hurry, see, and he just put that note on the door to tell us and never thought of saying we could start without him. He would have done, if he'd thought of it.'

They went into the church. The door was open from dawn until dusk but the door to the ground-floor ringing chamber, set in tall and elaborate railings across west end of the aisle, was padlocked. They tried it, just to make sure.

'We can climb over these,' Micky repeated, looking for footholds. 'Easy as winking.'

In a few minutes, both boys were on the other side, grinning nervously at each other. They looked at the six ropes, looped up on a central 'spider' that was fixed to the ceiling, and Micky unwound the cord from its hook on the wall and let the spider down. They took the ropes off and he raised the spider again while Henry tied the ropes up as he had been taught.

'We'm not really going to ring them, are we?' he asked uneasily.

'Well, we're not going to stand here admiring them.' Micky untied one of Henry's knots. 'Come on. This is the one I usually ring. You do the other one.'

'They'll hear us outside,' Henry pointed out, and Micky hesitated, but only for a moment.

'Well, that don't matter. They'll know it's us. It's all right for proper ringers.'

Henry continued to look doubtful, but as Micky coiled his rope and began to pull and he heard the bell chime above, the excitement of the adventure caught him and he coiled his rope as well, then paused.

'Wait a minute. I've got a better idea. Why don't we pull up the tenor and ring that? I bet we could.'

Micky stopped pulling so hard and the chiming ceased. He stared at Henry.

'That's a smashing idea. I bags first go.'

'It was my idea,' Henry began to protest, but Micky was already coiling the rope of the largest, heaviest bell in the tower. He began to heave but although the rope swung there was no sound from above.

'It's too heavy for you,' Henry said jealously. 'Let me have a go.'

Micky was red-faced and panting. He shook his head. 'Us'll have to do it together. Catch hold of the fillet.'

Henry did as he was told. They hauled with all their combined strength on the rope and suddenly the deep tone of the tenor sounded, making them both jump and almost let go. Micky let out a nervous giggle.

'Hang on tight. Ooh!' He yelped with surprise as the rope pulled them both off their feet. 'Let it out a bit.'

'I can't,' Henry panted. 'You've got the rope. You let it out.' It pulled them higher again and they clung on, afraid to let go. 'Micky, I can't hold it...'

'Pull it down,' Micky ordered, but that only made matters worse as the bell swung higher in its frame, dragging them both off the stone floor. This time, their feet did not touch the ground at all, and they dangled helplessly together, swinging in a panicky circle around the space of the tower. Every now and then their feet came near enough to one of the walls for them to push against it, but

292

their frantic kicks only made things worse.

'Stop it!' Henry begged, almost in tears. 'Make it stop!'

'I can't. I don't know how.' The bell was sounding loudly now. 'It's going up all by itself.'

'It can't! We'll never be able to ring it. We'll break the stay and go all the way up to the ceiling and fall down and break our legs. Oh, I wish we'd never come,' Henry babbled shrilly. 'I wish we'd just waited outside like we were supposed to. I wish I'd never thought of ringing the tenor. I wish–'

'Shut up!' Micky shrieked. 'Shut up and let go. It might stop if there's only one of us.'

'*You* let go. You're nearer the floor than I am.'

'I can't – I'm going too high–'

'What the *devil*,' a deep voice thundered from the other side of the railings, 'is going on here? What are you two up to, for God's sake?'

Startled, they almost did let go, but terror caused them to tighten their grip. Peering round, they saw Travis Kellaway glowering at them furiously. In another moment, he had climbed the railings. He reached up and snatched the coils from Mickey's clutching hands. 'Let go, you little fools. Let go at once.'

'We'll fall.'

'You'll be all right. It's only a foot or two.' Reluctantly, they loosed their fingers and dropped to the floor. Travis pushed them roughly out of the way and brought the rope under control. The bell stopped swinging and the deep note faded.

Travis tied up the rope and glared at the two boys.

'Now perhaps you'll tell me what you were

293

playing at.'

'We were early for practice,' Micky began in an injured tone. 'Mr Tozer sent to say he'd be late so we thought we'd start.'

'*You thought you'd start,*' Travis repeated heavily. 'All by yourselves, with no ringers present. Despite all you've been told about never coming here on your own, never touching the ropes without permission, despite all you've been told about the dangers of ringing bells when you don't know what you're doing, *you thought you'd start.*'

'We *do* know what we're doing,' Micky said indignantly. 'We've been ringing for ages now – weeks and weeks. We can ring up and down and rounds – Mr Tozer said we might start on a few changes soon. We'm proper ringers.'

'Oh, yes,' Travis said. 'You've proved that, haven't you, by half-killing yourselves. Do you realise what could have happened – both of you heaving away on that rope like that? You could have been swinging around halfway up the tower. Or suppose you'd managed to keep your feet on the ground and get it all the way up? You could have broken the stay. It's not funny when the stay of a big bell like the tenor gets broken. You could have been killed.'

The boys looked at each other. Micky muttered, 'It was only because Mr Tozer was late. We thought he'd be pleased.'

'Oh yes,' Travis said again. 'People always are pleased when you do things you've been expressly told not to do, aren't they? Especially when you might get hurt or even killed doing them.'

'We didn't expect it to swing like that,' Henry

294

explained, but Travis cut him short.

'You didn't know what you were doing, that's why. You're *not* proper ringers – you're learners and will be for a long time. That's if Mr Tozer lets you go on,' he added. 'I wouldn't be surprised if he banned you from the tower. Nobody can afford to have ringers who can't be trusted.'

Henry's eyes filled with tears. 'Don't tell him, Mr Kellaway,' he begged. 'Please don't tell him. Us *likes* ringing.'

'We'll never do it again,' Micky assured him. 'We'll never do anything like it again.'

'It's not up to me. Mr Tozer's the tower captain. And your father's the vice-captain, Micky. What do you think *he's* going to say about all this?'

Micky turned white. 'Are you going to tell him as well?' he asked in a small voice.

'I don't think I'm going to need to tell anyone,' Travis told him. 'The whole village will have heard that bell. I daresay Mr Tozer and your father are on their way here right now to find out what's going on.'

Micky gave a little squeak of panic and looked wildly at the gate.

'It's locked, isn't it?' Travis said. 'How are we going to explain that, do you think?'

Both boys were now in tears. Travis regarded them thoughtfully, then reached into the pocket of his jacket. 'As it happens I do have a key, to the outside door. Mr Tozer gave it to me the other day in case he had to be late.' He strode across to the big oak door that led from the base of the tower into the churchyard and unlocked it, swinging it open to let in the cool evening air. Then he turned back. 'Now look, I'll make a bargain with you. You've both been doing reasonably well as learners and you're keen. You've been bloody idiots this evening but if you promise never, ever – and I do mean *never, ever* – to do anything like this again, I'll say nothing about it. But one foot out of place and it'll be all up with the pair of you. Is that understood?'

They nodded, shaken as much by his use of a swear word as by his uncompromising manner. They looked at each other again and Micky said in a timid voice quite unlike his usual bossy tone, 'Yes, thank you, Mr Kellaway. And we'll never do it again – will us, Henry?'

Henry shook his head. His shoulders were still heaving with leftover sobs. 'I never wanted to do it in the first place,' he said, and Micky was so cowed that he didn't even scowl at him.

'Right,' Travis said. 'And now we've got that cleared up, we may as well start a bit of practice. You first, Micky. Show me what you can do – but not on the tenor, if you don't mind. The three's your bell, isn't it?'

Micky nodded gratefully and took the rope with fingers that still shook. He coiled them up to the fillet – or sally, as Travis always called it – and looked at his mentor.

'You can start,' Travis told him. 'Pull steadily and let your coils out gradually, just as you've been taught. And this time keep both feet on the ground.'

Travis locked the church and walked away down the path. Ted had not arrived and he'd spent the evening teaching the boys on their own. As they rested from their exertions, he'd told them about ringing 'up-country'.

'Scientific, Dad and Mr Tozer call it,' Micky observed. 'Why do they call it that, Mr Kellaway?'

'Because it's based on mathematic permutations, I suppose,' he answered, and saw from their faces that they didn't understand this. He took an envelope from his pocket and quickly wrote the numbers 1 to 6 in a row across the top. 'Those are the numbers of the bells, you see, in the order they ring in rounds, from the treble to the tenor. Now, in call-changes, just two bells change places at a time.' He wrote 132456 beneath the top row. 'But in "method" or "scientific" ringing, they all change places at every blow, according to a certain pattern which they all follow. And the patterns can be quite simple, or they can be very complicated indeed. Basically, that's all it is, but it does take quite a long time to learn and I don't suppose there's anyone who knows all the different methods. But once you know how to do it, you can learn most of them quite quickly.'

'It looks hard,' Henry said doubtfully as Travis wrote down more rows of figures, showing how the pattern evolved as the bells changed their order. 'Too hard for us.'

'It's not at all. You're quite bright enough to learn it.' Travis folded up the envelope. 'The hardest part would be persuading Mr Tozer to let a team learn it here. Devon people don't like method ringing very much.'

'If he did let us,' Micky began, looking at Travis with wide, imploring eyes, 'would you teach us?'

Travis laughed. 'I'd be pleased to, but I think it will be a long time before it happens. Meanwhile, you've got to learn to handle a bell properly – and treat it with respect,' he added sternly. 'It can be a lethal weapon if it's not used sensibly.'

'I'd like to learn method ringing,' Micky said, and Henry nodded vigorously. 'So would I.'

'Well, it'll be a while before you're ready so we needn't think about it just yet.' Travis gave Micky the envelope. 'You can have that anyway and see if you can work out the method. It's the simplest of all – Plain Hunt – so you shouldn't have too much trouble. If you can do that, I'll teach you Grandsire, where some of the bells dodge.'

'Dodge?' They looked at the ropes, and then back at Travis to see if he were joking. 'How do they do that?'

'I'll tell you what,' he said. 'We could do it in handbells. I'm sure Mr Tozer would let us borrow his. You can learn method on them while you're still practising rounds on the big bells.' He got up from the narrow bench that was placed along one wall for the ringers to rest on between peals. 'And now it's time to go. And remember what I said – always treat bells with respect.'

The two boys nodded and ran off, already chattering about their next lesson, and Travis smiled to himself as he walked down to the lych gate. He stopped there for a moment or two, lighting his pipe, and leaned on the ancient oak frame.

His mind was filled with thoughts of Jennifer Tucker. He knew now that he felt more strongly about her than he had for any of the other women who had passed through his life, and he was pretty

298

sure that she felt the same about him. Yet something was holding her back, and he wondered what it was.

She'll tell me, he thought, strolling across the green to the Bell Inn. She'll tell me eventually. I just wish she'd make it soon.

Jennifer Tucker was coming to the same conclusion. It was a long time since any man had affected her the way Travis did; for years now she had led such a quiet life, going to work each day in one of Plymouth's major department stores and returning to the little house in Devonport each evening, that she had scarcely had an opportunity to meet men, and she had told herself that she was happy that way. It wasn't until she had come to Burracombe, looking for the father she had never known, that her life had begun to expand.

Even so, she had never expected to fall in love. The prospect was quite alarming. Suppose Travis were really serious about her – suppose he asked her to marry him? Jennifer's heart quaked at the thought. It would mean a complete change in her life, of course – the move to Burracombe, dreamed about for so long, would become an instant reality and she would almost certainly have to give up her job in Dingle's. Even if they agreed to her continuing to work there (and she knew a lot of people would resent that, seeing her as taking a job from a single woman), there would be the journey into Plymouth on the bus every day. How could she be a proper wife to Travis if she was away from home nine or ten hours a day?

Most important of all, however, was the secret

she had carried within her for all these years – the secret that even Jacob had never been told, but that Travis would have to know if they were to be married.

You're jumping ahead, she told herself sternly. He hasn't asked you yet – and he might not be going to. The friendship which had deepened between them might never be any more than that. She might never need to tell him.

But that wasn't the point. Travis had a right to know *before* he decided to ask her. Once he knew, he might not want to marry her after all ... and it was unfair not to give him the chance to consider.

Jennifer was on the bus, on her way to Burracombe for the weekend, as these thoughts passed through her mind. The bus rattled across the cattle-grid and they were on Roborough Down, with Dartmoor spread out before them. She gazed across the broad fields to the hills and tors beyond and thought how beautiful it looked on this May evening and how much she loved it. All through her childhood, when her parents had brought her and her sisters – her half-sisters as she'd later discovered them to be – out on the bus for walks and picnics, this first view of the moor had caught at her heart. A warm excitement tingled through her body as she thought of living here always – in the village of Burracombe, which she loved so dearly, with Dartmoor all about her.

It had been her dream ever since she had found her father and Jacob Prout, and been left the cottage where Val and Luke were now living. One day, when they moved into the estate manager's house as Hilary had promised, she would live in it her-self, next door to Jacob. But now it looked as if Val and Luke wouldn't be moving to that house because Colonel Napier had said that Travis must have it.

And if Travis were to be living there...

No! Jennifer told herself severely. It doesn't matter *where* Travis lives – if he asked me to marry him, I'd live anywhere. I'd live in the shack that Val and Luke lived in before I let them the cottage. I'd live in a tent, if Travis wanted me to.

But first, she must tell him the truth about herself.

Chapter Twenty-Seven

Joanna was in the small sitting-room that she and Tom used for their own private space when Tom came in from milking that evening. She heard him go upstairs to wash and change, and then he peered warily round the door.

'Oh, Tom,' Joanna said sorrowfully, 'you don't need to look like that.'

'Like what?' He came in and shut the door behind him.

'As if you think I'm going to bite your head off.' She held out her hand. 'I know I've been rotten to you lately. I'm sorry.'

He was still standing just inside the door and she saw his expression change from uncertainty to cautious relief. He turned his head slightly, as

301

if half afraid to meet her eyes directly, and she felt a stab to her heart to think that this was what she had done to him, and an aching dread that it might be too late to break down the barrier which had grown between them.

'I really am sorry,' she said, with a break in her voice. 'I've just been thinking about myself and how miserable I've been. I couldn't seem to get over it – it's been so terrible. Losing our baby has been the worst thing that's ever happened to us.'

'I know.' He came across and knelt before her, and she took his hands. 'I couldn't imagine anything being this bad. She was so lovely – growing stronger every day, just starting to laugh and sit up. I still can't believe it happened.'

'Neither can I,' Joanna said soberly. 'I go and look at the pram a dozen times a day and it's always a shock to see that she's not there. We'll never be able to use it again, Tom.'

'No, we won't.' The pram had been put out into the small barn where it was supposed to be out of Joanna's sight. 'You shouldn't be torturing yourself like that,' Tom said gently. 'I'll take it right away – give it back to Miss Bellamy.'

She nodded, then said, 'Someone told me that one of the twins that had the pram in the first place – Miss Bellamy's nieces, I think they were, or maybe cousins – died. I didn't take any notice at the time, but I keep wondering...' Her voice shook and tears fell on to Tom's wrists.

He shook her hands and said urgently, 'Jo, sweetheart, you mustn't think like that. Even if it's true, the baby didn't die in the pram – Miss Bellamy told me they went to America. It's got nothing to do with what happened to Suzanne.'

'I know ... well, I think I know... But you know what they say about twins – if one dies... And knowing about the pram as well...' She looked up at him with eyes that swam deep in tears. 'I can't get it out of my mind,' she whispered.

Tom gathered her roughly against him and held her tightly as she wept against his shoulder. He laid his face against her hair, knowing that his own tears were soaking them both, and they clung together, sobbing out their heartbreak. At last she drew away a little and looked at him, and he gave her his handkerchief. She mopped both their faces, and even managed a tiny laugh.

'Look at us. All streaky. Oh, *Tom*...'

'I know,' he said again. 'It's been bad for us both. I've wanted so much to comfort you, but I couldn't seem to reach you.'

'I didn't think there was any comfort to be had,' she confessed. 'Nothing anyone said made any sense. The only thing that could have made it better was for Suzanne not to have died.'

'And that's just what we can't have,' he said sadly. 'We can never have our baby back, and somehow we've got to accept that and give all our love to the children we have.'

'Not all of it,' she said. 'There'll always be a part of my heart for Suzanne.'

'Mine too,' he said, and slipped his arms around her neck to draw her head closer to his.

'Oh Tom,' Joanna said as the tears began to fall once more. 'I've missed you so much.'

'But we're together again now,' he said, and made it a question. 'Aren't we?'

'Yes,' she said, and turned her head to him as he began to kiss the tears away. 'We're together again now.'

Maddy came home from her talk with Joanna feeling shaken and upset, all her grief welling to the surface once more. Sometimes, she thought, I wish I could just go away somewhere where nobody knows me or knows what happened, and maybe then I could just be myself, the old Maddy without a care in the world. But that Maddy never really existed anyway, did she? How could she have done, after losing her baby brother and both parents, and then being separated from her sister for so many years?

There had always been Fenella, though. Fenella had noticed the woebegone little girl at the Barton, and something about Maddy had touched her heart so that eventually she had adopted the child as her own. And she had left her with Dottie, one of the kindest people she could have found, to take care of her during the war while Fenella toured and entertained the troops. And after that she had taken Maddy abroad with her, showing her countries she could never have dreamed of visiting, introducing her to people she could never have dreamed of meeting.

Yet my heart was still with my childhood, Maddy thought. It was still the villages of Bridge End and Burracombe that were my home, even more than Portsmouth where I was born. That time is so bleak to me, so full of noise and dust; the bombing that destroyed our first home, then that horrible little house they sent us to, that was so dirty and stank of cats. And then losing even that, when our mother and little Thomas were killed. It wasn't until we went to stay at the vicarage at Bridge End that I began to feel safe, that I began to feel like a child once more. It's no wonder I fell in love with Sammy when I saw him again; he brought back memories of those happy times.

She wondered if there would ever be another man for her. It seemed impossible – yet people did fall in love again. Even people who had been happily married seemed to recover from their loss and found new partners. She wondered if she could ever love Stephen.

She could not even think of it now. Her heart was too full of Sammy and the sadness she could not yet shake off. She went back to Dottie's cottage and as she opened the gate she saw Travis Kellaway's Land Rover come to a halt outside Jed's Cottage, and Jennifer Tucker get out, laughing and happy.

Maddy turned away and went indoors.

Travis and Jennifer had planned to meet later that evening, when he was taking her to the cinema in Tavistock. Afterwards, they would walk up on to Whitchurch Down and watch the sun set from the Pimple.

The film was *From Here To Eternity*, starring Burt Lancaster, Deborah Kerr and Frank Sinatra. The audience sat transfixed but, gripping though the film was, both Jennifer and Travis were distracted by their own thoughts. They were quiet as they came out and got into the Land Rover for the short drive to Whitchurch.

305

'It was a marvellous film,' Jennifer said at last, as they got out of the car just past the church and began to walk up to the Pimple.

'I'm afraid it was pretty brutal in places,' Travis said apologetically. 'I hope it didn't upset you.'

'Well, not more than it was supposed to. And the love scenes made up for that.'

'Yes, the one on the beach was pretty steamy.'

They were talking in stilted voices, unlike their normal easy conversational tones. Jennifer had felt quite embarrassed sitting next to Travis as they watched Deborah Kerr and Burt Lancaster rolling together in a close embrace in the surf. Good though the film had been, she almost wished they'd chosen to see a Mickey Mouse instead!

The Pimple was a small, triangular building standing on a knoll on the top of Whitchurch Down. It was built of local stone and had a slate roof, and there were seats on each side. One faced the town of Tavistock in its valley, one across the moor towards Princetown and one across Whitchurch and Crowndale to the hills beyond.

The sun was going down over Tavistock as they reached it, and the skies flamed with scarlet, pink and orange. Narrow drifts of clouds hung above the horizon, lit by glowing colours as if a fire was burning somewhere out in space. The sun itself was a lustrous orb of deep gold, spreading its radiance over the dome of sky, so that the entire moor glowed with rich, sumptuous colour.

'Oh, Travis,' Jennifer whispered as they sat down, gazing westward over Tavistock and over the Cornish border, as far as Bodmin Moor. 'How beautiful.'

He nodded and they sat quietly for a while, watching the deepening splendour.

'It's like a wonderful painting, changing every moment,' she said at last, and he took her hand and turned her face so that their eyes met.

'Jennifer...'

'No. Don't say anything, Travis. Not for a minute or two. Please.'

'Jennifer, I must. There's something I want to ask you.'

Jennifer laid her fingers over his lips. 'Travis, before you say anything else there's something I have to tell you.'

He looked at her in surprise. 'What?'

Jennifer took a deep breath. 'It's something you have to know about me. Something nobody else knows – not even Jacob – but it's important. It may – it may make you change your mind about what you wanted to say.'

'I doubt that,' Travis said. 'I can't imagine what dark secret you could possibly have that would make me do that – but go on. And don't look so anxious. You're not going to tell me you've been in prison or anything, are you!'

'No, it's nothing like that. It's just that – Travis, I've been married.'

He stared at her. 'You've been *married?* When?'

'Years ago. It was during the war. I was in the Wrens and I met someone – a sub-lieutenant in the Navy. It was one of those whirlwind wartime romances. We were both over twenty-one so we didn't need to ask permission, and – well, we just got married. We didn't even tell our families.'

'I don't know what to say,' Travis said after a

moment. 'What happened to him? You're not still married, are you?'

'No. You see – we only had a week for our honeymoon. We found a little hotel and went there, and...' She stopped and took another breath. 'This is the hardest part, Travis. He – he wouldn't...' She stopped again, then went on determinedly. 'He wouldn't consummate the marriage.'

'He wouldn't...? You mean he wouldn't make love to you?'

'No. I mean, yes. It wasn't that he *couldn't*,' she went on, glad that the glowing colour all around them hid her blush. 'He just wouldn't. It was – it was awful.'

Travis shook his head. 'I can't believe it. A whirlwind romance and then... What was he thinking of? Why did he get married at all?'

'I don't know. I've thought about it over and over again and the only thing I can think is that he – well, he didn't really like women.'

Travis looked at her. 'You mean he was...?'

'Yes,' she said. 'I didn't even know about things like that in those days. We don't talk about them even now, do we? But he was very, very keen to get on in the Navy – his father was a rear-admiral – and if anyone had found out what he really was, he'd have been thrown out. And, of course, it's illegal so he might have gone to prison. I think someone was beginning to suspect, and the only way he could prevent the truth coming out was to get married. So he looked around for a wife and – well, he picked on me. He was very good-looking,' she added. 'And he was very nice, too. I mean, he was genuinely nice. It was easy to fall in love with him, especially in those days.'

There was a short silence. At last, Travis asked, 'What happened to him? Did you divorce? You can have a marriage annulled, can't you?'

'Yes, but that would have meant a scandal. In any case, it wasn't necessary. He went to sea immediately after our honeymoon and his ship was sunk. So it was all over, and I never told anyone, not even my mother.' She turned her head to meet his eyes. 'I had to tell you, though.'

'Yes,' he said, and she waited, wondering what he was thinking. Damaged goods, a lot of people would have said. How could any respectable girl have got herself into such a sordid situation? She felt the tears come to her eyes and blinked as she turned back to the sunset.

The sun was very low now and the sky afire. Flames of gold and ginger licked up from the narrow, ragged bands of cloud and the horizon shimmered, while at its at very edge there was a thin, barely visible, line of green.

In a moment, the sun would be gone and the colour would slowly fade. The magic would disappear.

Travis laid one hand against her cheek and turned her head back to face him. Their eyes met once more, but Jennifer's were swimming with tears and his expression was a blur.

'Travis...?'

'Don't say another word,' he said quietly. 'This is our moment, Jennifer. We'll talk about all that later, but for now I want it to be just you and me. I want to ask you this before the sun goes down, while the enchantment is still in the air.' He paused, then said very seriously, 'Jennifer, I love you. Will you marry me? Please? Will you be my wife?'

Chapter Twenty-Eight

The date of the Coronation was almost upon them. In London, the Mall was magnificently decorated, with great coloured hoops stretching over the road all down its length, and people were talking about spending the night on the pavement to make sure of a good position. Several coaches were going from Tavistock, and would be taking excited people carrying rolled-up sleeping bags and blankets, bags of sandwiches, cakes and fruit, and thermos flasks or bottles of lemonade or water. A few were going from Burracombe itself but most had decided to stay in the village to celebrate with their friends and families and either listen to the proceedings on the wireless or – for a few lucky ones – watch it on television.

Henry and Micky had been practising their bell-ringing with enthusiasm, and begged to be allowed to ring for the great event. Ted was doubtful about this, but discussed it with Travis.

'You been doing quite a bit of the teaching. What do you think?'

'I think it would be shame not to let them,' Travis said decisively. 'They've worked hard and they'd be very disappointed if they couldn't. It's something they'll remember all their lives.'

'Hm. They've only been learning for a few weeks, all the same. I know they can both handle their bells all right, but it's the striking I'm thinking about. Us got a good reputation for our striking and I don't want folk saying us couldn't make a decent team for the Queen's coronation.'

'I don't think anyone would say that,' Travis said. 'For one thing, Micky and Henry are going to make sure everyone knows they're ringing! And they're going to be useful members of your team, you know. You don't want them put off.'

'No reason why they should be! Why, when I was a tacker learning to ring, I wasn't allowed to ring on Sundays or for weddings and any other services for nigh on two years. I had to come along, mind, but I had to sit and watch all that time. *And* my dad was tower captain.'

'Yes, but that was quite a while ago, wasn't it? I'm not sure today's youngsters have got the patience.'

'Haven't got the discipline, you mean,' Ted growled. 'Allowed too much freedom, if you ask me. Even a bloke like Alf Coker, who you'd think would know better, lets that boy of his do more or less what he likes. Still, that's the way it seems to be going these days and there's not much chaps like me can do about it.'

'Probably not,' Travis agreed, hiding a smile. The idea of Alf Coker letting Micky do as he liked was a new one to him. 'So are you going to let them ring?'

'I suppose so. They can have a few rounds, early on. They can't join in for the main peals, mind,' Ted warned him. 'And there's to be none of that

311

scientific stuff you're teaching them on my handbells.'

Travis laughed. 'I can promise you that! The whole team has to know what they're doing – and anyway, Micky and Henry are nowhere near ready. I can't see you ever allowing it in Burracombe,' he added, but Ted pursed his lips judiciously.

'We might think about it some day. It don't sound too bad on the handbells. Quite pretty, at times. And it comes on the wireless sometimes, on *Bells on Sunday*. It can sound all right, if they strikes their bells proper.'

Travis went off to tell the boys the good news. As he walked through the village he met Jackie Tozer.

'Hullo, Jackie. Not in Plymouth today?'

'No, I've got two days off so I'll be here tomorrow as well. I'm looking forward to it.'

'Really? I'd have thought you might rather be in Plymouth – I'm sure their celebrations will be much more sophisticated than we can manage here.'

'No, I wanted to be at home. It's fun when everyone gets together. I wouldn't want to come back here to live,' she added quickly. 'I love being in Plymouth. In fact, I've had some rather good news – only I'm not quite sure how to tell Jennifer. You're friends, aren't you – maybe you could tell me what to say.'

Travis looked at her in surprise. He and Jennifer had agreed to keep their news quiet for a week or two, and as far as he knew she hadn't mentioned it to Jackie. In fact, Jackie had been one of her concerns since she was worried about where the girl would live if she gave up the house in Devonport. It was only rented, so it would probably still be available, but a young girl like Jackie wouldn't want to take it on.

'What is it?' he asked.

'Well, I've been offered a living-in job at the hotel. It was what I wanted all along but I couldn't have it straight away in case I didn't stay. But the housekeeper says I'm doing well and I've been given promotion!' Jackie's eyes were sparkling with excitement. 'The only thing is, I don't want to upset Jennifer – she's been ever so kind to me and I don't want her to think I don't like living with her. What do you think?'

'Oh, I shouldn't worry,' Travis said gravely. 'I'm sure she's enjoyed having you with her, but she always knew it wasn't for ever. I don't think she'll be at all upset. She'll be pleased for you. I think you should tell her straight away.'

'Do you really? I will, then.' Jackie glanced past him and along the street. 'Oh, there's Vic,' she added in a nonchalant tone. 'That's lucky – there's something I need to ask him. See you at the sports tomorrow, Mr Kellaway.' And she skipped past him, doing her best to look as if the meeting with Vic was purely coincidental.

Travis grinned and walked on. So that little romance was on again, was it? He knew they'd been keen on each other until Jackie had gone to work in Plymouth but it had apparently fizzled out when she began to get too independent for the possessive Vic. He wondered how Vic would feel about her news. Vic himself worked in Plymouth, so as far as Travis could see there ought to be no problem, but Jennifer had told him that

313

the young man had objected to the idea of taking his girl out for an evening in Plymouth and then coming back on the bus alone. It did rather destroy the romance, she'd said with a smile.

Val came out of her gate at that moment and gave him a friendly wave. He quickened his step.

'Hullo, Val. You're looking blooming.'

'Everyone says that. I don't know why they all use the word "blooming".' She looked down at her figure, which was beginning to bulge in what she considered a most satisfactory manner. 'Or maybe I do! How are you, Travis?'

'I'm blooming too, although perhaps not in the same way as you are! In fact, everyone seems happy at the moment. I suppose it's because the whole country is celebrating.'

'Well, not quite everyone,' Val said ruefully. 'Our Joanna's still suffering. But there doesn't seem to be anything we can do about that. I hear the Cherrimans are moving out soon, by the way.'

'Are they?' Travis asked in surprise. 'I didn't know that. Neither Hilary nor her father have said anything to me about it.'

'I don't think they knew until yesterday. Hilary came down to tell me yesterday evening. She'd promised the house to me and Luke, you remember.'

'Yes,' Travis said. 'I remember. So when will you be moving in?'

'Oh, we're not,' Val said, surprising him again. 'The Colonel says you've got to have it, and anyway we're happy where we are. We've got two bedrooms, so it's quite big enough for us.'

'But doesn't Luke use one as his studio?'

314

'Yes, but he's going to use the charcoal-burner's cottage – that shack on the way up to the Standing Stones. Didn't you know?' Travis shook his head. 'We've been doing it up. It's ideal for him and we can take the baby there as well, for picnics.' She smiled at him. 'So it looks as though you'll be the one to be moving in!'

She walked briskly on towards the village shop, and Travis stood looking after her, bemused.

Jackie's news, only a few moments earlier, had set him thinking again about his own living arrangements. Until now, he had been lodging at one of the tenant farms, but obviously when he and Jennifer were married that wouldn't do at all. Colonel Napier had told him that as soon as the Cherrimans had moved out of the estate house and back to their own home in Plymouth, which had been requisitioned during the war, he would be given that, but Travis had been aware that Hilary was against this, having promised it to Luke and Val. And now that Val was expecting their first baby, he'd been sure they'd be wanting something bigger than Jed's Cottage.

There was nowhere else vacant in the village or on the estate, and Travis was impatient to be married. He and Jennifer were both in their thirties and he knew she wanted a family – so did he, for that matter. They really couldn't afford to wait long and the problem had been on his mind since he'd first decided to ask her to marry him.

And now, as if by magic, it had been solved. The Cherrimans' house – which had always been intended for a manager – was soon to become vacant and surely Hilary would not begrudge it

315

to him now, especially as he was to be married, and Val and Luke no longer wanted it.

There must be something in the air, he decided as he walked on. The whole country is celebrating, and things are turning out right for everyone.

Nothing could ever turn out right for everyone at once, however, and for Joanna Tozer nothing had really changed.

She and Tom were closer again, of course, but there were still days when Tom seemed unreasonably cheerful and Joanna resentful of his ability to set his grief aside. On those days, she had to forcibly remind herself that he was just as upset and missed their baby just as much, but it was hard to believe it as she heard him whistling about the yard or making one of his silly jokes. One day, a week or so earlier, she had gone to talk to Basil Harvey about it.

'I can't bear to see people smiling or hear them being happy,' she said as she sat in the Vicarage sitting-room. 'I feel as if I want to drag them all down to be as miserable as me. I know it's selfish, but I can't seem to help it.'

'My dear, you mustn't expect too much of yourself,' he said. 'You've had a terrible loss and it will take you a long time to get over it. And it's no good trying to force it. You have to let it happen in its own good time. In *your* own good time.'

'But I'm making everyone else miserable,' she said despondently. 'I'm spoiling things for the whole family. And it's Val I feel worst about. I'm spoiling it for her, just when she ought to be so happy and excited.'

'I'm sure she understands,' he said gently. 'She knows you can't help it, and she won't let it spoil her happiness.'

'I don't see how she can help that, though. Having someone scowl at her every time she comes to her own home – sometimes I can't even bear to be in the same room as her. I know it's not her fault, but I just can't stop myself. I have to get up and walk out, or I'd scream.'

Basil Harvey sighed. He had come across a good many difficult situations in his time, but this was one of the worst. Here were two young women who basically loved each other, yet caught in a trap of misery that neither had wished for or caused. It wasn't as if they could simply agree not to meet – they were part of the same family. They would meet over and over again, for the rest of their lives.

'Time is the only thing that will help you,' he said. 'Time and our Lord, of course. If you can just hold Val in your prayers, as I know she holds you ... I promise you, it *will* get better.'

Joanna looked at him hopelessly and he patted her hand.

'I know it's difficult for you to believe me. Just try to remember it. Just hold on, Joanna. You're a brave young woman – a very brave young woman.'

'I don't feel brave.'

'You are, all the same. And everyone knows it, and loves you. We're all here to help you, Joanna, whenever you need whatever we can offer.'

Joanna nodded bleakly and stood up. She thanked the vicar and went out. But her heart was just as heavy as when she had arrived, and

317

Basil found his heart heavy too as he watched her go and wondered what more he could have said and done.

Chapter Twenty-Nine

The day dawned at last – not bright and sunny, as everyone had hoped, but grey and drizzly and even a bit cold for early June. But nothing was going to dampen the spirits of the British on this day, especially when they heard the news on the wireless.

'*Everest Conquered!*' George Sweet was first out in the street, just after seven o'clock, but he was quickly joined by a small crowd of excited villagers. 'On the very day of the Coronation! The British really are on top of the world.'

'It must have been a day or two ago, though,' Bert Foster argued. 'They'd never have got the news out that quick. I mean, someone must have got down the mountain pretty quick to get to a telephone. It stands to reason...'

George flapped an impatient hand in his face. 'Oh, shut up, Bert. They've got radio, haven't they? They can send these things round the world in a matter of minutes. And there's a time difference too, don't forget. I reckon it was early today – their time anyway.'

'Are they ahead of us or behind?' Bert began, but George had turned away. 'Anyway, who says it's the British? This chap Hillary, he's from New

Zealand, isn't he? And that other man, Tiger Tenzing, he's an Indian.'

'He's a Sherpa,' Alf Coker said. 'I don't think they're Indians, as such.'

'Well, whatever he is, he's not English and neither's Hillary.'

'Who says I'm not English?' Hilary Napier enquired, clattering into the group at that moment on her horse, Beau. 'Oh, you mean Edmund Hillary? Well, New Zealand's part of the Commonwealth, so I think we can claim him. Anyway, it's wonderful news, isn't it. They must be very proud. I wonder if anyone will ever manage to climb it again.'

'Shouldn't think so,' Bert said, still nettled by the argument. 'It's been done now, hasn't it? Not much point in doing it again.'

'It's a tremendous thing to hear about on Coronation Day, anyway,' Hilary said. 'And isn't the village looking marvellous?'

They stood for a moment looking about them. All the hard work of the last few months had come to fruition and the rather grey morning was brightened by streams of red, white and blue bunting strung between all the cottages and the displays of flowers in the gardens. It was surprising how many red, white and blue flowers could be found, and such plants as yellow roses, which their owners had refused to uproot, seemed only to enhance the festive air. Union Jacks (no amount of correction by Mrs Warren could persuade the villagers to call them Union Flags) hung from several upstairs windows, while the lower ones were festooned with striped ribbons and cardboard crowns. Quite a few people had woven ribbon into their garden fences as well and the Bell Inn was a glory of patriotism. Dottie's tubs, painted bright blue to set off the red and white begonias she had planted, made clumps of brilliant colour against the enormous flag that Bernie and Rose had spent afternoon after afternoon (their only time off) making from half a dozen old bed sheets, sewn together and painted in rather wobbly stripes. It hung across the entire front of the pub, drooping a little lower than they had intended so that it brushed the faces of the regulars as they went in and out. But nobody minded. It was almost as good as being brushed by the Royal Standard that they knew would be flying from the roof of Buckingham Palace. It was the flag of the Queen and her country and, on this day of her coronation, everyone was filled with a fervent pride.

At that moment, the bells began to ring. Like everyone else, Ted Tozer and his band had risen early and got as many of the day's jobs out of the way as they could. Surprised cows found themselves in their byres earlier than usual and poultry were gratified to be let out of their coops and given their feed at first light. Only essential tasks would be done today, just as at Christmas.

Constance Bellamy bustled along at that moment, resplendent in her best dark green costume and matching hat with a feather in it. This outfit had appeared every Sunday for almost as long as anyone could remember (Jacob Prout said he could remember her wearing a red one when he was a boy, but nobody really believed him) and today she had embellished it with a buttonhole made of red and white carnations bound in blue ribbon. She paused by the little group and automatically stroked Beau's nose.

'Off to church for the early service, Miss Bellamy?' Hilary asked, and she nodded.

'It will be nice to have half an hour of quiet before everything starts. There'll be plenty to do later on. I suppose you'll all be coming into church later, to hear the broadcast?'

'Those of us that aren't invited up to Mrs Warren's or the Barton to see it on the television,' Bert Foster said a little resentfully. 'Got their own posh friends coming in.'

Hilary flushed, and Miss Bellamy said severely, 'And when was the last time you invited either the Squire or Mrs Warren into *your* house, Bert? They both give a lot to this village, one way and another, but I don't see you doing much more than take. Anyway, I shall be going to the church to hear it myself, and I hope we'll see the rest of you there. We can join in all the hymns they're singing at the Abbey and it'll be almost as good as being there in person.'

She marched off and George Sweet grinned. 'That's you told, Bert, and I must say 'tis the first time I've ever heard Miss Bellamy side with Mrs Warren. At daggers drawn, they be usually.'

'That's because them sort always hangs together,' Bert said in a grumbling tone, but George flapped a hand at him again.

'Oh, put a sock in it. What's wrong with you, got out of bed the wrong side this morning?'

'Got out of the wrong bed, more like,' someone said with a snigger, and Bert turned furiously,

321

but George stepped in again.

'And that's enough of that sort of talk! We don't want none of that here, specially today. This is meant to be a happy day – us oughtn't to be bickering even before breakfast time.'

The others agreed and turned away, some to follow Miss Bellamy to church, some to go back to their homes and prepare for the busy day ahead. Hilary rode on through the village street to the turning to the Barton, meeting Val at the gate.

'Hullo. Where have you been, so bright and early?'

'Oh, just out for a walk,' Val said. She was looking pale and tired, and Hilary eyed her anxiously.

'Are you all right? It's a bit early for walking, isn't it?'

'I like it early,' Val said defensively. 'Anyway, I woke up and felt like a walk. There's nothing wrong with that, is there?'

'Of course not,' Hilary said. 'Val, what's the matter? Can't you tell me? I can see something's upsetting you.'

Val hesitated, then shrugged. 'Oh, it's Joanna. She can't seem to forgive me for being the one to find little Suzanne that day. And since she found out that I'm pregnant too...'

'But that's not your fault! Well – you know what I mean. You couldn't help Suzanne dying, poor little mite, and you being pregnant is nothing to do with it. It's not as if you've done it to hurt her. I'm not even sure why it should,' she added.

'I don't know *why*, either, but I knew it *would* – that's why I didn't tell the family until I had to. I was going to tell them that day, you know – on

Easter Sunday. And it's made everything so awkward. She won't speak to me, and if I go to the farm she walks out of the room as soon as I walk in – it's making a dreadful atmosphere, it's upsetting Mum and I feel as if all my own pleasure in it is being taken away from me. And that makes me angry, and being angry makes me feel guilty, because I know she can't really help it. It's still only a few weeks and she hasn't had any time to get over it yet. Well, she never will get over it completely.'

'Yes, I see,' Hilary said thoughtfully. 'And it must all be making her feel even more miserable, because I expect she feels guilty as well. Joanna's a good sort really.'

'Of course she is, and we've always got on really well before. As for poor Tom, he hardly knows which way to turn. He feels sorry for me but he's got to be loyal to Jo, and he's as miserable as she is about the baby. It's a dreadful mess, Hil.'

'And it's keeping you awake,' Hilary said sympathetically. 'I'm really sorry, Val, but you know, you've got to look after yourself too. You can't let it make you ill. You've got your own baby to think about. You need your rest. What are you and Luke doing today?'

'Oh, going to the church for part of the service, and then down to the field. I'm doing teas and Luke's helping organise the races. He says he'll have a go at the greasy pole as well.'

'That's something to look forward to then,' Hilary said with a grin. 'And what about Joanna and Tom? Will they be there too?'

Val sighed. 'I don't think so. I can't see Joanna

323

wanting to join in anything in her present state, and Tom won't go without her. Oh Hil, it's not just for myself I'm upset – it's for *them*. I want to be able to help them, to give them some support, but I can't get near. That's the worst of it. My own brother and sister-in-law and I can't go and give them a hug and just be *with* them.'

Hilary hesitated for a moment, then said diffidently, 'Have you thought of telling her about the baby you lost? It might help her to believe that you understand her feelings. It seems to me that that's one of the worst parts for Joanna – the thought that nobody really understands what she's going through. And if you confided in her – trusted her with your own story... Well, it might help.'

Val stared at her. 'Tell her about Johnny? But he was never properly born, Hil. It's not the same at all.'

'He was still your baby,' Hilary said quietly. 'And you loved him, and grieved for him.'

'I still do.'

'Well, it's for you to decide.' There was another brief silence, then Hilary added, 'I'll have to go, Val, I've kept Beau standing too long as it is. And you don't have to take any notice of me – I've never had a baby at all, and never likely to at the present rate. If there's anyone not qualified to give advice, it must be me!'

She rode on up the long drive, her face thoughtful. She had still not fully resolved her issues with her father. Although she had come to terms with his gift to Little Burracombe, she still resented the fact that he hadn't told her about it beforehand. It was clear to her now that she would never, try as she might, take the same place in his mind, and enjoy the same respect, as her brother Baden would have done. It just wasn't in him to feel the same about a daughter as about a son. Expecting it was expecting the impossible, and resenting that was forming a canker in her heart and mind, a canker that wasn't unlike the one forming in Joanna Tozer's heart and mind about Val. The circumstances and the causes were different, but the result was the same: a hard little nub of bitterness that wouldn't go away, and might grow and spread its poison through their whole lives.

What was to be done about it? She thought about it as she took Beau into his stable and began to remove his tack. Either you have to get over it, she told herself, or you have to do something else. But it wasn't just the gift, was it? It was the whole thing about the estate – the way her father still insisted on treating Travis as senior to her, simply because he was a man. The way he only included her in their discussions because she refused to be left out. The way he looked first at Travis when a decision needed to be made. Oh, not as openly as he used to do, much more subtly – possibly he wasn't even entirely aware of it himself – but it was there just the same. That underlying belief that a woman could not really do what he considered to be a man's job; that she was just filling in time while waiting for a husband to come along.

Well, it looks as if we're going to wait a long time before that happens, she thought, giving Beau a brisk rub down. She hadn't missed the increasing closeness between Travis and Jennifer over the past few weeks, and although she would have strenuously denied any hopes of her own in that direction, she knew that their friendship had come to mean a lot to her, and she might well have let it develop further, if Jennifer hadn't come into his life.

Always assuming *he'd* wanted it to go any further, she reminded herself, and tidied up quickly, determined to put all her problems out of her mind for the day. As someone had been saying as she rode down the village street, this was meant to be a happy day and she knew that it meant a lot to her father. She would not let her own petty resentments spoil it for him.

The church was full by the time the short service to be held before the broadcast began. Most villagers had been listening to their radios since early morning, when the BBC commentators had been describing the scenes outside Buckingham Palace and along the Mall on the route to Westminster Abbey. People had been camping out on the pavement all night, caring nothing for the drizzling rain in their excitement. The decorations were spectacular enough to keep them awed as daylight dawned and although those listening to the radio couldn't see them, the commentators' descriptions brought the scene to life.

At the Barton, and in a few houses – Joyce Warren's, the doctor's and one or two others – everything could be seen on the new television sets. The screens were only a few inches across and Henry Warren had bought a large magnifier to fix over his, so that everyone in the room could see, but owing to its strange green tinge and the distortion caused by the curvature of the glass, it looked rather as if the whole thing were taking place under the sea and after a while Joyce took it off again. Gilbert Napier had bought a rather more expensive set, and he and Hilary and a few friends sat in front of it watching as the State coach left Buckingham Palace and drove slowly through the cheering crowds; but as the time grew nearer to the beginning of the service itself, Hilary declared her intention of going to the church.

'Someone ought to represent the family,' she pointed out when her father began to protest. 'And Mrs Ellis and I have laid out sandwiches and sausage rolls in the breakfast room. I don't suppose I'll stay through the whole thing anyway.'

The Napiers' pew, at the front of the church, had been left empty as usual, but when Hilary sat down she looked around and beckoned to those standing to come and join her. They came uncertainly; Maggie and Arthur Culliford weren't regular attendees and had only come because their own elderly wireless accumulator needed recharging, and sitting in the Squire's pew right at the front made them feel self-conscious. But Shirley, who was accustomed to coming with the school and knew Hilary from last year's pantomime, led her brothers and sister in confidently and they squeezed in between Hilary and their parents.

Hilary passed them the programmes for the short service, which had been specially printed complete with a stern warning against 'shuffling, knocking of feet or jingling money in pockets'. She whispered, 'When Mr Harvey wipes his nose in the last hymn, that's to tell us to sing the last

327

verse, so keep your eyes on him.'

'Suppose he's got a cold,' Shirley whispered anxiously. 'He might have to wipe it before then.'

'I don't think he has,' Hilary said, thinking that Shirley actually had rather a good point, and hoping that Basil wouldn't have to sneeze at an inappropriate moment.

'Did you see it on your television?' Shirley asked, still in a hoarse whisper. 'Did you see the Queen in her golden coach?'

'Yes, although we couldn't really see that it was gold, of course. But it looked wonderful and the Queen looked beautiful. And I saw inside West-minster Abbey too. It looked like a huge, glittering palace.'

'Oh, I wish I could see it too!' Shirley exclaimed, and several people said 'ssh'. Her mother, who was on her other side, gave her a sharp nudge and she subsided, blushing.

Basil Harvey came in then and the service began. There were loudspeakers around the church so that everyone could hear the coronation service, and this short service was to give thanks, to ask for help and strength for the new young queen, and to lead into the main event. It was because nobody was quite sure of the exact timing that the last hymn might be shortened, and everyone watched keenly as they came to the middle of the hymn.

At the appointed moment, Basil took out his handkerchief and wiped his nose. There was a moment of hesitation as the congregation frantically searched its memory and some even wondered aloud whether this meant they were, or were not, to sing the last verse. A few stalwart voices carried on, some stopped, others joined in rather uncertainly and the hymn staggered to an untidy close before Basil, who hadn't been too sure himself, stepped forward for the Blessing and they all knelt in prayer before the loudspeakers, operated by Norman Tozer and Vic Nethercott, burst into joyous life and everyone could settle back and listen to the glorious music and to Richard Dimbleby's reverential commentary.

Chapter Thirty

Val too had been thoughtful after her talk with Hilary. Nobody in her family knew anything about the baby that she had been carrying after her affair with Luke in Egypt, during the war. Only Hilary and a few other VAD nurses had known at the time, and because she had miscarried early in the pregnancy, while they were on the voyage home, it had been quite easy to keep the secret. To tell her sister-in-law now, so many years later, would be one of the most difficult things she had ever done.

It was not that she feared that Joanna would tell anyone else. It was more that, having kept the secret for so long, it was almost impossible to let it go. Yet the more she considered it, the more she felt that Hilary was right. It would show some fellow-feeling for the bereaved mother, and it would show the trust that Val was placing in her.

It would show Joanna how valued she was.

I'll do it, Val decided. I'll do it this morning, when everyone else is at church. Joanna had already said that she wouldn't go – someone must stay with Robin and Heather – but the rest of the family was going, even Minnie, although they had agreed they wouldn't stay for the whole time. Just the beginning Alice had said, until Minnie started to feel tired.

It didn't leave very long, so as soon as the family had departed, Val went up to Joanna's room and knocked on the door.

'Jo. It's Val. Can I come in, please?'

There was a short silence, then Joanna said stiffly, 'What for?'

'I want to talk to you.' Val turned the handle and peeped in. Joanna was sitting on the bed, feeding Heather, while Robin was on the floor fitting a jigsaw together. Val came in and closed the door behind her and Joanna gave her a hostile look.

'What is it?'

Val sat on the bed beside her and looked gravely into her face. 'Look, Jo, I know you don't want to talk to me. You don't want me here at all. But please listen – just this once – and if you still want me to go away, I will. I'll never bother you again. But – I hope you won't want that. It's upsetting everyone – Mum, Dad, Gran … the whole family.'

'I can't help that,' Joanna said woodenly. 'I can't change my feelings.'

'I know. But maybe if you knew just why I said I knew how you felt–'

'And that's just it!' Joanna exclaimed, and the baby at her breast let out a protesting whimper.

330

Irritated, she bent to smooth the small, downy head and murmur words of comfort. Then she looked up again and said more quietly, 'I wish you'd stop saying that, Val. You don't know. Nobody can know, who hasn't lost a child.'

'But I have,' Val said, her heart beginning to hammer as she said the words. 'Lost a child, I mean.'

There was a moment of silence. Joanna turned and stared into her eyes. Val met her gaze, though it cost her an effort to do so, for until she had told Luke about the baby she had called Johnny, she had never talked about him to anyone.

'What do you mean?' Joanna asked at last.

'I was going to have a baby,' Val said painfully. 'On the way home from Egypt. It was Luke's – we knew each other there, he was a war artist – and, well, I fell for a baby. I didn't know until I was on the way home, and Luke and I had parted by then anyway. So he never knew. And then, on board the ship, I miscarried. I was far enough on to know it was a little boy and I called him Johnny. I know it's not the same as it was for you – you had time to get to know Suzanne and to love her. But I loved my baby too, even though I never did have time to know him, and to me that seemed to make it worse. He never knew me either, you see. We never even had time to look at each other.' The tears were sliding down her cheeks and she brushed them away with the back of her wrist. 'That's why we were so happy to know I was going to have a baby now – I'd been afraid I couldn't, you see. I thought I was being punished. And we were going to tell everyone that day – on

Easter Sunday.'

The silence lasted longer. Joanna looked down at her own baby, who had fallen asleep at the breast. Gently, she removed her, wiped her nipple, and drew her blouse together. She turned back to Val.

'Does anyone else know?'

'Not in the family, no. Luke knows, of course, and Hilary – that's where we really became friends, in Egypt, and she was on board the ship. Some of the other VADs knew too, but I've lost touch with most of them. Nobody ever mentioned it to me again, afterwards.'

'Afterwards...' Joanna said slowly. 'What did you do with – with the baby?'

'We gave him a sea-burial. We found a bit of flag and wrapped him in it, and said some prayers and – and put him in the sea.' Val's voice shook and she began to cry in earnest. 'I've told myself over and over again that we did it properly, that it wasn't like – like throwing away a bag of rubbish, but that's what it felt like. Oh, Jo – that's what it felt like.'

Instinctively, Joanna put her free arm around Val's shoulders and drew her close. Her own eyes were wet and she drew in a deep, shuddering breath. For several minutes, neither said anything; they simply wept in each other's arms.

'Oh, Val,' Joanna said at last.

'Yes. So you see – I do understand, a bit, how you feel. I've always thought of Johnny as my first baby – perhaps my only one. And I know it wasn't quite the same – not the same at all, really – and I won't say it again if it upsets you – but I wanted you to know.'

'Yes,' Joanna said. 'Yes, I see. And ... thank you, Val... Thank you.'

'Why in heaven's name,' Gilbert Napier demanded of his daughter, 'did you have to bring those Cullifords back with you?'

'Shirley was so longing to see the Queen in her golden coach,' Hilary said defensively. 'And I couldn't get out of the pew without disturbing them all, so I just invited them to come back here. Don't be cross, Father – they're loving it.' She had brought the family in just as the crown was being set upon the new Queen's head, and arranged them swiftly, the children on the carpet close to the set and Arthur and Maggie, looking even more uncomfortable, on upright chairs at the back. They had sat engrossed throughout the rest of the service and, apart from the youngest child suddenly discovering a need for the lavatory, had barely moved or spoken. It was only as the procession was leaving the Abbey that Hilary had left the room to see that the sandwich lunch was in order, and Gilbert had followed her to the breakfast room to upbraid her.

'We'll never get rid of them now, especially when they realise there's food on offer. And you know Culliford can't hold his drink. God knows what Arnold and his wife are thinking.'

'Quite frankly,' said Hilary, who didn't like Arnold Cherriman although she felt sorry for his mouse of a wife, 'I don't really care what they're thinking. It's time they went back to Plymouth anyway. That house of theirs must be nearly ready by now.'

'It is. Arnold was telling me they're hoping to move back in sometime in August. And before you say anything, Hilary, I'll be putting Kellaway there. It was always intended as the estate manager's house, and that's how it will be used from now on.'

Hilary bit her lip. 'Well, this isn't the day for arguments,' she said peaceably. 'And I don't expect the Cullifords will stay long. Arthur and Maggie are no more comfortable with it than you are, and once the Royal Family are back at the Palace, the broadcast will stop and everyone will be going down to the field.'

Gilbert grunted, but, short of throwing the Cullifords out, he had no option but to extend his hospitality towards them. Travis, who was also amongst the gathering, came to stand beside Hilary as she stood filling their plates with sandwiches and fruit cake, and murmured in her ear: 'Is this the start of a new Elizabethan age, and a levelling-out of classes?'

'Who knows?' she retorted, still feeling nettled about the house. 'It wouldn't be such a bad thing if it were. Not that Father will ever be able to understand that.'

He looked at her thoughtfully. 'Don't be too hard on him, Hilary. He's – what? Sixty-five? Nearly seventy? He can't cast aside the values he's grown up with just like that.'

'I suppose not,' she said grumpily. 'But he's getting more and more crotchety these days, and more determined to have everything his own way. I'm not sure I can stand it much longer. In fact–' she waited until she had handed the last plate of food to the smallest Culliford '–I might as well tell you now, I'm seriously considering whether I can go on like this. He could live another twenty-five years, and what sort of a life is that for me? And where will I be at the end of it?'

'You'll inherit,' he said. 'And then you'll be able to have everything *your* own way.'

Hilary gave him a sharp glance. 'Oh, I know what you're thinking – like father, like daughter. And maybe you're right. But it's not going to make a comfortable future, is it? Twenty-five more years of scrapping and arguing? Honestly, Travis, it just doesn't appeal to me.'

'You might marry,' he said, and she snorted.

'That's what he says! As if it would be the solution to everything. Why should it be? And who does he think I'm going to marry, anyway?' She caught his eye on her and felt herself blush. They both knew quite well that Gilbert half expected a marriage between them, and knew that he would probably accept it as the best of a bad job. Better Hilary married a man who understood and cared about the estate than one who would fritter the money away – or not married at all. Which is the most likely, she thought gloomily. 'Anyway, I don't know that I want to get married. If I did, I'd have done something about it before now. I'm happy as I am – or would be, if I could be left to live my life as I want to live it.'

'And just how is that?' he asked, and she shrugged.

'Quite honestly, I hardly know any more. It's so long since I've had any choice in the matter. Oh, let's forget it for today and enjoy ourselves. Are you going in for the sports this afternoon?'

'I am indeed. I'm leading the estate tug-of-war team, don't forget – the Barton Giants, we're calling ourselves. It looks as if we'll have quite a lot of competition too. There are a good half-dozen teams entering. How about you?'

'I'm running the pony club gymkhana in the other field. Mrs Ellis is helping with the teas, and then there's the dance tonight and the beacon being lit up at the Standing Stones – the whole village will go up for that, and the firework display. We'll be able to see beacons and fireworks for miles around.'

'It's going to be a good day,' he said. 'Starting with the Monarchs' Procession, of course. Speaking of which...'

'We'll have to think about getting ready soon,' she finished for him. 'We're starting off from the school sharp at three and Joyce will be going up in flames herself if we're not all there. Eat up, Betty,' she added, turning to the child who was standing behind her. 'You'll need to go home and wash before you put on your frock. You're going to be one of the little princesses, aren't you?'

'Yes, miss. I'm Princess Margaret Rose when she was a little girl, and Shirley's going to be Princess Elizabeth before she was Queen. And George and Eddy Crocker are going to be the Princes in the Tower. They get their heads cut off.' She took her plate away to a corner and sat on a small stool to finish her cake.

Travis grinned. 'Unfortunately, there's no actual proof of that.'

Hilary laughed. 'Those boys are the bane of

poor Stella's life.'

'They're going to be the bane of mine as soon as they're old enough to go poaching,' he said wryly. 'It's a pity, because old man Crocker's a decent sort and their parents are too. They seem to have bred a couple of wild cards with those two.'

The Crocker twins did look very good as the princes in the tower, Hilary thought a little while later as the procession began to move off. After a morning cooped up in their homes or crammed together in the church, listening to the broadcast, everyone felt liberated in the open air, even though it was still damp. It had rained harder in London, so the commentators had told them, but that hadn't prevented the people from cheering all along the route, and moving in a huge mass down the Mall to see the Royal Family on the balcony of Buckingham Palace. And the procession itself had been a spectacle too, with visiting heads of states and dignitaries from all over the world. Queen Salote of Tonga had been the star attraction, refusing to travel in a closed carriage or even to have an umbrella held over her head, and waving and smiling at the crowds with overflowing joy.

'She looked so jolly, and so pleased to be there,' Hilary told Val as they waited. 'I wished we could be inviting her to our party this afternoon! None of our monarchs look half as much fun.'

'Oh, I don't know,' Val said thoughtfully. 'Henry the Eighth looks jolly enough. He must have been quite a party lover in his day even if it did usually end in tears.'

'Yes, well, I don't think I'd have liked to be one of his wives. Not a man you want to lose your head

337

over!' Hilary said with a grin, and Val groaned. 'Oops, here we go. I wonder if our route will be lined with cheering crowds, like the Queen's.'

They moved off along the village street, to the accompaniment of more ringing from the bells. As Ted had promised, they had been sounding more or less all day, apart from while the service itself was being broadcast, and he had been particularly proud of the fact that they had timed their peal to coincide exactly with the Abbey bells as the Queen left the building and was handed back into her golden coach.

'All over the country,' he'd said afterwards, beaming with pride, 'ringers pulled off at the same moment, just like they do on New Year's Eve, and if the Queen had been able to hear them all—'

'She'd have been deafened,' Tom said, grinning. He tied his rope and said, 'I'll get back now, Dad. I promised Jo I wouldn't be long, and we've got to get young Robin dressed up for his part.'

'That's right, you go off now,' Ted told him. 'There's enough of us here for a second peal.' He watched his son depart and said to the others, 'It's good to see him smile and crack a bit of a joke. Us haven't had much of that these past few weeks.'

'Time heals all things,' Alf Coker observed. 'Mind you, I reckon it's got a bit of a job on when it comes to losing a kiddy. Always thought that must be the worst thing that can happen to anyone. It can't have been all that easy for you and Alice neither, Ted.'

'Can't say it has,' Ted agreed. 'But we've decided to put all that to one side today, if us can. Plenty of time for grieving afterwards. And now let's ring another peal and get down to the field. There's a lot more to enjoy before today's over.'

And enjoy it the two villages were determined to do. The two processions – Burracombe's Procession of Monarchs, and Little Burracombe's pageant of village life in the first Elizabethan age – met at the big field by the river, and the participants mingled with the crowds already there, resplendent in their costumes. Some of these were soon divested (in a screened-off portion of the marquee) so that their wearers could take part in the games, but some chose to remain dressed for the whole afternoon. Joyce Warren (as Queen Catherine of Aragon) was one of these, moving gracefully and regally about the field for all the world as if she were really royalty, and you had to admit, as Maddy said to Stella when they stood watching the antics of the young men on the greasy pole, she did lend a kind of panache to the proceedings.

'Are you enjoying yourself?' Stella asked. She had been anxious about Maddy, wondering if she had been right to persuade her to come to Burracombe when she had had invitations both from the Archdeacon and his wife, and from Dan and Ruth Hodges, to join them for the day. But Maddy smiled and nodded.

'I'm having a lovely time. Burracombe is always home to me, you know, more than anywhere else. And I spent last weekend at Bridge End with the Hodges, so they didn't mind.'

'How are they?' Stella enquired. 'I haven't had a chance to talk to you properly yet. They must still be very sad.'

'Yes, they are. But they're very good for each other, and of course they've got Linnet.' There was a wistful note in her voice, and Stella linked her arm through her sister's and gave it a squeeze. There was no need for words; she knew that Maddy was wishing that she and Sammy had had more time together, that they could have known what it was to be married, that she could have held his baby in her arms. None of that was to be, and never would be, but Stella hoped with all her heart that Maddy would find happiness again one day, with a husband she could love as much as she had loved Sammy, and with a family of her own.

'How's Stephen?' she asked, scarcely realising what had led her to think of him. 'I thought he might be here too.'

'He's coming later. They had special services at the station and he couldn't get away.' Maddy's face broke into laughter as Vic Nethercott finally lost his grip on the slippery ash branch that had been laid across the river and swung underneath it, his fingers scrabbling wildly for a hold before he fell with a splash into the tumbling water. 'D'you think anyone will manage to get all the way across without falling in?'

'I'd be surprised. Felix said they smothered it about two inches thick in grease. I'm surprised anyone gets as far as Vic did.' They watched as a dripping Vic climbed out on to the bank, to the cheers of the onlookers. 'Anyway, I can't stand here all afternoon – I'm supposed to be helping with the children's races. They're just starting over there, look.'

The older children, their feet and legs in sacks

which they held up to their waists, were already jostling for places at the starting line. Henry Bennetts and Micky Coker were in the middle, which was generally believed to be the best place, and the Crocker twins were complaining bitterly at not being allowed to take part.

'You'll have your turn in a minute,' Stella told them firmly. 'This race is for eleven and older.'

'We'm just as good as they,' they argued. 'Us could win old Micky Coker any day.'

'I've told you before, George, you do not *win* a person, you win a prize,' Stella said. 'And you can't go in this race, so stand back and let Mr Copley blow his whistle to start it.' She held the twins firmly by their collars, one in each hand, and after a wriggle or two they subsided, grumbling.

'I *am* impressed,' Maddy said. 'However do you tell them apart?'

The race was under way and Stella let them go. She grinned. 'I can't. I just assume that the first one to speak is George, and if it isn't, they tell me! And if I'm right, it makes them wonder if I actually can tell the difference.'

'And they haven't realised what you're doing?'

'Not so far. It can only be a matter of time, though. They're very bright little boys.'

'They did look sweet as the little princes,' Maddy said.

'So everybody says. The photographer from the Tavistock Gazette was here and he wanted to photograph them especially. I suppose they'll be in next week's paper, looking as if butter wouldn't melt in their mouths. Nobody in Burracombe will be fooled, though.'

341

Henry won the sack race by one leap, and Micky evened out the score by winning the egg-and-spoon. Together, they came third in the three-legged, and would have won that too if they hadn't been knocked over by two boys from Little Burracombe who appeared to be their arch-enemies. After that, the smaller children had their races and at last it was time for tea.

'It's the tug-of-war competitions next,' Felix said, joining the girls in the marquee. 'This is where I show off my muscles!'

'And which team will you be in?' Stella enquired, passing him a plate of jam and cream scones. 'Christians against the Lions?'

'Ha ha. As a matter of fact, I did suggest to Mr Harvey that we should have a contest between the Clergy and the Bell-ringers, but he took one look at Alf Coker and said he didn't think we'd have a leg to stand on – literally. So I'm in the Little Burracombe team against Burracombe itself.'

'Won't you feel rather torn between them?' Maddy asked, and they all laughed.

'I hope not! I don't want to end up in little bits. Could I have another slice of fruit cake, d'you think? I need to build up my strength.'

Dottie came past with a tray of pasties. 'I suppose you've had at least two of these?' she asked, and Felix admitted that he had. 'And how be you getting on, over the river?'

'Just as well as the last time you asked, sometime last week,' he said with a grin. 'They haven't eaten me yet, anyway.'

'More like you'll eat them,' she said, glancing at his plate. 'I'm not sure they realised what they

were taking on with you. Teas in Little Burracombe aren't too bad, taking all in all, but they'll
be hard put to it to keep up with your appetite.'

'I might remind you, Dottie,' Felix said with
dignity, 'that you are no longer speaking to a
curate still wet behind the ears. I am now a fully-
fledged vicar–'

'–still wet behind the ears,' Stella said neatly,
and filched a jam tart. 'You can't possibly want
this as well as all the rest.'

'For you, my love,' he said, 'I would give up my
whole plate. Well, apart from Dottie's fruit cake.
I draw the line at that. Anyway, I must go now
and get ready for the tug-of-war. I hope you're
coming to watch.'

'Wouldn't miss it for the world,' Stella said, and
finished her tea.

Little Burracombe lost the tug-of-war, despite
Felix's efforts, and when all the games were finished the prizes were distributed, ending with a
presentation to each child of a Coronation mug,
with a coloured picture of the Queen on each.
Most were immediately appropriated by mothers,
who declared that they would go on the mantelpiece, alongside the Coronation mugs for the
Queen's father, George the Sixth. However, Miss
Kemp had foreseen this and salved the children's
disappointment by handing out small bars of
chocolate.

It was time now for a short hiatus while the
marquee was cleared and washing-up finished,
and fresh sandwiches made for the evening's
refreshments. Tired children were taken home
and put to bed, and all those who were coming to

the dance changed into best frocks and suits. The men cleared away the remnants of the afternoon's games and sports, and the greasy pole was lugged up to the tor, where for the past fortnight the young men had been building a bonfire. Once again both villages had combined, to make a huge beacon and buy a fine assortment of fireworks.

'It'll be the best anyone hereabouts has ever seen,' Ted Tozer declared, setting up a sturdy pole for the Catherine wheels. 'And sparklers for all the kiddies, too. It'll be a day they'll never forget.'

Tom Tozer had already gone home, taking Robin with him. The little boy had behaved splendidly for his part as one of Queen Victoria's nine children, but he was tired and fretful now and needed his mother. Tom held his hand and urged him along gently as they walked up the path from the river.

'Soon be home now, Robbie. Have you enjoyed yourself?'

'I liked the tea best,' Robin said. 'I wanted a piece of cake for Heather but Granny said she was too young for cake.'

'Well, so she is. You know she hasn't got any teeth yet.'

'Will she be dead when we get home?' Robin asked, and Tom stopped in his tracks, shocked by the question put so casually, yet with an undertone of anxiety.

'No, of course she won't be dead! Why should she be?' But he knew that in Robin's mind there was every reason why she should be. Every bit as much reason as for Suzanne to die in her pram, that Easter afternoon. He felt a stab of anxiety himself and had to prevent himself from hurrying on in sudden panic.

'Suzie died.'

'I know Suzie died, but that doesn't mean Heather will as well. We don't always know when someone's going to die, but it doesn't often happen like that. Not to babies.'

'Will I die?'

'One day,' Tom answered, wondering what could have possibly happened on this particular day to bring on all these questions. 'But not yet. Probably not until you're a very old man.'

'I might,' Robin said matter-of-factly. 'I might die quite soon.'

Tom knelt down in front of him. He took Robin's hands in his and looked earnestly into his face.

'Robin, you mustn't think like that. You must think about living, not dying. Look how many old people there are about, people you know. Granny and Granddad. Great-granny. Uncle Norman.'

'You,' Robin said. 'You and Mummy. You're old. Does that mean you're going to die too?'

'No! Not for a long time. Look, I told you, we don't always know, but usually people are ill for a while first. And it really isn't a good thing to worry about it. We must just be glad we're alive and do the best we can with the life we've been given. Whatever happens to us, we can always do that. We can always be glad we're alive. And we can help other people to be glad, too.'

'Is that what you really believe?' Joanna said, and he turned in surprise to find her standing close behind him.

'Yes, I do,' he said. 'I can't see any other way of

living. Jo, you know people who've lived miserable lives – look at old Jed Fisher, who was never happy with anything. What good did it do him? What good did it do anyone else? And look at old Jacob, who could have been just as miserable after what Jed did to him when they were both young. He could have been just the same, but he wasn't. He's stayed cheerful and he's kept other people cheerful. You know as well as I do that it always makes us feel better to stop and have a word with Jacob, and the village will be a poorer place when he goes. And he knows what it's like to lose someone he loves.'

'Not a child, though,' Joanna said, but he detected a faint doubt in her voice.

'Not a child, no. But then he never had one, did he, and that was just as great a sorrow to him. That's why he's so fond of Jennifer. He thinks of her as the child he never had.' Tom rose to his feet and took her gently by the arms. 'We'll never forget little Suzanne, either of us. But life has to go on, and we have to make it as good as we can for our other two children. And for the rest of the family, too. They've all been suffering, Jo.'

'I know,' she said, and raised her eyes. He saw that her pupils were huge and swimming with tears, and he knew that she was looking directly into his heart.

'Oh, Jo, my sweetheart,' he said, and gathered her close against him. 'I know we can't grieve at the same rate all the time. Sometimes I feel a bit better, and sometimes you do. But we know where we're going now, don't we? We're helping each other through the bad times.' He kissed her wet face and whispered, 'We'll get through it together. We'll never forget our little Suzie – but we *will* get through it.'

Chapter Thirty-One

The dance began at half-past seven, and plenty of people from both villages were there on time. Little Burracombe's own country-dance band – Hop, Skip and Jump – were to play, with Jeremiah Harcup calling the dances. He did a good blend of English and American squares, with a few circle waltzes thrown in to mix things up, and was an entertainment in himself with his fast patter and singing calls, as he stood on the small stage they had rigged up at one end of the marquee.

'If he waves his arms much more, he'll fall off,' Stella said in amusement. 'Why don't we have a country-dance group in Burracombe?'

'It must be the only thing we haven't got,' Hilary said. 'There was a really active one before the war, when country dancing was all the rage, but it never seemed to get going again afterwards. You're right, we should have one. No use asking you to run it, I suppose, since you'll soon be living on the other side of the river?'

'No use at all,' Stella said firmly. 'Why don't you ask Travis? He told me once that he used to do some calling, and doesn't he play the piano-accordion?'

'Yes, I believe he does,' Hilary said a little

shortly, and Stella looked at her in surprise.

'Where *is* Travis, now I come to think of it?' she asked. 'I thought he'd be here with you.'

'Did you?' Hilary moved away to talk to Constance Bellamy and Felix came to Stella's other side and pulled her into the grassy space that was doing duty as a dance floor. She went with him, glancing over her shoulder at her friend.

'I wonder what's the matter with Hilary. She was quite cool to me then – almost rude.'

'Hilary? Rude to you? I can't believe that – why should she be?' They took their places as fourth couple and stood waiting for Jeremiah's instructions.

'I don't know. All I did was ask where Travis was. You don't suppose there's anything wrong between them, do you?'

'I don't really think there's *anything* between them,' he said. 'Perhaps that's the problem.'

Before Stella could ask what he meant, the dance began and she found herself whisking round the circle in a grand chain, arming left and right, do-si-doing with someone she had never seen before, and whirling away from Felix altogether in half a lady's chain. It wasn't until the dance ended and they were laughing and breathless that she had a chance to speak to him again, and by then Hilary was forgotten and they were listening to the instructions for the next dance.

Hilary, too, was dancing. She had a succession of partners, from Charles Latimer to Jacob Prout, and almost every other man in between. She enjoyed the dancing, yet she was bitterly aware that most of them were dancing with her

348

out of politeness, and that she was one of the few women in the place who had no partner of her own. She saw her brother, keeping a tight hold on Maddy Simmons, and wondered whether anything would ever come of that. She'd quite liked the idea of having little Maddy as her sister- in- law until that young man, Sammy Hodges, whom nobody else in Burracombe (apart from Stella and Felix) had met, had stolen her heart. A childhood sweetheart, Stella had said. Well, that had been a real whirlwind romance, started and ended within weeks, and might not have lasted. And if Sammy had lived and they'd broken up later, Stephen's chance might have come. But a live rival was easier to fight than a dead one, and now Maddy might never look his way.

Hilary sighed and shook her head as Vic Nethercott asked her for another dance. 'No, thanks, Vic. I'm having a rest this time. Go and ask Jackie.' He turned away without much show of disappointment and she saw him make his way over to the youngest Tozer, whose face broke into a smile as he reached for her hand. There was another couple who'd gone through a rocky patch and now seemed as if they might be getting together again, she thought, and sighed again. Much as she might insist to her father that she was perfectly happy single, she had to admit that there were times when she would have liked to have a man by her side.

At that moment, she saw Travis at the entrance. He was wearing dark green corduroy trousers and a checked shirt with a brown suede waistcoat, and his dark hair, flopping over his forehead, looked soft and thick, as if he had freshly washed it. She knew, without having to go close to him, that he would smell of soap with that indefinable, musky tang that was his alone, and her heart quickened.

She was just about to cross the marquee towards him when she saw another figure, and she stopped abruptly.

Jennifer Tucker, wearing a swirling, bright scarlet skirt and white blouse with a ruffled neckline, had come in and was standing close beside Travis. As Hilary watched, he stretched out his hand and Jennifer slipped hers into it. They smiled at each other and then moved further into the marquee and disappeared behind a group of dancers.

Hilary turned away. All this time, she had been telling herself that Travis was no more than a colleague and a friend, that she didn't want any more than friendship from him, that she had given up all thoughts of love and marriage – and now this. The moment she had seen him come in, taken in his appearance and known instinctively what his scent would be, and felt that quickening of her heart, she had known that her protestations had been merely a cover for her real feelings. I *could* love him, she thought, making her way blindly to one of the other doorways. Maybe I do. But I've left it too late.

'Hilary!' Val was in front of her, staring anxiously into her face. 'Hilary, are you all right? You look as white as a sheet.'

'How can you tell?' Hilary grabbed her cloak of self-respect and dragged it round her. 'Everyone looks pretty ghastly, in this light.'

Val looked dubious. 'Well, I could say you look

ghastlier than the rest of us, but I'm your friend so I won't. Honestly, are you OK?'

'Just a bit tired. It's been a long day.'

'Too tired to give me a dance?' Luke asked, as the square came to an end and Jeremiah announced a longways dance. 'Come on. They're doing Jack's Maggot and I've always liked that one.'

Hilary allowed herself to be led to the end of the long line of couples. She stood facing Luke, hardly listening to the simple instructions. She knew the dance well enough, anyway. It was only after it had begun that she realised that Travis and Jennifer were in the same line, and all too soon she and Luke were facing them and performing the sideways 'setting'.

'Having a good time?' Travis enquired, and she summoned up a smile.

'Lovely. And you?'

'Tremendous. It's been a good day.'

'Yes, it has.' In another moment, they would be in the star and passing on to other couples. 'You and Jennifer seem very friendly.'

Travis smiled. 'You noticed!'

'I should think everyone has,' she said a little caustically, and he laughed.

'Good! We don't mind who knows.'

He swung away to face the next couple, leaving Hilary and Luke to set to Norman Tozer and his wife. Knows what? she wondered, keeping a smile pinned firmly to her face. How serious was this friendship, and why hadn't she noticed before? And why did it matter to her? In fact – *did* it matter to her?

I don't seem to have got any further on, she thought as the dance came to an end and Luke thanked her and saw her back to her seat. I thought that managing the estate was all I wanted – and until Travis came along, it was. If only Father had left it at that and let me get on with it, I would have been perfectly happy. I could have spent the rest of my life running the estate, making decisions, improving it and keeping up with the times. But he couldn't allow it, could he. He had to bring in a man – and that man had to be Travis. And that's the whole crux of the matter.

To Gilbert Napier, a woman – even his own daughter – would never be a fit and proper heir for the inheritance he was going to leave. He wanted a male heir. Basically, he still wanted Baden – but failing that, and failing Stephen, he wanted Hilary to produce a son.

Hilary still wasn't sure how he would react if she were to marry Travis. But she knew that he liked and respected his estate manager, and Travis certainly had the best interests of the estate at heart. He would have made a better match than many of the chinless wonders that her father would have had her meeting at society balls and London functions.

Well, it wasn't going to happen now, was it. She could see Travis and Jennifer dancing together, their bodies close in a swing, and it was plain from their faces that something important had happened between them. He'd definitely be wanting the house in the woods now, she thought. And probably in a little while she'd be able to feel happy for them. But not tonight.

She got up and slipped quietly from the marquee. The evening had been soured and she just wanted to go home.

'Thank goodness for that,' Maddy said as Jeremiah announced the supper-break. 'I'm exhausted!'

'It's been good, hasn't it,' Stephen said, leading her through the throng to the long trestle-tables. 'You know, I don't usually go for this sort of dancing, but it's good fun for a party.'

'And what sort of dancing do you usually go for?' she enquired.

'You know what sort.' He slipped his arm round her waist and gave her a squeeze. 'The sort where I can hold a nice girl in my arms and just waltz round the room in our own little world.'

Their eyes met and then Maddy turned away, towards the table. 'Oh look, sausages.'

'Goodness me,' he said gravely. 'It must be all of twelve hours since I saw a sausage.'

'Oh, shut up and hand me a plate, will you? I'm starving.'

Stephen did as he was told and they filled their plates with home-made sausage rolls, cheese straws and sandwiches. There were large bowls of trifle too, and plenty of tea, coffee and orange squash. Bernie had sent down a barrel of beer and some of the men were getting quite merry.

'It's all right, you know, Maddy,' Stephen said as they found chairs and sat down. 'I know it's too early for you to think about anyone else. I'm not going to make a nuisance of myself.'

Maddy turned to him. 'I know. It's just that

353

sometimes, when you say things like that about dancing ... well, I don't know quite what to think.'

'I'm sorry. I'll try not to do it again. Can't promise, though, I'm afraid – these things just slip out. Just ignore me when they do.'

'I will.' They smiled at each other and Maddy put one of her sausage rolls on Stephen's plate. 'As long as you're happy to be just friends.'

'I'll always be your friend, Maddy,' he said seriously, and then gave her his familiar grin. 'Especially if you give me all your sausage rolls.'

Val and Luke went by at that moment and smiled to see them laughing.

'It's good to see Maddy enjoying herself. I wasn't at all sure she'd come tonight.'

'She knows life has to go on,' Luke said. 'And the best way to make that happen is to go on living it. It's hard for her, but I think she will get through it.'

'And what about Joanna? Will she get through it too? Such awful tragedies, Luke.'

'Well, we've had our share of those too,' he said gently. 'Or at least, you have as I didn't know anything about it at the time. And Joanna does know now that you understand. D'you think it's helped her?'

'I think it has,' Val said slowly. 'She didn't say much when I told her about Johnny, but she was different afterwards. I think she's stopped blaming me for Suzanne. It can't happen all at once, because she's still grieving and that takes its own time, but I think we'll be all right eventually.'

'It's bound to be hard for her when our own baby comes,' he said. 'We'll still have to be careful.'

'Babies bring their own love,' Val told him. That's what Mum always says, anyway. Nobody can be angry with a tiny baby.'

'And are you all right?' he asked quietly as they took their plates back to their chairs. 'It wasn't an easy thing for you to do.'

'Yes, I am now. It was upsetting to talk about Johnny – to go through it all again.' She looked down at her plate, feeling the tears sting her eyes. 'I never stop thinking about him, you know. Oh, not all the time of course – but at some time, most days. He's always there, in his own little corner of my mind. I think about how old he would be now, I think about the day he'd have first walked, the day he'd have started school, all the things he would have done as he grew up. I wonder if he would have looked like you.'

'Well, with any luck he wouldn't!' Luke said with a smile. 'But you've got our new baby to think about now. And we'll see all of those things happen. We're going to be a proper family, Val.'

'I think I'd like to go home after supper,' she said after a moment. 'It's been a long day. But it's been a good one.'

'The dawn of a new era,' he said. 'Isn't that what everyone's saying? A new Elizabethan age.'

They looked around the crowded marquee, at the familiar faces, all laughing and smiling as they ate their supper and waited for the dancing to begin again. It was a good place to live, Val thought. A good place to have grown up, and a good place to bring up their own children. For she and Luke would have more than one; she was sure of that.

They said their goodnights and went home. And as they lay in bed, they could hear the bells ring their final peal, bidding good-night to the day that had brought them more than a new Queen; the day that had brought to them, and to Joanna, Tom and the rest of the family, a peace that might at last begin to ease their grief.

'I want to say something before we go to bed,' Joanna said as the family sat round the big kitchen table drinking their cocoa. She looked round the circle of faces, thinking how dear they were to her. 'I want to say I'm sorry.'

They stared at her.

'Sorry for what?' Alice asked in a bemused tone.

'For being so horrible to you all these past few weeks. For being so nasty and bad-tempered, when you were all trying to be kind to me. I'm really sorry. I just couldn't seem to help it, somehow.'

'Why, my dear soul, of course you couldn't!' Alice exclaimed, jumping up from her chair and coming round to Joanna. She put her arm around the younger woman's shoulders and gave her a squeeze. 'Us all understood that. There's no need to apologise, no need at all.'

'That's right, there isn't,' Ted said gruffly. 'You and Tom, you been hit as hard as anyone could be. It was bound to set you at sixes and sevens, and 'tis still early days. It takes a long time to get over what's happened to you.'

'I don't think we'll ever actually get over it,' Joanna said, through a shower of tears. 'But it's no excuse for behaving as I've been doing, and it's been bad for you too. I've been forgetting that, and I'm sorry.'

'Well, I think 'tis every excuse,' Alice said staunchly. 'Of course it's been bad for us as well – me and Ted have lost our little granddaughter that we were so fond of, and Mother here has lost a great-granddaughter. Us all has our grief. But the thing is to give each other time and a bit of room to grieve in our own way, and hold each other up. That's all a Christian family can do, and I don't think we've been doing all that bad.'

'You've been wonderful,' Joanna said. 'It's me that's been awful.'

'Now look here,' Ted said in the sort of tone he'd have used to Tom when he was a small boy and was behaving badly, 'you can just stop that sort of talk right now. Nobody thinks you been awful, or horrible, or any of those other things you seem to think. You'm a young mother who's been through the worst thing that can happen to any mother, and all that matters is that you grieve in your own way and us is all here, standing by to help you whenever you wants it and in any way us can. And that's all I got to say on the matter, and I don't want to hear no more talk about being sorry.'

Joanna smiled waveringly at him, and Tom reached out and took her hand.

'There is one more thing I've got to say, though,' she said. 'And it's about Val. I don't care what you say, I *have* been horrible to her, and it was all because she was the one who found Suzanne, and that wasn't fair – and I *am* sorry.'

'Well, that's a good thing to hear,' Alice said after a moment's silence. 'I know it's been a sor-

357

row to her, you two always having been such good friends and all. Have you said anything to her?'

'She knows,' Joanna said, thinking of the conversation she had had with Val earlier in the day, and the tearful hugs they'd exchanged as they parted. 'I don't have to say anything else. She knows.'

'Then that be all that matters,' Alice said. 'And now I reckon 'tis time us was all in bed. It's been a long day and a special one. Where's our Jackie?'

'I'm here,' Jackie said, coming through the door. Her face was flushed and her eyes bright. 'I was just saying goodnight to Vic – he brought me home.'

'He did, did he?' Alice said, with a quizzical glance. 'Quite the gentleman these days, young Vic. I thought you and him was all over.'

'And so we are,' Jackie said offhandedly, turning towards the stairs. 'He just brought me home, that's all. No need to make anything of it. Goodnight!'

She disappeared and they looked at each other and laughed, and Joanna thought that it was the first easy, relaxed laugh they had enjoyed together since Easter.

'All over, indeed,' Alice said, gathering up the cocoa mugs and taking them to the sink. 'Well, us'll wait and see about that. There's nothing else we can do. If there's one thing I've learned this year it's that it's a young folk's world now. A young queen, and all manner of new things to look forward to. Time us old folk took a back seat, Ted.'

'And I'd be glad to, if I thought young Tom here was up to doing half the work I can get through in a day,' Ted observed, pushing back his chair. 'But it'll be a while before that happens, I reckon!'

They laughed again, and Tom and Joanna went up to bed while Alice washed up the mugs and Ted went outside to look at the stars that had at last appeared as the clouds of the day dispersed. After a few minutes, she came out and joined him.

'I'm right, though, Ted. It's a new world now. The war's over, rationing is coming to an end and there's going to be all sorts of new ways of doing things. Tractors instead of horses – we've seen that starting already. More folk with their own cars. New houses being built and new people coming to the country to live here. 'Tis going to be a different world for our grandchildren to grow into.'

'And not all for the better,' he said. 'But when has it ever been? With everything you gain, it seems to me, there's summat else you got to lose. But that's enough of this philosophising, my dear. Us can leave that to clever folk like the vicar and the schoolteachers. Our job is to keep our little bit of England sweet, and as long as I can do that I'll be a happy man.'

He slipped his arm round his wife's waist and gave her a kiss, and then they both went inside.

Chapter Thirty-Two

Breakfast was late at the Barton next morning. Hilary, who had gone to bed despondent and dispirited, slept restlessly and fell into a deep sleep at six, waking an hour or so later with heavy eyes and a dull headache. On any other morning she would have gone out for a ride, hoping that a swift gallop over the moors would set her to rights, but too often when she had done that she had encountered Travis on his own early-morning ride, and she was uncomfortably aware that she might have read too much into these meetings. It wasn't a risk she felt inclined to take today.

Instead, she slipped out through the french doors of the drawing-room and walked round the garden. I don't spend enough time out here, she thought, looking at the remains of yesterday's rain, glistening like dew in the cups of the roses. I'm out in the fields all the time, or in the office. I don't have time to stop and enjoy what we have. Maybe it's time I did; maybe I should be content to sit back a bit and let Father and Travis run the estate the way they want to, and just stop bothering.

But she knew she would never be able to do that. She was trapped here, whatever happened between herself and Travis, whatever happened to her father. Because there was nobody else to take on the estate. Stephen never would, and unless he had children – a son – who could inherit the estate, it was hers for good or ill.

As she thought this, she saw her brother strolling towards her along the grassy path between the rose beds. He waved and she paused to wait for him.

'So what ails you, all alone and palely loitering?' he enquired when he came closer. 'You look a bit fed up.'

'I'm all right. Just wondering what the future holds for us all. This new era everyone keeps talking about, you know. The New Elizabethans and all that.'

'Well, I can tell you what it holds for me,' he said, stretching his arms. 'A bit longer in the RAF and then off to Canada. A new country, that's what I want, and a life of my own without feeling that Baden's shadow is looking over my shoulder all the time.'

Hilary stared at him in surprise. 'D'you still feel that? I thought you'd got over it long ago.'

He shook his head. 'It's always there, especially when I come home and see Father looking at me as if I'd let him down. Let the whole family down, for generations back. It's like walking about with a huge sack of rocks on my back. I tell you what, Hil, if it wasn't for Maddy I wouldn't come home half as much.'

'Maddy? But I thought–'

'You thought right, unfortunately. Friends and nothing more – until she can get over young Hodges, anyway. But at least coming down here gives me the excuse to bring her down to see her sister. I don't kid myself she wants to see me for my own good self.'

'And would you still like her to want that?' Hilary asked quietly.

'Yes, I would,' he said after a pause. 'I thought I'd get over her too, you know – once I realised it wasn't really me she was interested in. But I haven't; and I've got a feeling I never will. So maybe the best thing for me would be to go away – right away, to Canada. Maybe in a few years' time ... I can always come back, you know. For visits. I'm not abandoning you and Dad for ever.'

361

'I'm glad to hear it.' But she didn't really feel much less despondent. Stephen had distanced himself from the estate, but he was still *there*, in a sense – he was still a Napier, and would still take an interest in what she had to tell him. Canada seemed very far away.

'You could visit me too,' he said, watching her face. 'If things get too much for you here ... I told you before, there are plenty of opportunities for someone like you.'

'As I remember it,' she said drily, 'you were offering me an opportunity to be your housekeeper!'

He grinned, a little shamefacedly. 'Well, maybe, but that's not what I'm talking about now. They're looking for people like you – men and women who have got some skills and experience. Honestly, Hil. And when I get my own air freight business going I'll be looking for someone to help me. A partner – not a housekeeper. Think about it.'

'Yes,' she said, turning to look around the garden and the fields, woods and moorland rising beyond, and knowing that she could never leave it – or if she did, she'd only have to come back again when her father died or could no longer manage without her. 'Maybe I will.'

They went inside to breakfast. Gilbert Napier was already at the table, reading the newspaper that was full of Coronation pictures and reports from Everest. He wished them good morning and they helped themselves to grapefruit and porridge and began to eat.

As always, Baden's portrait was hanging on the

wall above the fireplace. Hilary glanced at it as she sat down, thinking yet again how simple it would all have been if only he had lived. How different for them all – nothing to hold her back from her own life, no pressure put on Stephen all these years, no heartbreak for their father. She looked up at her elder brother's dark eyes and felt a sudden pang of sorrow. Even after all this time, she thought, I still miss you.

The doorbell rang and Hilary looked up in surprise. 'I wonder who that is. It can't be Travis – he never comes in that way. D'you suppose it's Maddy?'

'Might be, I suppose.' Stephen laid down his spoon and began to get up, but at that moment the door opened and Mrs Ellis put her head in.

'It's a young woman, Miss Hilary. Asking for you.'

'A young woman? Not anyone you know?'

'No, miss. I've never seen her before. Foreign, she is, but I don't know where from. I've put them in the small sitting room.'

'Them?' Hilary asked, following her out of the room, but Mrs Ellis was already on her way back to the kitchen. Shrugging, Hilary opened the door to the small sitting room and went in.

A dark-haired young woman about her own age was sitting on the couch next to the window. Beside her sat a boy of about twelve or thirteen, also with dark hair and eyes. In the first moment of looking at him, Hilary felt a tiny flicker of something – recognition? – and then it was gone. She regarded them both with some bemusement, wondering who they were and why they had come.

'Good morning,' she said a little doubtfully. 'I'm Hilary Napier. What can I do for you?'

The woman stood up and held out her hand. She was several inches shorter than Hilary and her hair was cut in a style that seemed unusual. Her clothes too were of a different cut from those Hilary was used to and looked like good quality, although somewhat shabby. But then, Mrs Ellis had said she was foreign, and when she spoke Hilary realised that she was French.

'I am pleased to meet you, Miss Napier,' she said. 'I have been wanting to meet you for a long time.'

'Have you?' Hilary felt her bewilderment increase. 'Why? Do we have mutual friends? I'm sorry – I don't know your name.'

'Before I tell you that,' the Frenchwoman said, putting out a hand to the boy at her side, who was also now on his feet, 'I would like you to meet my son. This is Robert.' She pronounced it in the French way – *Rob-air*. The boy smiled shyly and held out his hand and Hilary took it. She looked more carefully at his face, searching for that flash of recognition, but it was gone and left no clue. I've never seen either of them before, she thought. Who on earth are they, and why have they come?

'Would you like some tea, or coffee?' she asked. 'You must have had quite a journey to get here so early.'

'We came on the first train from London. It was very early. It brought the newspapers.'

'Yes, it would. Did you go to Plymouth or Tavistock? Plymouth's a bigger station, but Tavistock's nearer.' I'm blathering, she thought, but what am

I supposed to say? 'I'll get some coffee,' she added a little desperately. 'And something to eat too – you must be hungry.' And why she should be offering them food as well, she had no idea. I'll be asking them to stay to lunch next, she thought, wondering what had got into her. They could be anyone – why ever didn't she just find out what they wanted and send them packing?

'Nothing, thank you,' the Frenchwoman said, holding up her hand. She seemed much more self-possessed than Hilary, yet there was a nervousness about her, as if she were less sure than she seemed of their welcome. They stood looking at one another for a moment, then Hilary gestured towards the couch.

'Why don't we all sit down, and you can tell me why you've come – and how you knew about me in the first place.'

They sat. The silence stretched between them. Hilary looked first at one face, then at the other. The boy was looking down at his hands, but as she studied him he raised his eyes suddenly and again she felt that shock. But I *don't* know you, she thought, almost angrily. I've never seen either of you before. And she wished, very much, that they would state their business and go.

'I have known about you for a long time,' the woman said at last. She looked directly into Hilary's face and said, slowly and carefully, as if it were something she had rehearsed: 'Baden told me about you.'

Hilary caught her breath. She felt as if she had been dashed in the face with a bucket of icy water. She gripped the arms of her chair, struggling for

365

words, and at last, feebly, she echoed, '*Baden* told you?'

'Yes,' the woman said. 'Baden told me. I am Baden's widow, Miss Napier, Marianne, and this is our son – Robert.'

'Your *son?*' Hilary repeated slowly. She turned her eyes to the boy's face and their eyes met once again. Now I know why he looks familiar, she thought with another shock. Those are Baden's eyes. That dark, intense blue ... and those straight, black brows...

She looked at the mother again. There was something of her in the child's face too, and she had no doubt that the Frenchwoman was speaking the truth.

'But ... I don't understand. Baden wasn't married.'

'He was. He was married to me. We met when his regiment was billeted near our farm, and we fell in love. It seemed at first that there was plenty of time – but then the Germans came into the country and we knew that there was almost none at all. Baden had to have his colonel's permission to marry – it was all very quick, you understand.' She glanced briefly at the boy, and Hilary nodded in understanding. 'Baden was not quite twenty-one, but the colonel told us it was quite legal, and two days later the regiment was ordered to leave.' She was silent for a moment, before adding, 'I never heard from Baden again.'

Hilary nodded. 'He was killed in the retreat to Dunkirk. And his colonel too. So we never knew anything about you. We had no idea.' She looked at Robert. 'You must be my nephew.'

He smiled, and his resemblance to Baden caught her by the throat. Tears came to her eyes as she thought of the portrait she had been looking at, no more than half an hour earlier. The son Baden had never known he had. The grandson her father had thought would never be born.

And then the full significance dawned on her and she turned her head slowly back to the small, dark Frenchwoman who was her unexpected sister-in-law. Questions crowded into her mind: why had Marianne waited for so long? Why had she come now? What did she want from them, and what would her father not give? How, even, could she tell him, knowing what a shock it must be? She couldn't even be sure that it would be a welcome one, after all these years.

The questions would all be asked and, she hoped, answered over the next few days. For Marianne and her son would certainly have to stay here, at least for a time. The lives of every member of the family would be affected by this.

But overriding it all was one great truth, that it would take even Hilary time to absorb.

Here, sitting before her with Baden's eyes and Baden's smile, was the heir to Burracombe.